THE WENCH IS
In which Lt. Al W............ ....
+ a murdered Hollywood writer whose body is
  discovered at the bottom of a gravel pit with three
  bullet holes in him…
+ a cop who turns up shot to death the next night in
  the same gravel pit with $3,000 in his pocket…
+ and a Hollywood film crew that is shooting a
  western nearby, starring a cast of characters who all
  have good reason to see the writer dead…

BLONDE VERDICT
In which Lt. Al Wheeler must consider—
+ why a lawyer suddenly collapses and dies in a bar
  from curare poisoning?
+ why the lawyer's wife seems to be so unconcerned
  about the sudden death of her wealthy husband?
+ what has become of the handsome fiancée of the
  murdered man's mistress?

DELILAH WAS DEADLY
In which Lt. Al Wheeler must contend with—
+ the corpse of the social editor found in the safe of the
  prestigious fashion magazine, in his pajamas and
  strangled with a girdle…
+ a second body, stabbed in the back, this time a
  murdered cop who had been sent to the social
  editor's apartment to look around….
+ and two more bodies that pile up under similar
  circumstances, all pointing to someone who could be
  trying to steal the magazine's latest designs…

The Wench is Wicked

– – – –

Blonde Verdict

– – – –

Delilah Was Deadly

– – – –

Three Novels by
Carter Brown

Stark House Press • Eureka California

THE WENCH IS WICKED / BLONDE VERDICT /
DELILAH WAS DEADLY

Published by Stark House Press
1315 H Street
Eureka, CA 95501, USA
griffinskye3@sbcglobal.net
www.starkhousepress.com

THE WENCH IS WICKED
Originally published and copyright © 1955 by Horwitz Publications, Sydney.

BLONDE VERDICT
Originally published and copyright © 1956 as by Horwitz Publications,
Sydney; revised and reprinted by Signet Books, New York, as The Brazen,
1960. Horwitz edition reprinted herewith.

DELILAH WAS DEADLY
Originally published and copyright © 1956 as by Horwitz Publications,
Sydney.

Reprinted by permission of the Estate of Alan G. Yates, and licensed via
publishing representatives, Xou Pty Ltd, Australia. All rights reserved under
International and Pan-American Copyright Conventions.

"Carter Brown: An Introduction " copyright © 2017 by Chris Yates.

ISBN-13: 978-1-944520-33-5

Book design by Mark Shepard, www.SHEPGRAPHICS.COM

First Stark House Press Edition: October 2017

FIRST EDITION

Contents

Contents

Carter Brown: An Introduction

By Chris Yates

The story of Carter Brown is as remarkable as any of his books. It's the story of one of the most popular and prolific authors the world has ever seen. It's the story of how Alan G. Yates became Carter Brown. Of how Yates, born in England, became Australia's greatest literary export, writing stories mostly set in a fictional US city. Many of which were written long before he'd even set foot in the country. It's the story of how these books not only appealed to Americans and Australians but also had huge international success becoming the second most translated books after The Bible.

Just like many other stories, this one begins in World War Two. Alan G. Yates (1 August – 5 May 1985), was born in Ilford, Essex. An outer suburb of London. In 1942 he joined the Royal Navy. Firstly in elite landing craft designed for commando raiding before being transferred to HMS Euryalus in the Pacific. *'The ship arrived in Sydney around seven in the morning and I stood on deck with my mouth wide open just not believing it as vista after vista of the harbour unrolled in front of my enchanted eyes,'* Yates wrote in his autobiography. If that was the start of his love for Australia, it wasn't long before he found love for an Australian too. He married Denise MacKellar in Sydney before they both travelled to England after the war.

In London, Yates worked as a sound cameraman for a subsidiary of Gaumont British Films. He entered a newspaper short story competition for £1000. A fortune in those days. He didn't win but he was hooked. He continued writing short stories, sending them to only the best magazines—*Argosy*, *Blackwoods* and *The Strand*—and continually being rejected. Yates returned to Australia working as an encyclopaedia salesman, a wine company clerk and a hardware store supplier before joining Qantas Empire Airways Ltd as a publicity writer, producing the monthly flight magazine and the staff journal. All the time he continued to write.

Yates recalled that *'publishers had found great success with pulp novelettes around 20,000 words in length which sold for sixpence a copy. Westerns were most popular of all. I knew absolutely nothing about the American West but as I read on I became convinced that these authors didn't either. Right then I began to feel that if I couldn't write any better than that*

I sure as hell could write faster.' Very quickly he was to do both. Yates wrote his first western and sent it to Invincible Press. It was published and he was paid £20, £1 per thousand words.

Yates wrote westerns, horror stories, romance and sci-fi thrillers under a variety of pseudonyms. The editor of a short story sci-fi magazine, *Thrills Incorporated*, complained that one of his stories was more a straight detective story than a sci-fi thriller but they liked it and would he write more? In September 1951 *The Lady is Murder* was the first story to be published under the name Peter Carter Brown. 'Peter' was later dropped for the US market.

The Carter Brown stories became immensely popular so much so that Yates stopped writing any other genre and focussed entirely on crime fiction. In fact, Carter Brown's success grew to such an extent that Yates was able to give up his job at Qantas and write full time, signing a 30-year contract with Horwitz to produce one novel and two novelettes per month. An outrageously demanding schedule.

By the mid-1950's Yates was producing 20 Carter Brown books each year. Between 1954 and 1984 Yates created around 300 Carter Brown books and novella-length stories making him one of the most prolific authors the world has ever seen. And, with around 100 million copies in print, one of the world's most popular authors too.

Lyle Moore, a key figure at Horwitz throughout Yates's career, came up with two astounding facts. Firstly on Yates's prolificness. Moore estimated that by 1960 Yates had published 8 million words adding *'to get there he's probably written twice that number.'* And secondly, on Cater Brown's popularity. Moore revealed that *'at his peak in America, he was selling 350,000 copies a book and in Australia we were doing 30,000-40,000 a book....so you can see how he built up to 100 million copies. Yates was bigger than big...it was difficult to find a country he wasn't published in.'* Incredible output, incredible sales but what was it that made Carter Brown such a big success?

Yates had his own spontaneous approach to plotting and characterisation. *'There must be many writers who can sit at their desks and carefully plot out the whole book before they start. I have tried it a couple of times but it never works for me. One of the main projected characters is so boring the typewriter yawns every time I write his name, while that minor character who was supposed to have been killed on page eight is starting to sound like fun.'* Yates always maintained that if he knew who the murderer was so would his audience before the end of Chapter One.

Yet despite this spontaneity and his impressive output, Yates still had the traditional fear of writer's block and of course deadlines. A 1963 profile piece in *Pix* magazine revealed that he approached the dreaded deadlines *'with the reluctance of a long-distance swimmer shivering on the brink of a cold, grey English Channel. In the manic depressive moments of the third night without sleep – when the deadline is long past and the mental block has set solid as concrete, the writer inevitably descends into self-analysis. He knows, of course, that it will be no more help than the last Dexedrine tablet but still clings to the naïve hope that, somehow, sometime, he will find a way of avoiding the recurrence of his present hopeless situation.'*

Later, in his autobiography, Yates wrote *'A friend of mine, also a writer, had said he'd found dexadrine a great help for keeping the concentration going. I went on happily using dexadrine for years, sometimes working for forty-eight hours straight. It was like castor oil, I always thought, the after-effects were lousey but it did its job. I was surprised when it was banned and slack-jawed at the thought of people taking speed for kicks. What the hell kick was that, staying up all night and pounding a typewriter?'*

Carter Brown books are fast-paced with a driving first-person narrative. There's titillation too. The girls are always glamourous, always well-endowed and always ready to have a good time for one reason or another. Most covers featured semi-clad models with a promise of more to come. Yates wrote the sex scenes with a light touch and good taste but later books had a more graphic sexual element to them introduced by editors at New American Library (NAL). Something that didn't always sit easily with the author.

Yates wasn't American and Carter Brown wasn't traditional noir but that's where it all started from. For Art Scott writing in 20th *Century Crime and Mystery Writers,* Carter Brown had its roots in a 1940s sub-genre of pulp. *'The Brown Books are the direct descendants of the 'spicy' detective pulps like* Hollywood Detective *and* Spicy Detective, *which occupied the opposite end of the respectability scale from the revered* Black Mask. *Yates hews to the conventions of that school closely…'*

Like the women, the settings are glamourous. Often characters are larger than life bordering on the eccentric or zany. There was always humour and plots were never too intellectual but what they did have was a cinematic or televisual quality. Fans at the time said they reminded them of television series, *77 Sunset Strip* and *Surfside Six,* for example. Carter Browns were fast, funny, slick and always entertaining which gave them their universal appeal.

Yates also liked to play with the titles and occasionally dialogue to refer, usually ironically, to other works. For *The Loving and The Dead (1959)* see Norman Mailer's *The Naked and The Dead (1948). Murder is my Mistress (1954)* is not a million miles from Chandler's *Trouble is My Business'* and James Hadley Chase's *No Orchids for Miss Blandish (1939)* has a link to *Halo for Hedy (1956).*

Yates created a variety of protagonists but Al Wheeler was the most popular and the most frequent. Wheeler's a homicide lieutenant at the Sheriff's Office in fictional Pine City, California, not so far from L.A. The first Carter Brown published in the US was *The Body* in July, 1958. Yates remembered '*I had been writing stories with American backgrounds for the last 9 years so I thought it would be a good idea to see the place.*' On a publicity tour arranged by NAL, Yates met his lifelong hero Duke Ellington who came and sat at his table at The Blue Note. Gore Vidal joined him for cocktails at another engagement. But despite all this success, serious literary critics did not deem Yates's books fit for review. All except one. Writer, editor and critic, Anthony Boucher, consistently championed Carter Brown in the *New York Times Book Review.*

In January, 1964, Boucher wrote an article for the *New York Times Book Review* outlining an imaginary university course studying crime fiction, concluding the course '*will not overlook, among all these reprints, the original paperback novels, the legitimate heirs to the dead pulps in which Hammett and Chandler flourished—their serious and substantial authors, such as John D. MacDonald, Charles Williams, Donald Hamilton and Vin Packer (all Gold Medal), and their highly competent purveyors of light amusement, like Carter Brown (Signet), Richard S. Prather (Gold Medal) and Henry Kane (many publishers).*'

Yates and Boucher became friends although the fact that Yates wasn't American still occasionally took him by surprise. Yates recalled one such conversation over dinner.

'*One time in San Francisco Anthony Boucher had asked me where we were going next. Well,*' I said, '*according to our schedule...*'

'*You really say 'schedule' and not 'skedule'? He was mildly surprised. 'You know what Dorothy Parker said when she first heard somebody say 'schedule'? 'Oh skit!*'

Serious literary critics ignoring Yates didn't stop Carter Brown sitting among the literary greats. In France, Gallimard can count Marcel Proust, Simone de Beavoir and Jean-Paul Satre on their back catalogue. Série Noire is Gallimard's crime fiction imprint with authors such as James Hadley Chase, Peter Cheyney, Horace McCoy, Jonathan Latimer, Dashiell Hammett, Raymond Chandler, and James M. Cain. And since 1959, Carter Brown. The French saw the cinema in CB too with three French films being produced and Yates even won a French literary award for the most whiskies drunk in a novel.

The rest, as they say, is history and, as Lyle Moore said, 'Yates became bigger than big' with 100 million copies in print and the second most translated books behind The Bible.

A spin-off Carter Brown comic book series was produced. 'The Carter Brown Mystery Theatre' radio series introduced by Yates himself ran from 1956-58. It was rumoured that Yates was one of John F. Kennedy's favourite authors and there was also a Japanese TV series. In the early 1980s, Yates worked with The Rocky Horror Show creator Richard O'Brien on a musical of *The Stripper* with Al Wheeler as its star which has been performed in both Australia and the UK.

Despite all his success and achievement, fellow author, Morris West, found Yates to be a modest man who wore his fame lightly and who found enjoyment in sharing a joke and a beer with a friend. Lyle Moore remembers him as '*a superb man and quite a unique character. He had an amazing intellect and tremendous powers of concentration. But when he wasn't writing he was a very urbane and interesting person who you could spend a lot of time with. He and Denise were always a very dynamic couple, very, very charming and interesting people,* '

Yates died in 1985. He was posthumously awarded a Ned Kelly in 1997, Australia's leading literary award for crime writing, for his lifelong contribution to the art.

—May 2017

The Wench is Wicked

- - - -

Carter Brown

CHAPTER 1
One for the Morgue

"Lieutenant!" The phone crackled with his emotion. "I've just found a body."

"Well, go and lose it again," I snarled. "I don't want it."

"I ain't kidding, Lieutenant," he said. "It's got three bullet-holes in it and it's deader than dead—it's stiff."

"In ten minutes from now," I said slowly, "I am off duty. I have a date with a blonde whose hourglass figure I can spend hours just looking at. I don't want to be interrupted. Is that quite clear?"

"Aw, lootenant," his voice was pleading. "You're kidding, ain't you?"

Why the hell did I choose to be a cop when I might have been a heist-man with three apartments, five blondes and no interruptions?

"OK," I said resignedly. "Where is this cadaver?"

"I'm out on the State Highway," he said. "Just about a mile past the road-house, there's an old gravel pit that ain't been used for years. This stiff is down there."

"What the hell are you doing walking around a disused sandpit?" I asked him. "Looking for the Sandman?"

"Lieutenant," he said slowly, "I'm the patrolman out this way, remember?"

"OK," I said. "We'll come out and take a look at it—meet us on the highway."

"Sure, lootenant." He sounded happier.

I hung up and went along to Captain Parker's office, knocked on the door, then walked in. He took off his glasses and looked at me.

"What is it, Al?" he asked.

"Patrolman Macey has just turned up a stiff," I told him. "It so happens that I'm off duty in eight minutes and I also have a heavy date with a blonde, so ..."

"You now have a heavy date with a stiff,' he finished for me. "Go on."

I sighed. "Is there no place for romance in this precinct?"

"Not along with the stiffs," he said comfortably. "The place would get too crowded. Go on."

"A mile past the roadhouse on the State Highway," I quoted Macey, "there is an old, disused gravel pit. At the bottom of the gravel pit is an old, disused stiff with three bullet-holes in it."

"What the hell was Macey doing around the gravel pit?"

"I asked him that," I said. "He told me he's the patrolman out there."

"Digging sandcastles while autos are running into each other all over the highway," Parker grated. "I must have a few words with Patrolman Macey."

"Sure," I said. I lit a cigarette and wondered how the blonde would react to being stood up. I didn't think she'd like it. Come to think of it, outside of mink and diamonds, there wasn't much that Goldie did like.

Parker grunted sourly. "You'd better get out there and take a look. Get some photographs, then bring it into the morgue. I'll have the doctor look at it there."

"OK," I said.

"You want to take anybody with you?" he asked.

I shook my head. "If they really want to see a stiff, they can go look at it in the morgue. You'll send the meat-wagon to pick it up?"

"Sure," he said. "The photographer can ride with it, if you're keen on going alone."

"OK," I said again.

He looked at me sharply. "I'll check with Patrolman Macey what time you arrive out there, Al. No detouring to see this blonde on the way."

"What's the matter?" I said indignantly. "Don't you trust me?"

"In a word—no," he said emphatically.

I left the precinct, took one of the prowl cars off the curb and switched on the radio out of habit, as I drove.

Out on the west side of the city, a hopped-up kid had piled up a sedan on the sidewalk, killing a mother and child ... Downtown somebody had shoved a knife into somebody they didn't like ... It was a lovely golden afternoon with the sun still just above the horizon. I thought about Goldie and sighed deeply. Somebody was worrying Precinct Six because a bank messenger hadn't turned up at the bank he was supposed to, and he was carrying quite a lot of money with him when he left the first bank. There was another accident just being reported—on the State Highway the other side of town, this time. It sounded messy. I turned the radio off and concentrated on the golden afternoon.

A mile past the Eldorado Roadhouse I saw the patrolman sitting on his bike, waiting for me. I pulled into the curb and stopped. He came up to me as I got out of the car.

"Glad you got here, Lieutenant," he said. "Seeing that stiff sort of unnerved me and ..."

"What the hell were you doing in the gravel pit, anyway?"

He blushed. "It's the only place around here you can't be seen from the highway, Lieutenant, and ..."

"OK, OK," I said. "Let's go take a look. How far is it?"

"About a quarter of a mile down that track," he said.

"Can I get the car down there?"

"I guess so, Lieutenant."

"You lead the way, then."

His bike bumped down the track and I followed him in low gear. Finally we stopped beside the edge of the pit and I got out. Macey was standing at the edge of the pit and I walked up to him.

"There it is, Lieutenant," he pointed downward, "down there."

"You been down to have a look at it?" I asked him.

"No, sir," he shook his head. "I thought I'd better report it right away."

"I guess I'd better take a look," I said. "You go back to the highway and wait for the meat-wagon. Bring it up here when it arrives."

"Sure, lootenant." He seemed glad of the chance to go. A few seconds later he roared off on his motorbike—and I started the climb down into the gravel pit.

I scrambled down the steep side of the pit and lost my footing, so that I slid the last ten feet on the seat of my pants. That would do my new dacron suit a hell of a lot of good. I stood upright at the bottom, dusted off the seat of my pants and walked toward the corpse.

He'd been somewhere around the forty mark when he'd come to a full stop. Not a bad-looking character with a neatly trimmed mustache and that attractive touch of gray around the temples. He was wearing an expensive suit which the bullet-holes had spoiled. I counted them and there were three, just like Macey had said. He lay sprawled on his back, his arms flung out either side of him. There was no look of surprise or fear on his face.

I knelt down and touched his wrist—it was quite cold. I stood up again and looked at the ground around him. It was rough and uneven with water lying in patches close by. There were no signs of him having been dragged down there and I doubted that there would have been any signs, even if he had been dragged.

I lit a cigarette and after a while I heard the chug-chug of the patrolman's bike and then he came into view at the top of the pit. The photographer came scrambling down toward me and I felt disappointed when he managed to avoid sliding the last ten feet on the seat of his pants.

He took his flash-shots from every possible angle and then a couple more. "OK, Lieutenant?" he asked.

"Sure," I said.

He looked down at the stiff curiously. "Hell of a place to find a corpse, isn't it?"

"We should feel grateful that Patrolman Macey likes to commune with nature," I said. He looked at me blankly and shrugged his shoulders.

I knelt down beside the corpse and went through the pockets quickly. It was a job that would be done thoroughly back at the morgue and the lab boys would take the dust off his feet and out of his pockets and out of his ears and say, "Ah, yes. This man comes from number fifty-four, Morgan Street, Colombus, Ohio."

But sometimes a humble working cop like me can find all that out from the stiff's billfold, which may have his address in it.

He had a billfold. Inside was a hundred and fifty dollars in cash, a driving lice in the name of Robert Heinman with a New York address, and a photograph.

The photograph I recognized. Who wouldn't? A photograph of Deidre Damour would be recognized by any citizen of the United States over the age of five. I turned it over and written on the back was the inscription ... *To Bobby, this is forever—Deidre.*

Touching.

The only other things in his pockets were a pack of cigarettes, a silver-plated lighter and a key ring. I left them where they were, put the billfold into my own pocket, then looked up and saw the two white-coated ghouls with their stretcher, waiting sourly to take the cadaver away.

I got up on my feet again. "All right, boys," I said. "It's all yours."

"How are we going to get it up there?" one of them asked, jerking his head toward the top of the pit.

"Carry it?" I suggested helpfully and left them to work it out. I managed to scramble up to the top of the pit again, where Macey and the photographer waited for me. "You'd better come in and write out a report," I told Macey.

"Yes, lootenant," he nodded and kicked over the starter of his motorbike.

"You can ride back with me," I told the photographer.

"Be glad to, Lieutenant." He shivered as he looked around. The sun was a golden orb on the horizon and long shadows were creeping across the gravel pit. "This place gives me the shivers."

We got back to the precinct. The photographer hurried off to his darkroom and I went through to my desk. Detective Quinn grinned at me as I came in.

"A dame phoned you about a quarter of an hour ago," he said. "I told her you was out on a murder and she said she was glad you was getting the practice, because the next time she sees you there's likely to be another one."

"Yeah," I said sourly, then went into Captain Parker's office. This time he didn't bother to take his glasses off, he just looked at me over the top of them. "Well?" he demanded.

"Name of Heinman," I said. I tossed the billfold on his desk. He opened it and read the license, then saw the photograph of Deidre Damour and whistled softly. He turned it over and read the inscription.

"A guy who knows Deidre Damour that well," he said, "is just wasting his time being dead."

"Check," I agreed.

"By a remarkable coincidence," he said mildly, "there happens to be a …"

"Film unit on location here," I said, "and the star of the epic they're making happens to be Deidre Damour."

"Don't interrupt your senior officer," he said. "You'd better go out there and take a look."

"They're out in the valley," I said, "making a wide western for the wide screen. They won't be filming now—it's nearly dark."

I looked at him hopefully. "I'll get over there first thing in the morning, captain, and …"

"You'll get over there tonight," he snarled.

"Yes, sir," I said.

He lit a cigarette and sucked smoke into his lungs and from the look on his face, it tasted like sludge. "Anything else?" he asked.

"Three bullet-holes in his chest," I said. "No surprise on his face—maybe he was used to being murdered. No signs of anything—struggle, etcetera—around, but it's not the sort of ground that would show any signs, anyway."

"What was Macey doing around the gravel pit to find him?"

"My modesty forbids me revealing that fact," I told him. "How long have patrolmen been issued with field-glasses?"

"Huh?" he said blankly.

"When Macey phoned through, he told me there were three bullet-holes in the stiff," I said. "When I got out there, he told me he hadn't been down into the pit—he'd seen the corpse from the top and then left to phone through. From the top of the pit to the stiff was maybe seventy-five feet. His eyes can't be that good."

"Why didn't you ask him where he got his X-ray vision?"

"I thought I'd save it," I said. "I had him come in to write his report—maybe he'll explain it in that."

"I'll let you know," Parker said.

He took another draw on his cigarette and looked at me. "You got something on your mind about Macey?" he asked.

"Check," I agreed. "But I don't know what it is—I'd like to leave it simmer a little."

"You don't want me to ask Macey?"

"Not yet," I said.

He took another look at me. "You know why you got to be a lieutenant, when there are guys around almost old enough to be your father and still detectives?"

"Nobody else was sucker enough to take the job?" I suggested.

"Because you're bright," Parker grunted. "You're also the most un-orthodox cop I've ever met. The way I let you talk to me makes me the second most unorthodox cop I know, too. But handle this lightly, Al. Damour's a big name and if she's wrapped up with this thing in any way, we're going to hit the front pages throughout the country. So let's not do anything the district attorney would not like, eh?"

"No, sir," I said, like any orthodox cop would.

CHAPTER 2
No Motives, No Suspects

There were trucks and caravans and arc lights rigged over the lot. It looked like a carnival. I parked the prowl car and got out. A guy came over to me, swinging a heavy torch in his hand.

"You want anything, bud?" he asked.

"Who's in charge here?" I asked him.

"Marina," he grunted, "but he ain't here."

"Miss Damour here?"

"Sorry, bud," he grunted again, "she's working. She don't sign no au-tographs or give no interviews while she's working."

"This is police business," I told him and showed him my ticket.

He thawed a little at that. "Sorry, Lieutenant. She's up at the hotel. They're all staying there. All the big shots, that is."

"Which hotel?"

"The one down in the valley," he pointed vaguely, "about four miles from here."

"I know it," I said, "thanks." I turned away, back toward the prowl car.

"Trouble?" he asked curiously.

"You ever hear of a guy called Heinman, Robert Heinman?"

He shook his head disappointedly. "Not me. Why?"

"I just wondered," I told him.

I got behind the wheel and started the car again. I drove down the road that led into the valley. I'd forgotten the hotel existed. It's a hangover from the days the west was really wild. A two-story clapboard affair that looks as if it's overdue to fall over. It's run as a tourist place—I didn't know if it ever got any tourists. It must have hit the jackpot when the film crowd ar-rived.

Five minutes later I stopped outside the hotel. I walked up the steps and in the front entrance. The floor was wooden and the walls were timber-paneled. Stetsons, sombreros, lariats and six-guns were hung around the walls. There was a wooden reception desk but the dame behind the reception desk looked anything but wooden.

She was tall, blonde and wearing a white sweater that must have been painted on her by a Rembrandt—or some character who took a pride in his work, anyway.

"I'm sorry, sir," she said in a husky voice, "but there are no vacancies."

"You couldn't squeeze me in behind that desk?" I suggested hopefully.

Her nose tilted a couple of inches up into the air. "I told you there are no vacancies. Do you want me to call a cop?"

"You wouldn't have to call real loud," I told her. I showed her my ticket. "I was just kidding," I told her. "Surprisingly enough, blondes have that effect on me."

She thawed a little. "What can I do for you, Lieutenant?"

I sighed gently and she absentmindedly patted her hair.

"I'd like to see Deidre Damour," I said.

"I think she's in her room," she said. "Would you like me to find out?"

"I think that would he a wonderful idea," I said soberly.

She rang through on the house phone, waited a moment, then said in the honey-sweet professional tones of all desk clerks, "Miss Damour? This is the reception desk here. There is a Lieutenant Wheeler down here and he wants to see you."

She listened for a moment, then looked at me. "Miss Damour says she's too tired to see anybody."

"Tell her she can see me in her room now," I said, "or I'll take her down to the precinct and she can see me there—and all the other cops, too."

She blurted the words doubtfully into the phone. The earpiece quivered for about thirty seconds, then there was a sharp click as Deidre Damour hung up. The blonde desk clerk looked slightly shaken.

"She said to come up," she told me, "or words to that effect."

"What's the room number?"

"Eighteen—just turn to your left at the top of the stairs." She hesitated for a moment. "Does this mean trouble, Lieutenant?"

"Trouble?" I said. "What's trouble? You look like trouble to me. Interesting trouble."

She patted her hair again. "Why, Lieutenant. You don't sound like a policeman at all."

"I hope I don't even look like one," I said and headed toward the stairs. I found the room easily enough, knocked on the door, then walked in.

Deidre Damour looked everything in real life that she looked on the screen—which is saying quite a lot. She was the harem vision of office boys and the penthouse vision of financiers alike. And she still was in real life, without any soft-focus lenses or expert make-up to help. Her tawny-colored hair hung down below her shoulders, her eyes were dark and smoldering, like a forest fire ready to burst into flame again at any moment.

She was sitting on a stool in front of a dressing table with a huge mirror, doing her nails with a file as long as a bayonet.

She was wearing a housegown that didn't have the four bottom buttons done up, so that the gown parted six inches above her knees and draped carelessly either side of her crossed legs to the floor. The pose was too good to be natural. I seemed to remember it from her last movie.

"What is it?" she asked impatiently, without bothering to look around at me.

"This is forever," I said softly and she jumped as if I'd told her she was flat-footed.

She turned around to look at me then. "What did you say?"

"Just a phrase I heard some place," I told her. "I'm Lieutenant Wheeler, Miss Damour, city police."

"If you have some stupid traffic regulations that I broke," she said coldly, "'contact the studio about it—they'll fix it."

I have my pride. "I'm a lieutenant," I said. "You should feel flattered having a lieutenant call on you. An ordinary cop would come around if it were traffic regulations."

"So I'm flattered," she said. "What is it, then? Tickets for the Policemen's Ball?"

I leaned against the door and looked at her. "Do you know a man named Robert Heinman?" I asked her.

"Bobby? Yes, of course I know him."

"You know him well?"

"Reasonably well," she frowned. "Why? What has he done? What is all this?"

"Who is he?"

She sounded surprised. "You don't know?"

"Would I ask if I did?"

"After all," she said, "this is a hick town. Bobby's one of the most brilliant playwrights this country has ever produced."

"Was," I said gently.

She stared at me blankly for a moment. "Was?"

"When did you last see him?"

"A week ago—in New York. What did you mean—was?"

"We found him in a gravel pit this afternoon," I said. "Nobody was using the gravel pit, except him. He was dead—somebody had shot him."

"Poor Bobby." She turned away from me and buried her head in her hands. She seemed to remember that one from her last movie, too.

"Have you any idea why anyone would want to kill him?" I asked her.

"No," she said in a muffled voice, "he was a wonderful person. I can't believe it's true that anyone would kill him."

"He was awfully dead when I last saw him," I assured her. "He had your photograph in his billfold," I said, "with an inscription on the back."

She lifted her face, dabbing her eyes gently with a wisp of a handkerchief. "I was very fond of Bobby," she said. "He did the scenario of this film we're making."

"Why would he have come down here, do you think?"

She shook her head. "I don't know. Unless Baron sent for him."

"Baron?"

"Baron Marina—he's the director."

"I'll talk to him afterwards," I said. "What was Heinman doing in New York when you saw him there a week ago?"

"He lived there," she said. "I was in New York for a couple of days on business. I just stopped by to say hello to him. He seemed perfectly happy then. He was working on a new play."

"You haven't seen him since and you don't know what he was doing down here, or why anybody should want to murder him?"

"No," she said.

"Thanks, Miss Damour," I said. "You've been a great help."

I let myself out and went downstairs to the blonde. "Where do I find Marina?" I asked her.

"I think he's in the bar, Lieutenant," she said. "Shall I have him paged for you?"

"Don't bother," I told her, "I'll go find him. Where is the bar?"

"Straight through there," she pointed to an archway.

I went through into the bar. There were half a dozen characters grouped around the bar, all arguing violently. They stopped as I came in and looked at me.

"I thought we took over the whole hotel," one of them said belligerently.

"I'm looking for Mr. Marina," I said.

"That's me," a character with dark glasses and a large paunch grunted. "What do you want?"

"I'm Lieutenant Wheeler," I repeated the formula. "I'd like to talk to you."

"All right, Lieutenant."

I lit myself a cigarette. I thought if Heinman had written a scenario for the film they were doing, all of them probably knew him. So there was no point in getting Marina into a corner to tell him about it.

"I'm investigating a murder, Mr. Marina," I said. "A man by the name of Robert Heinman."

There was a stifled scream from someone sitting in the corner. I turned

and looked at her: a brunette with everything. "You knew him?" I said.
"Bobby." She nodded jerkily. "Yes, I knew him."

"We all knew him, Lieutenant," Marina said gravely, "and the news of his death comes as a great shock to us. He did the scene for the film we're shooting right here in this valley. Where was he murdered—in New York?"

"In a gravel pit about four miles from here," I said. "That was where we found his body, anyway. A patrolman turned it up this afternoon."

They all looked at each other. Marina cleared his throat. "But what was he doing down here?"

"I thought you might be able to tell me that,' I said.

He shook his head. "I have no idea. I don't know if anyone else has, but perhaps I'd better introduce you to these people, Lieutenant? They are, of course, all working on this film with me. This is Jon Clayton, the male star."

Clayton nodded. He was tall, wide and handsome, and dumb-looking, the way all western heroes should be.

"Moira Banks, who plays the second female lead," Marina said.

She was the brunette who'd screamed in the wrong place. She nodded and went back to biting her handkerchief.

"Wolf Ramos ..."

"Hello there, Lieutenant," Wolf Ramos smiled. He'd been playing character parts around Hollywood longer than I could remember, but he didn't look a day over forty-five.

"This is Ed Stultz, our cameraman," Marina introduced the last of the group. He was in his mid-thirties, with horn-rimmed glasses and an absentminded look.

"You will appreciate this is a preliminary investigation," I said. "The body was only found a couple of hours ago. I'm trying to ascertain what he was doing here instead of New York and why he was murdered. The obvious link between Heinman and this town is yourselves—the film you're making. Did any one of you know he was coming down?"

They looked at each other, then shook their heads.

"He had a very intimate relationship with Miss Deidre Damour, I understand," I said smoothly.

"No," Moira Banks said with unnecessary violence, then looked embarrassed again.

"Perhaps I heard it wrong," I said. "Would anyone have any ideas why he should be murdered?"

"The only reason I can think of," Wolf Ramos said cheerfully, "is the quality of the scenarios he writes." He saw the glare on Baron Marina's face. "But I suppose ninety per cent of Hollywood writers should end up in the morgue in that case," he finished.

I was getting nowhere fast. I lit myself a cigarette. "Has anyone got any information they think might be of some help? Does anybody know if he had any enemies? Was there any reason why he should come down here? To see somebody, maybe?"

I looked around the ring of blank faces. "No? Well, thanks for your help, anyway." I looked at Marina. "I'll be around again, no doubt. If anyone should think of anything, I'd be pleased to hear it."

I went out of the bar and saw the blonde was quivering with curiosity. I thought I'd be kind to her—who knows? I might need a room one day— or even a blonde.

"A guy by the name of Robert Heinman got himself bumped off today," I said. "That's what all the excitement's about."

"Him," she said scornfully. "I'm not surprised."

I stopped dead in my tracks and looked at her. "Why aren't you surprised?"

"Didn't you read his series in *Dynamite?*" she asked.

"No," I said slowly, "I didn't."

"He called it 'Hollywood with the Lid Off'," she sniffed. "The things he said about the stars and the directors. It's a wonder they didn't all club together to get him murdered."

"Thanks," I said, "thank you very much."

CHAPTER 3
The Wild, Wild West

It was eight-thirty when I got to the morgue. There's nothing I like better than seeing those rows of slabs on an empty stomach. Old Elmer, who looks like a ghost himself, met me at the door. He nodded when he saw who it was. He doesn't like me much—he doesn't think I'm a sober enough character to really appreciate a morgue.

"What do you want?" he grunted.

"You got that new stiff in here?" I asked him.

"Sure," he said. "Everybody's been down having a crack at it."

"Captain Parker down here?"

"He was—he's gone now."

"OK," I said.

"You want to see him?" Elmer asked.

"The captain?"

"The corpse."

"I saw it this afternoon," I said. "It's not my idea of fun, pal. I'm not like you."

Elmer sniffed, "That's where you'll end up one of these days, son. On a slab in here."

"Well, you lay me out good and nice," I told him, "otherwise I'll come back and haunt you."

I went back to the prowl car and drove back to the precinct. Captain Parker was still in his office.

"You've been down to the morgue, so Elmer told me," I said as I walked in.

He nodded. "Took a look. Doctor places time of death around four this morning. Kind of early."

"Or late," I said.

"Yeah," he said. "What did you find out with this film outfit?" I told him. He grunted when I'd finished, "You might just as well have stayed here."

"I got something from the blonde on the reception desk," I said.

"Spare me the sordid details of your life," he said.

"I mean information," I grinned. "Apparently Heinman wrote a series of articles for *Dynamite*, lifting the lid off Hollywood. My blonde wonders they all didn't club together to have him murdered."

"That sounds interesting," Parker said. "He was shot with a .45 caliber. Two bullets in the heart and one just above it in the lung. Whoever did it wanted to make sure."

"Nothing like finishing a thing once you've started it," I said.

He rang the cop on desk duty and told him to send in two cups of coffee. "You find out who Heinman was?" he asked me.

"Sure," I said. "A playwright—he did the scenario of this film they're making."

"I checked with New York," he said. "My information's the same. I've told the D.A. He's jumping around like a cat on hot bricks—wants the case busted, and quickly. He's releasing details to the press in about half an hour from now, so from then on the precinct's going to be lousy with reporters."

"I just remembered," I said, "I have to go out about then."

The cop arrived with the coffee. Parker broke off the lid of the container and drank.

"I've got Quinn out checking on the railroad and the airport," he said, "seeing if we can find out when he arrived. Nobody has turned in an abandoned car, so I'm presuming he came in by train or plane."

"Maybe he walked?" I suggested.

He gave me an ice-cooled look. "Save it for your memoirs," he said, "I'm in no mood, Al."

"OK," I said. I drank some of the coffee—hot and strong. It reminded me of Goldie again. "What do I do?" I asked him.

"You never were very hot on routine," he said. "I'll handle the routine from here. I'm giving you a roving commission, but don't rove for too long. We've got to turn in results, and fast, or we're really in trouble. The D.A.'s sweating and that means that city hall is sweating. They've got a nice clean town all ready for the elections—they won't want an unsolved murder draped across the landscape."

"Yes, sir," I said. "I mean—no, sir."

"And three bags full to you," he said. "OK—start roving."

"Did you get Macey's written report?" I asked him.

"Yeah—he didn't go down into the pit. He looked over the edge, saw the cadaver and went back to the highway and phoned in. You still want that to simmer?"

"For a little while, chief. While I'm roving, you expect to see me from time to time?"

"Yeah—every morning, every afternoon and every night."

"That's what I like about working for you," I said. "You don't care what I do, just so long as I'm working myself to death."

"Check," he agreed.

I went out of his office and over to my desk in the detectives' room. One of these days they'll give the Lieutenant of the precinct a room of his own. I've only been waiting two years for it now.

Detective Poleiski was booking a junkie. It looked like the stuff was just wearing off. The whites of his eyes were showing and he was screaming thinly while two burly cops wrestled with him, trying to hold him down.

It was too noisy to concentrate. I went out front and saw Sam Macnamara on the desk.

"Hi, Lieutenant," he grinned at me. "We got a brand-new murder, I hear?"

"That's right, Sam," I said. "The chief has given me a sort of roving commission, so I'm going to take a car and just rove."

"Some guys," he said.

"You know Macey?" I asked.

"Sure," he said.

"Where does he live?"

Sam thumbed through his books until he found the address and then gave it to me. I wrote it down. "Thanks," I said. "What sort of a cop is he, Sam?"

"Macey? Just a cop. He ain't bright—but then he ain't dumb, either. Average."

"Been in the force long?"

"About five or six years, I guess." He frowned at me. "Why? What's the matter with Macey?"

"He's got a bad memory," I said. "I'll be seeing you around, Sam."

I went out on the sidewalk and took the car off the curb again. Nine-thirty when I reached the Eldorado; left the car on the lot outside and went in.

Johnny Ralston was out front in the foyer, looking like an ad for some English tailor in his dinner suit. "Hello, Lieutenant," he grinned at me. It was strictly a facial contortion while his eyes still looked as if they belonged to a rattlesnake.

"Hi, Johnny," I said.

"Not business, I hope?"

"Strictly for pleasure," I said. "Goldie around?"

"Yeah," he nodded. "Last time I saw her, she was in the bar. It's her night off. I don't know what she's doing hanging around the joint."

"I do," I said. "Did I say pleasure?" I walked through into the bar.

Goldie was there, all right. She was sitting facing the bar, her chin propped up on her elbows, with one of the biggest glasses I had ever seen in front of her. I shuddered to think what the glass contained—probably neat alcohol.

She was wearing a black dress which had no back whatsoever. I wondered how it looked from the front, then she caught sight of me in the mirror and turned around. There was some gown in front—just enough. But I didn't have time to analyze exactly how much. The big glass described a neat spiral through the air in my direction.

I ducked hastily and it shattered against the wall behind me. "You louse," she said. "You heel."

"Listen," I pleaded with her. "I can explain."

Goldie wasn't listening to me, she was talking to the barman. "Charlie," she said pleadingly. "Give me a bottle—a full one."

"You're not breaking up my bar, Goldie," he said firmly. "If you don't like the guy, why don't you take him outside and cut his throat?"

"That's an idea," she said. "Got a knife?"

"Can I help it," I said loudly, "if a guy gets himself murdered and they find the corpse ten minutes before I go off duty?"

They both looked up at me. "Murdered?" Goldie said slowly. "Who was murdered?"

"Character by the name of Robert Heinman," I said.

"He had it coming to him," she said.

"You read *Dynamite*, too?" I said.

She nodded. "Sure I do. I wondered how he had the nerve to try and get away with it, when I read the stuff."

"Just goes to show," Charlie shook his head, "that he didn't get away with it. You drinking, Lieutenant?"

"I shouldn't," I said. "Scotch on the rocks, thanks, Charlie." He poured the drink and I sat on the stool next to Goldie. "I'm sorry, honey," I said. "You know how it is."

"I suppose so," she said. "I should have my head read, going out with a cop. Johnny gives me the fish-eye every time he sees you around."

"He does, does he?" I said indignantly. "Well, maybe I'll raid this dump a couple of times and then he can smile when he sees me around."

I picked up the drink and swallowed it down in a couple of gulps. "This case is hot, honey," I said. "I'm going to be busy till it's over. So if I don't see you for a few days."

"I can pour a can of water over that torch I'm carrying without any trouble at all," she said acidly.

"Yeah," I said and slid off the stool. "Well, so long."

"Goodbye—Lieutenant," she said coldly. Such is a cop's life.

I went outside. Johnny was still in the foyer. "I hear we got a murder," he said.

I looked at him. "Where did you hear that?"

He shrugged, "You know how it is, Lieutenant."

"No," I said, "I don't know how it is. You tell me."

"I just heard," he said.

I thought I'd let it ride. "You get any of this film crowd come in?" I asked him.

"There was a party of them here last night," he said. "They left around two."

"Anything interesting happen while they were here?"

"Not that I recall," he said. "Most of 'em seemed to get pretty drunk— that Ramos character in particular, though he held it all right. Looks like instead of going to bed nights, he just crawls into a vat of alcohol and stays pickled till morning."

"It's an interesting thought," I said.

Out into the car again. I sat behind the wheel and lit a cigarette. I was going to see Macey, I remembered, but I had another hunch and I wanted to see if there was a pay-off in it first. Macey could wait.

I pointed the bonnet of the car down the highway and headed back toward the valley. The blonde was still on duty behind the desk.

She gave me a warm smile this time as I came in. "Hello there, Lieutenant," she said. "Back so soon?"

"Since I saw you I can't stay away," I said. I leaned against the desk and looked around. "Nice place you got here."

"It is nice, isn't it?" she said enthusiastically. "We were very glad when the film crowd came. Business hasn't been so good lately and we certainly can use their money."

"This place is old," I said. "Quite a history?"

"It goes right back to the old days of the west," she said. She patted her hair. "You know—when men were men ..."

"And women were grateful for it," I said.

She laughed. "We've tried to keep the atmosphere," she said. "That's why we've got those hats and things around the walls."

"Good idea," I said. "Guns, too."

"And guns, too," she agreed.

"Have you got any bullets for the guns?" I asked her.

"What are you trying to do, Lieutenant?" she laughed nervously. "Tell me we should have licenses for the guns?"

"I'm not worried about licenses," I said. "I'm just interested in whether you've got any bullets?"

"I'd have to ask Pop," she said. "He'd know."

"Go ask him," I said.

She hesitated. "I shouldn't leave the desk—somebody might want some room service."

"I'll watch the desk," I said. "You go ask him."

She walked away with that nice tight swing that most blondes seem to have. I lit a cigarette and thought it was probably a lousy hunch, anyway.

The phone on the desk jingled. I picked up the receiver and said, "Desk," into it.

"Miss Damour here," a husky voice said. "Send up a martini, will you?"

"Right away," I said. "I'll have the helicopter tested."

"What?"

"I have a bad heart," I said. "I can't climb stairs."

"This is ridiculous," she said.

"I know," I said helpfully. "Would you like to come down and get the martini?"

"Don't be absurd. I'm just out of the shower."

"In that case," I said, "I'll bring it up—personally."

The receiver clunked in my ear as she hung up. I put my own receiver back on the cradle. What did she want to do—drink to Bobby's memory?

The blonde came back, followed by an old guy wearing rimless glasses perched halfway down his nose, and a worried look. "This is my Pop," she said. "This is the Lieutenant Wheeler I was telling you about, Pop."

"Howdy, Lieutenant," he said nervously.

"Miss Damour wants a martini," I said to the blonde.

"I'd better take it up to her," she said and headed toward the bar.

I looked at the old guy. He was fidgeting around, not looking at me. "Pop," I said. "Bullets?"

"Well," he said cautiously, "it's like this, Lieutenant. I set up a range at the back of the place—to amuse the guests, you know. I figured they might get a kick out of firing some of them old forty-fives and ..."

"You've got a stack of ammunition out there," I finished for him. "OK—let's take a look."

Pop shuffled off and I followed him through the hotel and out the back. We went down a concrete path for about twenty yards and into a shack. He switched the lights on and I saw the wooden bench with the rack above it and the guns neatly stacked there.

"The range is out there," he gestured toward the back door of the shack. "You want to see that, Lieutenant?"

"No," I said. "Where do you keep the ammunition?"

"In this drawer here." He opened a drawer in the bench and I saw the packs of slugs scattered around inside.

"How many guns you got?"

"Six," he told me.

I looked at the rack and counted. There were six guns there. "When did you last check the guns?" I asked him.

"Yesterday afternoon," he said. "Them film folk were out here, playin' around with 'em. It was rainin' and they said they didn't have anything else to do—couldn't go filming in the valley while it was rainin', they said."

"How about the ammunition—did you check that at the same time?"

"Well, Lieutenant," he scratched his ear and looked embarrassed. "I don't rightly know about that—you see, I never do check the bullets—sort of ain't no point in doin' so. When we're runnin' short, I buy some more."

I swore softly under my breath.

He was looking more and more worried. "Lieutenant—I been doin' something I shouldn't?"

"Oh, no," I said bitterly, "nothing—nothing at all. You're just six licenses short for a start. You realize anybody could walk in here, take one of those guns, load it, then walk out and murder somebody?"

"I never did think of that." He scratched his ear again.

"That's what happened last night," I said. "Somebody walked in here, took a gun, loaded it—then walked out and killed a guy by the name of Robert Heinman. Then they came back, put the gun back on the rack and went to bed."

"Maybe you could test for fingerprints," he said eagerly.

"Sure," I said. "You just told me they were all using the guns out here yesterday afternoon—so I'd expect to find their prints over all the guns, wouldn't I? So it wouldn't mean a damn thing, would it?"

"I suppose not," he agreed.

"Pop," I said, "let's get back to the hotel. The sight of this hut is beginning to depress me."

CHAPTER 4
Vive Damour

I got back to the reception desk and the blonde. Pop shuffled off, still scratching his ear and wearing his worried expression. The blonde was also wearing a worried expression. "I hope Pop didn't do anything wrong," she said.

"Skip it," I told her. "Is Miss Banks around?"

"I think she went up to her room," she said. "Do you want me to ring her?"

"Just give me her room number," I said.

"Fifteen," she said. She smiled uncertainly. "If there's anything I can do to help, Lieutenant."

"Just stay the way you are, honey," I told her. "You're good for my morale that way."

I climbed the stairs and went along to number fifteen, then knocked gently on the door.

"Who is it?" a muffled voice asked.

"Lieutenant Wheeler," I said.

"Oh." I heard the key turn in the lock and then she opened the door. "What is it, Lieutenant?" she asked.

"I wanted to talk to you for a moment," I said. I looked at her tear-stained face. "Sorry if it's an awkward moment, but murder creates a lot of awkward problems." I walked into the room and closed the door behind me.

She stood there, looking at me. "What did you want to see me about?" she asked.

"About Heinman," I said. I took off my hat and dropped it on the dressing table. "Tell me about him."

"I can't tell you anything," she said, "really, Lieutenant. I said downstairs that I didn't know anything that could be of any help to you and ..."

"Tell me," I said, "why are you carrying a torch higher than the Empire State for a guy you hardly knew?"

She stared at me for a moment, then she got a haughty look on her face—expression number four at the dramatic school. I wasn't impressed.

"I don't know what you're talking about," she said.

"Why the tears? Don't tell me you've been peeling onions."

"Do I have to put up with your insults, Lieutenant?"

"Heinman's dead," I said, "somebody shot him—and that makes it murder. I'm the detective who is investigating the murder. I expect co-operation. If I don't get it, then I can use other methods to try and get it. Methods like taking people down to the precinct and booking them as material witnesses, for example, questioning them under bright lights for a long time. All nice and legal, those methods. Do I make myself clear?"

"Painfully," she said.

"OK." I lit myself a cigarette. "Then let's get back to Robert Heinman."

"He was a nice guy," she said, "he was one hell of a nice guy."

"So he got himself murdered?"

"Yes," she said.

I closed my eyes for a moment. Maybe I'd worked too long or I was getting too old for this sort of business. Maybe Charlie would move over if I asked him nicely and let me help him tend his bar.

"He was a nice guy so he was murdered," I repeated. "Do you base your theory on facts, Miss Banks? Or don't little things like facts bother you?"

"Bobby was an idealist," she said.

"That's no crime," I said, "not in the statute book, anyway."

"All right," she said coldly. "If you really want to know what happened to Bobby, why don't you ask Deidre Damour? She knows."

"But you know, too," I said mildly. "Let's hear it from you, first."

She turned away from me and went to the window, looking out on the darkness that was the valley. "Bobby had a raw deal in Hollywood," she said in a low voice. "He was a brilliant playwright—brilliant."

"So everybody keeps telling me," I said wearily.

"But they didn't know it," she said. "They never do. They spend millions on the wide screens and stereophonic sound and things like that, when all they've got to do to make money is to make decent pictures. And to make decent pictures, they need decent scripts—but they don't use the good writers, the brilliant ones—like Bobby."

"Does Sam Goldwyn know all this?" I asked in an awed voice.

She ignored my comment. "It would have soured most men," she said. "It has soured a lot of them—but it didn't sour Bobby. He was too fine for that. He put it down to experience. Hollywood fascinated him—he set out to find what made it tick."

"And he ended up writing dirt for a dirty magazine?" I asked helpfully.

She spun around to face me with a look of fury on her face. "That's the way you see it," she almost spat the words. "That's the way all the morons see it. They don't realize what happened to him. They don't know that human vampire got her hooks into him and he was so blinded by her that he didn't even know what was happening to him."

I lit my cigarette. "You refer, I take it, to Miss Damour?"

"Yes," she told me, her voice dripping vitriol, "I refer to Miss Damour."

"Where was his willpower in all this?" I asked her. She didn't answer.

"Straighten me up if I've got my facts wrong," I said. "He was just a nice, clean, one hundred per cent American boy who was all set to point out that the only thing wrong with Hollywood was that they didn't recognize his genius. But then Deidre Damour lured him into her web and he ended up in the ashcan of *Dynamite*, writing a series of dirty articles that probably didn't make him any more than around fifty thousand bucks—which is running close to three years of my salary. You'll pardon me," I said nastily, "if I don't bust out crying."

"You wouldn't understand," she said in a small voice. "Nobody could understand him, except me."

"And he gave you the brush-off for a human vampire?"

"I may have to listen to your silly questions," she looked at me coldly, "but I don't have to listen to your insults. If you haven't any more questions, Lieutenant, will you please leave now?"

It was her point. I left.

I walked down the passage and thought now would be a good time to call on Macey. But I was thinking about what she had told me and I wondered what Deidre's version would be.

I also wondered if she'd remembered to do up those last four buttons yet—and I thought Macey could wait. I knocked on the door of number eighteen.

"Come in," the sultry voice said. I came in, closing the door behind me.

She wasn't wearing the housegown anymore. She was wearing toreador pants—they're pretty much like matador pants, except they fit tighter. She was also wearing a top. You weren't particularly aware of that at first, because her suntanned shoulders had a smoothness that sort of absorbed your attention for a while.

Finally you realized she was wearing an off-the-shoulder something that left her midriff bare and molded the bosom that had been the pride of Kentucky, her home state, when she carried off the title of 'Miss Curves' way back in her youth during the year 1953. She had come a long way since then—the bosom had stayed right where it was. You can't improve on perfection.

She gave me that Damour look—slanted at me from behind lowered eyelids. That look from the wide screen sends a million husbands home discontented, whenever one of Deidre's films has a national showing.

"What's the matter with you?" she said. "Don't you sleep?"

I remembered just in time that l was investigating a murder and I had the dignity of the city police force in my hands. I remembered that although Captain Parker recognized me as being unorthodox, there were limits even to that ...

"I wanted to ask you some questions," I said.

She yawned. Even her yawn was attractive. If she was a female vampire, she could have a quart of my blood anytime she liked.

"Can't it wait?" she asked.

"I don't want to go through my routine again," I said. "You know, the one that starts with, 'There's been a murder'?"

"All right," she said. "You don't mind if I have a drink sent up while you're asking the questions?"

"Not if you make it two," I said. "My throat runs dry asking all these questions."

"Why don't you have it slit?" she suggested. "It would save you a lot of problems."

She flowed over to the phone and rang down to the blonde, asking for two double martinis to be sent up. The word 'double' made me forget that nasty crack about slit throats.

I offered her a cigarette. She took it disdainfully and I lit it for her, then one for myself. A minute later there was a discreet rap on the door and a guy I presumed must be the barman came in with a tray and deposited it on the small table, then disappeared again. He gave me an envious look as he departed. It was wasted, but he didn't know that. I wasn't any closer than he was, really.

She picked up her drink from the tray and I picked up mine quickly in case she was really thirsty.

"Questions?" she said.

I tried to think of some. The only thing that had happened to 'Miss Curves' of 1953 was that she'd improved by 1955. Questions—and not the $64,000 one.

"I hear tell that Robert Heinman was the all-American idealist until he went to Hollywood," I said. "Even the fact they didn't recognize his genius didn't sour him. He was going to write a nice educated essay on what was wrong with Hollywood, but he met someone and somehow ended up writing dirt for *Dynamite*. And that someone, I'm told, had the name of Deidre Damour."

She smiled at me over the rim of her glass. "Lieutenant," she said, "you've been talking to Moira Banks."

"There's no prize for guessing," I told her.

"It isn't much of a story," she said. "I put Boby wise to himself, that's all."

"How wise was that?" I asked her.

"They gave him the runaround out there—they generally give most people the runaround in Hollywood. It's part of the system, I suppose."

"You're not thinking of writing about it yourself?"

She smiled at me again. "If I ever did that, they'd never be able to put the lid back on again."

"So you put Robert Heinman wise and he wrote that series for *Dy-*

mamite?"

"He got paid fifty thousand dollars for it," she told me. "In Hollywood he had a three-month contract."

"I wonder where he got all his material from?" I said.

She smiled again. I got the slanted look, the heave of the bosom—the works. "He dug around," she said.

"He must have dug pretty hard in the time he was there," I said.

"Bobby was a good digger," she said evenly.

"He didn't have time to dig a grave for himself," I said. "They left him in a gravel pit."

She looked away. "Do you have to put it like that?"

"What other way is there?" I asked her. "He's dead—he was shot, now he's in the morgue. How do you say all that politely so people don't get sensitive about it?"

"All right," she said in a hard voice, "you've made your point. Any more questions?"

"Plenty," I said, "but right now they can wait." I finished the martini and put the empty glass back on the tray. "Thanks for the drink."

"A pleasure," she said. The smile was back on her lips. "Call again, Lieutenant—anytime."

"That anytime," I said. "That's a figure of speech?"

"Why—no," she said and walked toward me. Kept on walking until she was standing in front of me, not more than a foot away. "I meant it, Lieutenant. I like big men."

"The trouble with you is you're not real," I said. "You're a celluloid image that a million guys carry around in their heads to cheer them up on a rainy day."

"The crock of gold at the end of the rainbow?" she mocked. "Why don't you reach out and find if the gold's real, Lieutenant? Nobody ever helped a guy who didn't help himself."

So I reached out and I found the crock of gold was real.

Her lips melted against mine and she came into my arms like she belonged right there. It was a clinch that would never have got past the Hays Office and how long we might have stayed in it I wouldn't know, because we were interrupted.

There was a knock on the door. I let go of her and she stood off a pace, reluctantly I hoped.

"I'd better find out what sort of opportunity this is knocking," she said in a low voice. "Wipe the lipstick off, Lieutenant. It looks sort of silly on a cop."

I took out a handkerchief and wiped my lips. Then she opened the door. Baron Marina stood there. He looked at me curiously, then at Deidre.

"Sorry if I intrude," he said in a smooth voice, "but we have altered the schedule for tomorrow, Deidre. The bureau says it's going to be fine and we could use a fine day right now. We're making the call for seven, instead of nine."

"I shall be haggard," she said, "but haggard."

"I'll keep your face out of the picture," he grinned. "The fans would never notice."

"I should be going if you're starting work so early," I said. "Thanks for your information, Miss Damour."

Her eyes were mocking. "It was a pleasure, Lieutenant." The tone of her voice left no doubt as to what had been a pleasure.

I brushed past Marina and went down the stairs to the reception desk. The blonde looked at me expectantly. "Did you find out, Lieutenant?" she whispered.

"What?"

"Who did it?"

"Who did what?"

She began to look annoyed. "The murder, I mean."

"Oh," I said, "that." I shook my head. "Not yet."

"Do you want to see any of the others?" she asked hopefully.

"Not now," I said, "I've seen enough of them for one night." I thought about Deidre Damour for a moment. "And you can say that again."

I went out to the prowl car and sat in the front seat, lit myself a cigarette, then called up on the two-way radio and asked to speak to Captain Parker.

His voice crackled in my ears a moment later, "Yes, Al?"

"What gives?" I asked him.

"I've just got the reporters off my back," he said sourly. "They're heading out to the valley now to interview that film outfit. This is red-hot news, for your information, Al. They kept on telling me that until I swore I'd never read a newspaper again."

"Thanks for the good word," I said. "I'm out at the hotel now. I'll get out of their way before they arrive."

"You find out anything?" he asked.

"He was killed with a forty-five," I said. "The old man who runs this place has half a dozen forty-fives out the back, with a miniature range—ammunition lying around in a drawer where anybody could get their hands on it. The film outfit amused themselves yesterday afternoon taking pot-shots in the rain.

"My theory is that the murderer helped himself to one of those guns last night, then returned it after he'd shot Heinman. Every gun will have been fired recently and every gun will probably be plastered with fingerprints—

it helps a lot, doesn't it?"

Parker swore briefly and to the point. "What else?" he asked.

"This Heinman wrote a series of articles for a magazine called *Dynamite*," I said. "The old expose stuff—only dirtier, I understand. That could be a good reason for killing him, don't you think?"

He didn't say anything for a moment and I listened to the radio hum and crackle in my ears. "You seem to be tying it down nice and tight to this film outfit," he said finally.

"Looks like it," I agreed. "You got anything new?"

"Not yet," he said. "If you want to quit for tonight, it's OK. Anything breaks and I'll let you know."

"OK," I said and signed off.

I drove the car back down the valley toward the highway.

About halfway along a dozen cars screamed past me. That would be the *Voice of the People* going to get their interviews. The film outfit wasn't going to get much sleep before their seven o'clock call.

I drove home remembering Deidre Damour and thinking was that me?

When I parked the car outside my house, I remembered something else. I'd been going to call on Patrolman Macey.

CHAPTER 5
Two for the Morgue

I went into the house—it's seven squares and four rooms, but I like to call it a house. You live in an apartment and people who live in the other apartments think it's immoral for a cop to have a private life. So every time they see you bringing a blonde home, they write an anonymous letter to the captain of your precinct, the D.A., the mayor, or some guy they think can boot you in the ribs. It didn't really worry me but it started to get monotonous, so I bought this place. It will be mine, all mine, in another twenty-two years, if I live that long and keep up the payments.

I switched on the lights, put a twelve-inch Ellington L.P. on the turntable and let it drift. That was another thing about living in a house. When you've got a hi-fi set up with five speakers, you like to hear it. In an apartment, the rest of the block think the men from Mars have arrived. Maybe I do Ellington an injustice.

I drifted, with the strains of *Caravan* gently bending the walls into the kitchen, and guess what? That's right—I poured myself a drink. I looked at my watch. It was just after eleven.

I thought maybe I should go to bed or maybe I should go over to the Eldorado and see what Goldie was doing. I shuddered at the thought—she was probably sharpening an ax against the next time she'd see me.

What I should do, I thought regretfully, is go see Macey.

The idea didn't appeal to me very much, but the time had its advantages. I'd probably drag him out of bed and he'd be half-asleep and frightened, wondering what the hell was so important that he had to be dragged out of bed. That way it might be easier to dig the truth out of him—if the truth was important. He could have forgotten he'd told me there were three bullets in Heinman, which meant he must have been down into the gravel pit.

I finished the drink and poured myself another. I listened to the Ellington disc play itself out and I thought that they don't make music like that anymore. You don't get that muted brass and sweet, sweet reed with the ivories giving you the beat. All you get is the big band stuff where they figure thirty saxophones are better than twenty, because they make more noise.

Or maybe I'm getting old. But I can't be really old. I'll know that day when it comes—when I'm really old, I'll be able to look at Deidre Damour without thinking a single thought.

I thought Macey could enjoy his sleep for a little while longer. I flipped the disc and heard the other side of Ellington. I had one more drink and looked at my watch again. Midnight.

The witching hour, when graveyards yawn. I thought I'd go see a cop and stop him yawning.

Out into the prowl car again. I started the motor, switched on the radio and then listened for a couple of minutes. Nothing very exciting was happening. I switched it off, engaged the gearshift and moved away.

The street where Macey lived was nice and neat. There were cut front lawns and cement pathways and driveways beside the houses. They all looked unpretentious but solid. Here, you would say, lives a citizen—a solid citizen.

I stopped outside the house. There was a light shining through the blinds against the front window. So maybe Macey wouldn't be yawning, after all.

I opened the gate and walked down the path to the front door. I pressed the push and chimes sounded inside. How any guy can live with a noise like that, beats me. It's a noise he doesn't even have any control over—someone comes to the front door, presses the push and bingo. You got chimes again.

The door opened and a woman stood there, looking at me. She was coming up at a fast run to the forty mark. She had a pleasant face—or a face that could have been pleasant if it hadn't been so worried. Right now it was worried.

I remembered I was wearing a hat so I lifted it. "Mrs. Macey?"

"Yes," she said.

"I'm Wheeler," I said, "Lieutenant Wheeler. I'd like to see your husband."

Her face cleared a little. "Come right in, Lieutenant," she said.

I followed her into the living room, which looked as neat and unromantic as Mrs. Macey herself.

She turned to face me, her fingers laced together in front of her. "He isn't home, Lieutenant," she said.

"That's bad luck," I said, "I particularly wanted to see him. Where is he?"

Her mouth twisted. "I don't know. I wish I did. I was just wondering whether I should ring Sergeant Macnamara when you called."

"There's trouble?" I asked her.

"I don't know, Lieutenant," she said dismally. "I can't figure him out. At first I thought it was finding that body this afternoon that depressed him. I could understand that upsetting anybody. He's been on the force nearly six years now, but that's the first time he ever walked in on a corpse. I guess things like that can upset you, can't they, Lieutenant?"

"I guess so," I said.

She looked at me, then looked away. "He hardly said a word from the time he got in the door, except to tell me what had happened. He seemed sort of worried and when I asked him, he shouted at me to leave him alone."

Her face twisted again. "He's never done that before, Lieutenant, in all the four years we've been married. Never."

"He probably was just upset," I said.

"Then about nine he said he had to go out," she went on as if she hadn't heard me. "He didn't say where he was going or why. He'd changed out of his uniform and he took the car. After he'd gone, I went into the bedroom—he's never very tidy and I was going to hang his clothes on a hanger for him. His belt was there but the gun was missing. He's never taken his gun with him before when he's gone out—except on duty, of course."

"Maybe he's just feeling upset," I said.

"I don't like it, Lieutenant," she said, "I don't like it at all. He's got something on his mind, something he can't even tell me about. He went out about nine and he hasn't come back. He's been gone three hours, Lieutenant."

"Don't you worry, Mrs. Macey," I told her. "He was probably upset at finding the body that way—it would be a terrific shock to anyone, cop or no cop. He's probably drinking in a bar someplace to forget it. By breakfast time he'll be his old self again."

"He doesn't drink," she said dully.

"Then maybe he has broken a rule," I said. "I'll tell Sergeant Macnamara over the radio that it's past your husband's bedtime and if any of the boys see him, to tell him to come home."

She smiled for the first time. "Would you do that, Lieutenant? It eases my mind such a lot to think I'm not just worrying by myself. I'd be so grateful."

"I'll do it just as soon as I get back to the car," I promised her. "Good night, Mrs. Macey."

"Good night, Lieutenant," she walked to the door with me, "and thank you again."

I walked down the path, out of the garden, then into the car. I drove a hundred yards down the street and stopped. I switched on the radio and asked the cop on duty if Parker was there. The captain had gone home, he told me, and Sergeant Macnamara had the desk. I told him to put Mac on the line.

I heard his voice after a short while. "Yeah, Lieutenant?"

"I just called on Macey," I said. "His story about finding that cadaver this afternoon stank."

"Yeah?" Mac sounded interested. Interested enough to forget the "lieutenant". What the hell—he'd been twice as long in the force as I had—he was entitled to.

"I just called on him," I said. "He's not home—went out about nine, his wife says, and she's worried about him. He was wearing plain clothes and he took his gun with him. Put out a tag on him, Mac, I want him brought in. Bring him into the precinct and hold him there. If you get him or get a line on where he might be, broadcast it. I'll tune in from time to time and listen."

"OK, Lieutenant." Mac's voice had a wondering note in it. "You think that Macey's mixed up in the killing?"

"I'm not thinking anything right now," I said. "Ring his wife. I told her I'd let you know so you could tell the boys that if they saw him, to tell him to come home. That's the story, Mac, so far as she's concerned—and don't forget it. Ring her and ask what he was wearing and get the license number of his car—OK?"

"OK, Lieutenant," he said.

I switched off the two-way, leaving the speaker live, and a few minutes later I heard the general call going out to pick up Macey. Mac hadn't wasted any time. The message said he was wearing a light-gray suit and a panama hat. His car was a blue Chevrolet, '53 model, and the license plates were NAT-10653.

Being a cop, I could have asked Mrs. Macey those questions, but I never thought of it at the time. What the hell? I don't take dope like that character Holmes did—I don't even play a violin, although I might fiddle a little. Sorry.

Another of those hunches had crept up on me while I wasn't looking. Patrolman Macey was a shy cop, there was no doubt about it. He'd gone off the highway all the way to the gravel pit that afternoon, just to make sure he wasn't seen. I wondered if the gravel pit had a different sort of fascination for him. Even at night? Or the early hours of the morning?

It was one hunch I could find out and if I was wrong, nobody could laugh at me. I turned the nose of the car around, left the radio on in case they found him and saved me the trip.

By the time I reached the turn-off from the highway, they hadn't found him. I had the headlights on high beam and the car bumped crazily over the track in low gear.

I turned the last bend of the track and ahead of me was the edge of the pit itself—and something else.

It was the second hunch that had paid off that night. I began to feel a little uneasy—if my luck held like this, I could quit being a cop and play the racehorses for a living.

The sedan was caught in my headlights and I edged closer to it, reading the rear license plate, NAT-10653, without any trouble at all. I stopped the prowl car with the front bumper nudging the rear bumper of Macey's car, then I took the flashlight from the dashtray and got out. I left the headlights on so they illuminated his car like it was the Fourth of July or something.

The sedan was empty. I shone the flash down on the floor and saw nothing of any interest. I walked to the edge of the pit and shone the flashlight downward.

"Macey!" I shouted. "Where the hell are you? Macey!"

There was a sharp crack and something whined past my head. My memory served me, remarking that it was a bullet. But my memory was way behind my automatic reflexes. By the time old memory had it figured out I was flat on my stomach, hugging the ground with the flashlight out.

I eased my right hand inside my coat and got out the .32 Smith & Wesson, then thumbed off the safety. I felt a little better with the gun in my hand, but not much. I had no idea where the shot had come from, but Macey or whoever it was had fired at me would have a very accurate idea where I was—or where I had been, anyway.

I edged sideways on my stomach like a crab with the gripes, maybe a dozen yards, then I stopped and listened again. The only thing I could hear was the silence—one hell of a silence. Away on the highway, a car went past and the faint sound of the engine and tires rubbing on the concrete only served to emphasize the silence.

Johnnie Ray could have had a hell of time with that silence, busting it into little pieces and throwing the pieces around. And I almost wished he was there to do it. That gives you an idea how happy I felt.

I listened hard, but all I could hear was that silence again. I didn't have any ambitions to spend the rest of the night flat on my stomach at the edge of a gravel pit. As Cleopatra might have said, it wasn't my idea of fun.

I got cautiously to my feet and still no sound broke the silence. My eyes were getting used to the starlight and I could make out the edge a couple of yards in front. I thought if I went any closer, I'd be silhouetted against the starlit sky and I'd be easier than a day pigeon for the guy below. I needed a diversion.

I hunted around for a hefty stone—and found one without too much trouble. I hefted it in my hand, then threw it in a long arc toward the bottom of the pit.

The theory was simple. The noise would make the guy with the gun nervous—he'd jump and maybe fire a shot at the noise. Then I could get a better idea, from the flash of his gun, where he was.

But I never did get to hear that stone drop. A moment after I'd thrown it, a voice from somewhere below me shouted, "Wheeler! Lieutenant Wheeler! For Pete's sake." There was the hammering sound of another shot and the voice stopped abruptly.

The voice belonged to Macey—I recognized it. He sounded like he was in trouble—bad trouble. I jumped forward to the edge of the pit, shone the flashlight down for a moment, then switched it off again. Here went the seat of my pants for the second time that day, I thought.

I started downward, slithering and sliding until I finally lost my balance and rolled over and over until I came to a quick stop at the bottom. I'd kept hold of both the gun and the flashlight and apart from feeling like I'd been put through a mincing machine, I was OK.

I scrambled to my feet and started running in the direction I thought Macey's shout had come from. I had to switch on the flash again to see where I was running. It was smart of me to do that—I was heading straight for a pool of water. I kept going, the flash leapt ahead of me—and then I saw a crumpled-looking heap which had all the signs of being a body— head, torso, two arms and legs but I wasn't sure whether it was living or not.

I came up to it and stopped. I played the flashlight all around me, but I couldn't see anyone else. Then I knelt down beside the crumpled heap and I was able to give the body a name. Macey.

He had been shot through the back of the head and it wasn't pretty. From here on he was always going to know just where he was—he was never going to move again of his own accord.

I heard another shot.

I spun around, thinking it must have come from the top of the pit. I heard the whirr of a starter motor and then the roar of the engine as it turned over.

I watched helplessly.

I saw the headlights of my car back away slowly from Macey's car, then the prowl car gathered speed in reverse and went bumping backward down the track which led to the highway. There was nothing I could do about it.

"Sucker," I said bitterly to myself.

I had to admit I was right.

CHAPTER 6
Ex-cop

I lit a cigarette and saw the headlights of the prowl car slowly fade away. I wondered who was driving it? Whoever it was had played me for a sucker and won hands down. The shout from Macey had brought me running. And while I was running, the killer had probably passed me, running the other way toward the cars—which meant escape.

He must have come with Macey to the gravel pit. I thought I wasn't being very smart at all that night. I could have figured that out earlier. And if I had figured it out, all I had to do was call up on the radio inside the prowl car and get a squad of men out here, while I just sat tight and kept the killer bottled up in the gravel pit. I had a nasty vision of trying to explain to Captain Parker just why I didn't figure it out before it was too late.

I put the flashlight on and knelt down beside Macey: he was dead, as I said before. He was also wearing the gray suit his wife had said he was wearing. I went through the pockets. There was a bulging wallet on his hip.

I opened it and then shook my head and looked again. It was still there, so I counted it. It came to three thousand bucks. That's a lot of hay for any cop to carry around with him. Too much.

I shoved the wallet in my pocket and went through the rest of his pockets. There was nothing else of any particular interest. But there was something notable by its absence—his gun that his wife said he'd taken with him. It was missing.

I walked back slowly, climbed the side of the pit even more slowly and reached Macey's car out of breath and out of temper. I slid into the driving seat, saw the keys were still in the ignition and felt a little better. I turned it over and the starter motor whirred without anything else happening. So I tried it a dozen times and still nothing happened. I got out and took a look.

I should have remembered the shot I heard fired when I was standing beside Macey's body. There was a neat hole in the petrol tank and the ground was wet underneath the car. So I walked along the track, cursing steadily and carefully.

I hadn't repeated myself by the time I got to the highway. I must admit I cheated a little—throwing in some Spanish words I had learned from a Mexican chick when she discovered I didn't have a rich uncle about to die and leave me his fortune.

I stood on the highway, thumbed eight cars and the eighth one stopped. The guy gave me a lift to the Eldorado and I dropped off there.

It was two o'clock in the morning and the place was beginning to die a little, but it never shut down much before four. I went in and the hat-check girl, wearing the mink one-piece and the tired eyes, smiled at me.

"Hello, Lieutenant," she said. "You looking for Goldie?"

"I'm looking for a phone, honey," I said, "a private one."

She raised her eyebrows. "You've come a long way to make a phone call."

"You never said a truer word," I said. "Give me one of the booths, will you?"

I dialed Parker's home number and the phone rang a dozen times before his wife answered. I often wondered why guys got married until I got to know the Parkers—that's the answer. Wives are to answer the phone when it rings in the middle of the night.

"It's Al Wheeler," I told her. "Could I speak to Captain Parker? It's urgent."

"Hold the line, Lieutenant," she said.

Parker seemed to get to the phone quickly. "What is it, Al?"

"I'm at the Eldorado," I told him. "I went to see Macey around midnight—he wasn't home ..." I told him the rest of the story and I gave him the number of the prowl car.

"OK," he said. "You'd better get back to the precinct as fast as you can. I'll have a call put out for that prowl car. It's probably been dumped by now, anyway. I'll take care of the other details. But get back to the precinct as fast as you can." He hung up with a bang that nearly punctured my eardrum. I went back to the hat-check girl.

"Johnny around?" I asked.

"I think so," she said. "I think he's up in his office."

"Ring through and if he's in, get him to come down here for a minute," I said. "Tell him it's urgent—police business."

"Yes, Lieutenant," her voice was almost respectful. She rang the office, found Johnny there and told him the message.

He was down in the foyer a minute later. "Trouble, Lieutenant? What is it?"

"Lend me a car, Johnny," I said. "I've got to get back to the precinct in a hurry."

"Why—sure," he said. "What happened?"

It wouldn't be any secret by daylight. "Patrolman Macey just got himself shot down in the gravel pit," I said.

Johnny whistled softly. "That's two of 'em in one day—things are sure humming, aren't they?"

"Looks like it," I agreed.

"You found him?"

"Check," I said. "What about the car?"

"Sure," he said and took a key ring from his pocket and gave it to me. "The green Cadillac at the end of the line. What were you doing walking around the gravel pit, Lieutenant—just taking exercise?"

"I took a car," I said. "I heard Macey yell and went down to find him dead—while I was down, the murderer came up."

"And took the prowl car?" A grin creased his face. "Well, that sure is tough luck, Lieutenant. And you had to walk all the way back."

"Don't break your heart over it." I snarled. "I'll survive." I turned around and walked out, my face burning.

I got into the green Cadillac and drove back to the precinct.

It was two-thirty when I arrived. The place seemed to be humming with activity. Macnamara looked down his nose at me as I came in.

"Captain wants to see you right away, Lieutenant," he told me. "Said to tell you as soon as you came in. He doesn't sound very happy."

"That," I told him, "I can believe."

I knocked on Parker's door, then walked in. He was sitting at his desk looking as if he'd been welded to it. It was almost impossible to believe that he'd been sleeping soundly in his bed an hour before.

"Sit down," he growled at me.

I sat down on the visitor's chair, sitting on the edge of it, then waited for the volcano to erupt.

"They found the prowl car you mislaid," he said. "It may ease your mind a little to know that?"

"Sure," I said.

"It was dumped on the highway just a mile out of town," he said. "Whoever took it could have gone this way, that way, any damned way."

"Yes, sir," I said.

Parker lit a cigarette and still glared at me. "You, my bright, unorthodox detective, were going to talk to Macey. I said I might talk to him, but you said you'd take care of it—you'd like to let him simmer a little. Has he simmered enough yet?"

"I ..." That was as far as I got.

"And that brilliant episode at the gravel pit." He was really getting into his stride now. "Deduction. You get there and find one car—Macey's. You're in a prowl car which has all the latest devices—even a two-way radio. But do you ask for help—get a couple of carloads of good beefy cops down there to look around the gravel pit? Oh, no. Dick Tracy has to handle it on his own. That lost us a murderer and a prowl car—temporarily, anyway." He took a breath.

"All right, captain," I said, "I asked for it and I got it. The thing is ..."

"The thing is one of our own men got killed tonight," he said, "and you let his murderer get away with it. The D.A. will be in at nine sharp this morning—and so will I—and so will you." He raised his voice to a shout. "Macnamara!"

Ten seconds later Mac came almost running into the office.

"Sergeant," Parker snarled, "from now on I'm not risking losing another prowl car. Any request for a prowl car from Lieutenant Wheeler is to be referred to me personally. Understand?"

"Yes, sir," Mac said wonderingly.

"That's all," Parker said.

Mac went out slowly, his mouth still hanging open slightly.

I got to my feet. "Is that all—sir?"

"I guess so," Parker said. "Don't be late for the appointment we have with the D.A."

"I wasn't bright," I said, "I admit I was entitled to a bawling-out. But did you have to give the sergeant that order about cars?"

"Are you questioning my orders?" he barked.

"That one," I said.

"You've been using prowl cars for your own convenience too long, Wheeler," he said. "I could bear with that while you didn't lose them, but now ..."

"Nuts!" I said and headed toward the door. I reached it; had my hand on the knob.

"Wheeler."

I turned and looked at him. "Yes?"

"If you ... Nothing."

"Nothing," I said and walked out of his office.

Detective Quinn was sitting in his chair, his feet on his desk, smoking a cigarette. He grinned when he saw me. "Can I offer you a lift home, Lieutenant?"

I got one arm under his feet and jerked upward. The chair tilted backward and Quinn described a neat backward somersault onto the floor.

I walked out and stopped by Macnamara's desk.

Mac licked his lips slowly. "Good night, Lieutenant," he said huskily.

I had to walk four blocks before I found a cab home. When I did get home, I felt like doing something dramatic. I also felt damned tired—so I went to bed. Then I remembered I could have taken Johnny's Cadillac.

It was ten after nine when I walked up the steps of the city hall. It was fifteen after nine when a thin redhead who wore too much lipstick showed me into the district attorney's office.

District Attorney Jordan had one hero—and that was District Attorney Jordan. He was a small guy, dapper, with a neat little mustache.

When I came into his office he was sitting behind his desk—looking like a bird of prey whose breakfast is overdue. I had an idea I was the breakfast.

Sitting comfortably in deep chairs were Captain Parker and another guy whom I knew—Commissioner Lavers. Seeing him, I knew that I was the sacrifice. It didn't improve my mental out-look.

"I'm sorry if we disturbed your breakfast, Lieutenant," Jordan said with a thin sneer on his face. "But then, you're only fifteen minutes late. I hope you didn't lose another prowl car on your way?"

I didn't say anything. I just looked at him.

"Sit down, Wheeler," Lavers growled. "We've wasted enough time already."

I sat down, felt in my pocket for a cigarette, found one and lit it, ignoring Jordan's disapproving stare.

"Well," Jordan said, "now that Wheeler is here, I suppose we can get on with it."

"All yours," the commissioner said to Parker, "or it has been up to now."

Captain Parker gave them a quick resume of the case; of everything that had happened up to date. There was a short silence after he had finished.

"It seems to me," Jordan said, "that we haven't got anywhere at all. Already there have been two murders—one of them a cop. And we don't know a damned thing."

"I wouldn't say that," Parker grunted. "We know some things. The suspects seem to tie down pretty well to that bunch of film people. That's where the murder weapon came from. The articles that Heinman wrote probably provide a motive."

"Hasn't anyone even read them yet?" Jordan asked coldly.

"The editor will be here in about an hour," Parker said, equally coldly. "I talked to him long distance last night. He was catching the first plane out this morning."

Jordan tapped one neatly manicured nail on the blotting pad which lay in front of him. "We shall have to release the story of Macey's death," he said, "and how his body was found."

He glanced at me for a moment. "That means, of course, that a lot of people will start asking questions—the obvious questions—about Wheeler's behavior. I don't think that his behavior as a lieutenant of police is going to inspire the people with confidence in the force."

Nobody argued with him.

"So," he went on, "I suggest we anticipate their reaction. I put it to you, Mr. Commissioner, that Wheeler be dealt with immediately or at least suspended immediately until he can be dealt with."

Lavers shifted irritably in his chair. I almost felt sympathetic toward him. As commissioner, his appointment was a political one and subject to re-election just as the district attorney was. Yet it was irking him like hell to have the D.A. telling him what to do.

"I agree that Wheeler should be suspended immediately," he said finally. "We'll see what else we can do later."

"All right," the D.A. seemed satisfied. "I don't have to tell you the amount of publicity this case is getting. Unless we catch this murderer, and fast, our chances at the next election aren't worth a row of beans."

"I know that," Lavers agreed.

"Well," the D.A. shrugged his shoulders, "it's up to you."

Lavers hoisted his bulk on his feet and Parker followed him to the door. I followed Parker at a discreet distance. When they had gone into the outer office, I turned back and looked at the district attorney.

"Well?" he demanded sharply.

"Frankly," I said, "comes next election and you don't get my vote."

When I came down the steps of the city hall, I saw Lavers and Parker talking together, then Lavers left. I caught up to Parker.

"I take it I'm on my own time from now?" I said.

"Get in the car, Al," he said. "I want to talk to you."

We got into the back seat of the car and the cop who was at the wheel started the motor, pulled out from the curb and headed back toward the precinct.

"I've been talking to the commissioner," Parker told me. "He's sorry about this, Al, but you know how things are. You're suspended as from now. But once this murder's cleared up, you'll be back. It won't mean anything worse than the loss of pay while you're suspended and ..."

"Skip it," I said.

He looked at me, frowning. "Now, listen."

"You listen," I said. "I quit."

"Don't be stupid, you're ..."

"I quit," I repeated. "I can still resign, can't I? Even the D.A. can't stop me doing that."

"What the hell's got into you?"

"Jordan," I told him. "If you want an answer to that. I can't stomach it anymore. So I didn't think very brightly last night, OK, but I heard a guy yell for help—a cop, remember? I went to help him. I don't think that's so bad."

"It's not only that ... If we'd talked to him earlier, we might have found out ..."

"You think he'd have talked with three thousand bucks in his wallet?" I asked him impatiently. "Or if he didn't have it then, he knew he soon would have it. What about all the time I wasted finding out where the murder gun came from? And what about Heinman's articles that provide the motive for the killing?"

"You don't have to convince me," he said.

"I have to convince Jordan," I agreed. "No, thanks. I'm resigning as from now."

He knuckled his chin irritably. "I've got enough worries on my mind right now, without you adding to them, Al. You want to throw away nine years of your life? In six months' time we could have a new district attorney—a new commissioner, even. Nobody will even remember you were suspended."

"I don't like being the fall guy for a character like Jordan," I said. "Compared with our illustrious district attorney, a snake is a noble creature. Do I make myself clear?"

"All right," Parker said. "You quit." We rode the rest of the way in silence.

When we reached the precinct, I went to my desk and wrote out a formal resignation. I took it into Parker's office and tossed it on his desk. He looked at it for a moment, then looked at me. "I'd like to tear this up, Al," he said.

"That would mean I'd have to write it out all over again."

"All right," he said wearily. "What are you going to do?"

"I really haven't had time to plan anything," I said. "I might go into the private-eye business."

"The D.A. would have to issue a license," he said.

"That takes care of the private-eye business," I said. "Maybe I'll break into films—I could get a job playing stooge to someone like Jordan."

"Until your resignation is accepted, you're still officially only suspended," he said. "Go home, Al, and think about it."

CHAPTER 7
Dynamite and Damour

I drove the Cadillac back to the Eldorado. Morning is not the time to see a nightclub—or a roadhouse. They should be seen only at night, when the neons give them some glamour. In the morning, they look like a week's wet weekend.

I left the Cadillac outside and took the keys with me. There was a tired-looking woman scrubbing the floor of the foyer. I asked her if she'd seen Ralston around. She said she thought he was in the main room, so I went in there.

Up on the dais, a pianist in shirtsleeves was banging out a tune and Goldie was rehearsing. She was wearing a lemon-colored sweater and black tights.

Why a blues singer needed to wear tights when she rehearsed might be a mystery to you, but if you could have seen Goldie's legs the mystery would have been solved. She'd be crazy to keep those legs covered, and she knew it.

Johnny Ralston was sitting at the nearest table, watching, and he had one of his gorillas with him—a guy named Rudi. If you think that sounds romantic, all I can say is you should have seen Rudi.

I waited until Goldie got through the ballad, then walked over to the table and dropped the keys on it. "Thanks, Johnny," I said.

He grinned. "Anytime, Lieutenant." Rudi just stared at me with those cold fish-eyes of his.

Goldie sauntered over to the table. "Well," she said, "look who is here. Where is my wandering boy tonight?"

"Free as a bird," I said hopefully. "You doing anything?"

"I work for a living. Last night was my night off. I wasted it hanging around for some jerk who was too busy to worry about me."

"Jerk is right," Rudi said.

I looked at him, then I looked at Ralston. "Johnny," I said, "you get a license for him or put a muzzle on him."

"Rudi's old-fashioned." Johnny's grin broadened. "He doesn't like coppers." Rudi just kept on staring at me.

Goldie walked back to the dais. "Let's take it again, Henry," she said to the pianist. "Slower tempo this time."

I'd been given the brush-off, nice and clean. "See you around," I said to Johnny.

"Sure," he nodded. "So long, Lieutenant."

I walked back into the foyer and used the phone to call a cab. I smoked a cigarette until the cab arrived, then went home. I was a free man, so I went to bed when I got home.

It was late afternoon when I got up again. I walked down to the book-stall on the corner and bought the evening newspapers. I asked the guy behind the counter if he had any back copies of *Dynamite*. He unearthed one which had the last of the three-part series Heinman had written. I took it home with me.

I poured myself a drink, put a mixture of discs which included some more Ellington, Eartha Kitt, Frank Sinatra and Dinah Shore on the turntable and switched it on. Then I settled down in an armchair with my reading.

The papers first. That had the story on the front page, with a picture of Macey and the grief-stricken Mrs. Macey. They also had the story of a certain Lieutenant Wheeler who had mislaid a prowl car and was subsequently suspended.

I finished with the papers and opened up *Dynamite*. It didn't have the smell of bad fish that I'd half-expected. The final episode of Robert Heinman's story consisted almost entirely of thumbnail sketches of Hollywood personalities—drawn in vitriol. I found some that were particularly interesting.

Baron Marina, the director who has been on the skids for the last eighteen months, hit an all-time low with his last picture, which was a box-office stinkeroo. Marina's gimmick is the dark glasses he's never seen without, day or night.

The good word in the celluloid city is that the same dark glasses hide the pin-pointed pupils of the drug addict. Baron Marina's other claim to fame is his well-known enthusiasm for rising stars (female). It is a cliché in Hollywood that any rising star who works for his studio needs to reflect the warmth of the Marina sun if she is to rise to any great height.

I wrinkled my nose after reading it. From the five speakers, Eartha Kitt whispered confidentially, "C'est si bon." I wasn't at all sure about that. A page further in I hit another little gem ...

Jon Clayton, the good-looking dope who plays the part of good-looking dopes so naturally, is another of nature's gentlemen. Thrice-divorced, they say no woman has any appeal for him unless already married. The latest story going the rounds concerning Clayton states that an ex-drive-in waitress who was permanently crippled from a beating given her by Jon Clayton settled out of court for fifty thousand. There's one thing, if it's true, Jon can certainly afford it. His new contract gives him a guaranteed eighty thousand and two per cent of the gross.

I was beginning to feel I needed a bath. I'd stopped wondering why Heinman was killed—I was wondering how he managed to live as long as he did. There was more ...

They say that luscious Deidre Damour is no better than she should be. That impression she gives of being a sucker for a guy with muscles is no more than the truth. Where she came from originally is her own and her studio's well-kept secret.

Could be she's the ex-girlfriend of a hoodlum who returned into legitimate business—or almost legitimate business. That's one of the things that interests your reporter. I'm going to check on that soon. It should prove an interesting story for the readers of this magazine.

One thing about Heinman ... he always saw the best in people. There was more.

Ed Stultz, ace cameraman, he of the horn-rimmed glasses and campus-professor looks. Ed is undoubtedly a wizard with the lens and is also rumored to be a wizard with the girls. How much he paid out to the local gendarmes to forget the teenage girls they found living in his house when they raided it three months back is between Ed and those cops. Could be quite a wad, judging from the worried look Ed carries around with him these days.

Then there's that fine character actor who has been around the celluloid city for so long that he's almost part of the scenery. Wolf Ramos is a guy who lives up to his Christian name off-screen. The girls go around in threes if Wolf's within seeing distance. Even so, it doesn't always do them any good. Wolf never refuses a picture and they say he needs the money.

Settling all those paternity suits out of court is an expensive business, I hear tell. All I can say is that if Wolf's having a last fling, it's a marathon.

There were six pages more after that. There weren't many names that were names in Hollywood that Heinman had left untouched. I imagined the libel suits in the offing would be worth millions.

I tossed the magazine on the floor, then went and had a shower. But afterwards I still had a nasty taste in my mouth. I was feeling that whoever bumped off Heinman should be given a gold medal.

The phone jangled and I picked up the receiver.

"Mr. Wheeler?" I would have recognized the sultry voice anyplace. "I should say 'Mr.' and not 'Lieutenant' now, shouldn't I? Or have the newspapers got it all wrong?"

"You and the papers are right," I told her.

"Bad luck," she laughed, "I thought you were much too nice to be a policeman, anyway. What are you doing now you're not a policeman any longer, Mr. Wheeler?"

"A little of this, a little of that," I said. "Drinking, mostly."

"Why don't you come over and drink with me for a while?" she suggested. "I have a proposition that might interest you."

"You've got a lot of things that interest me, honey," I told her. "But a proposition is something new."

She laughed. "Will you come?"

"I'm on my way," I said.

I put the receiver back on the cradle and felt a little brighter. It isn't every guy who gets an invitation from Deidre Damour. "One for my baby," Frank Sinatra sang gently, "and one for the road." It was a good idea. I poured a drink and took it into the bedroom with me to keep me company while I got dressed.

I walked four blocks to a rent-a-car place and rented a little black MG sports with tartan seat covers. It's not the sort of car a lieutenant of police would drive—but I felt it suited an ex-lieutenant of police.

Then I drove out to the hotel in the valley. It was just after seven when I got there. The blonde on the desk patted her hair carefully when I came in.

"Lieutenant. This is a pleasant surprise," she said.

"It is?"

"The place has been full of policemen all day," she said. "There was a Captain Parker out here and lots of detectives and people."

"How nice," I said.

She pulled a face. "I don't know what it's going to do to our business."

"The publicity will be wonderful," I said. "You don't have to worry about it."

"I hope you're right," she said. "And I have to say thank you, too."

"What for?"

"Pop," she said. "Captain Parker gave him a bawling-out about not having licenses for those guns, but he didn't do anything about it. I know it's you we've got to thank for that."

"No," I said, getting a guilty conscience, "not me. You thank Captain Parker."

"You're just being modest, Lieutenant," she smiled and patted her hair again. "If there's anything I can do for you, you just let me know."

I swallowed hastily. "Is Miss Damour in?" I asked her.

The smile on her face slipped half an inch. "Miss Damour? I think so." She picked up the house phone and rang through. "Miss Damour? The desk here. There's Lieutenant Wheeler here to see you." She listened for a moment, then said, "Very good," and hung up. She looked at me, her face expressionless. "Miss Damour says will you please go straight up."

"Thanks," I said.

"You're welcome," she said coldly.

I walked up the stairs and along to Deidre Damour's room. I knocked on the door and the husky voice said, "Come in." So I went in and closed the door behind me.

She wore a cocktail frock. It wasn't much bigger than a cocktail—throw in a cherry and they would have come out even for size. The Pride of Kentucky was dressed to kill.

She smiled at me. "I'm glad you could make it. Do I have to keep on calling you Lieutenant?"

"Al is the name," I said.

"What will you have to drink, Al?" She gestured toward an impressive array of bottles on a tray.

"Scotch?" I said hopefully.

She pulsated across to the bottles and began to pour the drinks. The cocktail frock clung to her closer than a finance company to a deposit.

"Now that you're suspended from the police force, Al," she said, her back toward me, "I suppose that means you'll have a lot of time on your hands?"

"Check," I agreed. "The days stretch ahead of me like a wasteland."

"What are you going to do about the wasteland?" she asked.

"Populate it with blondes," I said, "I hope. Also brunettes and redheads."

Deidre turned around with the drinks in her hands. "Then my proposition won't interest you?"

"If it has anything to do with figures," I made a survey of the cocktail frock's curves, "I think it could."

"It has to do with murder," she said. She handed me my drink and looked at me steadily.

"You disappoint me," I told her.

She sat down and crossed her legs, so that the frock slid up a couple of inches above her knees. It was probably an automatic reflex with her—if she sat down wearing a floor-length flannel nightie, it would do the same.

"I liked Bobby," she said, "I liked him a lot."

"You must have been on your own," I said.

She ignored that. "I'd like whoever killed him to wind up in the chair," she said. "It wouldn't be a lot of consolation but it would be some. I don't think the police are going to get very far with it—particularly now you've been suspended. I wondered if you'd consider continuing your investigation—unofficially, of course."

"I've got a coarse mind," I said. "What's in it for me?"

"Name your price," she said.

"You mean—money?" I asked her.

A faint smile curved her lips. "What else?"

"Once upon a time," I said, "there were three bears—Father Bear, Mother Bear and Little Baby Bear. Goldielocks gets into the story, too, because she was after her oats and ..."

"I'll pay you five thousand dollars if you get whoever killed Bobby," she said.

If I'd still been working for the police and I managed to catch a murderer in, say, a fortnight, they would pay me my salary over two weeks that was roughly two hundred and twenty bucks. On a percentage basis, her offer was quite a lot more. Hell. On any basis it was quite a lot more.

"I'll take it," I said.

"Thought you might." The faint smile played around her lips again. It gave her a Mona Lisa look—a cheesecake Mona Lisa, of course. I've always had a theory that's why the lifespan was so short in the olden days. No cheesecake. The boys had just nothing to live for. I'm talking about the period that came after the Sabine women—naturally.

I lifted my drink. "Here's to catching whoever knocked off Heinman," I said. I drank, then lowered my glass again. "I caught up on the last installment of his stuff in *Dynamite* this afternoon. Reading it makes you feel that whoever knocked him off deserves a gold medal."

"You don't understand," she said. "Hollywood is like that—like the way he wrote it. The people he wrote about—the way they behave. It's quite true—they do behave that way. That's the reason they couldn't afford to have him go on writing that way. That's why one of them either killed him or had him killed."

"Was he planning to go on writing that way?" I asked her.

"Of course," she nodded. "That series lifted *Dynamite*'s circulation by a hundred thousand on the second issue. He was going to do another series on Hollywood, then he was planning a series on TV people and maybe after that a ..."

"You know," I said wonderingly, "if you climbed down into a drain with a spade, nobody would give a dime however much you dug up."

"People like to know the truth," she said. "Why shouldn't they? And if they will pay to read it."

"That reminds me," I said. "Who was the racketeer you associated with in your earlier days?"

"That," she laughed. "That was a figment of Bobby's fertile imagination."

"I thought you just told me it was all true?" I said. "Every line he wrote?"

"So it was," she said easily, "except that stuff about me. He had to throw something in about me, otherwise people would start yapping about our association. They could have said that I'd made sure he didn't write anything about me by being ... friendly with him."

"It could have been an idea, couldn't it?" I said.

Deidre lowered her eyelids, "Al. I'm surprised at you—I don't have ideas like that."

I lit a cigarette. "How about Moira Banks?" I said. "She seems to be carrying a flaring torch for his memory."

"He met her when he was being given the runaround as a hack writer on the payroll," she said. "That was before he met me."

"Now I'm working for you," I said, "and not asking questions as a cop—is there anything else you'd like to tell me that you might have thought was none of my business when I was a cop?"

She got out of the chair slowly. "Why, yes, Al—there is." She walked toward me, then took the cigarette out of my hand and carefully crushed it in the ashtray. She removed the drink from my other hand and stood it back on the tray. Then she came back again and leaned against me.

"I wanted to tell you," she told my chest in a husky whisper, "that you're the biggest hunk of man I've seen in a long time."

"And you're the biggest hunk of ..." I started again hastily, "Honey, I'll bring the killer's head to you on a silver platter."

"That's my man," she said. She nestled still closer. "Al?"

"Hmm?"

"Tomorrow will be a nice, bright, brand-new day."

"It will?"

"Just the time to start working on an investigation. Today's all used up—there's only some of tonight left."

"Why," I said, "that's so right."

"You aren't in a hurry to go anyplace?" she asked.

"Only when that brand-new day is here," I said. "I'm going to start an investigation then."

"That's what I thought," she said.

The phone jangled sharply.

"Damn," she said. She reached out a hand and lifted the phone. "Yes?" She listened for a moment, then gave me the phone. "It's somebody who wants to talk to you," she said and walked away from me.

"Al?" a hard voice snapped in my ear.

"Yeah—who's that?"

"Parker."

"Not old Nosey Parker?" I sneered.

"You can cut the comedy," he said impatiently. "I need you ... As from now you're un-suspended, Al. Get down to the precinct right away."

"What?"

"You heard me. You can forget the suspended business entirely. I've cleared it with Jordan and the commissioner approves."

I looked up from the phone. Deidre had moved fast. The cocktail frock had gone—in its place was a negligee, white nylon and lace. She was sitting in front of a mirror, combing her hair slowly. She took a deep breath and quite a lot of the lace flattened out momentarily.

"You going to be long on that phone, Al?" she asked me. "I'm missing you over here all by myself."

"Not long, honey," I said.

"What?" Parker yelped in my ear. "What did you call me?"

"I wasn't talking to you," I said.

"I don't care who you were talking to!" he roared. "You grab your hat and get down to the precinct right away. You hear me?"

There it was, it couldn't have been plainer. The choice between duty and beauty. Parker and the precinct or Deidre and Damour.

I'm proud to say I didn't hesitate for a single second.

"Go boil your head," I told Parker and hung up on him.

I walked over to where Deidre sat and put my hands on her shoulders. "Did you miss me while I was gone?" I asked her.

She turned her head and looked at me, that faint smile on her lips again. "You were gone an awful long time," she pouted.

"I never stopped thinking of you, honey," I said, "the whole three minutes I was away."

"I wonder if you always just make love with words?" she said slowly.

I stopped her wondering.

CHAPTER 8
Reprieved

That nice, bright, brand-new day was just coming up over the horizon as I buzzed the MG back along the valley road at a steady seventy. The sun coming up had a nice, bright, brand-new look about it. The trouble with me was that I hadn't changed at all. I was still the old, beat-out, bleary-eyed Al Wheeler.

It was a healthy young morning with birds whistling and the citizens taking showers by the time I parked the MG outside my house and walked inside.

I wondered about breakfast and decided on coffee. When it was made, I took a cup with me into the living room. I sat there drinking the coffee and thinking about going to bed. Then I had a second cup and a third cup. I was still thinking about going to bed when the prowl car stopped outside.

I saw through the window Captain Parker walking toward the front door. I got up and opened the door for him as he reached the porch. He glared at me and walked straight past me into the living room. I shut the front door and followed him.

He stood there, glaring at me.

"Hi, cap," I said. "Like some coffee?"

"Go boil your head," he said distinctly.

I smiled feebly. "You know how it is. A man just feels ..."

"That he can't be disturbed?" he finished the line. "Particularly when he's with a blonde, redhead or brunette, whichever it might have been."

"How about that coffee?" I said.

"I guess so," he growled. "Make it black."

I went into the kitchen, organized him some coffee and some more for me. Then I brought it back into the living room.

"What did you come to tell me?" I asked him. "That I don't need to resign—I'm fired?"

He stirred his coffee carefully. "I've got troubles, Al, lots of troubles. So many troubles that I'm even prepared to forget what you told me to do last night."

I sat down opposite him and lit a cigarette. "You must have troubles," I said.

"You can say that again." His face looked haggard. "I spent all day yesterday out at that hotel, questioning those film people. I saw the editor of *Dynamite* before I went out there. All those film people are red-hot suspects. But do you think I could crack one of them or get even the hint of a lead?" He shook his head despairingly. "I didn't have a hope."

I drank some more coffee and waited for him to go on. "You know what this Heinman character said about them?" he asked.

"Sure," I said. "I got a copy of the last issue of the magazine yesterday."

"That gives them all good motive," he said.

"It also gives about another two-thirds of Hollywood names good motive," I said.

"But they weren't in this town when his body was turned up."

"A point," I admitted.

He lit himself a cigarette, getting that sour look that he always does when he inhales. "Let's run over the facts that we've got," he said. "Patrolman Macey turns up Heinman's corpse in the gravel pit. Macey obviously lies about having been down into the pit. It's afternoon when he turns up the body—Heinman was killed at four in the morning.

"Macey gets himself killed down in the gravel pit the following night. The killer gets away. We find three thousand bucks on Macey. His wife said he was worried all evening until he went out and when he went out, he took his gun with him. So what does that add up to?"

"It adds up to the fact that Macey knew who murdered Heinman and he was going to meet the killer that night and get the pay-off to keep his mouth shut," I said. "He didn't trust the killer so he took a gun with him—and I'll take a bet he was killed with his own gun."

"Check," Parker nodded. "So that takes care of Macey, but it doesn't help any in finding the killer."

I stubbed out my cigarette. "What else did you find out about Heinman?"

"He must have come into town in a flying saucer," Parker said bitterly. "Nobody saw him come—not by train and not by plane. If he drove in, the car must have been painted with invisible paint because we haven't found it yet, and brother we've been looking for it."

"What did the editor of *Dynamite* have to say?" I asked him.

"That Heinman died a hero's death and he was going to tell his readers all about it." Parker's mouth twisted wryly. "And if we don't get his murderer quickly, he's going to tell his readers all about that, too."

"He thinks one of the film mob killed Heinman?"

"Nothing surer, he says. He claims that Heinman told him he was working on a new series, covering a very famous personality, that would rock the whole country."

"No details of the new series?"

"None at all," the captain sighed. "We've had his New York apartment taken apart but whatever he had in mind, he hadn't put any of it down on paper."

He finished his coffee. "None of them up at the hotel have any alibis. They all went to the Eldorado that night and they all left there somewhere just before two and got back to the hotel about a quarter after, then they all went to bed—they say. That means any one of them needn't have gone to bed but could have gone out, met Heinman and killed him, instead. I think you're right about the murder gun being one of those forty-fives the doddering old fool out there keeps in that miniature range of his. So we've got the murder weapon—any one of six."

"What about the time when Macey was killed?" I asked him. "Anybody got an alibi for then?"

"No," he shook his head. "That's what makes it so easy."

"You have my sympathy, captain," I told him. "I feel almost glad I'm no longer with you."

His head came up and his jaw stuck out dangerously. "That reminds me—that's what I came to see you about."

"Yeah?"

"You're suspended—I had you on—suspended last night but you told me what I could do about that."

I smiled modestly. "I didn't really mean it. Sticking it in hot water would have been enough."

He made a choking noise, then struggled on. "This morning I got a better idea. Officially, you're still suspended. So anything you might do is strictly off your own cuff and the department can't be held responsible in any way—get it?"

"You want me to go and shoot the D.A.?" I asked. "It would be a pleasure."

"That will have to wait," he said flatly. "You're an unorthodox cop at the best of times, as I've said often before. Now, I figure, is a good time for you to be unorthodox. I want you to get out among those film people and stay with them. Harass them, annoy them—I don't give a damn what you do to them—but keep at them and maybe if you try hard enough, you might break one of them down for long enough to learn something worthwhile."

I thought about it. "It could be done," I said. "But what's in it for me?"

"You've had twenty-four hours to cool down—twenty-four hours to get over being mad at the D.A., mad at Lavers and mad at me. You know you're a cop at heart and basically all you want to do is go on being a cop.

"You get a lead out of this and I'll play ball with you—so will the commissioner, and the D.A. won't have any choice but to play ball, either. We'll write you up big as acting as an undercover man for the department. Everything about the suspension gets wiped off the record and ..."

"OK," I said. "You don't have to play the whole symphony. I get the drift."

"Will you do it?" he asked anxiously.

"I guess so," I said.

I didn't really have to think about it. What he said was true. I was a cop at heart, even if I wasn't an orthodox cop, I liked being a cop. I didn't want to change it for street-sweeping, not through choice, anyway.

"I'm glad you've come to your senses at last," he growled. "All right, the sooner you start moving, the better."

"Are they filming today?" I asked him.

"I guess so," he said. "That Marina was beefing all day yesterday that we were costing his studio a fortune, holding them at the hotel for questioning when they should have been out in the valley filming. So I imagine they would have started today, bright and early."

"I might go take a look," I said.

"Let me know if you get anything, Al," he said. "Anything at all."

"I'll send a carrier pigeon," I promised him.

After he'd gone I thought about it. Right then all I wanted to do was go to bed and sleep, but it looked like that would have to wait.

I showered, shaved, put on a clean shirt, a suit fresh back from the cleaners. I felt a little better but not much. If I was going to work, I ought to have some breakfast. I made some more coffee, broke a couple of raw eggs into a glass of whisky and had that before the next round of coffee. I lit a cigarette and it tasted like straw somebody forgot to clean out of the stable.

I put on a pair of dark glasses and went out to the MG again. It was a revoltingly sunny morning. Just the weather to make a western, I thought. They'd be having fun out in the valley. Good clean fun. Maybe. I aimed to sour it a little.

I got one break. The guy on duty was the same guy I'd seen the other night and he recognized me. "Morning, Lieutenant," he nodded almost respectfully. "Who did you want to see?"

"Marina," I said.

"You'll find him down there," he pointed past the trailers and trucks. "They're shooting—he'll be pretty busy."

"I guess I can wait till he stops being busy," I said.

I parked the MG between two trailers and it looked like a bug sandwiched between two elephants. Then I walked along the line until I saw them—the film-makers actually making a film.

There was a camera on a crane and a couple of microphones suspended from booms. There was Marina shouting his head off through a megaphone and there were lots of cowboys all around and a couple of cowgirls. I came up behind Marina's chair and watched.

"OK!" he shouted hoarsely. "Let's get a take this time. We've spent two hours of the morning horsing around already—with nothing in the can. Jon."

A weather-beaten but handsome cowboy looked inquiringly from the saddle. "Yep?"

"Hell," Marina said. "You don't have to talk westernese to me. Save it for the take. And please. Try and remember all your lines this time."

"Yep," Clayton said easily.

Marina groaned, "OK, then let's roll it. Moira."

A nice line in cowgirls looked up at him. "Yes, Baron?"

"You come riding along happily," he said, "not a care in the world, and suddenly you find him—lover-boy—the guy you're going to marry, hidden away here with the dancehall girl you wouldn't even deign to recognize in the street."

"I know," she said.

"Well," he took a deep breath, "this time look mad, will you? Look as if it really burns you up. Act like it really burns you up, not as if you've just come upon a Sunday school picnic."

"Sure, Baron," she said.

He looked away wearily. "You set, Deidre?"

"I've been set all morning," she said tartly. "Why don't you get yourself some actors and actresses to help me out with this picture?"

"Don't let's go into that right now," he pleaded, "my ulcer just wouldn't stand it." His voice rose to a bellow again. "OK, let's shoot it. Start 'em rolling."

A boy appeared magically from nowhere with two pieces of wood in his hands. "Scene nine," he said, "take three." Then he clapped the two pieces of wood together sharply and disappeared again.

The horse came steadily into camera range, being ridden by a smiling, open-faced girl who bore a remarkable resemblance to Moira Banks. Suddenly she stopped, staring—the smile disappearing from her face.

Down in the hollow was tall, wide-shouldered Jon Clayton and smoldering, short-skirted Deidre Damour. Moira looked, then got off her horse and walked slowly toward them.

Jon had Deidre clutched in his arms in the closest thing to a passionate embrace that Marina thought they could get past the censor.

"Ah'm crazy about you, Rita," Jon drawled. "Plumb crazy."

Deidre laughed in his face, "So you say. But tonight, in the saloon when I dance, you will not be there. You will be with her. She is for you, you think. Her father is a rich cattleman. You will marry her and Rita will still dance at the saloon for her living."

Jon took a firmer grip on her. "Ah'm not marryin' her," he said. "Ah love you, Rita. I guess you sure know that by now."

Moira stepped up to them. "Don't worry. I wouldn't marry you now, Clem Peters, if you were the last man left alive on this range. You ... you lowdown snake."

She stepped up to him and swung her hand toward his face. Jon jerked his head back instinctively so that Moira missed. The swing of her arm carried her on and jerked her off her feet, and she fell flat on her face.

"Cut!" Marina shrieked. He held both hands to his head. "I don't deserve it," he said in a broken voice. "What did I do to deserve such hams? Did I eat little children for breakfast—no. Did I rob blind men—no. Then why," his voice rose to a shriek again, "why do you do this to me?"

"Take it easy, pal," I said from behind him. "Why don't you take another shot of heroin and stop worrying?"

CHAPTER 9
Eddie Comes Clean

He jumped as if I'd put a bullet through him. Then he turned around slowly and looked at me. "You," he said. "What the hell are you doing out here?"

I couldn't see the expression in his eyes behind the dark glasses.

"I just came along for the ride," I said, "and to ask some more questions."

"Not more questions." He shook his head helplessly. Then he picked up the megaphone and bellowed, "Take a thirty-minute break."

He turned back to me. "Didn't I read someplace that you were no longer a cop?"

"I'm still asking questions," I said.

"Well, go ask someplace else, pal," he said, "I'm busy."

The other three came toward us, followed by a smiling Wolf Ramos, wearing a silver star pinned to his shirt and a pair of Colts slung around his hips.

"Hi, there," Deidre smiled warmly at me. "We don't need a sheriff around here, we've already got one." She pointed at Wolf.

"We don't need a cop around here at all," Marina said. "And just what was that crack you made about heroin or something a while back?"

"I just wondered how much truth there was in the article I've been reading," I said. "You know the one—written by the late, lamented Robert Heinman."

Ramos took a step toward me, his face serious. "There was no damned truth in it at all," he said bitterly.

"No paternity suits?" I grinned at him.

His face darkened. "I don't have to take that sort of crack from anybody."

"You can take it from me and another million or so readers of *Dynamite*," I told him.

"We don't have to take it from him," Marina said. "He's been suspended—he let the killer get away in his own prowl car. He isn't even a cop anymore."

"Do you really take dope?" I asked him. "Are you on the skids like Heinman said you were?"

"Go to hell," he said.

Jon Clayton looked at me, a serious expression on his handsome face. "There's been enough trouble caused by that guy Heinman, without you making it any worse, mister."

"Fifty thousand dollars," I said softly. "Did you really have to pay that much to keep it out of court?"

"You say just one thing more," he said evenly, "and I'll punch your jaw for you."

I grinned at him, "Don't be a dope—beating up girls is your line—not fully-grown men."

He took a quick step toward me and drew back his fist. I just waited, ready to ride the punch that he telegraphed. I saw it coming and swayed to the left. Too late I saw him shift his stance and too late I realized the telegraphed punch had been the feint. The next moment what felt like a load of iron connected under my jaw and I had a brief Fourth of July fireworks display for free. Then everything turned into blackness.

I probably wasn't out more than a minute. I came round and found my head was cradled in Deidre's lap. I felt a few drops on my face.

"Don't cry for me, honey," I said huskily, "I'm OK."

"You dope," she said. "It's starting to rain."

I sat up, rubbing my jaw tenderly.

Marina was looking up at the sky. "I'm fated," he said bitterly. "Looks like a storm coming. Another day's shooting lost."

The rain began to come down steadily. Overhead, a long black storm cloud looked like it was getting set to enjoy itself. Deidre straightened up, the skimpy, Western-style dancehall dress she was wearing not quite reaching her knees.

"If you're in one piece, Al," she said, "I'm not staying around to catch pneumonia."

"I'm in one piece," I admitted and staggered to my feet.

Clayton looked at me impassively, then turned on his heel and walked toward a trailer, followed by Moira Banks.

Wolf Ramos grinned at me. "Didn't you know?"

"Know what?" I asked sourly, rubbing my chin.

"Jon's an ex-pug," he said. "Before he got the breaks in Hollywood, they were starting to talk of him as a new hope for the heavyweight championship."

"Why doesn't someone tell me these things?" I said bitterly.

"You found out, anyway," he chuckled. He was still laughing when he walked away.

I realized I was steadily getting wet. I headed back to the MG. I'd nearly reached it when I heard someone running along behind me. I turned around and saw Ed Stultz, the cameraman, running toward me.

"Wait a minute, Lieutenant," he said. "I wanted to talk to you."'

"OK," I said, "but there's no reason why we should drown while we talk. Get into the car."

We both squeezed into the MG. "Where are you going?" I asked him.

"Back to the hotel," he said. "Marina's had it. He's canned any shooting for the rest of the day."

"I'll drive you back," I said, "and we can talk on the way."

"That would be fine—thanks," he said.

I gunned the engine, backed the car out from between the two trailers and we bumped our way back to the road. When we were headed for the hotel at a steady sixty, I said, "OK—what's on your mind?"

"Heinman," he said promptly.

"What about Heinman?" I said.

He lit himself a cigarette, inhaling nervously. Then he turned to look at me, his eyes bulging behind his hornrims. "I overheard the conversation before Clayton hung a punch on your chin," he said. "I don't think you'd get the right slant on Heinman from the way the others talk."

"The only slant Clayton gave me was a horizontal one," I said. "What are you trying to say?"

He paused for a moment. "Well," he said nervously, "take what Heinman said about me in that article. Remember? That piece about the teenage girls living in my house and so on?"

"I remember," I said.

"It was true—in a sense," he said. "I've got a teenage sister. She's the only family I've got. At the time Heinman was talking about, I was on location down in Mexico. I was a fool to leave the kid on her own in the house but I thought she'd be OK. Apparently she got bored on her own and threw some parties—normal parties." He emphasized the word "normal."

"Tell me more," I said.

"That's all there is to it," he said. "She invited some of the kids in from around the neighborhood, kids she went to school with. Like all kids' parties, they got noisy. They had the phonogram going full blast into the small hours and they were dancing and shouting and so on. The neighbors complained about the noise to the cops and when I got back, the cops weren't very happy about it.

"So I had to square off. It cost me liquor and food for one night when I gave the cops a party at the house, by way of an apology and also to introduce them to a housekeeper I'd just hired to make sure there weren't any more noisy parties the next time I went on location."

He flicked the stub of his cigarette through the side curtain. "You see, that was where Heinman was clever—if you can call it being clever. What he said was true, so far as it went. There were teenagers in my house and they were having parties. I did square off with the police, in a way anybody would. But Heinman wrote it so it sounded like something out of De Sade."

"You think everything he wrote was based on the same sort of facts?" I asked him.

"I'm sure of it." He nodded vigorously. "I don't expect you to take my word for it—I know there've been two murders, but you can check on my story with the Los Angeles police, if you like. My lawyers are suing the editor of *Dynamite* for publishing the article, but they aren't too happy that we'll win. It's not easy, they say, to establish in law that the magazine actually committed a libel. I feel I've got to make the gesture, though. I'm worse off than any of the others."

I ran the MG up alongside the front steps of the hotel and stopped. "How do you work that out?" I asked him.

"Well," he laughed without any humor in his voice, "as you probably know, so long as a star has box-office appeal, their studio don't worry too much about their past or their private lives. But I'm not a star—I'm a lighting expert; a cameraman, if you like. I'm a technician and a good one. But Hollywood's crowded with good technicians. They could much easier sacrifice me than they could a star."

"What about Marina?" I said. "He's not a star."

"That's not quite true," Stultz said carefully. "His name as the director of a film still carries some weight. Frankly, I think Heinman was right about one thing—Baron is on the skids. His last two pictures were flopperoos and he knows it—and the studio knows it. He's sweating his own blood on the western—if this one misses, he's finished."

"How's it coming?" I asked. "The picture? What else?"

"Confidentially," he said quietly, "I think it stinks—so far, anyway. I could be wrong but I've been around pictures too long not to have a sixth sense when I see a stinkeroo being made."

The rain beat down on the canvas hood of the MG. "Let's go inside," I said, "and I'll buy you a drink."

"Thanks all the same," he said, "but I don't drink. I think I'll go up to my room and rest. I just wanted you to know about Heinman."

"Sure," I said, "I appreciate it. But he must have got too close to the truth about somebody, to get himself murdered."

He smiled wanly. "Well, I can assure you it wasn't me." He got out of the car. "Thanks for the lift," he said and walked inside.

I lit myself a cigarette and thought that as an unorthodox cop, I'd certainly been trying. I'd thought I'd try shock tactics—get them hopping mad and they might say something they hadn't meant to. And all I had got was a punch on the jaw. I thought Parker would roll around his desk screaming with laughter, when he got to hear about it.

I smoked the cigarette down, then pitched the butt away and thought that if I couldn't buy Eddie Stultz a drink, I could buy myself one.

I went into the hotel. The blonde was behind the desk and I wondered if she ever slept. She smiled tentatively at me. "Good morning, Lieutenant."

"Hi," I said. "I was just going to buy myself a drink. How about I buy you one as well?"

"I'm afraid not," she said coldly. "I couldn't possibly leave the desk, Lieutenant. But the rain will have stopped them working on the film, so I expect Miss Damour will be back quite soon—and I'm sure she would just love for you to buy her a drink."

I shrugged my shoulders and walked on into the bar. It was deserted except for the barman. "Yes, sir?" he asked gloomily.

"I'll have a straight cyanide," I said.

"With a dash of hemlock, sir?" he suggested.

"What the hell," I said, "make it Scotch. I might as well try living till this afternoon—maybe it'll fine up by then."

He looked out of the window and shook his head firmly. "Not a chance, sir. I know the valley."

He poured me a Scotch and put the glass on the bar in front of me. I drank it down and pushed the empty glass toward him.

"Would you mind refilling that?" I asked him.

"A pleasure, sir," he told me.

I drank the second one a little more slowly. I heard people come into the foyer and a moment later Marina came into the bar, with Wolf Ramos following him.

They looked at me and then ordered their drinks. "How's the jaw?" Ramos asked.

"Still tender," I said.

"You picked the wrong guy in Jon Clayton," Marina said with some satisfaction.

"Check," I agreed.

"What I don't get," he said, "is if you're suspended from the police department, then what are you doing running around asking questions and insulting people?"

"I read Dale Carnegie back to front," I told him. I finished the second drink and thought I might as well go home and blow my brains out.

Marina was studying me thoughtfully from behind his dark glasses. "You're the screwiest cop I ever met," he said.

"Ed Stultz took a lot of time explaining to me how Heinman operated," I said. "He said that Heinman took a lot of true but harmless facts and distorted them into implying something quite different and very sinister."

"You could say that," Marina agreed.

"So I suppose you don't take dope at all," I said. "You probably just can't keep away from Coca-Cola, that's your weakness. And you aren't on the skids, you're just slipping a little, picture by picture?"

Once again the dark glasses foiled me. I couldn't really see the expression in his eyes as he looked at me. "What are you trying to do?" he asked slowly. "Get me so mad that I'll accidentally admit I killed Heinman?"

"I didn't know it was that obvious," I said in a hurt voice. "Now I'll have to go away and read the manual all over again."

"Just so long as you go away," he said, "I don't care what you read."

He looked at the gaping barman. "Give me a double Scotch," he said, "and a triple heroin. And while you're about it, you had better give me a marijuana chaser."

He looked back at me. "If you really think I'm slipping," he said, "ask my studio how much it cost them to renew my contract three months ago."

I walked out of the bar into the foyer. I was no match for Baron Marina. It was probably my own fault for being a moron. The blonde looked at me coldly and I wondered if she'd checked what time I left the hotel that morning. While I was wondering, Moira Banks came in.

"You're just the girl I wanted to see," I said. "Can I ask you some questions?"

She looked at me like I was something the cleaner forgot to remove. "It must be my lucky day," she said. "I suppose I can't stop you asking questions—it seems to be a general hobby in this town. Come up to my room and ask them there while I change." She walked on past me toward the stairs and I started to follow her.

"My, my," the blonde said loudly to no one in particular, "who said Casanova wasn't a cop?"

CHAPTER 10
Questions

We got into Moira's room and I closed the door behind me and lit a cigarette. She was still wearing the cowgirl's outfit and it suited her. She picked up a robe off the bed and headed toward the bathroom.

"I'm going to have a shower," she said. "If you want to do any snooping while I'm gone, this is your chance." She disappeared into the bathroom and a few moments later I heard the shower running.

I walked over to the window and looked out. The valley was shrouded in rain. The storm seemed to have gone and the rain settled in.

Something tugged at my memory. It had rained the morning that Heinman had been killed. It hadn't been raining in the afternoon when I'd gone out to the gravel pit and met Macey, then seen the corpse. That should mean something, I felt, but it didn't.

I finished the cigarette and lit another. The noise of the shower had stopped. The bathroom door opened and Moira Banks came back into the room. She was wearing the toweling robe, wrapped tight around her. She went over to the dressing table, sat down in front of it and started to comb her hair.

"You'd better ask your questions," she said, "then when you've finished, you can go and I can get dressed."

"Sure," I said.

There was a knock on the door. Moira stood up and walked across to open it. When she did open it, Deidre Damour stood there.

"Honey," Deidre said, "I wondered if you ..." Then she saw me and stopped speaking suddenly. "Well, well," her smile was sad, "if it isn't the little butterfly that wings its way from blossom to blossom."

"Hello." I smiled wanly at her.

"What a man," Deidre said. "Who are you having dinner with tonight—Jane Russell?"

"I don't think her husband knows me," I said.

"You surprise me," she said coldly. "I didn't think a little thing like that would deter you."

"Was there something you wanted?" Moira asked impatiently.

"I forget," Deidre said and turned around, then walked slowly away.

Moira slammed the door shut. "That woman," she said.

"Woman," I said, "is the easiest way to describe her—in one word."

"I could think of another," she snapped as she sat down again in front of the dressing table.

"Questions," I said, "I was going to ask you some questions."

"Go on," she said.

Rain, I thought, then no rain. A corpse that had become a corpse around four in the morning, but wasn't found until late afternoon—and it had been dry. Did that mean anything?

"I said, go on," she repeated.

It meant that it hadn't been in the gravel pit, in the open, from four that morning. It meant that Heinman hadn't been shot in the gravel pit. It meant that his corpse had been dumped there afterwards—after it had stopped raining. But did that mean anything?

"I'm getting very tired of this, Lieutenant—or whatever you are now," Moira snapped. "Either ask your questions or leave my room."

I tried to think of the questions I'd wanted her to answer. I remembered. "Your life," I said, "it's been blameless?"

"Just exactly what do you mean by that crack?" she demanded.

"Heinman couldn't find a single piece of dirt to throw at you," I told her. "You didn't even get a mention in his series on Hollywood."

"I told you before," she said, "Bobby was an idealist, a wonderful guy, and he loved me. Would he write something nasty about the woman he loved?"

"From what I can see of him," I said, "if there was money in it, the answer's yes for sure."

She put the brush down on the table. "You're just being cheap and cynical," she said. "I can afford to ignore it."

"I can't have the story right," I said. "I thought you told me that the bad, bad Deidre lured him away?"

"There was that time in New York," she said, "just over two weeks ago.

I guess I wasn't thinking straight when I said that to you. I realize now she was trying to stop him publishing anything about her—but she didn't." There was an ugly note of triumph in her voice.

I watched the back of Moira's neck for a moment.

"There was going to be a red-hot new series from Heinman," I said, "according to his publisher. A series on a Hollywood personality that was going to sear the pages it was written on. But Heinman got himself murdered before he started to write it. You have any ideas who the series could be about?"

"I'd bet my last dollar it was that Damour woman," she said. "What Bobby said about her is dead right. Only he didn't go far enough. He said she likes big men, but she likes any sort of men so long as they're men."

She spun around to face me, her eyes eager. "I'll bet he was going to write that new series about her," she said. "And he told her when they were in New York together. So she killed him to stop the series from getting published."

"Maybe," I said.

"I'll bet I'm right," she said.

"Maybe nobody killed him to stop the series getting published," I said slowly. "Maybe he got killed because somebody was jealous of that time he spent with Deidre in New York? Maybe somebody didn't appreciate an idealist like him associating so intimately with an idealist like Deidre?"

Her tongue moistened her lips. "Get out," she said.

"Did you kill him?" I asked interestedly.

"Get out." The hairbrush hurtled through the air toward me and I ducked. It thudded against the wall behind me and dropped to the floor. I reached out and grabbed the door handle.

"Get out." A mirror described an arc through the air. I ducked again. It hit the wall and seven years' bad luck ended up on the carpet. I opened the door hastily and stepped into the corridor.

"If he was an idealist," I said, "I am Tarzan of the Apes."

"That," she shouted, "I'll believe." She picked up a vanity case and made like a pitcher. I shut the door hastily and walked down the corridor.

I went down the stairs into the foyer. "What have you been doing up there?" the blonde asked interestedly. "Murder?"

"Don't forget to charge her for the dents in the wall," I said.

"My problem was whether to call a cop or not," she said. "You aren't a cop anymore, are you?"

"It's remarkable the number of people who can read these days," I said.

"It's only one of my accomplishments," she said and patted her hair complacently.

"You must show me your accomplishments," I said. "We'll wait for a nice, long winter's evening when there's snow outside and Pop's gone to bed early."

"You're the most conceited character I ever met," the blonde said wanderingly. "You think you're irresistible, don't you?"

"Yes," I agreed modestly. "But right now I don't have the dime to spare in proving it. Whenever you feel like a demonstration, honey, ring me." I looked at her searchingly. "You need another blonde rinse—it's showing dark at the roots again."

I walked quickly out of the hotel before she threw a bellhop at me.

I got into the MG and drove down the valley, back toward the highway. The rain still swirled down and the wipers clicked monotonously. The sky was gray and so was life. I remembered I was feeling hungry and I thought maybe I could eat now.

I stopped at a diner and had a hamburger and two eggs. After I'd eaten them I regretted the hunger I'd had. But it was too late then. I got back into the MG and drove on until I reached the gravel pit.

I bumped along the track and then parked where I'd parked the prowl car that fateful night. I got out and walked over to the edge of the pit and looked down.

A gravel pit is a gravel pit is a gravel pit. Yeah—I know Gertrude Stein said the same thing about a rose—you think I'm all illiterate? Don't answer that.

What was so attractive about this gravel pit that it had to yield two corpses? I stood there for maybe five minutes, looking down, and at the end of that time I wasn't any the wiser. Only wetter.

I walked back to the car and stopped beside it for a moment, looking along the track I'd just come. There were two distinct tire tracks gouged out of the gravel. I stared at them while the rain beat down on me, gradually soaking my suit. I closed my eyes for a moment and I could see the track as it had been the afternoon I'd followed Macey along it.

It had rained all morning and the gravel had been wet then as it was wet now. There had been two wavering lines along the gravel, criss-crossing in places. The lines made by Macey's bike. He'd been up there once, then come back again and phoned in, reporting his discovery of the corpse.

Well, that was OK, wasn't it?

Except that meant, as there weren't any other tire marks, that no other cars had gone along the track. And that meant what?

I slid behind the wheel of the MG, lit myself a damp cigarette and watched the rain sliding down the windscreen. If a car hadn't been along the track, then whoever murdered Robert Heinman had carried him along it—only there weren't any footprints, and to carry a corpse all that way made the murderer a superman.

So if the corpse wasn't dropped off by helicopter, and I figured I could discount that—and there weren't any car-tire tracks or footprints—then how did the corpse get into the gravel pit?

And as that's an exercise in logic, you don't get any prize for working out the solution.

Check—Macey had taken the corpse in on his motorbike. That didn't mean that Macey had killed him, of course. Macey hadn't committed suicide the following night. There'd been someone else in the gravel pit, someone who had shot him. I should know because that same character stole my prowl car and made a getaway.

The damp cigarette fizzled out between my fingers and I didn't notice. The theory was beginning to make sense. Macey had taken the corpse and dumped it in the gravel pit. And he'd come back the following night to meet the killer and collect the pay-off.

He had collected the pay-off, all right. Three thousand bucks. He had collected a double pay-off, in fact. Three thousand bucks and a slug in the head. Something that would keep his mouth shut permanently.

I started the car, turned it around and drove back on to the highway, then headed for home.

Why had Macey taken the corpse in? I could discount any idea that Macey had killed Heinman in the first place, I thought. Therefore he had taken the corpse in, either because he had been forced to, or because of the pay-off. He'd got the pay-off but how in hell had he been in the right place at the right time, just when the murderer came along with a corpse over his shoulder or a corpse in the back of his car?

I was still thinking about that, without getting any answers, when I parked the MG outside the house and went in.

I took off my wet clothes and had a nice hot shower, then got into a shirt and a pair of slacks. I made some coffee and laced it with brandy to counteract the effects of the caffeine. I lined up a collection of Dave Brubeck discs on the turntable, then I phoned the precinct before I let the discs spin.

Captain Parker was there and I was switched through to him.

"Well, Al?" he barked. "What's new?"

"The bruise on my chin," I said. "Why didn't somebody warn me that Clayton was a potential heavyweight champion before he started playing Cowboys and Indians?"

Parker chuckled. "Do you good, Al. You find out anything of interest?"

"Not much," I said. "You check on Macey's bank account?"

"Yes," he said.

"More than there should be?" I asked.

"Not in the account," he said, "but he had a safe-deposit box. There was three thousand in there—in cash."

"That's interesting," I said. "Thanks."

I could hear his heavy breathing for a moment. "Just a minute," he snarled. "Why is it interesting?"

"It just is," I said.

"You're holding out on me."

"It's only a theory—a half-baked theory," I said. "Let me think about it some more."

"You think."

"Now you're starting to sound like the D.A.," I said. "Anybody found out how Heinman got down here from New York?"

"No," he said.

"Maybe he flew in by helicopter?" I suggested.

"Maybe he de-materialized himself in New York and materialized himself in that gravel pit," he snarled.

"Why, captain," I said, "that's a wonderful idea. Why didn't I think of that?"

"Because Captain Marvel thought of it first," he rasped, then banged his receiver down.

He was winning on points.

I started the turntable spinning and got myself some more hot coffee laced with brandy. The rain was still making the windows wet and it was getting toward the middle of the afternoon. My head felt as if someone had driven three sharp spikes into it—I wouldn't have minded that so much, only they kept on jerking them up and down.

I finished the coffee and went into the bedroom. I took off my shoes and stretched out on the bed. There was something in the whole set-up that was screwy and I couldn't see it. I could feel it nudging the back of my brain but that was as close to it as I could get.

I let it worry me for about ten minutes, then gave up. I relaxed and let Brubeck play me off to sleep.

CHAPTER 11
Eldorado

It was nine-thirty when I woke up.

I was hungry again—hungry and thirsty. But no more greasy hamburgers and eggs—no, sir. Tonight Wheeler was going to live it up a little.

I was remembering that I had a regular girlfriend here by the name of Goldie—and that regular girlfriend of mine sang in a place called the Eldorado—and that place where she sang served some of the best meals you could get around the town.

Somebody said something once about killing two birds with the one stone. I could have chicken for dinner and listen to a thrush emote. That was near enough, wasn't it?

I had a shave and another shower just for the hell of it, then dressed in a tuxedo with the trimmings. The last time I'd worn a tuxedo was to the Policemen's Ball and I ended up taking a policewoman home.

Me, I should have known better—they teach them jiu-jitsu and instead of ending up with my arms around her, I ended up with my arms tied in knots a boy scout couldn't have undone. And if you don't believe me, how come I can hold my arm straight up in the air and touch the elbow with my fingers at the same time?

I went out to the MG, trying not to think how much it was costing me in mileage, and drove across to the Eldorado.

The hat-check girl gave me a welcoming smile as I came in.

"You sure look smooth, Lieutenant!" she said.

"I not only look smooth, I am smooth," I told her. "Why don't you come out with me one night and let me prove it?"

"I'd like to," she said.

"Fine," I said enthusiastically.

"But my husband wouldn't like it."

"Who cares about your husband?"

"When he's through wrestling," she told me, "he likes to come home and have me waiting there for him."

"I care about your husband," I said quickly. "I think he's quite entitled to have you home waiting for him. What division does he wrestle in?"

"Heavy," she said.

"I must go out one night and catch him," I said.

"I wouldn't," she said, "he weighs two hundred and forty."

"I didn't make a pass at you, did I?" I asked quickly.

"Not that I remember, Lieutenant," she smiled. "Here's your tag." She gave the hat-check to me and I beat it just in case her husband wasn't wrestling that night.

I stood in the doorway and Toni, the head waiter, came over. "Good evening, Lieutenant," he said. "A pleasure to see you."

"Thanks, Toni," I said. "I'm celebrating tonight."

"Celebrating what, Lieutenant?" he asked.

"I'm not sure yet, Toni," I told him, "but I'm bound to think of something. I'm in time to catch Goldie's act, aren't I?"

"Another ten minutes," he said. "I will give you a table beside the floor."

"Throw in a chair with it and we're highly organized," I said. "Lead on, MacDuff."

Toni gave me a floorside table and a waiter appeared a moment later. I ordered half a chicken and told him to tell the chef not to throw away the other half, in case I still felt hungry. I also told him to bring me three double Scotches on the rocks—in three separate glasses because I didn't want to look greedy.

I thought that if I ever did find out who killed Heinman and collected the five thousand bucks from Deidre Damour, at the rate I was spending I ought to break even.

The first of the three doubles appeared on the table in front of me and I sipped it slowly and took a look around. It's a small world, as Columbus said when he fell over the edge of it. Sitting at a table on the other side of the floor were some familiar faces.

Baron Marina, Moira Banks, Wolf Ramos and Eddie Stultz. I looked at the couples dancing on the floor and saw Deidre dancing head to foot with Jon Clayton. Head to foot is a phrase like cheek to cheek is a phrase.

I finished the first double just in time for the waiter to serve the second. The music finished—then as everybody started back to their tables, a voice said from behind me, "It's a pleasure to see you as a paying guest, Lieutenant."

I looked around and saw Johnny Ralston standing there, a grin on his face. Just behind him stood Rudi—with no grin on his face. The last time Rudi grinned was probably when he saw somebody fall over and break a leg.

"Join me in a drink, Johnny," I said, pointedly not including Rudi in the offer. "I know the proprietor here—we might be able to get some real Scotch, instead of that bathtub stuff he serves the rest of the customers."

"Thanks," he said. He came around and sat down opposite me, waving Rudi away.

The waiter came over at a fast trot. "What will you have?" I asked Ralston.

"Scotch," he told the waiter, "the same way the Lieutenant has it—double."

The waiter disappeared and reappeared with the drink. Nobody got service in the Eldorado like Johnny Ralston got service. He lifted his glass. "'Luck, Lieutenant."

"Cheers," I told him.

"How's the murder case going?" he asked.

"I wouldn't know," I said. "I got suspended—remember? Just because I mislaid one small prowl car, they suspended me. Is there no justice in the world, Johnny?"

"Not now you're suspended," he grinned.

I finished the second drink and saw the waiter hovering with the third.

I nodded and he brought it over.

"Now I'm not busy being a cop anymore," I said, "I'm doing a little research all of my own."

"Sounds fascinating," he said.

"I want to know why thrushes sing," I said.

"The ones I know only sing when they hear the nickels clinking," Johnny said.

"I have one particular thrush in mind," I said. "I feel I should devote a lot of my time to researching with that thrush. The trouble is that in days gone by, I haven't always had the time. I seem to remember when the thrush was kept waiting a couple of times. If you should be talking to her, Johnny, you might just mention that I am hopefully waiting for the chance of a little research."

"Sure," he said. He looked at me for a moment. "You aren't just stringing me along, Lieutenant? The real reason you're here would not be sitting over at that table across the floor from us, would it? Those film people having a night out?"

I looked across at them. Deidre Damour looked up, saw me and waved. I waved back. "No," I said. "Cross my heart, I didn't know they were coming here tonight."

"They were all here the night that guy Heinman got himself murdered," Johnny said.

"I remember you saying so," I said. "They all left around two, or was it Captain Parker who told me that?"

"Probably," he said. "Yeah—they left around two and most of them seemed to be pretty high."

"Heinman got himself knocked off around four—two hours later," I said. "None of them have an alibi, which means any one of them could have done it. I'm glad I'm suspended and don't have to try and work out which one did it."

"Yeah," he said.

He finished his drink and got up from the chair. "Thanks for the drink, Lieutenant. I'll try and see that thrush you mentioned, before she starts her act. I'll just mention there's a researcher out front." He grinned. "I don't think she's crazy about researchers, one of them stood her up a number of times—but you never can tell with dames, can you?"

"No," I said, "I hope."

Ralston wandered off and I applied some serious concentration to the Scotch. My chicken and Goldie appeared simultaneously, one on the floor and the other on the table—which seemed to support this two-birds theory.

Goldie was wearing a jet-black gown, which I can't describe because the censor's getting gray hairs already, trying to cut out the undue stress on violence and brutality in 'Jack and the Beanstalk' and still leave a story.

Let me say just this. There was Goldie and there was the black gown, but you saw much more of Goldie than you did of the gown. I didn't hear any of the customers objecting.

Goldie's style is somewhere between a ballad and a blues singer. She's good, but she'll never be really good until she forgets all the top pop singers she's heard. She can't help a lacing of corn here and there and it just takes off the icing.

She sang half a dozen numbers, finishing up with 'Melancholy Baby,' which always reminds me of a dame we had in this town a couple of years back who was known as 'Gentle Nellie' and she got all melancholy one day because her boyfriend was neglecting her. So she took a submachine gun with her and cut him down in the street—and also five innocent bystanders who were waiting for a bus.

By the time Goldie had finished and taken her bows, I'd finished the chicken. Goldie disappeared and the lights came up. The band started playing and couples drifted onto the floor.

Five minutes later I saw Goldie heading toward me, still wearing the black gown. I got to my feet and held a chair for her, then sat down again.

"It's good to see you, honey," I said. "How have you been?"

"Good—you haven't been around," she said.

The waiter came over and I ordered a martini for Goldie and a double Scotch for myself.

"I've been thinking about you," I told her.

"Since when?" she said.

"Since I saw you in that gown—you look terrific."

The waiter brought the drinks, then went away again.

"That's nice of you, Al," she said. "To think of me, I mean. From what I hear, I wouldn't have thought you had the time."

"I don't get it, baby," I said.

Her fingers beat a tattoo on the tablecloth. "I hear you've been busy over at the Valley Hotel," she said coldly. "You have even been working nights over there."

"Who told you that?" I asked her.

"Irma," she said.

"Irma?"

"She's a girlfriend of mine. She helps her father run the hotel."

"Oh," I said.

I felt I'd just been kicked by a mule. Irma would be the blonde on the reception desk. It was getting to be such a small world, I wondered why Columbus ever bothered.

"You can't believe everything you hear," I said.

"Yes, I can," her voice was still deep-frozen, "when I hear it from Irma. She never tells a lie."

"You can never be sure," I said.

She looked around disdainfully. "I see she's here tonight, what a remarkable coincidence!"

"Who—Irma?"

"Don't play dumb, Al—even though it becomes you."

"Who are you talking about?"

"Deidre Damour, of course—as if you didn't know."

"It's purely coincidental," I said. "I swear it."

"Don't make me laugh," she said.

I gave her my pleading look. "There's never been anyone else but you—you know that."

"Oh, sure," she said. "No one else but me, except that policewoman you took home from the ball that night, the manicurist from the Embassy, that lady wrestler who threw a double nelson on me when I said hello to you. Nobody else but me. How about that Chinese girl who wore those slit skirts?"

"She was teaching me Chinese," I said.

"Chinese what. How about that redheaded taxi dancer?"

"I yelled out for a taxi," I said defensively, "and she came along. Maybe I should have yelled, 'Cab'."

She sipped her drink broodingly. "Then there was that French girl."

"I was teaching her English," I explained. "When I first met her she couldn't say no in eight different languages."

"I bet you taught her a lot."

"Sure I did—after she'd met me she couldn't say it in nine."

Goldie finished her drink. "No, Al. I've been thinking about it. I'm through with you. I'll be old before my time, worrying about what you're doing and who you're out with when you're not with me. So I quit—as of now."

"You're the most beautiful dame I ever met," I said, "and I'm not kidding. Don't stay mad at me, honey. Sure—I might have just looked at another dame here and there, but you're the only one for me. From now on, I'm not going to even look at another dame. If a dame comes right up and speaks to me even, I shall ignore her completely."

"Al," a warm voice said from right behind me.

I felt the hair rise at the nape of my neck. The voice was warm and feminine. I had a nasty feeling that I recognized it.

"Al," the voice said again, slightly louder.

I looked around and there she was. Deidre Damour, wearing a gown that made Goldie look overdressed and the reason Kentucky was so proud abundantly clear.

"Er ..." I said.

"I have to talk to you," Deidre said. "It's terribly important."

She looked at Goldie, then back at me. "It's about ... you know what."

"But I don't," Goldie said in a high, clear voice. "Do tell me."

Deidre smiled sweetly at her. "I'm afraid this is strictly a private matter between Al and myself. We share a little secret."

"How nice for you." Goldie swept back her chair and got to her feet. She glared at me. "Brother," she said bitterly. "That's certainly what I'd call completely ignoring someone." She started to walk away from the table.

"Oh," Deidre said in a honey-sweet voice. "Must you go?"

"I'm afraid so." Goldie spun around and glared at her. "I'd hate to intrude on your little secret that you share between you."

"Please don't be rude." Deidre said loftily.

"Oh, I'm not being rude," Goldie smiled sweetly back at her. "I was always taught never to be rude to anyone old enough to be my mother." Then she swept away, her head high in the air, and with her went my chances of a celebration.

I glared at Deidre. "What are you trying to do to me? Ruin my love life?"

She sat down opposite me in the chair that Goldie had vacated.

"Please be serious, Al," she said. "You're trying to earn that five thousand, remember?" She looked at me closely. "Or are you?"

"Sure I am," I said sourly.

"Well, this is important. I just had to come and tell you." She looked around. "But not in here—too many people might listen. Can't we go where it's more quiet?"

"I guess so," I said. "Why not come to my place? I could give you a drink."

"All right," she said. "I'll just collect my purse from the other table and tell them I've got a headache and I'm leaving. I'll see you in the foyer."

"OK," I said. I watched her go, back to her table, then called the waiter and paid the bill. It came to roughly one week's salary and I shuddered as I paid it.

I got up from the table and walked out into the foyer and got my hat. Johnny Ralston came out and saw me. "You leaving so soon?" he asked.

"You know how it is," I said.

"The thrush won't sing?"

"Not for me," I said.

"That's bad luck," he grinned. "Maybe another night?"

"I can't afford to eat in this place more than once a leap year," I said. "With Goldie and me I'm afraid the song is over and there isn't even a melody lingering on."

"Brother," he said admiringly. "You've got the corniest line of dialogue I ever heard."

Deidre came out just then. She walked up to me and tucked her arm through mine. "I'm ready to go, Al honey," she said.

I smiled at Johnny. "You should have a line of corny dialogue like mine," I told him.

Then Deidre and I walked out into the night and the MG. I proudly held the door of the car open for her and she looked at it incredulously, then looked at me.

"Do you have a shoehorn?" she asked.

CHAPTER 12
Cutie With a Colt .45

We got back to my place just after midnight.

I took Brubeck off the turntable—he doesn't make music for midnight and Deidre Damour—then substituted a couple of Kostelanetz L.P.s, all throbbing strings, the sort of music that keeps a girl from wondering what time it is.

I established Deidre in a chair and organized some drinks. I gave her a drink and took my mine to a chair opposite her. "OK," I said. "What's on your mind?"

"Have you got anywhere with the investigation, Al?"

"Is that all you wanted to know?"

"You're supposed to be working for me, aren't you?" she asked coldly.

I supposed she had a point there. "I haven't got very far at all," I told her.

"You must have found out something," she said.

"A few things," I said. "A few things that don't add up."

"What are they?" she asked.

"Ed Stultz told me that Heinman's story was based on a few quite innocent facts that were distorted until they sounded really terrific. Do you believe that?"

She shook her head. "No. Ed is just the boy to try and sell you that version. He has a nice innocent look—I think his glasses help him."

"Maybe," I said. "You know that Heinman was shot with one of the forty-fives from the miniature range behind the hotel?"

"No," she looked interested, "I didn't know that."

"It doesn't help much," I said. "All the guns there were used the afternoon before he was killed and that means we can't check any of the guns—

they all have different fingerprints on them and they all have been fired recently."

"I wonder ..." she said slowly.

I looked at her. "You wonder what?"

"You know the night before Bobby was killed, we all went to the Eldorado?"

"I heard about it," I said.

"We left there just before two, as I remember," Deidre said slowly. "When we got back to the hotel it was about two o'clock. Everybody was tired, so the party broke up in the foyer and we went up to our rooms."

"So?"

She studied her glass carefully. "When I got up to my room I found I wasn't as tired as I thought I was, so I went along to see if Jon would care to have a drink."

"Clayton?"

"Yes," she said. "He wasn't there."

"Maybe he was asleep?" I suggested.

"No—I looked. His door wasn't locked so I went into his room and it was empty. I thought he must have gone downstairs again or something, so I didn't worry any more. I went back to my own room and went to bed."

I lit myself a cigarette. "Why didn't you tell somebody about this before?"

"I didn't think it was important, Al," she said. "But I've been watching him today and he seems to be under a terrific nervous strain—the way he attacked you this morning, for example. And when you mentioned about the gun that was used to kill Bobby, a forty-five. It ties in so closely with a western, doesn't it? With Jon playing the hero and having forty-fives strapped around his waist all day long while we're shooting."

I thought about it. "Could be," I said. "Heinman's publisher says he was going to do a new series on a Hollywood personality that would lift the lid off. Maybe the personality was Jon Clayton—and Clayton killed Heinman rather than be exposed."

"It does sort of add up, doesn't it?" she said.

"Sort of," I agreed. I took her empty glass and my own to the kitchen and refilled them. "Summertime," I sang with the strings, "an' we're livin' so easy now."

I came back into the living room with the refilled glasses and gave Deidre hers.

"I was wondering," she said, her eyes sparkling. "Couldn't we set some sort of trap for him?"

"With what as bait?" I asked her.

"I don't know," she said. "But if we try, we ought to be able to think of something."

"OK," I said, "let's think."

We sat in silence for a couple of minutes. "I've got it," Deidre said triumphantly.

"All right, genius," I said. "Let's hear it."

"Supposing I told him that Bobby had started to write this new series of articles," she said slowly, "and that he mailed part of the manuscript to me—and I've got it."

"Then?"

"I'll tell him I'll take money for it—say fifty thousand—and keep my mouth shut."

"It would be very dangerous," I said.

"Not if we handled it right," she persisted. "If you think there's any danger, you could tell him."

"Me." I laughed. "He'd be sure to think that Heinman would send his manuscript to me—a guy he didn't meet until he was a corpse."

"Don't be a dope," she said. "You and I could be in it together. You could stifle your cop's conscience for twenty-five thousand dollars, or you could make Jon believe that, anyway. Particularly as he knows you've already been suspended from the police."

"You could have something there," I admitted.

She got to her feet. "We could do it tonight," she said, "there's no reason why not. If I go back to the hotel now, I'll be back before them. I'll tell you what, Al. I'll tell him the story and I'll say you're already waiting for him with the manuscript. If he'll pay you the money, he can have the manuscript right away."

"Where will he get fifty thousand bucks this time of night?" I asked her patiently.

"We don't need the cash," she said, "he can write a check. He might think we're fools to take it, but we aren't going to try and cash it, anyway—are we? We only want to catch him."

"I guess so," I said. "OK—if you really don't want to sleep tonight."

"There's only one other thing," she said. "Where will you meet him?"

I thought about it for a moment. "At the gravel pit," I said. "It seems the right place."

"The gravel pit?" She frowned. "How will he know the way?"

"Don't you be a dope, either," I said. "If he dumped Heinman's body there, he'll know his way back—won't he?"

She giggled. "Of course. I never thought of that."

I finished the second drink. "I'll call a cab and get it to take you back to the hotel—I won't have time to drive you and then get to the gravel pit."

"All right," she said. "What time will you be out there?"

"From two-thirty onwards," I said.

I went over to the phone and dug out the number of an all-night cab service from the book. I dialed the number and they promised a cab within ten minutes.

"Just don't forget," I told Deidre. "The first thing you tell him is that I know all about it—so he knows that it's no use getting tough with you."

"Don't worry," she said, "I'll tell him that, all right."

She walked toward me, her eyes sparkling. "This is the most exciting thing that's ever happened to me," she said.

"I feel insulted," I said.

She laughed. "I'm serious, Al. To think we might have caught Bobby's murderer before morning."

"If we haven't we'll have probably caught a cold, anyway," I said. "Or I will—it's going to be awful cold out there in that gravel pit."

Deidre put her arms around my neck and clung to me. "Don't worry, honey," she whispered, "I'll keep you warm."

There was a sharp blast on a horn somewhere outside.

"If it's not the bell tolling, it's the taxi waiting," I said. "You be careful when you talk to Clayton."

"I will, honey," she promised. She kissed me fiercely for a long moment. The horn sounded again.

"I'd better go," she said. "We will have plenty of time, Al, after it's all over." Then she turned and hurried out of the room.

I heard the front door open, then click shut behind her. The sound of the cab's engine faded in the distance. The house seemed suddenly still.

"Bess, you is my woman now," said the strings from all around the room.

I went into the bedroom and took the shoulder holster and .32 from the drawer. I took off the tuxedo and put on the holster, then shoved the gun into it. I put on a nice dark jacket instead of the tuxedo—white is a nasty color to wear at night—it makes a target so much easier.

I went into the kitchen, poured myself a drink, looked at it and then poured it down the sink. There was some coffee left from the afternoon. I reheated it and drank it, black and strong. I felt comparatively sober.

I checked my watch. I'd give it another half-hour, I thought, then drive over to the gravel pit. I wasn't liking this, not one little bit.

The half-hour dragged by. I was on my feet, ready to go, when the phone rang. I grabbed the receiver off the cradle.

"Al?" Deidre's voice was hardly more than a whisper.

"Yeah?"

"You on your way?"

"Check."

"They've just come in—I'm going along to Jon Clayton's room right now. I thought I'd better ring you and make sure you'd be there, in case he goes out there straight away."

"I'll be there," I told her, "and you be careful."

"I always am," she giggled. "I've given up trying to be good. It's too difficult." Then she hung up.

Twenty minutes later, I was driving along the track once more. There was no moon and the night was darker than a black cat. The gravel showed ahead of me the glare of the headlights. I came up close to the edge of the pit and stopped at the edge. I lit a cigarette and wondered how I'd got that nasty empty sensation in my stomach. I switched off the headlights and sat there in the dark, listening.

After a few minutes, it began to get on my nerves. I took the flashlight out I'd brought with me and got out of the car. I found a rock to sit on about ten feet away from the car, and sat on it. I heard a scampering noise somewhere close and flicked the flashlight on just in time to see a rat vanish.

I hoped Clayton wasn't going to be too long. It could be, of course, that Deidre was way off beam and when she broke the news to him, he'd bust a rib laughing and tell her she must be crazy. In which case, I'd probably sit around the gravel pit all night waiting for somebody who wasn't coming and end up with double pneumonia.

I was busy thinking cheerful thoughts like that when I saw the distant flash of headlights as a car turned off the highway and started up the track.

I stood up and moved behind the rock—it stood about three feet high and gave me some sort of cover. The headlights came nearer as the car bumped its way along the track. I ducked down behind the rock and stayed there, so that I wouldn't be seen.

Then I heard the car stop. The headlights were still on but they weren't hitting the rock—they were focused right on the MG. I straightened up cautiously. I couldn't see beyond the headlights and I cursed softly. I heard a car door slam and then there was silence for a moment. I eased the gun out of the holster and thumbed back the safety, then waited.

"Wheeler?" It was Clayton's voice, harsh with tension.

"Here," I said and as I spoke, I ducked down behind the rock again, fast.

A gun boomed and lead whined over my head. I stayed right there behind the rock. A dead cop is not only dead but he misses out on his pension, as Macnamara always says.

Then there were two more shots in quick succession, but no lead whined anywhere near me this time. A moment later there was a shrill scream—a feminine scream.

So I had to come out from behind the rock. I came out, moving fast, the flashlight in one hand and the gun in the other. I sprinted toward Clayton's car as fast as I could.

When I got close, the flashlight picked out two figures—one motionless on the ground and the other standing up. The one standing up had both hands to its face and was weeping hysterically.

I ignored her for the moment when I got there. I knelt down beside Clayton and I didn't need to take more than one look at him to see he was dead. There were two bullet-holes in his chest and the cloth of his suit was powder-burned. The shots had been fired at point-blank range.

I got to my feet again and shone the flashlight on Deidre's face. She was moaning and sobbing. She looked at me bewilderedly, but the moaning stopped and after a little while she began to cry quietly.

I put my arms around her and held her close, letting her cry it out on my shoulder.

"It was horrible," she whispered finally, "horrible. When I told him, I thought he'd go berserk. But he got control of himself and said he'd go to meet you—and he'd take me with him to make sure there was no double-cross."

"I couldn't do anything about it, Al. He just dragged me along with him and almost flung me into the car. When he got out of the car just now, he pulled me with him. I had no idea he had a gun with him. Then he called out your name and when you said, 'Here,' he shot at you. I went crazy, I guess. I thought he'd kill you and afterwards he'd kill me. So I grabbed the gun out of his hand and I don't think he was expecting it—he was too surprised to hang on to it."

She started to weep again. "He got his hands around my throat and I thought he was going to strangle me. So I pushed the gun into his chest and fired twice."

I shone the flashlight on the ground and saw the gun she had dropped—it lay alongside Clayton.

A Colt forty-five.

CHAPTER 13
A Hunch—I Hope

The thin redhead wasn't there. I went through into the inner office. District Attorney Jordan was sitting behind his desk. Captain Parker and Commissioner Lavers were both sitting in visitors' chairs, facing him. The set-up was as before, except for the smile on the D.A.'s face.

"Come in, Lieutenant," he said genially, "and have a chair." He pushed a box across the desk toward me. "Cigar?"

"No, thanks," I said. I sat down and looked at Parker, who let one eye-lid droop momentarily.

The D.A. took out a cigar and carefully nipped off the end, then concentrated on lighting it. "Well," he said, "all's well that ends well, eh?"

Nobody said anything.

He leaned back in his chair and puffed his cigar luxuriously. "I have issued a statement to the press," he said. "This will really rock the whole country. Clayton's name is a household word, of course. But I think, on the whole, that we haven't come out of it too badly. Not too badly at all. We've cleaned it all up in about seventy-two hours from the discovery of the first body. We've even saved the State some expense," he chuckled. "They don't have to worry about indicting Clayton and sending him to the chair now, do they?"

Lavers moved his bulk and the chair creaked protestingly. "The credit for this goes to Lieutenant Wheeler," he said.

The grin slipped a little from the D.A.'s face. "Quite, quite. I've forgotten all about that suspension business—it's cleaned out of the record now, of course."

"Of course," Lavers rumbled. "I didn't get to see that press statement before it was released?"

"There wasn't much time," Jordan said. "We had to catch the morning papers—there was hardly any time at all."

"Normally, on a police matter," Lavers went on slowly, "my department would make any statements to the press. Seems to me that murder was a matter for my department."

"It's no use getting all department-conscious about this, Mr. Commissioner," Jordan said testily. "The statement had to go out in a hurry and I—that is, my department—sent it out. It was a job to do and it had been done."

"I hope Wheeler gets the credit due to him," Lavers rumbled, "and Parker here, too."

"I can assure you," the D.A. said stiffly, "that credit has been given where credit is due."

Lavers heaved himself to his feet. "Can I have a copy of this statement?"

"Naturally," Jordan said. "I'll have one sent to you."

"Don't you have one here?"

"No." Jordan cleared his throat. "As a matter of fact, they were got out in such a rush that I haven't even got a file copy for myself—but that will be attended to. You'll get your copy in due course, Mr. Commissioner, don't worry about that."

Lavers grunted and walked to the door. Parker and I followed him out, past the redhead's desk and into the corridor. Lavers turned and looked at Parker. "Something stinks," he said.

"Yes, sir," Parker agreed.

"He hasn't even got a copy of the press statement to give me," Lavers snorted. "He doesn't want me to see it."

"Another hour or so, commissioner," Parker said, "and we'll be able to read it in the papers."

"I might have a few more words to say to District Attorney Jordan then," Lavers said. "Well, I'm going home to try and get another hour's sleep before the day starts."

I walked with Parker down the steps toward the waiting car. We got in and the driver pulled the car away from the curb.

"You going home to get some sleep, Al?" Parker asked me.

"I reckon so," I said.

"You did it all right anyway," he said.

"Any credit due is to Deidre Damour," I said. "And the D.A., of course."

He grinned. "If what I think has happened, has happened, the commissioner will have taken care of the district attorney in an hour or two from now."

"You mean, when he's read the papers which tell how Jordan brilliantly planned to snare the killer, knowing all the time who it was, of course."

"Of course," Parker agreed.

I lit a cigarette. "I'm going to look forward to seeing the D.A.'s face a bright red."

"You mean, when Lavers has finished with him?" Parker asked.

"Not particularly," I said.

He stared at me. "Then what in hell do you mean, Al?"

"I'm not sure," I said and he shrugged his shoulders disgustedly and gave up.

The prowl car dropped me at home. I went in and my watch said it was a quarter after five. I switched on the lights and then I saw her huddled in an armchair.

"I thought you'd be asleep at the hotel by now," I said.

"I got the shakes," she said, "just thinking about it. And the reporters kept ringing and some of them were coming out to the hotel. I couldn't have stood an interview, so I came here."

She was huddled inside a polo coat, her shoulders hunched, her hands thrust deep into the pockets, but she still looked like a million dollars.

"You'd better go back to the hotel, honey," I told her. "If a reporter found you here, it wouldn't look good."

"I don't care what would look good and what wouldn't," she said. She shivered suddenly. "Every time I close my eyes I see Jon Clayton's face staring at me. If I'm by myself for any length of time I'll go raving mad, I know I will."

"Take it easy," I said automatically.

She got up and walked toward me. "Hold me close, Al," she pleaded. "Hold me tight. Make me forget all about it."

She took off the polo coat. Underneath she was wearing a tight sweater and a pair of tight slacks. She was still the dream girl of two-thirds of the male population.

"Hold me." She stood in front of me, her eyes closed. "Kiss me, Al. Love me. Make me forget."

I measured the distance carefully, then hit her with a neat right to the point of the jaw. I caught her as she sagged forward, then I carried her into the bedroom and put her into the bed, rocking the covers around her.

Make me forget. That's what she said, didn't she? She lay there breathing peacefully and sleeping like a babe. I went back into the kitchen and poured myself a drink. I had been promising myself that drink ever since I saw the rat at the gravel pit.

I finished the first drink and poured another one. I took it back with me into the living room. I drank it, then stretched out on the sofa. I was asleep a couple of minutes later.

When I woke up the sun was streaming into the room. I looked at my watch and it said midday. I sat up and stretched, then saw the piece of paper on the table. I got up and walked over, then read it.

You looked so peaceful snoring away there, I didn't like to disturb you. I don't feel so bad now that it's daylight. I'm taking your advice and going back to the hotel. Will you give me a ring there when you wake up?

PS What hit me?

Deidre

I grinned and went into the bedroom. The bedclothes were still crumpled where she had slept. I stood there looking at them for a moment and the grin faded off my face. I went into the kitchen and put on some coffee and while it was percolating, I rang the hotel.

The blonde connected me with Deidre's room and a moment later her husky voice said, "Hello?"

"It was me that hit you," I said.

"You louse," she said.

"You said you wanted to forget," I reminded her. "You needed sleep more than you needed Al Wheeler."

"I don't suppose," Deidre said sweetly, "that Al Wheeler also needed sleep more than he needed Deidre Damour?"

"Could be," I admitted.

"I must be getting old," she said, "when a man thinks of sleep before he thinks of me."

"It's me that's getting old, honey," I said. "How do you feel this morning, anyway?"

"I feel better, Al," she said, "much better."

"No filming?" I asked her.

"Shooting," she gurgled with laughter. "You should see Baron this morning—he looks as if he's just come through the Flood. We're packing up on location here, anyway. He doesn't have a male star anymore—they'll have to junk everything they've shot with Jon Clayton in and shoot it again with a new male star. For me, they could junk the whole lot and not start again."

"So that means you're going back to Hollywood?"

"In a couple of days, I guess," she said.

"When do I see you?" I asked her.

She made an appreciative gurgle. "That sounds more like my boy. Not today, honey. I've got to go and make all sorts of statements to your D.A. this afternoon, and I think I'll have an early night tonight. Ring me tomorrow, Al."

"Sure thing," I said. "So long."

"Bye, honey." Deidre hung up. I hung up.

I un-hung up.

I rang the hotel again. One of those compulsional neuroses that splay-footed character Carter Brown is always talking about.

"Valley Hotel," the blonde said wearily.

"Lieutenant Wheeler," I said.

"Oh—you again," she said.

"Just remember that I am a lieutenant again," I said, "and this is police business."

"Yes, Lieutenant." There was a shade more respect in her voice.

"Miss Damour is going out this afternoon to see the D.A.," I said. "She should come back around five, I'd imagine. She says she's going to have an early night ..."

"Doing what?" the blonde asked interestedly.

"I didn't ask," I said wearily. "But I have a theory she'll go out again. As soon as she does, I want you to ring me at this number." I gave her the number.

"All right, Lieutenant." The curiosity broke through her voice. "What are you doing—checking up on her?"

"That's right," I said. "Her radio license is overdue." Then I hung up.

Shower, shave—the routine. I went out and had some lunch, then came back around three and read the papers for the first time. It was a whale of a story. The whole thing had been planned by the district attorney and executed with the co-operation of Miss Deidre Damour and an unnamed lieutenant. Captain Parker's had been so right.

The version was pretty well much the same in all three papers. I tossed them away, then rang the precinct. Parker wasn't there, Macnamara told me, he was with the commissioner and the D.A.

I hung up again and imagined the sparks flying all around the place. The redhead with too much lipstick would have improved her vocabulary no end, I imagined.

I sat around gnawing my knuckles and wondering.

If my hunch was right, I should have told Parker all about it this morning. The last time I'd played a hunch, I ended up losing a prowl car and letting a murderer slip through my fingers. But this hunch was much stronger.

The trouble with this hunch was that if I was wrong, I would embarrass a lot of people including the commissioner and Captain Parker. Whereas if I handled it myself and I was wrong, nobody would be any the wiser. And if I mishandled it myself and I was right—well, I wouldn't be worrying about the consequences, anyway, because I'd probably be dead.

I hope I make myself clear?

I checked the Smith & Wesson, then put it in the shoulder holster under my left armpit. I took the MG down to the nearest gas station and filled the tank. Then I came back to the house and waited some more.

I put some Ellington discs back on the turntable and spun them. But my mind wasn't on the music.

The phone rang at seven. "It's Irma here," an excited voice said.

"Who the hell's Irma?"

"You know—at the Valley Hotel."

"Oh—sure," I said. "Sorry."

"She just went out," Irma said breathlessly. "She got me to call a cab for her and it's just leaving now."

"Did you hear where she was going?" I asked.

"Yes—the ... "

"Eldorado?"

"That's right." She sounded disappointed. "How did you know, Lieutenant?"

"I'm psychic," I said. "Thanks, thanks very much." I hung up quickly.

I raced out of the house and into the MG. I gave it its head and it did over eighty on the highway for me and wriggled its way around corners at seventy. I reached the Eldorado in ten minutes flat.

I went straight on past it a couple of hundred yards, then pulled the car right off the road in the shelter of some trees. It wouldn't be seen by anyone passing, unless they were really looking for it.

I left the trees, jumped over the fence that separated me from the driveway, then hurried down it. I rounded the corner of the building just in time to see Deidre get out of the cab—and go into the roadhouse through a side door.

The cab made a sharp U-turn and came back. I flattened myself against the building and the headlights missed me. The driver went on past without seeing me.

I started walking again. I reached the side door where she had gone in and stopped. I thought if I got caught, I could always say I was looking for a steak. I tried the handle of the door and it wasn't locked. I pushed the door open a foot and waited. Nobody said anything or made any sort of noise inside. So I pushed it open a little further and stepped inside.

I was standing at one end of a corridor that led through to the kitchen at the far end. The corridor was in darkness, but there was light in the kitchen and I could see waiters passing to and fro, carrying trays.

There was a door fairly close to me and it wasn't properly shut. A thin shaft of light lay across the floor in front of me. I edged closer to it and I could hear voices. I came closer still until my ear was almost pressed against the crack between the door and jamb. Then I could hear what the voices were saying.

"All men are the same, honey," Deidre was saying. "To a girl like me, that is."

"I guess so," Ralston said. "I have to hand it to you, Deidre. You sewed it up like a gunny sack."

"And just as tight," she said evenly. "No cracks in the seams, no nothing. With the district attorney and the entire police force falling over me to say thank you."

So the hunch was paying off.

"I go back to Hollywood tomorrow afternoon," she went on. "That poor dope of a Wheeler is looking forward hopefully to seeing me tomorrow. If they're showing one of my films locally, then he might be lucky—but otherwise he'll be lonesome."

"He's not a bad sort of guy," Johnny said tolerantly. "Sure, he's dumb. More dumb than most cops and that's saying something. But I can live with him if he doesn't get wise."

"He won't get wise in a million years," Deidre said. "Guiding him along by his nose is like taking candy from a kid."

"Or a prowl car from a cop." Johnny chuckled.

I thought a guy should listen only so long to people insulting him. If he listened too long it was liable to undermine his morale.

I took the gun out of the holster—it was already off the safety—and held it in my right hand. I put the flat of my hand against the door and pushed gently, so that it swung wide open. I stepped into the room.

Johnny Ralston had his back to me. He was standing up, a glass in his hand. Deidre was sitting down in a chair, facing him, also with a glass in her hand.

She saw me over his shoulder and her eyes widened. The glass twitched suddenly in her hand and good liquor spilled on to the carpet.

CHAPTER 14
Always a Lady?

Johnny turned around slowly, the grin wiped off his face, and stared at me. "Back up against the wall and make it fast," I said. He didn't argue—he backed up against the wall. I looked at Deidre. "You can join him, too," I told her.

"Al," she said, her eyes wide. "What is this all about?"

"Murder," I said, "three murders, to be precise. You want me to list them?"

She got out of the chair and backed slowly toward the wall. When she reached it, she stood alongside Johnny—and there was concentrated hatred in her eyes as she looked at me. I thought I could stand up under the strain.

Johnny took a deep breath. "All right, Al," he said. "What's this all about?"

"You've got the same line of small talk as the Pride of Kentucky," I nodded in Deidre's direction. "Why can't you be original? You're so smart, both of you. I'm dumb—dumber than most cops, but even I don't keep on repeating myself."

"OK," he said. "So you listened at the door before you came in."

"Now you're getting smart," I told him.

Deidre laughed softly. "I think we should cut the dramatics, Al. Where do you think they'll get you?"

"I don't know about me," I said, "but I know where they'll get you two, OK—straight into the electric chair."

"For what?"

"Murder."

"Whose murder?"

"Heinman for one, Macey for two and Clayton for three."

Deidre shook her head slowly. "Don't you read your papers?" she said. "That's all history now, Al. Clayton killed the other two and I had to accidentally kill him—you should remember, you were there."

"I was there," I said, "but I didn't see anything. I only heard the shots."

"Then how do you know it didn't happen the way I said it happened?" she asked sweetly.

I juggled a cigarette into my mouth with one hand and lit it, also with one hand—and a match, of course.

"Don't think you're both too smart," I said. "I can take this thing apart and leave you with the pieces."

"Quit stalling, Al," Johnny said. "Go ahead—try and take it apart. You show us that Clayton wasn't the murderer, after all."

"It'll be a pleasure," I said, "and while I'm talking I'm likely to get thirsty—so you can pour me a drink, Deidre. Just pour the drink and leave it on the bar. I don't want to shoot you but if you try any bright tricks like throwing liquor in my eyes, I'll have to shoot—and that would be a pity for the magazines, wouldn't it? No more cheesecake pictures of Damour—only slightly messy pictures that nobody would want to look at."

"I get the drift," she said sourly. "You don't have to write a novel about it."

She walked over to the bar and poured out a drink, then went back to the wall again. I moved over to the bar and leaned against it, raising the drink with my free hand.

"Here's to a short life and a merry one," I said.

"You're still stalling, Al," Johnny said coldly. "You couldn't prove the earth was round if they gave you Christopher Columbus and an orange."

I grinned at him. "Let's take something easier to prove first. Something like the fact that you two killed Heinman, Macey and Clayton."

Deidre heaved a deep sigh, which did interesting things for the low-cut top of her dress. "Tell it, for Pete's sake," she said.

I had a long swallow of rye which moistened my throat a little. "Take Heinman," I said. "He left New York to come down here and nobody seems to know why. Nobody knows how he got here either. He didn't come by plane or train and if he drove a car, he parked it two miles up in the air because nobody found it and we were looking for it."

Deidre shrugged her shoulders. "I thought you were telling us the answers, not asking the questions."

"So I am, honey," I said, "so I am. If he didn't come by any of those means, there's only one logical answer to the way he did come—he was brought. Brought in somebody's car by somebody. And that somebody killed him and had him dumped into the gravel pit."

"Had him dumped?" Johnny asked softly. I told them about the tracks in the wet gravel.

"Macey slipped up when he phoned in," I said. "Maybe he was nervous. He said the corpse had three bullets in it and described exactly where they were ... When I got out to the gravel pit, we stood on the edge and looked down. Heinman was a long way down and Macey told me he hadn't been down the pit. He was obviously lying, because he couldn't have seen where the bullet-holes were from the top of the pit.

"Then I went checking up on Macey that night and found he'd gone out. I had a hunch he might have gone to the gravel pit—so I went looking for him. I found him—dead. I heard the shot that killed him. And I lost a prowl car, as you know. Macey had three thousand dollars on him and he also had another three thousand in a safe-deposit box in the bank."

"Go on," Johnny said.

I finished the drink and put the glass down on the bar. "So I supposed a lot of things. That Macey had been taking bribes for a while. And he'd been bribed to dump that corpse. Maybe he happened along the highway when the car with the corpse in it was just coming into the gravel pit turn-off. Maybe he stopped to pass the time of day and saw the cadaver. Got any ideas why he stopped then, Johnny?"

"These are all your ideas, copper?" he said. That "copper" meant he was reverting to type.

"He stopped because whoever was driving the car was known to him," I said. "That's the point. It wasn't a stranger—it was somebody he knew, somebody who was already paying him graft.

"So I thought about that one. The film crowd at the Valley Hotel had only been there a couple of days—it couldn't possibly be one of them. So I never was really sold on the idea that one of them murdered Heinman, although they all had such nice motives."

"Who was the guy in the car, then?" Johnny grated.

"Come, come, Johnny," I said. "Don't be so modest. Who, on Macey's patrol, would be the guy most likely to be bribing him and for what? That's what I asked myself. And without any effort at all I came up with the answer: Johnny Ralston. Johnny because he looks like a racketeer and employs hoodlums and runs a roadhouse and probably was a racketeer and maybe even sells a little marijuana and snow on the side."

I paused for breath. "That was interesting stuff Heinman wrote for *Dynamite*, wasn't it?" I asked.

They both stared at me blankly.

"You remember, Deidre, that stuff he wrote about you? About you having been the ex-girlfriend of a racketeer? That passage stuck in my memory. I thought it was very interesting. There you were—the girlfriend or ex-girlfriend of a racketeer—inside the Valley Hotel, and here Johnny was in the roadhouse not too far away—and him looking just the way you'd expect an ex-racketeer to look."

They looked at each other, then looked back at me.

"Somebody was trying to sell me the film crowd as suspects," I said. "I could feel it from the word go—but they were trying too hard. No one had an alibi. Why? Because coincidentally they had all had a night out here at the Eldorado on the night of the murder and arrived at the hotel around two, then gone to bed.

"Heinman was killed a couple of hours later, which gave each one of them a chance of not having gone to bed—but gone out and shot him, instead.

"It stank." I said.

"And then Deidre tells me what a great guy Bobby Heinman was and how he saw him in New York a couple of weeks ago. But Moira Banks told me he was her guy until somehow Deidre got her hooks into him. I'm inclined to believe that he didn't write anything about Moira, but he did give Deidre a little push along."

"Is this getting us anywhere?" Deidre yawned openly. "Is it proving anything? I'm getting tired of standing here."

"This is deduction," I said in a hurt voice. "This is the way that real detectives do it. You ought to be glad of the opportunity to listen."

"We don't have much choice," Johnny said flatly. "Is there any more?"

"Some," I admitted.

I discovered I could keep them covered with the gun and pour myself a drink with the other hand. I did that.

"I thought some about Heinman," I said. "He was a writer who went to Hollywood and didn't do any good—he only made about twice what I'm making a week, but he didn't do any good. And from being a nice American boy, he became a hundred per cent American tramp and started writing dirty articles for a dirty magazine."

"I got to wondering where he, as Moira Banks described to me, suddenly got his switch. Three months or so in Hollywood and he's suddenly digging up dirt that other people have tried to dig up for a couple of decades and haven't succeeded. So I thought maybe he had a little help.

"I also had a smart thought. Maybe he was given that help deliberately by someone. Someone who had all the dirt and gave him some of it so that it would get printed and scare the hell out of the people it concerned. Then Heinman, having done his job, could be pushed off somewhere to try and make a living digging ditches or something, and the other people could really get their racket going.

"One of those nice clean rackets that blackmail is a polite word for. They'd approach the people concerned and ask them whether they'd like to see the rest of the dirt about them printed or would they rather pay up? My bet is that ninety per cent of them would pay up.

"Yet I started thinking," I said, "'Which one of the suspects would be likely to be running a racket like that?' Well, though I just love the Pride of Kentucky, you have to admit, Johnny, that you could print her morals on a postage stamp and still have enough room left over for the Gettysburg Address."

Deidre nearly choked. "Why, you ..."

"Gently," I said. "Remember, always the lady. Even unto the bitter end. I went on thinking ... and what better partner could a dame like Deidre Damour have in a racket than a racketeer? So that sort of tied you in together. Then the one thing left was to work out why Heinman had to be bumped off after he'd served his purpose.

"That didn't take a lot of figuring, really. He'd been wised up somehow. Maybe he heard something he shouldn't or maybe he read something he shouldn't, and he suddenly realized he was on to the greatest racket of all. He didn't have to bother to squeeze the people you were going to squeeze. He could just sit back and let you do the hard work. When you raked in the dough, he'd squeeze you. And if you didn't play ball, he was going to write another article for *Dynamite*—he had already hinted at it to the editor—one that would make the last article look like a Sunday school appeal.

"And that would explain why Deidre went to New York. I'll bet she threw everything she could at him to try and make him change his mind, but being a determined character he stuck right where he was—all or nothing at all and he was going to have the all.

"That was when the two of you decided he had to die. Having decided that fate gave you an overripe orange in sending the other film people on location here. So here in this city was the obvious place for Heinman to die. Where there were ready-made suspects.

"How you got him down here is immaterial. Maybe you told him you'd make a pay-off here, or you told him something—but you got him to agree. You brought him down here and you killed him. On the way, when you were going to dump the corpse in the gravel pit, a cop came alongside you on a motorbike and asked how were you. Macey probably recognized that Cadillac of yours—which all goes to show that a good car has its disadvantages."

I looked at Johnny expectantly. "Am I right or am I right?"

"Not quite," he said. "You forget I was here in the roadhouse until two o'clock that morning, anyway. But you're basically right, copper—I take back what I said about your being dumb. It wasn't me who picked up Heinman from New York, then killed him on the way down."

"No?" I said.

"No," he agreed. "It was Rudi. You remember Rudi, don't you, copper?"

"The guy with a cement block instead of a head?" I said. "I remember him—how is he these days?"

"Why don't you ask him?" Johnny said, a grin spreading across his face. "He's right behind you."

I could feel my spine tingle. "That's the oldest gag in the book, Johnny," I said. "You don't kid me into looking around."

"There ain't no need, pal," a harsh voice grated in my ear. "You can feel this, can't you?"

I could feel it, all right. The spine is remarkably sensitive to the nose of a gun being poked into it.

"Drop your gun, pal," Rudi said. "Nice and gentle, otherwise I'll blow a hole right through you."

I opened my fingers and dropped the gun.

Johnny came across quickly and picked it up. "You didn't quite finish your story, copper," he said. "But then you weren't at the D.A.'s office this afternoon, were you?"

I looked at him—it was his pitch now.

"Deidre explained to them how she'd found out that Clayton was worried because the article that Heinman had hinted at to his editor was about him. And Clayton had invited him to come down here and talk it over. When Heinman did come down, Jon Clayton met him secretly and murdered him, but the cop saw him putting the body down in the gravel pit and he got him to keep his mouth shut by promising him that three thousand the following night. When the cop turned up, Clayton killed him as well, which in the long run is generally cheaper."

He grinned at me. "That was the story Clayton told Deidre on the way down to the gravel pit—so she said. And the D.A. was delighted to hear it. He swallowed every word of it and the case is closed, finished, wrapped up and thrown away now. So you're a little late, copper, just a little too late."

Deidre sauntered across to the bar and poured herself a drink. "The trouble with him now is that he makes for a problem," she said coldly. "What do we do with him?"

"I even thought of that one," Johnny said. "While we were standing there waiting for Rudi to show and listening to his gab, it gave me a chance to think."

"It had better be good," she said. "Another corpse after all the murders have been cleaned up is going to be hard to explain."

"Murder?" Johnny raised his eyebrows. "Who said anything about a murder?"

"You can't leave him in any other condition than one where his mouth is shut permanently," she said.

"You amaze me, honey," he said sarcastically.

"All right, genius," she said. "Tell it."

All the time the hard reality of Rudi's gun still bored into my back.

"This guy Wheeler," Johnny said complacently, "he's known around the town as the most unorthodox cop you could meet in a row of Sundays—unorthodox but a guy who does a lot of work, nevertheless. A guy who checks and rechecks. A guy who's very thorough."

"Why don't you get rid of him first and write the obituary notice afterwards?" she suggested.

"So, being a painstaking sort of guy," Johnny went on, ignoring her, "what should be more natural than him going back to the gravel pit tonight and having a look around? And that's where he hits a streak of bad luck. Trips over the edge, a little further along where it's almost sheer, and breaks his neck."

"Can you guarantee he'll break his neck?" she asked coolly.

"Oh, yes," Johnny said softly, "I think I can guarantee that all right. In fact, I think I can guarantee his neck will be broken just before he starts his fall. Can't I, Rudi?"

"Boss," Rudi said, "it'll be a pleasure. I never did like coppers and this one," he jabbed my spine to emphasize his words, "I never liked at all."

CHAPTER 15
"Ladies First"

They left me tied to a chair with my hands braced around the back of it and my ankles tied to a leg each, while Rudi went to bring the car around and Johnny went back into the main room of the roadhouse just to establish the fact that he was around—in case anyone should remember later on that he wasn't.

Johnny was a guy after my own heart—he was thorough. It was a pity he was after my neck, too, because he looked like getting it.

Deidre poured herself another drink and smiled at me. "Would you like a drink, Al? For old times' sake?"

"Fine," I said. I should have known better. I got it OK—in the end.

"I like to think of you lying down there in that gravel pit," she said. "That's where you belong."

"Who—me?" I said.

She walked over and slapped my face hard a couple of times. "It's a pity we have to get rid of you so quickly," she said. "I'd have liked to work you over a few times before we finally got rid of you."

"Who did you graduate with?" I asked her. "The werewolves or the vampires?"

She slapped me again another couple of times just to prove that I wasn't funny.

Johnny came back into the room. "We should be OK now," he said. "The place is nearly deserted—it's still too early for the mob to get in."

Rudi stuck his head through the doorway. "OK, boss. I got the car waiting."

"Fine," Johnny said. He bent down and untied my feet. "On your feet, Al."

I got to my feet and a gun jabbed back into its familiar niche in my spine. "One whisper out of you and I'll let you have it," Johnny said. "There's a silencer on this gun and it won't make any more noise than a champagne cork being drawn."

Rudi looked down the corridor, then nodded. We went out to the car. Deidre slid behind the wheel and Johnny stared at her.

"We don't need you along, honey," he said.

"This I wouldn't miss for a million dollars," Deidre said. "I'm coming with you."

"OK," he shrugged his shoulders. "If you want it that way, I guess it doesn't make any difference."

The motor purred into life and she made a U-turn and headed toward the gateway. A few seconds later we were out on the highway and picking up speed.

Five minutes later we came to the turn-off. Deidre slowed and changed down into second, then the Cadillac was bumping along the track. The headlights picked up the edge of the pit and she stopped and switched the engine off.

We got out, Rudi behind me, with the gun pressed tight into my spine as usual. Johnny had a flashlight with him and he led the way, Deidre followed and I and the gorilla brought up the rear.

We climbed along the higher ground, still keeping close to the edge of the pit. Johnny stopped after we'd been walking for five minutes and shone his flashlight down.

"This is the place," he said.

"OK," Rudi said. "I take him now?"

"Sure," Johnny said, "but take that rope off his wrists first. We don't want him found tied up—it would sort of upset the theory, wouldn't it?"

"I guess so," Rudi said, after thinking about it.

The rope around my wrists was untied and the next moment, before I could make a move, his massive hands were around my neck.

"Wait a minute!" Deidre squealed. "I want to enjoy this. I want to take a look first and see just how far down it is."

She walked to the very edge of the pit and peered down, bending forward to do so. "It sure is a hell of a long way down," she said exultantly. "You can hardly see the bottom at all. If we count the number of seconds it takes him to reach it, that gives you the number of yards or something, doesn't it?"

"All right," Johnny growled irritably. "You've had your fun, now stand back and let Rudi finish it."

As he spoke, Rudi automatically propelled me forward again. And for the first time in his life, so far as I was concerned, Rudi did the right thing.

He pushed me forward so that I was within reach. And I didn't hesitate. If "ladies first" was going to save my neck being broken, then it was going to be a case of "ladies first."

I lashed out with my foot and it connected with the seat of her skirt, sending her plunging forward. She screamed once, wildly, a terror-ridden scream that I still hear in nightmares, and then she disappeared over the edge.

She kept on screaming and the sound came floating up to us, growing fainter and fainter. Johnny was screaming himself, like a demented thing, and it wasn't surprising that Rudi slackened his grip on my neck.

It was a time when I had a split second to make a decision.

Johnny had a gun and he was going to use it now the first opportunity he had, that was for sure. And use it on me. And I had both him and Rudi to contend with and no gun.

I reached backward over my head and dug my fingers into Rudi's hair. He let out a squeal of surprise as I pulled viciously. He jerked forward a fraction, just enough to pull him off-balance, and I lunged toward the edge of the pit, taking him with me.

For one hair-whitening moment, I saw the abyss and then we were over, plunging downward. I heard the sound of shots from above us, but right then I wouldn't have really noticed an atomic bomb if someone had dropped it on us. I was too busy concentrating on what was going to happen when we hit the bottom.

I hung on to Rudi's hair for maybe three seconds, hearing his frantic shrieks as we fell, then his superior weight pulled his hair free of my grip and he started to fall faster.

The next moment, it seemed, I landed with agonizing force on something which gave momentarily. I landed sideways and then bounced off whatever I'd fallen on and started to roll.

Tree branches scratched my face as I rolled, then I was stopped suddenly by something that bashed into my ribs and I thought I felt something give inside me.

I lay there for what seemed a long while, until I finally dared to think that I was still alive. I moved my arms and they moved. I moved my legs and they moved. But when I tried to stand up, the pain in my chest brought me back to my knees.

I managed to lay on my stomach and I started to crawl slowly up the slope I'd rolled down a moment before.

The moon appeared suddenly over the edge of the pit and it seemed to be a hell of a long way away from where I was. But it gave me light. Light enough to see a motionless shape up ahead of me, maybe a dozen yards away.

I crawled toward it, slowly and painfully, feeling the blood running down my face from the scratches and the agonizing pain in my chest that shot through me every time I moved.

I don't know how long it took me to reach the shape but finally I did reach it. It was Rudi, all right—and it had been Rudi who broke my fall. He must have landed directly underneath me.

I groped through his pockets and found it in the hip. It was still there. I pulled it out with trembling fingers and could have kissed the barrel.

A gun.

I lay still for a moment, wondering how I was ever going to get enough strength to climb out of the gravel pit. Then I heard a slithering noise off to my left. I listened bard and heard it again, only louder.

That would be Johnny, I thought. He's come down into the pit looking for me. And then the question of how I was going to get out suddenly became academic.

The slithering noise sounded again, a little closer. "Rudi." His voice sounded cautious. "Rudi."

I leveled the gun and fired. The gun sounded frighteningly loud inside the pit and I heard the bullet hit rock and ricochet away with a whining noise.

Two shots sounded in return, neither of the bullets coming near me. Then silence again and a slithering sound occasionally. Each time it sounded closer.

Then Johnny's voice. "Al. I'll do a deal with you. If either of them is alive and needs help, I'll throw away my gun and you throw away yours and we'll get them up to the top of the pit."

He sounded almost sincere—almost.

I laughed out loud—until it hurt me so much that I had to stop.

"Al." His voice was guarded. "You taking my proposition?"

"Rudi's dead," I called out. "I don't know what's happened to Deidre, but I'm betting she's dead, too."

There were two more shots and this time they did come close. Two and two makes four, I told myself. How many in the gun?

Eight? He had all the advantage—he could move around while I was stuck where I was, with that pain in my chest. Only Johnny didn't know that—yet.

The slithering sound again. I took a shot in the general direction of the sound, then cursed myself for a fool. I should be counting my own bullets.

I heard him laugh and he sounded frighteningly close. There was a movement behind me and I swung around in a frenzy, forgetting my chest for
a moment, and fired two more shots.

Johnny's laugh sounded louder—from the opposite direction.

"You're getting jumpy, Al," he said. "That was rock. How many bullets
you got left in that gun? It's Rudi's, eh? I don't think it had a full magazine when you started."

He was moving around all the time while he talked. The pain in my chest
after the sudden movement had become unbearable.

I lay flat on my face, feeling the sweat pour off my forehead and pray-
ing that I wouldn't pass out.

His gun fired and a bullet thumped into the ground six inches away from
my head. "What's the matter, Al?" His voice had a jeering note. "You hurt
or something? You haven't got a very good position down there—I can see
you."

Maybe he could and maybe he couldn't. Maybe he was hoping to kid
me into moving and showing him where I was. Either way, it didn't make
much difference to me. I couldn't move—I had to stay where I was.

Then I grew conscious of another sound. It came from somewhere
above the pit. The sound of motors—auto motors coming nearer.

They got louder and louder, then they died away suddenly. Lights appeared at the edge of the gravel pit. I stared up at them, straining my eyes.

A swivel-light suddenly appeared over the rim of the pit, shining down.
"Hey!" a voice boomed. "Anybody down there?"

I couldn't have shouted if I tried. I pushed my elbow into the ground and
leveled the gun barrel into the air, then pushed the trigger.

The noise of the shot reverberated around the pit and I heard Johnny
curse. He was trapped and he knew it. I fired another shot in the direction
where the curse had come from and I heard him laugh again.

"That's your last bullet, Al," he shouted triumphantly, then I heard him
plunging through the undergrowth toward me.

My finger tightened on the trigger again instinctively and then just in time
I stopped myself. I'd forgotten to count—I didn't know whether he was
right or wrong. Maybe he was banking on that—banking on making me
jump and trigger wildly at him until my gun was empty.

So I waited.

More swivel-lights appeared at the top of the pit—then they began to play
down and across the pit, bathing swathes of gravel and dense undergrowth
in brilliant light.

The crashing grew louder and louder, then suddenly Johnny appeared almost directly in front of me. I had both elbows dug into the ground at my
sides, and I raised the gun slowly.

"This is it, copper," he said. His voice was high-pitched, an octave above normal. "I don't care if they get me, but I'll get you first if it's the last thing I ever ..."

I squeezed the trigger carefully and the shot boomed out. I squeezed the trigger again and the gun clicked emptily.

Johnny stood stark and still against the backdrop of moon and probing lights. "You hit me," he said in a little boy's voice. "You shot me," he whispered.

He began to back away slowly, still looking at me. "You shot me," he repeated in a high-pitched voice and then suddenly he broke and ran. He ran round and round in circles that widened all the time.

The swivel-lights caught him and held him in their beam. He looked up at them crazily and shouted his defiance at them and waved his fists in the air.

The lights were momentarily obscured as men began to slide down the side of the pit toward him. He stood motionless and screamed curses at them.

"Drop that gun!" a sharp voice ordered him from somewhere close and he spun around and fired in the direction of the man's voice.

The next moment a dozen guns seemed to reply. Among them was the staccato chatter of a tommy gun.

For a moment Johnny seemed to stand motionless, as if he was beyond the effect of mere bullets. Then he crumpled to the ground suddenly and lay still.

I opened my mouth to shout for help but just as I opened it, I saw an enormous pool of darkness straight ahead of me and I had no choice—I fell into it and let it swallow me up.

CHAPTER 16
Blonde Blackmail

The nurse went around the bed, pummeling the covers like she bore them a personal grudge.

"You're going to have a visitor," she said brightly.

"A dame?" I asked hopefully.

"Captain Parker." She frowned at me disapprovingly. "Can't you think of anything else but women?"

"No," I said truthfully. "How long have I been here?"

"Three weeks," she said.

"Three weeks," I said. "Three weeks without seeing a dame."

"What do you think I am?" she asked coldly.

"Do I have to answer that?"

She straightened up and then gave the covers one more vicious punch, like she wished it was my face.

"You're not to get excited," she said. "Doctor says that if you look as if you're getting excited, I'm to shoo the visitors away."

She smiled a Giaconda smile. "So if you get any feminine visitors, I'll make sure they don't get in ..." She departed triumphantly before I could think of an answer to that one.

Captain Parker came in gingerly and looked at me. "How are you, Al?" he asked.

"Not bad," I said.

"You shouldn't be alive, Al," he said comfortingly. "That's the theory, anyway."

"I heard it from the doc yesterday," I said. "Four busted ribs, internal bleeding and lots of things in the wrong places."

"But they say you're going to be OK now," he said. "Another eight weeks in hospital and ..."

"Another what?"

"Eight weeks. Then four weeks' convalescence. There's just nothing you can do about it, Al. For once in your life, you'll have to be orthodox."

"I'll say," I said feelingly.

"Can you smoke?" He waved a pack of cigarettes.

I took one and he lit it for me. "Tell me what's happening in the great outer world," I said. "What happened that night—the night Johnny Ralston got his? That's the last thing I remember, seeing him shot down."

"Rudi was dead—you probably know that," he said.

"How about Deidre?" I asked him.

"She was dead, too. She must have hit something on the way down that deflected her—she was about twenty yards away from Rudi."

I thought about it for a moment. "You've waited a long time to get a statement from me telling you what it was all about. Don't you damned well care?"

"Don't get excited, Al," he grinned at me. "The doctor says I have to leave if you start getting excited. We got a statement from you. I didn't think you'd remember it. It was after we got you up the side of the pit and into an ambulance. You started babbling and when I heard what you were saying, I persuaded them to let you keep on babbling for a while. What you didn't tell me, which wasn't much, I pieced together afterwards."

I shook my head slowly. "What I don't get," I said, "is how did you get there, anyway?"

"That dame in the Valley Hotel," he said. "You know—the blonde on the desk with the popgun father. Well, she must be carrying a torch for you someplace. She rang the precinct and asked to speak to me, told me what had happened and said she was worried—she knew you were going to do something stupid on your own. I waited an hour and then as a matter of routine, I sent a car over to the Eldorado.

"When they reported back that you hadn't been seen around the place and neither had Deidre Damour or Johnny—and then when they couldn't find Rudi, either—I thought it was time to go looking for you. We found the tire tracks of the Cadillac on the turn-off to the gravel pit and that was it."

"I must remember to thank that dame," I said. "And talking of dames, that reminds me. What's happened to the Eldorado?"

"Under new management," he said.

"Do they retain the old act?" I asked.

"If you refer to a certain female by the name of Goldie," he grinned again, "she departed for parts unknown the day after it all happened."

"The lousy double-crosser," I said.

Parker stubbed his cigarette. "Don't you want to hear any more than what's happened to the dames around the town?"

"Since you make the point," I said, "no."

He grunted. "Well, you're going to, anyway. You can imagine just how pleased Lavers was when he heard the true story. Surprisingly enough, the same day the D.A. had a heart attack and had to resign his office. And I think the commissioner definitely approves of the new D.A.—he calls the commissioner 'sir'."

"Fine," I said. "Where does that leave you and me?"

"In the same old precinct," he said. "Where in hell else would it leave us?"

"That's the trouble with being a cop," I said. "Nobody thinks you want a 'happy ever after' routine. If we'd been private dicks, somebody would have paid us a fabulous fee and we'd be in Miami now, with half a dozen blondes each and ..."

"Please remember I happen to be a married man," Parker said with quiet dignity.

"OK," I said. "Me with half a dozen blondes and you with five and a wife."

But he wasn't listening to me. "That does remind me of something," he said. "That film crowd—they were so glad to see it all cleaned up and themselves out of a mess, that they donated five thousand bucks to the widows' fund."

"What chance have I got of becoming a widow?" I asked him disgustedly.

"And they thought they ought to do something for you, too," he beamed at me.

"So they bought me a cigar?"

"No," he said. "They paid for four weeks' board at the Valley Hotel for you when you go out of hospital. They said they liked the place themselves, and anyway, that blonde told them she'd spike their drinks with poison if they didn't."

"The blonde, eh?" I said thoughtfully.

"I saw her this morning," Parker told me cheerfully. "Looking pretty as paint. She was telling me they haven't got a single booking for the four-week period you're booked in. She seemed quite cheerful about it, too."

"She did, eh?" My voice was getting stronger.

"Don't shout at me," he said. "Yes, she was telling me she'll be able to devote all her time to you, because her father's going away for a couple of months and he won't be there."

"Well, that's ridiculous," I said. "She might as well pay off the staff over that period."

"That's what she's going to do—she says."

"Then how the hell is she going to keep the hotel open?"

"She's not. She says it's the slack season, anyway. She's closing it down. She says that way she's sure she'll be able to give you her undivided attention."

The nurse stuck her ugly head around the door. "Time's up."

Parker got to his feet. "I can see you next week for a while, Al," he said. "You've got nothing to worry about except getting better. From here on you're one of Lavers' white-haired boys, so you'll have to commit murder to get into trouble."

"And don't worry about your house," he went on. "My wife went over and cleaned up. The patrolman keeps an eye on it, so it's OK."

"Thanks, captain," I said. "You cheer a man up—do him good. Tell the patrolman to keep an eye on that blonde up at the Valley Hotel, will you? See she doesn't run away or anything."

"I'll tell him," Parker said and walked toward the door. And that left me with only one worry.

How long is eight weeks?

The End

Blonde Verdict

- - - -

Carter Brown

CHAPTER 1
Minding My Own Business

I was just sitting there minding my own business, when this guy dropped dead at my feet.

I was spending good money on a blonde I regarded as an investment and I didn't want any cadaver taking the gilt off my investment, so I decided to ignore it. But the blonde was curious. "What's with that guy, Al?" she asked. "Drunk?"

"Dead," I explained. "Dead."

Her eyes got a glassy look in them, then she slid gently off her chair onto the floor and stretched out beside the corpse. It made an embarrassing situation for me. One stiff I could ignore—two were impossible.

A crowd started to gather round my table, chattering excitedly and looking at the two of them on the floor. The band was playing 'Miss Otis Regrets,' which would have been a coincidence if my blonde's name had been Miss Otis, but it wasn't.

The manager pushed his way through the crowd, looked at the two of them on the floor, then glared at me.

"If your friends are drunk," he said coldly, "will you please get them out of here at once."

"They aren't drunk," I said mildly. "The blonde has fainted and the guy's dead."

"Dead." His eyebrows would have disappeared if he'd had any hair. "But—but ..."

"At least," I said, "I think he's dead. He had that look about him just before he hit the floor."

The manager went down on his knees beside the cadaver and felt for heartbeats. His face was white when he got up onto his feet again.

"You're right," he said, "he is dead. I'd better call the police."

"I wouldn't holler real loud," I sighed deeply and got out my billfold.

He looked and brightened up a little. "Then you'll take care of it, Lieutenant?"

"This is one hell of a thing to happen to a cop when he's off duty," I said. "I'll take care of it—you take care of the blonde. She's an investment of mine and I wouldn't like to see her depreciate."

"Of course," he said. "I'll have a couple of girls look after her."

"You'd better move that cadaver out into a private room, too," I said. "I'll use your office and phone."

A waiter escorted me to the manager's office. I sat down at the desk and picked up the phone, then rang the Precinct. Sergeant Macnamara answered.

"Wheeler," I said.

"Yes, Lieutenant?"

"Who's got the desk?"

"Captain Parker's here," he said.

"Doesn't that guy ever sleep?" I said. "OK—let me speak to him."

Parker answered a moment later. "No," he said. "You can't have a prowl car."

"I'm at the Cordon Bleu," I said, "feeding a blonde I hope to get better acquainted with later on in her apartment ..."

"You live your life and I'll live mine," he told me, "but don't bother me ..."

"And," I said, "if you wouldn't keep on interrupting me, a guy drops dead."

"So?"

"So I do my duty even though I'm off duty," I said. "Which goes to show what a conscientious cop I am."

"Ignoring those lies," Parker grunted, "who is he?"

"I haven't looked yet," I said. "I thought I'd give you a ring, then I could go back to my blonde."

"Wrong," Parker said.

"What?"

He grunted again. "No dice. Rigorski went home sick—that's why I'm here. I'll send you out a car and the doc with it. I'll even tell the morgue to send the meat-wagon over. You can do the rest, Wheeler. Tell somebody about it—the guy might have a wife."

"He might have a wife," I said bitterly, "but one thing is for sure—I won't have a blonde after this."

"You're breaking my heart," Parker said simply. "Report back here when you've notified his next of kin, or if that isn't possible, report back here anyway." Then he hung up.

The door opened and two waiters carried the corpse in awkwardly, and put it down on the couch that stood against one wall. They seemed to be glad to be rid of it and beat it fast.

The manager came in, the worried look still on his face.

"Your lady friend recovered, Lieutenant," he said, "but she was still very upset. She said she wanted to go home. I told her you were busy for the moment, so one of the cigarette girls has gone home with her in a cab. She said maybe you'd ring her later?"

"Sure," I said. "Thanks."

I moved over to the couch. The manager watched me, wringing his hands together like he had somebody's neck in between them.

"Don't worry," I said, "they'll be here to take him away soon."

"It's bad for business," he said.

"Depends whether he was drinking your liquor or not," I said, just to cheer him up. Then I took a look at the cadaver.

He was, or had been, a guy somewhere in his middle forties. He was well dressed. I took his wallet out of his pocket. He was well heeled, too. There was something over three hundred bucks there. He had a bunch of cards. One said *Wallace J. Offenheim, Offenheim & Berkeley, Attorneys-at-law*. There were two down at the end of the bunch which said *Mr. and Mrs. Wallace J. Offenheim* and gave a Cone Hill address.

I turned the card over between my fingers, then looked at the manager. "You ever see this guy before?" I asked him.

"No," he said.

"His name's Offenheim," I said. "A lawyer."

He shook his head. "It must be the first time he's been here."

"And apparently on his own," I said. "Nobody's been making any inquiries for him?"

"Not that I've heard," he said.

"Go down and find out which one of your waiters served him and send him up here," I told him.

The manager disappeared. I lit a cigarette and wondered how quickly I could get rid of this business and back to my blonde.

Heavy feet clumped up the stairs and Patrolman Rorke came into the room, followed by Doc Walker.

"Evening, lootenant," Rorke said.

"This one's a natural, huh?" the doc asked.

I moved away from the cadaver to let him in.

"I wouldn't know," I told him. "He's walking across the floor toward the bar and then he drops dead. Maybe somebody told him to drop dead, or maybe he thought of it all by himself."

Walker grunted and went on with his examination.

I finished my cigarette and stubbed it in the manager's brass ashtray. Walker put his things back into his bag. There was a knock on the door and the vultures from the morgue came in.

"What's the verdict, doc?" I asked.

He shrugged his shoulders. "Looks like heart failure—can't tell until we do an autopsy. Might as well take him away. You know who he is?"

"Offenheim," I said. "A legal eagle."

"I've heard of him," he said. "Married?"

"Yeah."

"Your job to tell his wife?"

"Yeah."

"Not nice."

"I'm used to it," I said, "I think. You mind traveling back on the meat-wagon, doc? Parker says he's short-handed or something—then I could take the car straight out to the wife."

"Sure," Walker nodded. "It's good for a doctor's soul to take a look at the morgue once in a while."

The two boys in white removed the cadaver and Walker went with them. The manager came back a minute later and looked relieved to see his couch empty again.

"Nobody served him, Lieutenant," he said. "I checked with all the waiters—he must have just come in."

"He looked like he was walking toward the bar," I said. "All right. What's your name?"

"Lindsay," he gulped, "but honest, Lieutenant, I don't know a thing."

"Relax," I said. "Somebody might want you in the coroner's court, that's all."

I walked toward the door. "I wouldn't worry too much," I told him. "The doc thinks it was heart failure—just bad luck he chose your place to drop dead in."

I looked at Patrolman Rorke. "Straighten your tie," I told him. "We're going up to Cone Hill."

It took us thirty minutes to get there. Rorke whistled softly when he turned the car into the drive and saw the house ahead of us.

"He wasn't hard up for chips, was he, Lieutenant?" he said.

"The only guys who make money out of law are lawyers," I said. "You're a cop, you should know that."

He parked the car opposite the front door. I got out and rang the bell. I looked at my watch while I waited—just on eleven. To a blonde who looked the way my blonde looked, the night would still be young, I hoped.

The door opened and a butler stood there. I'd expected a butler ... people who live on Cone Hill would feel naked without a butler.

"Yes, sir?" He gave me a fish-eyed look.

"I'd like to see Mrs. Offenheim," I said.

"I'm sorry, sir," he said stiffly. "She has retired for the night."

I took out the billfold. "This is police business," I said. "I have to see her."

"Yes, sir." He looked worried. "If you wouldn't mind waiting in the library, sir, I'll tell Mrs. Offenheim."

"Sure," I said.

I waited for exactly five minutes in the library, then she came in. I felt my mouth drop open as I saw her. She was blonde and fragile-looking, but not so fragile she didn't have curves where every woman worthy of the name has curves. She was wearing a wrap over nothing very much, I guessed, and she looked as if she had just woken up.

"You wanted to see me, Lieutenant?" Her voice was husky.

"Mrs. Offenheim?" I stood up. "I'm afraid I have bad news for you."

"Yes?" Her voice was impersonal.

"It concerns your husband," I said. I was sweating slightly—this was going to be a little more difficult than I'd thought.

"He's had an accident?"

"Well, sort of."

"Is he dead?" Her voice was still impersonal.

"Yes," I said. "It looks like a heart attack."

Her face was still expressionless. "Where did it happen?"

"The Cordon Bleu—it's a sort of restaurant cum nightclub. He had only just got there, apparently—walked in for a drink—he was making toward the bar."

"I suppose you'll want me to identify the body?"

"I'm afraid so."

"If you wouldn't mind waiting, Lieutenant, I will go and get dressed."

"Sure," I said.

She walked from the room, leaving me standing there with my mouth hanging open.

What sort of dame was this?

CHAPTER 2
Little Brown Men

The phone jangled in my ear.

I lunged out with one hand, grabbed the receiver and took it under the bedclothes so I could keep the daylight out of my eyes.

"Yeah?" I said.

"Al," it was Parker's voice, "I want you to get down to the Precinct right away."

"Don't be stupid," I said. "I'm not on duty till ten."

"You heard me. This is urgent." He hung up before I could argue.

I put the phone back, crawled out of bed and looked at my watch. Exactly six a.m. I had a shower, ran a razor over my face, then got dressed.

I had a prowl car outside, which was some consolation—at least I didn't have to walk. I lit a cigarette to go with my morning cough as I drove. I thought life was a fake. From the time that guy dropped dead the night before until now, I hadn't taken a trick.

By the time I had returned Mrs. Offenheim to her Cone Hill home and got back into town, it was after one in the morning. I'd rung my blonde and all she did was to lift the receiver off the cradle and leave it off. So I'd gone home to bed. Bed. I couldn't have been in it more than a couple of hours.

I left the car at the curb and went into the Precinct. Parker was waiting for me in his office. He had Doc Walker with him.

"Greetings, zombies," I said. "Shouldn't you two have disappeared back into the graveyard by now? Dawn cracked some time ago."

"Sit down, Al," Parker said wearily. "We've been working, or the doc in particular has. We're not in the mood for your corny humor."

"Yes, sir," I said and sat down.

Captain Parker put on his glasses and studied some typewritten sheets that lay on his desk in front of him. I lit a cigarette and found I still had my morning cough.

"This Offenheim," Parker said. "You saw him die?"

"Sure," I said. "Grandstand seat. He was just level with my table when he keeled over."

"Tell us exactly what happened," Parker said.

I shrugged my shoulders. "That's about it—he keeled over and dropped dead."

"Did you notice the expression on his face, Lieutenant?" Walker asked.

"He stopped suddenly," I said, "and his face looked almost frozen—then he keeled over." I looked at him. "What is this? Since when have we all been so fascinated by heart failure?"

Parker took off his glasses again. "It wasn't heart failure, Al," he said. "It was murder."

I did a double take. "I was there," I said. "No shot, no knife, no nothing. What killed him? There wasn't even Nelson Eddy on television."

Doc Walker studied his fingernails carefully. "You ever hear of curare, Lieutenant?"

"Sure I did," I said. "Every kid who ever read a comic has heard of ... now wait a minute. You're not going to give me that poison dart routine—and little brown men in sarongs running in and out of the traffic."

Parker winced visibly. "I wish you wouldn't say that, Al. It makes me see all the newspapers saying it—and I can hear right now what the D.A. and the Commissioner will say when they read the newspapers."

"You mean you're serious?" I said.

Parker gestured toward Walker. "Ask the doc," he growled. "The whole thing is his idea."

"I wasn't too sure," Walker said apologetically, "though there were certain signs. I have a friend, a chemist, he made some tests for me. There was a scratch on the back of Offenheim's hand obviously where the poison entered."

I closed my eyes for a moment, then opened them again. "What makes you so sure he was murdered?" I asked.

"It's not only the 'little brown men' in South America who use curare," he said. "It's used quite a lot in modern anesthetics—tubocurarine is one good example. But no one could accidentally scratch their hand on something containing pure curare: therefore the scratching must have been deliberate."

"Maybe he committed suicide?" I suggested hopefully.

Parker shriveled me with a glare. "You've been a cop long enough to know how people take their own lives," he said. "And this certainly isn't one of the ways in which they do it. Would a man who knows he's just administered a deadly poison to himself walk into a crowded nightclub and go toward the bar to buy himself a drink?"

I had to admit Parker was right.

I just sat and looked at him, hoping that this wasn't one more time when I didn't take a trick.

"So you see, Al," Parker said carefully, "this gives us quite a problem."

"Yeah," I said cautiously.

"A most unorthodox way of murder." His voice grew a little more hearty. I didn't like Captain Parker when he was being hearty—he always sounded like Cassius saying good morning to Caesar. "We'll keep this quiet for a while if we can—the D.A. and the Commissioner will have to know, of course. But the press and everyone else needn't know."

"Sure," I said, still cautious.

"Yes," he sat back in his chair, rubbing the tips of his fingers together. "A most unorthodox murder. You know what my first reaction was, Al, when the doc here told me?"

"You thought it was an unorthodox murder," I grunted.

He nodded benignly. "That's right, and ..."

"If you'll excuse me?" Doc Walker got up from his chair. "You don't need me anymore. I'm going to get some sleep."

"Sure, doc," the captain nodded, "and thanks again."

Walker went out, closing the door behind him.

Parker leaned back again in his chair. "Now—where was I?"

"You'd got to an 'and,'" I reminded him.

"That's right," he nodded. "An unorthodox murder needs an unorthodox cop to solve it."

"Oh, no, you don't," I said.

"And what more unorthodox cop have I got than Al Wheeler," he went on. "The guy who loses prowl cars, dates blondes instead of interrogating suspects, the guy the D.A. just loves ..."

"Find yourself another boy," I said. "I'm not going to ..."

"Lieutenant Wheeler." His eyebrows came together and formed one straight line. "I'd like to remind you of two things. One is I happen to be the Captain of this Precinct and secondly, even lieutenants can be put back into uniform in less time than it takes to say 'Curare.'"

"Yes, sir," I said.

He relaxed a little. "That's better. I'm going to stick my neck out on this one. I'm giving you a free hand ..."

"And a prowl car?" I asked hopefully.

"Why don't you buy yourself a car?" he snarled.

"I can't support an automobile along with that hi-fi setup and all those blondes," I assured him.

"All right—and a car. But you turn in a written report every twenty-four hours. And if I don't think you're making progress fast enough, I'll put Rigorski on the case."

"I thought he was sick?"

"Sick or dying—I'll put him on the case."

"OK," I said. "When do I start—as of now?"

"As of now," he agreed.

"When I go round talking to people," I said, "what do I say?"

"You can tell them we suspect he was murdered, if you want to," Parker said. "I don't imagine anyone associated with him would want to tell the newspapers about it."

"OK," I said. "Anything else?"

"I can't think of anything," he said. "Once the newspaper boys get hold of this one, it will be a riot. Let's make sure that by the time they do, we've got the case licked."

"Can I call in Dick Tracy if the going gets really tough?"

"Oh, sure," he said. "You know where to call him?"

"You don't think I wear a two-way wrist radio for nothing," I said. Then I heaved myself out of the chair and out of his office before he heaved something at me.

I picked up the prowl car again and drove away from the Precinct. I figured that with a tough case like this one, the most important thing was to bring a fresh, alert mind to it. I didn't know anybody with a fresh, alert mind, but the next best thing to do was give my own mind a rest before I started anything. So I drove straight home and went back to bed.

I got up for lunch, showered again, then dressed. By three p.m. I was in the offices of Offenheim and Berkeley, attorneys-at-law. Their offices were nice and fresh-looking and so was the redhead on reception. She gave me a smile which showed she cleaned her teeth regularly.

"And what can I do for you, sir?" she asked.

"Would you like me to make a list?" I asked her thoughtfully. I showed her my billfold. "I'd like to see Mr. Berkeley," I said.

"Yes, Lieutenant." The smile was still on her face. "I'll tell him you're here."

I lit myself a cigarette and waited. A couple of minutes later the redhead showed me into Berkeley's office.

Berkeley was fat, bald and fifty. He shook me by the hand, pushed me into a chair, then retreated to his own chair behind his desk.

"And what can I do for you, Lieutenant?" he asked. It was beginning to sound like a stock legal phrase.

"Your partner died last night," I said.

"A tragedy." His face sobered. "Wally was a brilliant lawyer, Lieutenant, brilliant."

I thought I hadn't come to join the wake. "We have reason to believe he was murdered," I said.

"What." His jaw sagged, making another couple of chins.

"We're keeping it quiet—for now, anyway," I told him. "But naturally, murder requires investigation."

"It's—it's fantastic," Berkeley stuttered. "Who would want to murder Wally?"

"That's my question," I said irritably. "I came up here to ask you that. Any reason you might have wanted to murder him? You get his half of the business or anything?"

He swallowed a couple of times. "Really, Lieutenant. This is too much. I ..."

"Well—do you?"

"No," he said jerkily.

"Then who benefits directly from his death?"

He stared at me for a moment. "That's a crude sort of question, Lieutenant."

"You could call it a crude sort of murder," I said. "Come on, how much did he have and who gets it?"

"You always conduct an investigation in this manner?"

"No," I said. "Sometimes I get tough. Who gets it?"

"His wife," Berkeley said, "and a Miss Laverne. His estate is divided equally between the two of them. He was an orphan, you know. He has no other family than his wife. There were no children."

"Just this Miss Laverne," I said. "Who's she?"

Berkeley looked embarrassed. "I don't really know," he said. "But apparently some lady he was quite attached to."

"How much would his estate be worth, roughly?"

Berkeley pursed his lips. "About two hundred thousand dollars, roughly—less taxes, of course."

"That's a lot of attachment to Miss Laverne," I said. "About a hundred thousand dollars' worth."

"Wally's private life was his own," he said stiffly.

"What happens to your partnership?" I asked.

"We had an agreement that should either partner die, a valuation should be arrived at. We evolved a formula based on five years' average of profit as the price. The share would be first offered to the surviving partner but should he refuse it, it could then be offered on the open market."

"Are you buying?"

"Of course," he said.

I lit myself another cigarette. "Would you have Miss Laverne's address?"

"Yes," he nodded. "I can get that for you."

"Was Offenheim handling any case or did he handle any case recently that would have given anyone a reason for wanting him dead?"

He thought for a moment. "I don't think so, Lieutenant."

"What sort of business do you handle?"

"Criminal cases, mostly," he said. "We specialize in those. We handle plenty of other business too, of course. Routine stuff, you know."

"Did Offenheim have a criminal case proceeding now?"

"As a matter of fact, I think he did," Berkeley said reluctantly.

"What was it?"

He straightened up the blotter on his desk. "Our work is highly confidential, Lieutenant," he said. "You know that."

"And I'm investigating a suspected murder," I told him. "You know that."

He sighed gently. "I guess so. We're handling the defence of a man—Rafe Rubens," he said. "He is indicted for a first-degree homicide charge."

"Yes?"

Berkeley fidgeted with the blotter again. "John H. Rowlands is paying for the defence," he said reluctantly.

"Rowlands?" I concentrated. "It rings a bell somewhere."

"He only came here recently," Berkeley said. "A financier from Chicago. He makes gambling machines, you know?"

"One-armed bandits?"

"Pin-tables, all of them," Berkeley added.

I stubbed my cigarette. "It sounds like he's trying to muscle in on an existing racket," I said. "The way you say it, I could almost think this guy Rubens shot somebody trying to convince them it was better for them to run Rowlands' machines than the machines they were already running."

Berkeley was pink. "He is a client of ours, you understand, Lieutenant. But when you tell me my partner was murdered, I feel I must give you any information that may help you. Though I cannot see any possible connection between the Rubens case and Wally being murdered."

"Thanks for your co-operation," I said. "Any other business you can think of?"

He thought for a moment, then shook his head. "I don't think so, Lieutenant." He pulled a file off the shelf behind his desk and leafed through it. "Ah. Here we are—Miss Lola Laverne, apartment 7A, 1426 East Street."

I wrote it down. "Thanks." I got to my feet. "Where's Rubens now?"

"Out on bail," Berkeley told me. "You can reach him through Rowlands."

"And where would I find Rowlands?"

"His office is downtown—the Security Insurance Building. His home is on Cone Hill—it's listed in the phone book."

"Good," I said. "Thanks, Mr. Berkeley—you have been most co-operative."

He shook hands with me. "You'll let me know what progress you're making, Lieutenant?"

"Sure," I said. "I'll probably want to talk to you again soon, anyway." I looked at him for a moment. "Just for the record," I said, "where were you last night around ten o'clock?"

"I was home," he said.

"Where's that?"

"Cone Hill."

"Who else was there?"

"Only me, I'm afraid," he said. "I have a valet and a cook—it was their night off." He managed a smile. "If you're looking for alibis, Lieutenant, I'm afraid mine isn't very good, is it?"

"Innocent people generally don't have a very good alibi," I said, "if it's any consolation, Mr. Berkeley."

The redhead still had that smile on her face as I walked through the outer office.

"Were you doing anything tomorrow evening?" I asked her.

"Is this business, Lieutenant?" she smiled.

"You could call it that," I told her. "I'll pick you up around eight—we could eat and get our business done at the same time."

"I suppose I can't argue with a policeman," she said.

"If only every girl believed that." I sighed. She gave me her address.

CHAPTER 3
Lovely Laverne

I had a couple of drinks in a bar, then dinner in a Chinese joint. I had one more drink in the bar afterward for the drive, then drove up to Cone Hill.

The butler opened the door. The butler showed me into the living room, then disappeared.

A little while after, Mrs. Offenheim came into the room.

She was wearing a simple little number in black, which was probably an original with a price tag equal to six months of my salary. If it was mourning, all blondes with a figure like hers should mourn. It fitted her tightly all the way down past her hips, then flared slightly to give her enough room to walk in it. The neckline plunged, proving that what she had was her own.

She looked at me as if I'd called for the garbage. "What is it, Lieutenant?" Her voice was cold and bored.

I wondered if the icicle ever melted.

"Last night," I said, "when I called to tell you your husband was dead, Mrs. Offenheim, you seemed singularly uninterested."

"Isn't that my own affair, Lieutenant?" she asked coldly.

"Last night it was," I said, "because it looked like your husband had died from a sudden heart attack. But now we believe he was murdered. And that means it isn't your own affair any longer."

"Murdered." She seemed mildly surprised. "Who did it?"

"That's what I'm trying to find out," I said. "Perhaps you can help me, Mrs. Offenheim. I imagine you'd like to help us find the murderer?"

"If I found him, I'd shake him by the hand," she said.

I lit a cigarette. "Did you hate your husband that much?"

"I made no secret of it," she said. "The whole marriage was a mistake—we realized that very quickly. And when he began to spend whole weeks away from home, it was quite obvious there was another woman."

"Lola Laverne?" I suggested.

Her lips twisted. "I never interested myself in the name," she said contemptuously, "or in what sort of person she was. I could imagine what she'd be like—bold and brassy. Probably a dancer in a burlesque show."

"You didn't try to divorce your husband?" I asked.

"No," she said. "Our marriage was cold-blooded in many ways. I gave him social prestige in return for his money. I didn't want to lose that money, Lieutenant—he had too much of it."

"You're frank about it, anyway," I said. "Do you know the terms of his will?"

"No," she said flatly.

"You get half of his estate," I said. "Lola Laverne gets the other half."

"I shall contest it," she said, her lips tight.

I blew a thin stream of smoke toward the ceiling. "When did you last see him alive?" I asked.

"Yesterday evening," she said. "He came home from the office about five. He said he had to go out again, that he wouldn't be home until late. I wasn't particularly interested."

The butler knocked, then came into the room. "I beg your pardon, madame," he said deferentially, "but Mr. Kirkland is outside."

"Ask him to wait," she said.

The butler bowed and went out again.

"The only unusual thing was that he didn't take his own car," she went on as if nothing had happened. "He called a cab."

"Do you know if anyone would have reason to want to take his life?" I asked her.

"Almost anyone that had anything to do with him," she said. "He was a vile man, Lieutenant. Now I think of it, I wonder he lived as long as he did."

"You're very frank," I said.

She almost smiled. "Why shouldn't I be? I have nothing to hide, Lieutenant."

"Thanks, anyway," I told her. "I might come back later and talk to you again. Did he tell you he had any worries on his mind—his work, or anything?"

"We didn't talk very much," she said.

"OK," I said. "Thanks again."

I picked up my hat and walked out of the room. The butler showed me out. As I walked down the hall, I passed a guy on his way to the living room. A tall, nicely built character with curly hair and blue eyes. He looked like a kid out of college or a football pro, maybe. I thought this would be Kirkland. He smiled at me as he walked past.

Outside, I got into the prowl car and lit a cigarette. Parker figures me a screwball and therefore the right guy for a screwball job. I have a theory which I figure isn't screwball—if you follow your nose long enough in a murder case, you'll find something that smells.

I followed my nose back into town and out to 1426 East Street. It was an apartment block and that was all you could say for it.

I pressed 7A's buzzer and the door opened almost straight away. I walked up the stairs to 7A and knocked. The front door of her apartment opened straight away.

If this was Lola Laverne, I would have left her a hundred grand if I had it. If I didn't have it, I'd go get it and bring it straight back to her.

She was an uninhibited brunette with hair that hung down to her shoulders in soft waves. She had skin as white and almost as transparent as ice. Her lips didn't look anemic. They were full and soft and red.

She was wearing a peach-colored slip. Her lips made an 'oh' of surprise when she saw me. "I was expecting somebody else," she said softly.

"Offenheim?" I suggested.

"If you're one of Johnny's boys," she said, "you can tell him from me that ..."

"I'm Lieutenant Wheeler," I said, "State Police." Her mouth made that 'oh' again.

"I'd like to talk to you, Miss Laverne," I said.

"Won't you come in?" She held the door open a little wider. I walked inside the apartment. A one-room with bathroom and kitchen annex attached. The bed came out of the wall and if you were lucky the termites didn't. But with the hundred grand she had coming, she wouldn't have to worry about termites much longer.

I took off my hat and tossed it onto a chair. She watched me silently. I lit a cigarette and sat down in the chair, putting my hat on the arm.

"You figuring on staying long, Lieutenant?" she asked.

"A while," I said. "I've got some questions I'd like to ask you. Finish getting dressed if you want."

"Well—thanks," she said coldly. She peeled off the slip in a graceful gesture that left her standing there in what could be termed the basic fundamentals of clothing. "I was getting undressed, Lieutenant," she said. "To take a shower."

"I might join you," I said, running a finger round the neckband of my shirt. "I could do with cooling off."

"Anything you say, Lieutenant." Her hands went behind her back and snapped the fastener of her bra.

I gave in fast. I spun around so I faced a blank wall. "When you're all through with your shower and dressed again," I said, "we'll carry on from there."

"What's the matter with you, Lieutenant?" she laughed gently. "Nervous?"

"Only when I'm on duty," I told her. "Off duty, I'm what the girls nervously refer to as a ..."

I never did finish the sentence because someone dropped the ceiling on my head right then.

I woke up with a headache in an empty apartment.

I got to my feet, stepped into the kitchen annex and drank a glass of water. I thought I'd fallen for some routines in my time, but this was a new one—getting slugged on the head because I wouldn't watch a dame take her clothes off.

I picked up the phone and rang the Precinct. Parker was still there. I often used to wonder why he never went home until one day he introduced me to his wife.

"Wheeler," I said.

"Yes, Al?"

"Put out a call for a dame named Lola Laverne," I said. "Height around five-four, brunette, fair complexion, aged maybe twenty."

"What do you want her for?"

"Assault."

'Who did she assault?"

"Me. Dammit."

Parker gurgled with laughter. "It's all your fault, lover-boy," he said. "You shouldn't be so handsome."

"It wasn't that sort of assault," I said coldly. "She hit me with a blunt instrument when I wasn't looking."

"How you ever worked your way out of traffic duty, I'll never know," he said wonderingly.

"Will you put out the call?" I asked with great restraint.

"If you say so, lover-boy," he chuckled.

I hung up while he was still gurgling with laughter.

I had another glass of water, then lit a cigarette. I mooched around the apartment. There was a dressing table—the drawers full of clothes. A wardrobe full of dresses—none of them looked original models. They looked as if they belonged to a working girl.

In one drawer were a couple of photographs—one of Offenheim with a scrawled inscription: *To my darling Lola, with all my love—Wally.* I thought it was touching and tossed it back in the drawer.

The second photograph was of a nice-looking hunk of man who I also recognized. *All my love, darling, from Jim,* was that inscription.

I thought Kirkland certainly got around—from Lola Laverne to Mrs. Offenheim. I also thought I should talk to him sometime.

I left the apartment and went back to the prowl car. I switched on the radio while I drove. They were putting out the call for Lola at ten-minute intervals.

I got back to Cone Hill but not back to the Offenheim house. The house I went to was even bigger. It had a four-car garage at the end of the drive, with a big Cadillac standing on the concrete outside. I left the prowl car in front of the Caddy and walked up the six steps that led to the front door.

I rang the bell and waited for the butler. When the door finally opened, I took another look and thought that if this was what Cone Hill considered the smartest line of butlers this year, I would have to get me a butler.

She was a silver blonde, wearing a black halter top and a pair of skintight, silver matador pants. She wore long black jade earrings that swung gently in the breeze.

"Yes?" she said politely.

"I'd like to see Mr. Rowlands," I said. "Mr. John H. Rowlands."

"Is it business?" she asked.

"You could call it that," I agreed.

"I'm sorry," she said. The earrings swung some more as she shook her head. "Mr. Rowlands never sees anyone on business at home—only in the office."

I produced the billfold again. "Ask him to make an exception in my case," I said.

"I don't know, Lieutenant," she looked doubtful. "But I'll ask him."

"Tell him I'm a sensitive character," I suggested. "Tell him my feelings bruise easily. So if he doesn't see me now, I'm liable to come back with a carload of cops and drag him away for a cozy chat."

She walked away with a rhythmic sway and the sharp *clack-clack* of high heels. It's the thing that always appeals most to me about a life of crime— the blondes, I mean. I get along all right with roses and a night out at a dump like the Cordon Bleu. I often wonder how I'd make out with mink and the Waldorf.

The silver blonde came back. "Mr. Rowlands will see you now, Lieutenant—in the library."

"You mean he can read?" I asked incredulously.

Her lips tightened. "He also doesn't have flat feet, Lieutenant."

I followed her along the hall, then into the library. You could tell right away it was the library—it had books in it. Then she left me.

I lit a cigarette and realized I could use a drink. There was plenty of it, bottled, just hanging around the bar in the corner. I was debating whether he counted his bottles when the door opened and a guy came in.

He looked healthy the way a concrete slab looks healthy. He glowered at me for a moment. "What are you doing here, punk?" he grated.

"Waiting for a bus into town," I told him.

"The boss don't like strange characters nosin' around da joint," he said. He started to walk toward me with a curious, lumbering gait.

The door behind him opened suddenly and a crisp voice said, "Elmer." The baboon stopped and turned around.

"That will do," the voice said firmly. "It's all right—please leave us." Elmer glared at me for a moment, then lumbered out of the room. The second guy came across toward me, his hand outstretched.

"I'm John Rowlands," he said pleasantly. "Pleased to meet you, Lieutenant."

I shook hands with him. He was medium-sized, fair hair, crewcut. In his middle thirties, young to be what Berkeley had said he was.

"I must apologize about Elmer," he said. "He's a sort of watchdog around the place. He didn't know who you were, of course, and ..."

"Sure," I said.

"Elmer's an ex-pug," he went on. "Took too heavy a beating one fight and that was it. He was an up-and-coming contender for the middleweight championship, but that beating ..."

"Sure," I said again.

He nodded. "Well, I haven't had the pleasure of meeting you before, Lieutenant. Will you have a drink?"

"Love it," I said.

"Then let's go to the bar," he said.

So we went to the bar. He poured and I drank slowly.

He watched me carefully. "You're from Homicide, Lieutenant?"

I shook my head. "Twelfth Precinct."

"Off your beat up here," he grinned.

I finished the drink. "There was a man called Offenheim died last night," I said. "I'm conducting some inquiries concerning his death."

"Wally Offenheim," Rowlands' face sobered. "I knew him—a nice guy."

"He was defending somebody—Rafe Rubens," I said. "Charged with a first-degree murder, I understand. I also understand that you are paying for the defence."

Rowlands looked at me for a while before he answered. Then he picked his words carefully. "That would be common knowledge, I suppose, Lieutenant. But why question me—is there some charge involved in this? Maybe I should have a lawyer ..."

I shook my head. "I'm investigating the circumstances of his death—that's all," I told him. "I'm trying to find out if he had anything on his mind—anything that was particularly worrying him."

He refilled our glasses. "I wouldn't know, Lieutenant," he said. "He was a good criminal lawyer. He seemed confident that Rafe wouldn't have to worry—that he'd be able to get him off. Is there a possibility of suicide, Lieutenant?"

I shrugged my shoulders. "Maybe."

"Sorry I can't help you," he said. "Twelfth Precinct you said you were from, Lieutenant?"

"That's right," I agreed.

"And who's the Captain of the Precinct?"

"Parker," I said.

"I don't think I've met him," he said.

"This Rubens—where is he now?" I asked.

"He's staying right here," Rowlands said. "He's out on bail—the case comes up next month."

"Just out of curiosity," I said, "I'd like to know where he was last night around ten-thirty."

"I'll get him in here," Rowlands said.

He went out of the room. I finished my drink and stepped away from the bar. Rowlands came back, followed by another man. A tall, lean guy—good-looking if you didn't notice his eyes and the thin lips. Rowlands introduced us.

Rubens nodded. "You wanted to talk to me, Lieutenant?"

"I was wondering where you were last night," I said.

"Right here," he answered. "What's the matter—the cops not sure they're going to make this one stick, trying to find something else to pin on me?"

"Calm down," I told him. "Who else was here with you?"

"Elmer," he said, "and Johnnie."

"Johnnie?"

"My housekeeper," Rowlands said smoothly. "I think she opened the door to you."

I was out of my league. "OK," I said to Rubens. I turned to Rowlands. "Thanks for the drinks. I'll be on my way."

"Drop in anytime, Lieutenant," he said. "Anytime at all."

He walked me to the front door. There was no sign of his housekeeper, which was a pity.

CHAPTER 4
I Forgot the Bathroom

I thought I'd call it a day—or a night. I got back to my house, put some Doris Day on the hi-fi and poured myself a drink.

I was pouring the second drink when the phone rang. I debated whether to answer it or not—then thought maybe it was the blonde I'd stood up for the cadaver the night before.

I picked up the receiver and said who I was.

"Al." It was Parker, it wasn't my night for blondes. "Get over here right away."

"I was just going to write that report," I said. "Honest."

"Never mind that," he said. "Get over here as fast as you can."

"OK," I sighed. I put the phone down and finished my drink.

"Give me something to remember you by," Doris sang softly from the five speakers spread around the walls.

"Honey," I told her, "if you were within grabbing distance, I sure would."

I regretfully switched her off and went out to the prowl car.

When I walked into Parker's office, there was somebody else there as well. A somebody who made me straighten my tie as I saw him—Commissioner Lavers.

He shifted his bulk in his chair and nodded briefly. "Evening, Wheeler."

"Good evening, sir," I said politely.

"Sit down, Al," Parker grunted. So I sat.

He looked at me sourly. "How are you handling it?"

"You get a call from Mr. John H. Rowlands, by any chance?" I asked. "Saying are you Captain Parker of the Twelfth Precinct and do you have a certain nosy lieutenant by the name of Wheeler?"

"What makes you think that?" Parker said.

I looked at him, then I looked at Lavers. "You don't mind my saying this in front of the Commissioner?"

"He'll be very interested in anything you say," Parker grunted. "That's why he's here."

I nodded. "Fine. OK—what gives?"

"What do you mean?"

"I may be a dumb lieutenant," I said, "but once Doc Walker came up with his curare analysis, then it was a case of murder, right?"

"So?" Parker said.

"So it belonged to Homicide and not to the Precinct anymore," I said. "That is, under the rules as I understand them. But Homicide didn't get it—I got it. I got a pat on my curly hair and was told I had a free hand and a prowl car to nose around the case, in my celebrated unorthodox manner."

Lavers lit a cigar carefully. "What else?" he asked.

"In nosing around," I said, "I see a certain John H. Rowlands, who I've been told earlier on is muscling in on the gambling racket—one of his guys is out on bail for a murder rap. A certain Rafe Rubens—and Offenheim was going to defend him. Mr. John H. Rowlands is surprised that a cop calls to see him at his home. But he brightens up a little when he realizes that I'm not from Homicide—sort of feels that no one from Homicide would make a mistake like that. So he checks which Precinct I'm from and who the Captain of the Precinct happens to be. The obvious moral being that it shouldn't happen again."

Lavers and Parker looked at each other, then looked at me. "Sometimes," Parker said wonderingly, "he's almost bright."

"You've more or less got it, Wheeler," Lavers said. "Rowlands hasn't been in this city very long, but he has moved fast since he got here. He's virtually taken over the gambling in toto. And he's got a pipeline in Homicide. I don't know how much money he's spent to achieve it, but I think it must have been a lot—a hell of a lot."

He chewed his cigar for a moment. "The D.A. is ..."

"A four-letter word," I said.

Lavers almost grinned. "I wouldn't say that—but then again, I'm not sure if I wouldn't. Anyway, Wheeler—the thing is this. I haven't given this Offenheim case to Homicide—yet. They will scream about it. You can bet that John Rowlands has told them already. But I can stave them and the D.A. off for another three days, anyway. If you can bust it open by then, I'd be very happy. Because I feel sure that Rowlands is tied up in this thing somewhere."

"I see," I said. I didn't think I did.

"What did you find out today?" Parker asked me.

I told them the story of where I'd been, who I'd seen and so on. I lit a cigarette when I'd finished and brightened up a little when Parker had some coffee sent in.

Lavers wrinkled his brow. "This Laverne woman," he said. "I don't understand it. If she stands to make a hundred thousand from Offenheim's will, then why does she run out on you—even hit you over the head to do so?"

"I can't figure it, either," I admitted. "It's been bothering me all night. And there's something else about it that's bothering me, as well."

"What?" Parker asked.

I shrugged my shoulders helplessly. "I don't know—something in the back of my mind ... I've got it."

They both looked at me as if I was nuts and maybe they were right.

"What?" Parker asked suspiciously.

"The blunt weapon," I said. "Whatever she hit me with—it wasn't there afterward."

"Maybe she took it with her?" Lavers suggested.

I shook my head. "Why? She must have lammed out of there fast—and she had to be dressed again before she went, unless she walked down the street in a bra and a pair of panties."

I sat bolt upright. "The bathroom. I never looked in the bathroom."

"Did you mislay the soap?" Parker asked heavily.

"Maybe the weapon was in there," I said. "I never even tried the door— maybe she was still in there. Maybe she never took it on the lam at all."

I got to my feet. "I'm going to take a look."

"This Laverne woman intrigues me," Lavers said. "I might come and take a look with you. You'd better come along as well, Parker."

"I've already got a wife," Parker grunted.

"If we find this Laverne woman, you might want to swap," Lavers grinned. "Come on—let's see how a lieutenant lives."

So the three of us piled into the prowl car and I drove down to East Street again.

I pressed all the buzzers and somebody opened up for us. We went up the stairs to 7A. The door was shut. I knocked and we waited. I knocked twice more and still no one answered.

"No skeleton keys?" Lavers asked me. He looked as if he was beginning to enjoy himself.

"There should be a caretaker somewhere," Parker said.

I took a step back, then lunged forward, hitting the door with my shoulder. The lock gave way and the door swung inward.

"Dear, dear," Lavers said. "Breaking and entering. Lieutenant, I'm surprised at you."

"Sometimes, Commissioner," I told him, "I even amaze myself." I stepped inside the apartment and switched on the lights. It didn't look any different to the way it had earlier on.

Lavers looked around him interestedly. "Neat, isn't it?" he said.

I went over to the bathroom door and turned the handle. The door swung open. I felt for the switch, found it and the light came on.

I turned back to where Lavers and Parker stood in the center of the living room.

"Find your blunt instrument, Wheeler?" Lavers asked.

"I've done better than that," I said soberly. "I've found Lola Laverne."

"What." Lavers gaped at me for a moment, then both of them hurried toward me. They followed me into the bathroom and looked.

A girl in her underwear, particularly a girl like Lola Laverne, can be exciting—alive. Dead, she's pathetic. She lay in the bath, on her back, her head pillowed on the end of the bath. The cold-water tap leaked slightly and dripped down onto the big toe of her left foot.

We looked at her for a long moment.

"No marks," Lavers said hoarsely.

"I'll get the doc over," Parker said, "and the rest of the details taken care of."

"Just as well you had your hunch, Wheeler," Lavers told me. "Why do you think she was murdered?"

"Because I called on her," I said.

He looked at me blankly. "What?"

"There was somebody else with her," I said. "Remember, when the buzzer went she had to press the switch to open the front door for me. She had plenty of time before I arrived here in the apartment. Whoever was with her hid in the bathroom. I came in. He heard what I said. When I turned away to let the girl finish undressing, he slugged me. That might even have been planned."

"How could they plan it, not knowing who you were?" Lavers asked.

"They might have planned it for somebody else," I said. "They could still put it into effect for me. But the person who was here with her decided for some reason that she was better dead. So he killed her and left her in the bathroom."

Lavers shook his head bewilderedly. "This is moving too fast for me," he said. "Too fast altogether." He looked down at the bath again. "There's no mark on her."

"I wouldn't want to touch her before the doc arrives," I said, "but I'll take an even bet with you, Commissioner, that somewhere there's a scratch on her."

"You mean curare?"

"It's a logical thought," I said. "Isn't it?"

Parker rejoined us. "The doc will be here soon," he said, "and the rest of them."

We all moved back into the living room. Parker got out his pipe and started to fill it. I lit a cigarette. Then the buzzer went.

Parker nearly dropped his pipe. We all jumped. "Who the hell is that?" Lavers said tautly.

"It's an interesting problem," I said. "Somebody's down there, outside the front door right now. If it's the murderer, he's being cute—if anyone answers, then he disappears. But if it isn't the murderer, then he'll come up and that could be interesting, too."

The buzzer went again, impatiently.

"Take a chance," Lavers said. "Let's have him or her up."

I pressed the button which would open the front door. "We going to wait as a reception committee?" I asked.

"Why not?" Lavers said. "I'm getting quite a kick out of this, I must admit."

Footsteps sounded on the stairs. "So it wasn't the murderer, after all," Parker said.

"Unless he's going to brazen the thing out," I said. "That's possible."

Somebody knocked lightly on the door. "It's me, darling," a male voice called gently. "Open up. It's your golden-haired boy back from the wastes of Cone Hill. Open up. I don't care if you haven't got any clothes on—it's cold outside."

I went and opened the door. "I'm sorry, honey," I simpered, "but I'm all dressed."

Kirkland stood there, his jaw sagging. "What—what ..." he stammered.

"Why don't you come inside?" I suggested.

"But where's Lola?" he asked.

"She's here," I told him.

He stepped past me into the room and then he saw the other two and turned around.

"May I introduce you gentlemen?" I asked. "Mr. Kirkland, Commissioner Lavers and Captain Parker."

"G ... Good evening," Kirkland said weakly.

They just looked at him and said nothing. He turned around to me. "I saw you up at the Offenheim house earlier on tonight. You're Lieutenant Wheeler, aren't you?"

"That's right," I agreed.

"What's going on?" he asked.

"Just a policemen's convention," I told him.

"I thought you said Lola was here?"

"So she is—in the bathroom," I said.

He looked at the bathroom door, then back at me. "I don't get it," he said.

"Take a look," I said.

He looked at me again, uncertainly, then walked slowly to the bathroom door. He went into the bathroom and you could have put bells on the silence while he was in there.

Then he came out again. His face was drawn and white. He looked suddenly old. I had the feeling that he'd lost his college-boy look for all time.

"Who did it?" he asked hoarsely.

"That's what we're trying to find out," I told him. "Maybe you can help us."

He shook his head numbly. "I don't know anybody who could have any reason for wanting to kill her."

"Would she have any reason for taking her own life?" Parker asked softly.

Kirkland shook his head violently. "That's ridiculous. She was happy. We were going to be married."

A siren died as a car skidded to a stop outside the building. A couple of seconds later the door buzzer sounded violently. Lavers pressed the button to let them in.

Doc Walker was the first one into the apartment. He glared at us as he walked in. "What is this—a conspiracy to stop me from sleeping nights?" he growled.

"In the bathroom," Parker said laconically.

"Nice and hygienic, anyway," Walker grunted.

I looked at Kirkland. "I would like you to come down to the Precinct,"

I said, "and answer some questions."

CHAPTER 5
Getting No Place

Rorke brought me in some coffee, looked curiously at Kirkland, and then went out again. I drank the coffee and lit a cigarette. I'd made a point of not offering Kirkland anything. He sat there, just looking unhappy. By the time I was through with him, he was going to look even more unhappy, I hoped.

I looked at him for a long moment. "OK," I said. "We will start at the beginning. What's your full name?"

"James Hanford Kirkland," he said.

"What do you do for a living?"

"I'm a manufacturing chemist."

"In business on your own?"

"No," he said. "I work for Morgan and Scheer."

I took a draw on the cigarette. "How long have you known Lola Laverne?"

"About six months," he said.

"And you were going to be married?"

"In about a month from now."

"How did you get to know her?"

"I had an apartment in the same building until about a month ago."

"What did she do for a living?"

Kirkland looked at me blankly without answering.

"Come on," I said impatiently. "You knew her well enough to marry her, you knew how she earned her living."

"She wasn't working for the last three months," he said. "But before that she was a private secretary."

"For whom?"

"Wallace Offenheim."

"Why did she leave?"

"I—I don't know."

"You're lying."

He took out a cigarette and lit it, his hands shaking slightly.

"She was his mistress," I said. "She left his office because she didn't need to work anymore."

"Yes," he said sullenly.

"And you were going to marry another man's mistress?"

"I loved her," he said. "Maybe you don't understand that. I loved her."

"And when he was dead there was no need to worry about him anymore?" I suggested. "You and your sweetheart could live on the hundred grand without any trouble at all."

"What are you talking about?"

I grinned at him. "Don't play it naive, Kirkland—it doesn't become you. Offenheim left half his estate to her and half to his wife. His partner estimates a half as being worth a hundred grand. The girl and a hundred thousand, Kirkland—that adds up to two good reasons why someone would want to murder Offenheim, doesn't it? Somebody like you, for example."

"I never knew about the money," he said. "I swear it."

I yawned loudly. "Sure—you never knew. Mrs. Offenheim—where does she come into the picture?"

"Mrs. Offenheim. What do you mean?"

"You were seeing her earlier on tonight," I said. "Why?"

"She wanted to see me, that's all. You see, when I first knew that Lola was his mistress, I nearly went crazy. I wanted to break it up somehow—anyhow. I went to see her—I thought his wife might be able to help me. But she didn't seem even interested when I told her about it. Then today she rang me and said could she see me tonight. When I saw her she said she had been worried about how Lola would get on now that her husband was dead, but since she rang me she'd learned that she had no need to worry. It didn't make any sense to me at all, but I guess she'd heard about the will. I didn't stay there long—I left about ten minutes after you left."

"Where were you last night?" I asked.

"With Lola."

"From what time?"

"About eight o'clock."

"Until when?"

Kirkland blushed. "This morning."

"Anybody verify that?"

"No," he bit his lip, "only Lola."

"And she's dead," I said brutally.

He bit his lip again and nodded.

I lit another cigarette from the stub of the first. "You don't know any reason why anyone should want to kill her?" I asked.

"No."

"You know a man called Rowlands—John Rowlands?"

"No," he said.

"OK," I nodded. "That's all."

"You mean I can go now?"

"Leave your address with the desk sergeant on your way out. Don't leave town."

"All right, Lieutenant," he said. He got to his feet and walked slowly out of the room.

I went back to Parker's office. Commissioner Lavers had gone. The Captain had his glasses perched on the end of his nose and his pipe in his mouth.

"You look like an advertisement for Father's Day," I told him.

"Huh," he grunted.

"That Kirkland guy," I said. "He's a manufacturing chemist."

"I knew a manufacturing chemist once," Parker told me, "in Detroit."

"That curare," I said. "I have news for you. Maybe we don't have little brown men flapping their sarongs in the streets, after all. Maybe guys like manufacturing chemists can get their hands on it."

Parker looked up at that. "OK, wise guy," he growled. "Did Kirkland get the curare?"

"I don't know," I said. "I didn't ask him."

"You didn't ..." Parker's pipe gurgled violently. "Then what the hell have you been doing?"

I pulled over a chair and sat down. "Lola Laverne was Offenheim's mistress," I said. "She used to be his secretary. Kirkland lived in the same apartment block and bingo. Pure, sweet love at first sight. Or so he says. They were going to be married—so he says. He didn't know about Offenheim's will—so he says."

"And he doesn't know anything about the curare," Parker said heavily, "or if he does, you were too polite to ask him."

I nodded. "I have a feeling that it's a little premature to talk curare to Kirkland. I also have a feeling that he was genuine about that pure, sweet love he had for Lola. So now she's been murdered and maybe he'll have some ideas about who murdered her. He might start to follow them up."

Parker grunted and shoved his glasses back on the bridge of his nose. "You put a tail on him?" he asked.

"No," I said.

"*What.*" The window vibrated.

"Let's face it," I said. "Tailing is a job for an expert. Not a flat-footed cop. And all we've got available here are flat-footed cops."

"So how are you going to find out—television?"

"We'll find out soon enough," I said. "We'll watch the ripples."

"Ripples?"

"You know, drop a stone into a pool and the ripples start—they widen and widen until they reach the edges of the pool."

"Al," Parker took off his glasses, "go home and get some sleep. You need it."

"OK," I said. "I'm still on my own in this thing?"

"I guess so," he said. "But go and get that sleep first."

I walked out of his office and was just closing the door when I heard him explode.

"Ripples!"

I closed the door gently and went on my way.

I slept in until eleven in the morning. I got up and did all the necessary things including eating breakfast. At twelve I rang Berkeley's office.

"Offenheim and Berkeley," a sweet voice cooed in my ear.

"I bet you look just as beautiful as you sound," I said enthusiastically.

"Who is this calling?" she asked.

"We have a date for tonight," I said, "and I have to confess I don't even know your name."

"Lieutenant Wheeler," she said. "Well—it's Mona Gray."

"Fine, Mona," I said. "And I pick you up at eight?"

"Sure," she said. "You have my address?"

"I have it," I assured her.

"All right," she said. "Do I have to keep calling you Lieutenant Wheeler?"

"Al is the name," I said.

"Al," she said. "Short for what?"

"Never mind," I said. "Just Al."

"All right, Al," she said. "See you at eight."

I hung up and put Doris back on the hi-fi.

"I'm in the mood for love ..." she sang gently.

"Me, too, honey," I told her. "But save it for tonight—redheads are impulsive, aren't they?"

"Funny, but when you're near me ..." Doris and I finished it up as a duet.

Lunch in town, then the prowl car up to Cone Hill again. I was getting so used to the district that I felt I almost lived there. Only a twenty thousand dollar difference in annual income stopped me.

The butler opened the door to me again. "Good afternoon, Lieutenant," he said politely.

"Hi," I said. "Mrs. Offenheim in?"

"Yes, sir," he hesitated. "She's at the pool at present."

"In the billiard room?"

"The swimming pool, sir," he told me. "It's at the back of the house."

"Don't bother to announce me," I said as I walked past him. "I will announce myself."

"But ..." he started to protest.

He was too late. I walked past him, down the length of the hall and found my way out to the back terrace.

It was quite a terrace. At the end of it was a kidney-shaped pool. I walked toward it, lighting a cigarette as I went. When I got close, I saw a figure cutting through the water with a nice, fast crawlstroke. She stopped at the edge of the pool and climbed out. Then she saw me.

She pulled off her cap and shook her hair free. She was wearing a black bikini, simple in its brevity. What wasn't so simple was the contours the bikini molded. She had looked nice the night before—this morning she was terrific.

"Where did you come from?" she asked coldly.

"I used to keep on asking my mother that," I said. "But no one ever explained things to her and she'd keep on telling me about the gooseberry bush."

"You're the most ridiculous policeman I've ever met," she said.

"How does it feel?" I asked her. "To be a hundred thousand dollars better off?"

"What." She stared at me.

"Lola Laverne was murdered last night," I said. "Somebody must be on your side."

She hesitated for a moment, then picked up her robe and put it on. "Murdered?" she said.

"Dead," I said, "as your husband."

She winced at that. "How did she die?"

"I haven't heard the autopsy report yet," I said. "Where were you last night?"

"Are you accusing me of killing her?" she asked coldly.

"You must admit you're the prime suspect," I said. "She was your husband's mistress, you directly benefit by the money—and a hundred grand is money in anybody's language."

"You're abominable," she said acidly. "I shall complain to the Commissioner."

"Why don't you complain to Johnny Rowlands?" I suggested. "He might have more pull than the Commissioner."

"That's absurd," she said.

"You do know Rowlands, then?" I said genially.

She glared at me for a long moment. "I've met him," she said. "I don't know him."

"He was a client of your husband's," I said. "Your husband was going to defend a character named Rafe Rubens, who is facing a murder rap."

"I heard some talk of it," she admitted.

She started to walk toward the house. "If you don't mind," she said, "I'm going to put some clothes on."

"I do mind," I said, "but I don't suppose there's anything I can do about it."

I followed her as she walked along the terrace. "Next time you call, Lieutenant," she said, "I shall be glad if you have the butler announce you."

"Let's stop playing games, shall we?" I suggested.

She stopped and looked at me. "Just exactly what do you mean by that?"

"I am Lieutenant Wheeler, State Police," I explained patiently. "I have reason to believe you are withholding vital information concerning the death of your husband and one Lola Laverne. I must ask you to accompany me to the Precinct for further questioning, Mrs. Offenheim—and if you refuse, it will be my regrettable duty to take you in and then book you as a material witness."

"You wouldn't do that," she gasped.

"Not unless I'm forced to," I agreed. "But I will if you don't can this high-hat attitude—I'm beginning to find it just a little wearing."

"All right," she said. "Let me get into some dry clothes and then I'll talk to you, Lieutenant."

"Fine," I said. "Where?"

"Why not here, out on the terrace? I'll have Cedric bring out some chairs."

"Cedric?"

"The butler."

"Oh," I said.

She disappeared into the house. Cedric came out and mustered two chairs and a table. Then he came back with a tray containing all the essentials, including ice. I thought the day was brightening a little.

Finally Mrs. Offenheim came back. The bikini had gone and in its place was a halter top and a pair of shorts. They covered a little more territory than the bikini had, though not very much. She sat down on one of the chairs and I sat on the other, beside her. She poured the drinks and handed me one.

"Now, Lieutenant," she said, "ask your questions."

"Kirkland was here last night," I said, "arrived as I was leaving. Why?"

"I asked him to come," she said. "I knew he was in love with the Laverne girl. When I knew that Wally was dead, I thought the girl would be left without any money. I asked Kirkland to call—I was going to offer to help the girl for a while, anyway, until she got on her feet again. But then you told me the terms of my husband's will, so I told Kirkland there was no need for me to help the girl."

"It was a generous thought," I said.

She shook her head. "Not really. The girl had my sympathy. Anyone who had to live with Wally had my sympathy."

"I wonder you didn't divorce him," I said, "feeling that way about him."

She stretched her arms above her head leisurely. "This is a nice house, isn't it, Lieutenant?" she said.

"Sure," I agreed.

"And a nice swimming pool—and the butler, the cook and the maids are efficient, too. I have quite a wardrobe—I must show it to you sometime."

"I get the drift," I acknowledged.

"So if anybody was going to divorce anybody," she said silkily, "this body took a large settlement in cash with her. But Wally seemed satisfied—I couldn't figure out why, until I got to hear about Lola Laverne."

"And Kirkland was where you got to hear it from?"

"That's right," she agreed lazily.

It was a hot afternoon. I had a comfortable chair on a comfortable terrace, a drink in my hand and conversation with a beautiful blonde. Should I ask for anything more? I thought I should.

"Did your husband ever talk to you about his work?"

"Wally?" She laughed incredulously. "He never talked about anything—not to me, that is."

"So you don't have any idea why somebody should want to kill him."

"If he treated them the way he treated me, I'd have a good idea," she said slowly. "I wanted to kill him—but I didn't."

We had been around the track and now we were back at the starting gate. I thought this was where I got off the merry-go-round.

I finished my drink, put down the glass and got to my feet.

"Going, Lieutenant?" She looked up at me, leaning back in the chair, her arms still above her head.

I put my hands on the arms of her chair and leaned down, so that my eyes came within twelve inches of hers.

"I'm going, Mrs. Offenheim," I said. "I only came along for the ride and I got it. You don't mind if I tell you I don't believe a word of it?"

She looked up at me and smiled. "I'd hate to feel you came all this way for nothing, Lieutenant," she said softly.

Her hands came down from behind her head and twined round my neck. She pulled me forward, raising her head slightly so that our lips met. She kissed me the way I like to do my own kissing. Then suddenly she pushed me away.

I straightened up, then took out a handkerchief and wiped the lipstick off.

"If you must go, Lieutenant." She smiled.

"I really must," I said, "and I still don't believe a word of it."

"You're just making excuses so you can come back," she said. "Make it tomorrow night, Lieutenant—it's the servants' night off."

CHAPTER 6
Make Yourself Comfortable

I got into the prowl car and drove away. I reached the end of the drive and was going to turn into the street when a blue prowl car pulled to a stop, blocking my exit. A heavily built guy got out and came over.

"Don't look now," I said, "I'm a cop, too."

He grinned. "Lieutenant Wheeler, Twelfth Precinct?"

"You have me," I said.

"I'm Skip Cameron," he said. "Commissioner Lavers sent me looking for you. He wants to talk to you, pal, pronto."

"Did he see me chewing gum on duty?" I asked.

He shrugged his beefy shoulders. "He don't tell me any secrets. He said to bring you back fast. Mind if I ride back with you? This car I've got has something else to do."

"Sure," I said.

He waved to the driver of the other car, who nodded. The car accelerated away, leaving me free access to the street again.

Twenty minutes later we were parked outside the city hall. Cameron led the way in and I followed him. We walked for what seemed a long way and ended up in the basement. Cameron finally stopped and opened a door.

"In here, Wheeler," he said.

"What's the Commissioner doing?" I asked him. "Hiding out?"

Cameron shrugged his shoulders. I shrugged mine to keep him company and went into the room. Cameron followed me in and I heard the door click shut. There were two other guys in the room and neither of them was the Commissioner. I began to smell something.

"Here he is," Cameron said from behind me. "Wonder Boy himself."

"Yeah," one of the other two guys nodded. "We should get acquainted, Wheeler. You've already met Lieutenant Cameron, I presume?"

"We're almost buddies," I said.

"This is Sergeant Podeski," he nodded to the shortish, broad-shouldered guy with a crew cut, beside him, "and I'm Lieutenant O'Malley."

"How nice for you," I said.

The two of them just looked at me. I felt for a cigarette, found one and lit it. "Since we've met," I said, "what's the gag?"

"Can you read, Wheeler?" O'Malley asked curiously.

"If the words aren't too long," I said.

"You read the afternoon papers?"

"Not yet."

"You should." He picked up a paper and tossed it at me. "You really should—try page three, pal."

I tried page three. It was part of a column written by Phantom. I would have liked to meet Phantom—preferably in a dark alley someplace. It read:

Rumor has it that a certain criminal lawyer who died the day before yesterday didn't die a natural death. The rumor says he might even have been murdered. This rumor (you have no idea how persistent this rumor is) says that's the way Commissioner Lavers figures it. The sixty-four-dollar question is then why doesn't he give it to Homicide to unravel, rather than leaving it to the white-haired Lieutenant of Twelfth Precinct ... which is exactly what he has done.

I folded the paper carefully and tossed it back to O'Malley. He beat it to the floor with an impatient swipe of his hand:

"Wheeler," he said, "we figure you're just the boy to answer the sixty-four-dollar question."

"Why don't you ask the Commissioner?" I suggested.

Cameron had a look of perplexity on his face. "Listen, Wheeler," he said. "You know that's the one thing we can't do—no cop can go ask the Commissioner why he does things or don't do things. He's the boss."

"I can't ask him, either," I said. "I don't go for the idea of traffic duty in a blue uniform any more than you do."

He grinned wryly. "I guess that's right. But I'm putting it to you this way, Wheeler. We're all cops—it don't make no difference that we're Homicide and you're a Precinct Lieutenant. We're all cops. We don't like it when some columnist can take a crack at us. If Lavers thinks we aren't competent to handle a homicide, he should do something about it. Toss us back into blue uniforms. If he thinks you're the boy to handle it—well, OK, give you to Homicide."

"But he hasn't done either," Podeski said.

"That's it exactly," Cameron said, "and we would like to know why."

He was looking at me squarely and I thought Cameron was a guy I could like. A cop who was proud of being a cop and didn't like the vague insinuations of the columnist.

"Look," I said, "I don't know. I don't know any more than you guys do. I know how you feel—I'd feel the same way. It's tough enough being a cop and trying to do your job without being left open for people to take cracks at you. But that's the truth—I don't know what Lavers' angle is."

O'Malley looked at me with a sneer on his face. "The way he says it, you could almost believe it," he said.

"Shut up," Cameron said coldly. "I believe what Wheeler says."

"Yeah," Podeski nodded slowly. "I think the Lieutenant is leveling with us. Maybe the Commissioner just don't like us—or something."

"Maybe this white-haired boy of the Twelfth Precinct has been telling him how incompetent Homicide is," O'Malley sneered.

"Can it," Cameron said impatiently. "We only got Wheeler down here to see if he could tell us anything. He says he can't and I believe him—so that's that."

"You guys would believe in Snow White," O'Malley said.

"With you around, they've only got six of the dwarfs left to find," I suggested. "Haven't they—Dopey?"

O'Malley took a step toward me and raised his clenched fist. Cameron caught his wrist and swung him round without apparent effort, so that he faced Podeski. The Sergeant put the flat of his hand against O'Malley's chest and pushed, so that O'Malley went stumbling backward trying to regain his balance.

"It's Spanish blood or something," Cameron explained, "he gets excitable. OK, Lieutenant, we're sorry we bothered you."

"That's OK," I said. "I wish I could help." And I meant that, too. I turned around and walked toward the door.

When I got home I had a shower, remembering I had a date, which brightened my outlook somewhat. The phone rang just as I was getting out of the shower. I wrapped a towel around my middle and padded out to the living room.

It was Parker. "I've been trying to raise you all afternoon," he said indignantly. "Where the hell have you been?"

"Working," I said. "And if you had raised me at home, you'd have also raised hell wanting to know why I wasn't out working."

"OK," he said. "We got the result of the autopsy on Lola Laverne this morning."

"Curare?"

"Yeah—and there's no prize for guessing."

"So what?"

"You read that columnist's crack in the paper?" he asked me.

"Yeah," I said.

"The Commissioner doesn't like it one little bit. The D.A. is asking awkward questions and Homicide is hopping mad about it. They've got a Lieutenant O'Malley down there—he rang up, asking where you were."

"Yeah?" I tried to sound surprised.

"I told him to mind his own damn business." Parker chuckled. "Fine thing, this cop-eating cop."

"Yeah," I said again. "Is that all?"

"You in a hurry?" he asked.

"I've got a date," I told him.

Parker growled ominously. "Now listen, Al. You keep your mind on your job. You don't have the time to go."

"This date is with a suspect," I said. "You can relax." Then I hung up.

I dressed carefully. The phone rang a couple of times while I was dressing, but I ignored it. I thought it was probably Parker again. I left the house at seven-thirty and I was ringing the buzzer of Mona Gray's apartment by eight.

She was ready and waiting for me. She was wearing a gold lamé number that had no back, no shoulder-straps and the bare minimum of front—with plenty of support. She didn't look like a secretary—she looked like a million dollars.

I told her so and she smiled. "I never knew policemen ever said nice things about anybody."

"I can see you have a lot to learn about policemen," I said. "I shall consider it my duty to teach you."

"Just be careful how you teach," she said, "or I'll call a cop."

We went to the Eldorado, which is a dump. It was a dump when Johnny Ralston was running it, and it still is a dump. We had dinner, we danced, we had a couple of drinks.

We sat over a drink while the three-piece outfit gave out with what they imagined was a rumba and the Latins would have thought must be Dixieland.

"That sounds terrible," Mona said.

"I know a place," I said, "where you get the sweetest music this side of heaven. You can make your own choice—they play what you want."

"Sounds good," she said.

"It's piped out of the walls," I said, "five speakers—and with these L.P. discs you only need to change a stack once every four hours."

"Sounds even more wonderful," she said. "Where is this place? Can we go there?"

"Sure we can," I said. "Like to?"

"I can't stand much more of this." Mona gestured toward the three-piece outfit. "Let's go."

So half an hour later we stopped outside the house. We got out of the prowl car and Mona looked dubiously at the house.

"It seems awful quiet," she said.

"We can take care of that," I assured her.

"Does it belong to a friend of yours?" she asked.

"You could call him that, I guess."

We walked up the front path and I took out my key and put it into the lock.

"Oh. Oh," Mona said.

"What's the matter?"

"Now I get it," she said. "You live here."

"Sure," I said, "and the hi-fi is all here, too."

"My mother warned me about situations like these," she said.

"Your mother never went out with me," I told her, "otherwise she wouldn't have warned you."

I opened the door and switched on the lights. She walked into the living room.

"What would you like?" I asked her. "Sweet music, hot music, Dixieland, swing, bop, boogie?"

"Something sweet," she said, "to give my ears a rest from that three-piece outfit."

I planned the music with care. A woman is a sensitive thing, as a female wrestler once said. I stacked the discs on the turntable. First up, Eartha Kitt—that would persuade Mona she was bright and sophisticated. Then Sinatra—still sophisticated, but with a throb of tenderness.

Afterward, Doris Day, and the ones that always send them wild: 'Body and Soul,' 'Tenderly,' and then the last L.P. as a clincher. No vocals. Ellington: 'Caravan,' 'Mood Indigo,' 'Creole Love Call.'

Hell. If Mona wasn't crying in my arms by the time we got around to Ellington, I'd sell the hi-fi setup and buy a TV set.

I started the Kitt disc playing and went into the kitchen to get some drinks. I loaded a tray with two glasses, ice, bourbon. Some people drink martinis and some manhattans, some old-fashioneds, and some like me just drink. What I like about bourbon is that you pour it from the bottle, add ice, and you got you a drink. It saves a lot of time.

I carried the tray with me back into the living room.

Mona was sitting in an armchair, chuckling at 'Monotonous.' A few laughs are always good for a girl—it reassures them. I poured the drinks, gave her hers and me mine. We drank. The Kitt L.P. ran out and Sinatra took over.

We were on our third drink.

"How come you're so beautiful?" I asked her.

"Sssh," she said. "I'm listening."

"Sorry," I said sourly, and poured myself the fourth drink. I thought that was a hell of a fine thing for Sinatra to do to monopolize the conversation.

But time took care of him—the disc ran out. Doris Day drifted into the room. Mona's eyes got dreamy. I moved over and sat on the arm of her chair.

"No conversation?" I asked her.

She shook her head. "No conversation. This setup of yours is terrific, Al. I could sit here all night and just listen."

"Fine," I said weakly. I went back and poured my fifth drink. She was still dawdling with her third.

Doris drifted away and Ellington's reeds and muted brass filtered through the air. At least she didn't have to listen to the words.

I moved back to the arm of her chair.

"You like Ellington?"

"I'm crazy about Ellington," she said. "The old Ellington—this sort of stuff."

"I sort of figured you might be," I said. I went back and poured myself the sixth drink.

But then the Ellington disc ran out. I thanked my stars I hadn't loaded the turntable. The four sides had taken just under two hours to play—my watch said it was just after midnight.

"I'll get you another drink," I said, and lifted her glass out of her hand.

"That was wonderful, Al," she said, her eyes still dreamy. "Play some more."

"I'm all out of discs," I said hastily. "The rest of them are at the drycleaners."

I gave her back her refilled glass. "Thanks," she said. Then she looked out of the window. "The night's getting old outside. I'll have this, then I'd better go."

"Sure," I said bleakly. "I'd hate to keep you out late."

"I've enjoyed tonight, Al," she said enthusiastically. "It's been such fun."

"That's what I thought," I said. "Such nice clean fun."

"I have to get up early in the morning, Al," she said. "I'm a working girl, you know."

"Yeah," I nodded. "How do you like working for a firm of lawyers—criminal lawyers?"

"It's very interesting," she said.

"It must be a riot when they lose a case and a client goes to the chair."

She made a face at me and handed me her empty glass. I refilled it quickly.

"I said that was the last," she protested.

"One for the road," I said. "It's an old policemen's custom."

She took the refilled glass back. "Well, all right. But this one definitely is the last."

"Sure," I said.

"Mr. Berkeley is a funny man to work for," she said musingly. "Poor Mr. Offenheim was much nicer, really."

"He was?"

"I liked him," she said. "It was quite a mystery when I started there. The girl before me left the same day I started. Her name was Lola Laverne—

she was a brunette and really beautiful. She didn't say she was leaving and no one else ever told me why she left. But she used to ring up Mr. Offenheim quite often. Whenever it was her on the phone, he'd get quite a stupid look on his face and shush me out of his office." She laughed, remembering.

"He was going to handle this Rafe Rubens case, wasn't he?" I asked her casually.

She sipped her drink and nodded. "That's right. I suppose Mr. Berkeley will handle it now. We get some funny people in the office at times. That Mr. Rubens scared me, just to look at him. There was another one in this afternoon. He didn't scare me—he looked quite nice, really. But he was terribly worried. Demanded to see Mr. Berkeley at once. I told him Mr. Berkeley was engaged—he wasn't really but that's a sort of routine we have ..."

I refilled my glass. I wondered how much longer she was going to babble. I thought I'd have been better off seeing a movie that night.

".... Anyway, he just brushed past me into Mr. Berkeley's office." She giggled. "It was really quite dramatic. I walked after him, trying to stop him, but he didn't take any notice of me at all. He just threw Mr. Berkeley's door open and rushed in. Mr. Berkeley got an awful shock."

She finished her drink and giggled again. Then she held her glass out. "The service round here is something awful."

"I can fix it," I told her and took the glass.

"He just stood there," she went on regardless, "and stared at Mr. Berkeley. Then he said in a low voice, 'All right, Berkeley. So you thought you'd stand me up as the dummy, did you?' And Mr. Berkeley told him to be quiet—but he wouldn't."

I handed her back her glass, full to the brim. I raised my own.

"Sounds exciting," I said unenthusiastically.

"But you haven't heard it all yet," she said.

"That's what I was afraid of."

"You see, then he said, 'I didn't do it. But they think I did. They've been questioning me. I had a look at her—I saw what it was right away. Those men aren't fools. I had to tell them who I was and who I worked for. They'll come round to the plant, asking awkward questions. But if you think I'm going to take the rap, then ...'"

I dropped my glass on the floor and didn't even notice the good liquor seeping out over the carpet.

"And then?" I asked eagerly.

"Mr. Berkeley shut the door in my face," she said in a disappointed voice, "so I didn't hear any more."

"What a pity."

"Wasn't it?" She looked at me, her eyes bright. "But don't you think it's intriguing, Al? You're a policeman—what do you make of it?"

"I'll lay you twenty to one that I know the name of the guy."

"You couldn't possibly," she said flatly. "He never came near the office before."

"You want to bet?"

"Of course I want to bet," she pouted. "I'll bet ten dollars."

"I'm giving the odds," I said, "I call the bet."

"All right—what?"

"Twenty to one," I said. "You bet ten dollars, I bet a kiss."

"I don't get it," she said.

"It's quite simple," I assured her. "If you win, you get two hundred dollars. Ten dollars at twenty to one—check?"

"Check," she said solemnly.

"And if I win, if I'm right, I get twenty kisses, one kiss at twenty to one—check?"

"I suppose so," she said. "Anyway, you can't possibly win—you were only trying to be smart."

"James Kirkland," I said.

She stared at me, her eyes bulging. "But—but how ..."

"It's a sort of mental telepathy," I explained. "All policemen have it. You only have to open a bottle of beer within a three-mile radius of a prowl car and the cops inside know about it straight away."

"I don't know how you did it," she said, "but I've got a feeling you cheated somewhere."

She finished her drink and got onto her feet. "Well," she said casually, "I really must be going home, Al."

"You wouldn't welsh on a bet, would you?" I asked her.

She flushed. "You would know this red hair goes with Irish blood. Never let it be said a Gray welshed on a bet."

I took the glass out of her hand and put it down on the arm of the chair. Then I took her into my arms. I kissed her the way Mrs. Offenheim had kissed me that afternoon. For a while she was stiff in my arms, then she melted suddenly. She trembled and her fingernails dug into my shoulders.

A long time later I let go of her.

She took a deep breath. "Well," her voice was shaky, "I didn't know policemen could kiss like that. Now I really have to be going ..."

"You've got nineteen to go," I said. "Remember?"

She looked at her watch. "That was the first one and that took ten minutes. At that rate, I'll be here all night."

"Is that bad?" I asked her.

She didn't answer. Suddenly I got remorse. I'm stupid like that. I can get remorse at the stupidest times.

"Look, honey," I said, "if you want to go home, that's OK—I'll take you. We'll consider the debt paid in full."

She looked up at me. There was a sparkle in her eyes that hadn't been there before.

"I don't get you, Lieutenant Wheeler," she said. "All evening you've been building to a climax. Eartha Kitt for laughs and that bright, sophisticated feeling. Sinatra introducing the sentiment, Doris Day piling it on, then Ellington as the clincher with the wild stuff. You call a bet you knew you could win ... and now you want to call it off."

"And I said I was telepathic," I muttered.

She walked away from me to the switch on the wall and flicked it off, killing all the lights except for a table lamp. Then suddenly she was back in my arms, snuggling against me.

"No redhead welshes on a bet," she said. "And neither do they allow any-one else to welsh—not even a cop."

She pouted her lips at me. "Nineteen more, please."

CHAPTER 7
No Kirkland

Sunlight filtered through the windows.

"The last time I looked out there," Mona said in a wondering voice, "the night was growing old. Now there's a bright new day there already."

"How about that bet?" I asked her. "Is that all paid off?"

"With about five hundred percent interest." She leaned across and kissed my forehead. "And well you know it."

"Would you like me to make you some breakfast?"

"I should get back," she said, "before the tattered shreds of my reputation are gone forever. Besides, I'd look stupid turning up at the office in gold lamé."

"Why don't you turn up there the way you are?" I suggested. "Nobody would say you looked stupid then."

She blushed. I watched it start around her face and keep on spreading. It's surprising just how far a blush will spread.

"I'm going to have a shower and put on a new face," she said firmly. "Then will you kindly transport me home?"

"Sure, honey," I said. "And I've got news for you."

"What's that?"

"You aren't going to work today."

"But I have to."

"Or tomorrow or the day after," I added. "Or ever again—not at Offenheim and Berkeley, attorneys-at-law, you're not."

"Are you crazy?" she asked.

I shook my head. "I hate to drag this into the conversation just now— but I'm a cop. And right now I'm being a cop. That conversation you over- heard was dynamite. Sooner or later Berkeley is going to remember you heard it. I don't want you to take any chances, kid."

She stared at me. "You're really serious? You think I'm in some sort of danger from Mr. Berkeley?" She started to laugh. "Al. That's too ridicu- lous."

"Offenheim didn't die a natural death," I told her. "He was murdered. And last night Lola Laverne was murdered. The conversation you heard ties in strongly with those two murders. Do I begin to stop being ridicu- lous?"

Her face sobered. "I keep forgetting you're a real Lieutenant of police, Al. No, it doesn't sound ridiculous anymore."

"Then stay away from the place," I told her, "and get another apart- ment—today."

She thought for a moment. "Al?"

"Yeah?"

"If I went back there, knowing what you've told me, I might hear some more. Something that could be useful to you, couldn't I?"

"I suppose so," I said, "but ..."

"Then that's what I'm going to do," she said firmly. "And no arguments will make me alter my mind, so you can be quiet."

She leaned over and kissed me again, then walked quickly out of the room. A few moments later I heard the shower running.

I went out into the kitchen. I made some coffee—it was ready by the time Mona came in. She had put on a new face and the gold lamé. She looked fresh and beautiful.

I made a dive for the bathroom, showered, shaved, and got dressed.

By the time I got back to the kitchen, Mona had made some toast to go with the coffee.

When we'd finished breakfast, I drove her home. I told her to ring me if anything happened at Offenheim and Berkeley, and in case it didn't, I'd ring her. Then I kissed her good morning and she disappeared into her apart- ment building a minute before the milkman appeared.

I drove home. It was seven a.m. when I got back. I hadn't been up so early in a long time. I made myself some more breakfast then tidied up the place. Came eight-thirty and I was back in the prowl car.

I thought I'd do what Kirkland expected me to do—pay a visit to Mor- gan and Scheer, his employers.

The plant was about twenty miles out of town. I got caught in the down-

town traffic and it took me over an hour to get there. When I did get there
I found that Mr. Morgan had died some ten years back, but there was a
Mr. Scheer. So I saw Mr. Scheer.

He was a German with thick glasses and a trace of an accent. He had
lived in the States for thirty years, he told me, but his English still wasn't
quite perfect. But his son was playing quarterback for Yale this year and
he couldn't speak a word of German.

I said that was nice.

Then Mr. Scheer cleared his throat and said he guessed I hadn't come out
to visit him to hear about his son, and I said it just so happened I hadn't.

Then I told him about the murders. Without the names, but the findings
of the autopsies. I told him one of his employees was under suspicion, then
asked him would it be possible for anyone to have access to curare.

Scheer took off his glasses and looked at me. "Is it permissible, Lieutenant, to ask the name of the employee?"

"I guess so," I said. "You won't repeat any of this conversation, naturally?"

He nodded. "Naturally."

"James Kirkland," he said.

He shook his head slowly. "I wouldn't have believed it," he said. "He
seems such a nice lad ..."

"Would it be possible?"

He nodded again. "Quite possible. He is engaged primarily in the man-
ufacture of tubocurarine—an anesthetic. We obtain our supplies of raw curare from South America—we have an agent in Buenos Aires who sends
us our supplies. I would say it was quite possible, Lieutenant Wheeler.
James Kirkland has charge of that particular processing plant. It would be
easy for him—very easy."

"Thanks, Mr. Scheer," I said. "That's what I wanted to know. Is he working today?"

"I can find out for you," he said.

He rang through while I lit a cigarette. He spoke a few words, then hung
up.

"No," he said. "He's not here. He wasn't in yesterday, either. He rang
to say he had a bad cold and would be away a few days."

"Thanks," I said. I got to my feet. "I won't bother you any longer, Mr.
Scheer."

"I am glad to have been of help, Lieutenant," he said. And he sat there
shaking his head while I let myself out.

I drove back into town. I went straight to the Precinct, into Captain
Parker's office. He looked over the top of his glasses at me as I came in.

"Where's that written report?" he asked.

"I came to deliver it verbally," I said.

I told him of the conversation between Kirkland and Berkeley that Mona had repeated to me. Then the conversation I'd just had with Scheer.

"So if it's all the same to you," I finished, "I'll go out and pick him up."

"You could have done that the same night the Laverne woman was knocked off," he snorted. "Instead of fooling around with Berkeley's secretary."

I shook my head. "Remember that stone in the pool?"

"I'm more concerned with the rocks in your head," he snorted.

"If the stone hadn't been dropped, the ripple that tied Berkeley into this wouldn't have reached us, would it?" I said.

He snorted some more. "All right, wise guy. Go and bring him in. We'll book him on suspicion. That's plenty to hold him—and while you're gone, I'd better ring the Commissioner."

"I'll go find Kirkland," I told him.

I picked up the address Kirkland had left with the desk sergeant the other night.

Macnamara looked at me. "Nice-looking young man, that one. Don't see many honest faces around here—made a change."

"I'm just going out to pull him in," I said, "on suspicion of a double murder. Like you say, Mac, it's nice to see an honest face around here." I left him staring after me.

I got out to where James Kirkland lived. A rooming house in a district which wasn't a slum, but you wouldn't bet on where it would be ten years from now.

A fat woman with gray hair and tired eyes answered the door.

"I'd like to see Mr. Kirkland," I said.

"And so would I," she said tartly. "He hasn't been here since yesterday morning and he's owing me a week's rent."

I pulled out my billfold and showed it to her.

"Police." She looked indignant. "I hope he's not in any trouble. I run a respectable place here."

"I'd like to look at his room," I said.

"All right," she sniffed. "I've got a key. I haven't had a look myself yet. Shouldn't be surprised if he's taken his things with him ... and owing me a week's rent, too."

I followed her up two flights of stairs. She unlocked the door for me, then followed me in. She looked around, sniffing like a bloodhound.

It was just a room. A gas ring in one corner, next to the washbasin. A bed against one wall. A couple of chairs and a desk. I went through the drawers of the desk, finding a lot of junk but nothing of much interest.

There was a photograph of Lola Laverne, with a scrawled *To my dar-*

ling Jimmy across it. The landlady sniffed excitedly when she saw it.

"That's a wicked-looking girl," she said triumphantly. "All the good-looking ones you can't trust."

"She's dead," I said. "We think that Kirkland killed her."

She gave a scream and reared back a pace. "Murdered. And him with his nice manners and everything." She sniffed again. "How was she killed?" she asked eagerly.

"With an axe," I said gravely. "Hacked into little pieces."

She screamed again. "With an axe."

"A blunt one," I told her.

I finished with the desk and started on the wardrobe. It was bare—so were the drawers underneath. I had a final look around. There was nothing else. I headed toward the door.

The landlady followed me, sniffing agitatedly. I got downstairs and she was still at my shoulder.

"What happens if he comes back?" she asked in a quavering voice. "We might all be murdered in our beds."

"I don't think he's coming back," I said, "but I'll send a man out just in case."

"Oh." She sounded mollified. "Well, tell that man of yours to hurry up."

"Sure," I said. "And do me one favour, will you?"

"What's that?" she sniffed.

"Blow your nose," I told her.

I got back into the car and operated the radio. I told Parker what I had found and asked him to send a man to the rooming house. He made some caustic remarks about how this wouldn't have happened if we'd held Kirkland when we had him. I didn't want another argument so I turned the radio off while he was still talking.

I drove home. I felt tired and I thought a rest might do me some good. I went to bed and slept the sleep of the unjust—like a top.

When I woke it was just after five in the evening. I opened a can of spaghetti and made some toast and coffee to go with it. I had a shower, no shave, and got dressed again. I put some Stravinsky on the turntable. I felt like something zany and I certainly got it. Stravinsky sounds like a merry-go-round gone mad and that's just the way I felt.

I was going to ring Mona Gray and see what she was doing when I suddenly remembered I had a date up on Cone Hill.

I heard the Stravinsky through, had a couple of drinks and it was nine when I left the house. I didn't hurry—I drove leisurely and it was ten when I parked the car on the drive. I rang the bell and waited on the step.

She took a while to open the door. Then she didn't open it very wide until she saw who it was. It brightened my ego a little that the door opened wide when she recognized me.

"So you remembered," she said. "Well—come in."

I walked into the hall and she closed the door behind me.

"I'm glad you came," she said. "I was watching the fights on television and getting awfully bored."

I looked at her. She was wearing a pair of silk lounging pajamas that shimmied as she walked.

"The boredom," I said, "we can take care of."

We went into the library and across to the bar.

"Here there's no television," she said. "What are you drinking?"

"Bourbon, thanks," I said. "Ice and no water."

She poured me a drink, then poured one for herself. "How is the investigation going, Lieutenant?" she asked.

"It's going along fine," I said, "and the name is Al."

"Short for what?"

"Just Al."

"Nobody calls a child Al," she said. "So it must be short for something."

"Skip it," I said.

"Come on," she persisted. "Don't hold out on me—short for what?"

I took a deep breath. "Aloysius."

"Oh, no." She rocked with laughter. "That's wonderful. A tough cop like you hiding under a name like that."

"Very funny," I said. "And what's your name?"

"Gail," she said.

"Short for Abigail?"

"It so happens it is," she said coldly.

"I'll make a deal with you," I said. "I won't call you Abby if you don't call me Aloysius."

"It's a deal, Al," she said solemnly. We shook hands on it.

My glass happened to be empty so she refilled it.

"So the investigation is going along all right," she said. "Going to arrest somebody soon?"

"Sure," I said. "When we find him—and that won't be hard."

"Who?" she asked breathlessly.

"It's a departmental secret," I said. "I am sworn to secrecy by the gray hairs of my Precinct Captain."

"But you can tell me," she said.

I looked around the room: there was a comfortable sofa against the far wall. I got up from the stool I was sitting on.

"I'd have to whisper it," I said. "Even the walls have ears."

She followed me across the room. "Well, all right—whisper."

I sat down on the sofa and patted the empty space beside me. She sat down there, a puzzled look on her face. I moved closer until I was crowding the peignoir.

"Lean this way," I told her.

She leaned this way. I grabbed her and kissed her the way she had kissed me the previous morning. I thought fair was fair, as the brunette said when she dyed her hair and it came out mauve.

She didn't respond. So after a while I gave up.

"All right," she said, "now that's over—who?"

"Kirkland," I said.

"Kirkland." She looked amazed. "But why him?"

"Your late husband and his late mistress were both poisoned," I said, "by a poison called curare."

"Not the stuff the ..."

"Little brown men in South America poison their darts with," I finished for her. "That's correct. Only it's brought into this country and processed into a number of things, including anesthetics. Kirkland is a chemical boy— a manufacturing chemist working for a company of manufacturing chemists—in charge of—guess what? The processing plant that processes curare."

"I see," she said slowly. "But why on earth."

"He loved Lola," I said. "He hated your husband because of what he'd done to her. Maybe he hated her finally because of what she'd let your husband do to her. So he knocked off one and then the other."

It didn't sound very convincing, even to me.

"It sounds screwy to me," she said.

"But then, Gail," I patted her knee, "you aren't a cop. That's the way we figure it. It gains strength by the fact that Kirkland has run out. We can't find him—but we will, of course."

"If you say so," she said.

She walked toward the bar and topped up her drink. I lit a cigarette. I was beginning to feel like a passed-over Casanova.

"This date we had for tonight," I said. "What was that for?"

"I just wondered if you'd come," she said. "A girl likes to be reassured that she's still got what it takes." She patted her hair. "I've been out of circulation a long time."

"And now you're back?"

She smiled sweetly. "Not tonight—sorry."

The bell sounded outside. She frowned. "Who's that?"

"Why don't you go answer the door and find out?" I suggested helpfully.

She went out. I heard a murmur of voices and then she came into the room again, followed by John Rowlands and his housekeeper, Johnnie.

She didn't look like a housekeeper. She was wearing a black, short evening gown with a plunge neckline. She had a mink jacket over that. Spear-shaped brass earrings contrasted with her silver-blonde hair.

Elmer brought up the rear.

"You folks know each other?" Gail asked in a conversational voice.

Rowlands smiled. "How are you, Lieutenant?"

"Fine," I told him.

His housekeeper and his goon didn't say anything. They just looked at me.

CHAPTER 8
Cone Hill Capers

We handed drinks around. Then we sat and looked at each other.

"How is the case progressing, Lieutenant?" Rowlands asked.

"Just fine," I said.

He raised his eyebrows. "As good as that? You expecting to make an arrest soon?"

"Anytime now," I assured him.

"I suppose I can't ask who?" he smiled.

"No," I smiled back at him, "you can't."

His smile started to show holes all over the place.

I got to my feet. "Well, I guess I ought to be running along. Thanks for the drink, Mrs. Offenheim."

Rowlands also got to his feet. "Hope we haven't disturbed you, Lieutenant. I was a client of Offenheim's, as you know. I thought I should drop over and offer my sympathy to his wife. I brought Johnnie along so that Mrs. Offenheim wouldn't misunderstand my intentions."

"Sure," I said. I walked past him toward the door.

The silver-blonde gave me a frosty look. Elmer glared at me.

"I'm sorry," I told him, "I don't have any dog biscuits with me."

He made an inarticulate noise, just like a dog, and I kept on walking. Gail came into the hall with me.

"Fancy Mr. Rowlands calling on me," she said, "and bringing his retinue with him."

"Just fancy," I said.

She put her hand on my arm. "You're sore with me, Al," she said sympathetically. "Aren't you?"

"Who—me?" I said. "I like the drive up here to Cone Hill. The air is so stimulating."

"Call me tomorrow," she said. "My mood might have changed by then."

"In a word," I said, "nuts."

I opened the door and stepped out into the night. The door slammed shut behind me. I got into the car and drove away. I had a bright idea ... an idea that Captain Parker would never approve of, but then he's a married man and respectable—well, almost.

I drove over to Rowlands' house—or, to be exact, I drove a block past and made a left-hand turn. I left the prowl car parked in that street and walked back.

I thought that while he was busy visiting, I might just take a look at his house. People as experienced as Rowlands don't generally leave things lying around, but it could be worth taking a look just in case.

I catfooted up the drive, keeping close to the fence. There were no lights showing in the front of the house. I followed the drive down the side and around to the back. There was a light on in one of the downstairs rooms. I wondered if anyone was home or whether they just had forgotten the light. There was an easy way to find out.

I came up close to the house and moved along until I stopped in front of one of the unlit windows. I tried lifting it and it slid upward without any trouble. I listened for a few seconds, but no alarm bells jangled anywhere inside. So I threw one leg over the sill, then climbed in.

I closed the window behind me carefully. It was quite dark inside the room. After a while my eyes got used to it and I could pick out the dark bulk of furniture. There was a desk against one wall. I walked over to it gently and felt along the surface, my fingers touching the cold base of a lamp.

I went back to the window and pulled the curtains across, then came back to the desk. I switched on the lamp. It looked like I'd hit the jackpot—this was Rowlands' desk. I sat down in the chair in front of the desk and opened the first drawer.

There was a click and the overhead light went on. My stomach flapped around, looking for some visible means of support.

"All right, pal," a voice said from behind me. "Turn around slow—try anything and you're morgue meat."

I turned around slowly, still sitting in the swivel chair. I was the bright boy, all right—the brain, the unorthodox cop with a hole where his head should have been. I'd seen that Rowlands, Johnnie and Elmer were out of the way, over at Gail Offenheim's house. The guy I'd forgotten was Rowlands' permanent houseguest—Rafe Rubens.

He stood there in the doorway, a business-looking Mauser in his hand, pointing at the spot where my stomach was still looking around for support.

"Well, well," Rubens said. "If it isn't the nosy cop. You got a search warrant, of course?"

"It so happens," I said carefully, "that I must have left it behind someplace."

"Yeah?" he grinned. "That's too bad, isn't it, Lieutenant?"

I sat there, watching him. There wasn't much else I could do.

"When Rowlands gets back," he said, "he ain't going to like this, copper."

"That's too bad," I said.

"Yeah." He came forward into the room and kicked the door shut behind him.

We didn't seem to be getting anyplace very much.

"You mind if I light a cigarette?" I asked him.

"Just don't make a mistake about what you pull out of your pocket," he said. "I'm sort of nervous, copper." He moved the gun suggestively.

I took the pack out of my pocket carefully, put a cigarette in my mouth and lit it.

"The boss is over at the Offenheim house, isn't he?" Rubens asked me.

I shrugged my shoulders and took a draw on the cigarette.

"Yeah," he said. "I'll ring him."

He came toward the desk. He picked up the phone, then put it down again. He pulled a directory out of the bottom drawer and checked the number. Then he dialed it. His gun never even wavered. My stomach was having hysterics just watching it.

"Like to speak to Mr. Rowlands, please," he said, then waited. "Boss? Rafe here. Guess what? We got a visitor—yeah, comes in through a window and I find him sitting at your desk—sure, I got him right here, at the end of a gun." He grinned. "Yeah, you know him, all right—it's that nosy cop. Yeah, that's right. No, he don't have no search warrant. I figure it's strictly his own idea. Sure, I'll wait."

He stood, watching me, the grin still on his face. "The boss is thinking about this," he said. "I figure he's cooking up something good for you."

I took another draw on the cigarette. There's nothing that makes you feel quite so stupid as having a gun pointed at you.

Rubens was listening intently. "Yeah—yeah, boss? What." The grin disappeared off his face. "Yeah—OK. You sure about this?" He listened for maybe ten seconds without speaking. "OK, boss, if you're sure it'll work out. I got this other rap hanging. I know, sure he says he can fix it."

The grin reappeared on his face. "I didn't know that, boss. I'll take care of it—be a pleasure. You know how I like cops. You'll be back in fifteen minutes? OK, I'll check the time." He looked at his watch. "Ten to midnight now—on the dot of the hour, eh, boss? Sure." He hung up.

I stubbed my butt in the brass ashtray. "All right, bright eyes," I said.

"What have you got cooked up?"

"That Rowlands," he said admiringly. "He's a genius."

"That must be nice for him," I said.

"He figures you're getting in his hair," Rubens went on cheerfully. "He don't like you, copper. And when John H. Rowlands don't like somebody, that somebody don't live long."

"Why don't you say something instead of just talking?"

Rubens' face contorted into a snarl. "Sure, I'll say something, copper. The boss has it all worked out. He figures that I'm here on my own—right. I hear somebody breaking into the place. So I get a gun—his gun, you understand, copper? And I get into the room. This guy has a gun in his hand. I tell him to take it easy and he takes a shot at me, so I shoot back—strictly in self-defense, you understand, copper? It just so happens that I kill the guy. The boss and the others come back and they find out what has happened—they see the guy with the gun in his hand and the bullet in the wall where he shot at me."

I felt my throat tighten. "You've already got one murder rap hanging over your head, Rubens," I told him. "You think any cop will believe a story like that?"

"Listen, pal," he said, "I got news for you. There's a certain cop who'll be glad to believe it. You ain't got friends in this town, copper."

If somebody in Homicide was playing along with Rowlands—and Commissioner Lavers had tipped that way back—he might be glad to believe the story. I had no right to break into the house if I was mistaken for a hoodlum and shot—well, nobody would cry for me.

"That dumb ox," Parker would say and shake his head. "I told him that sooner or later he'd have to start acting like a real cop, or wind up dead."

And that would be that.

Rubens looked at his watch. "Five minutes to go, copper. You want another cigarette before you knock off?"

"It wouldn't be a bad idea," I said. I lit another cigarette. "Since we've got a whole five minutes to waste, maybe you'd tell me something?"

"Maybe," he grunted.

"Who killed Offenheim?"

He shook his head. "If I knew I'd tell you, copper. But I don't. I work for the boss and he don't tell me why he does things, or even if he does things. I don't know if he was in on that Offenheim deal or not. He figures I'll beat the rap OK with the other guy—Berkeley—handling it." He grinned. "The boss has a lot of friends, copper. A lot of friends."

"Yeah," I said.

Rubens looked down at the gun in his hand, then back at me. "John H. Rowlands is a big man," he said, "a big man. We came here from Chi. The boss is a big man in Chi. But things get a little warm down there and the boss figures it's time to pull out. We have to pull out fast. When we get here, he says he's going to build up an organization here—and that's just what he's doing, copper. A year from now, anybody in this town wants anything, they'll come to John H. Rowlands."

"There would be some other boys in this town who wouldn't like that," I said.

"They'll be taken care of," he said confidently. "The word's getting around. The boss has a theory about that. He figures it's kind of old-fashioned to bump off your opposition the way they used to. Tommy guns and grenades are old stuff, he figures."

"What does he figure is the new stuff?"

Rafe shrugged his shoulders. "He's smart, the boss. He figures if you frighten 'em, you don't have to kill so many. He figures that the ones you do bump off, you bump off in a way that scares hell out of people. That way, he says, it's economic."

"Like curare?" I suggested.

"Huh?"

"Skip it," I said.

He looked at his watch again. "You got a minute to go, copper. How you liking it, huh?" he grinned.

"It's just fine," I told him.

"Get up out of that chair, copper," he said.

I got up out of the chair.

"I got to figure this right," Rubens said. "You get over by the window again, huh?"

"What's the idea of that?"

"So you just got in when I bump you," he said. "You're awful dumb— even for a copper."

"Yeah," I said.

I took a long, last draw on the cigarette. Then I leaned across the desk toward the brass ashtray again. I stubbed the butt carefully. For the moment I was turned away from Rubens, my arm shielded by my body.

"Hurry it up, copper," he said. "It's time."

I picked up the brass ashtray and turned toward him quickly.

I flung the ashtray at his head and he jerked his head back, but not quite fast enough. It caught him a glancing blow on the temple and he staggered for a moment. I threw myself sideways, my right hand clawing for the .32 in the shoulder-holster.

The Mauser fired and lead plowed into the floor beside me. I got the .32 in my hand, steadied my wrist against my stomach and fired twice.

Rubens straightened up, a surprised look on his face. The gun spilled out of his hand to the floor, then he toppled forward and fell flat on his face. He didn't move.

I went over to where he lay and turned him over with my foot.

Rubens wasn't going to have to worry about the other rap—it's surprising what a couple of .32 slugs can do to a guy's chest at close range. In a word, he was dead.

I looked at my watch—a minute after midnight. In another four minutes, Rowlands and his friends would be back.

I started out—fast. Then I came back—fast. I took the handkerchief out of my top pocket and wiped off the desktop. Then I went out the window again, closing it behind me and wiping off the frame with the handkerchief.

I went down the drive at a fast run and didn't stop running until I was back in the prowl car. I drove back into town as fast as I could, which was fast. I didn't go home.

At twelve-thirty, I parked the car outside Mona's apartment block. At twelve thirty-one, she opened the door of her apartment and stared at me.

"Well," she said. "This is a surprise."

She was wearing what the ads call a shortie nightdress. This one was a short shortie nightdress. Her legs were nice and tanned. I thought that sometime we should take them to Miami for a week or two, so they could get some more tan. When I had the time.

I stepped into the apartment quickly and closed the door.

"Take it easy, Romeo," she said tartly. "I happen to live here, remember? I also like to have my life reasonably organized. Hi-fi and twenty-to-one shots are all right—when they are reasonably organized. Tonight I'm organized to catch up on my beauty sleep, so hit the road."

I took her into my arms and kissed her. It stopped her talking and she looked as if she should be kissed. What else could I do with a redhead in a shortie nightdress—use her as a doorstop?

I made, in all modesty, the thorough Wheeler job of kissing her that is referred to in feminine circles as the ultimate. When I let go of her, she didn't move anyplace—she stayed there hard up against my chest.

"Why did you have to come and disorganize my organization?" she asked softly. "You must know I like it."

I moved away from her. "You have a drink around the place?"

"There's a bottle of bourbon somewhere," she said. "You prefer liquor to me?"

"Not really," I said, "but I need a drink."

"OK," she sighed. "It's nice to know my rival only comes out of a bottle, anyway."

She found the bottle and two glasses, then poured us a drink. "Here's to your beautiful eyes," I told her, "and your beautiful legs."

She looked down at them complacently. "They have got a nice tan, haven't they?"

"Lucky sun," I said, and gave her my empty glass as a subtle hint. She refilled it and handed it back to me.

"You remember what time it was when I got here?" I asked.

"Something after midnight." She looked at me curiously. "You have a watch—what do you care?"

"You're wrong," I told her. "It was ten after eleven when I got here." She stared at me for a moment. "I don't get it," she said.

"Honey," I said, "you don't have to do this—you can tell me to go to hell. You can tell me to go peddle my badge someplace else—that's OK."

"I wish you'd start making sense, Al," she said.

I finished my drink. "I need an alibi," I said. "I need to have been here since ten after eleven. It so happens you remember the time exactly because I told you I'd be here at ten, and it got later and later and you thought I wasn't coming. One hour and ten minutes late. You told me as soon as I arrived."

I finished the second drink and reached for the bottle.

"What do you need an alibi for?" she asked. "It sounds sort of stupid—a lieutenant of police asking for an alibi."

"I shot a guy," I said. "I killed him."

"But can't policemen do that? I mean, you did it in the course of duty, Al?"

"I did it to save my neck," I said. "Because I wanted to go on living and see you in a shortie nightdress again."

"Again?"

"Well, to see you again, honey."

"I like that better," she said.

I told her the story of what had happened.

"You arrived at ten past eleven," she said when I'd finished. "I remember the time exactly because you'd said you'd be here at ten. An hour and ten minutes late. I told you as soon as you got here."

"Honey," I said, "you might save my badge even yet—and my neck."

I kissed her again, thoroughly. Then I started to head for the door. I looked at my watch. "I left at twelve-fifty," I said. "Get your beauty sleep, Mona. I'll call you tomorrow."

"Al?"

"Yeah?" I turned around and looked at her.

"A really good alibi," she said, "one that would hold up to close scrutiny, wouldn't end at twelve-fifty."

"It wouldn't?"

Mona shook her head demurely. "I wouldn't think it could possibly end before seven a.m."

"You don't?"

"But then I'm not a policeman," she said.

"You don't know how glad I am about that," I said. "What about your beauty sleep?"

"I've reorganized myself," she said. "That's tomorrow night."

CHAPTER 9
My Time's My Own

I arrived home at eight a.m.

At eight-five a.m. the phone rang.

I answered it.

"Where the hell have you been all night?" Parker bellowed into my ear.

"That's none of your damn business," I told him. "I have some private life, don't I?"

"This is serious, Al," Parker said. "I don't know what the hell you've been doing, but the Homicide boys have been looking for you all night."

"A party?" I suggested.

"They say you broke into Rowlands' place and shot Rubens," he said soberly. "You were at the Offenheim house last night?"

"Sure," I said.

"You left around ten-thirty?"

"Sure," I said again.

"Rowlands got a call from Rubens," Parker went on. "Rubens told him he'd caught you breaking into the house and was holding you at the point of a gun and what should he do. Rowlands told him to wait until he got home. When he got there he found Rafe Rubens dead on the floor, with a couple of .32 slugs in him."

"He's got an imagination," I said, "that Rowlands."

"The Homicide boys seem to think he's got more than imagination, Al," Parker said. "They want you—and they want your gun for the ballistics experts."

My stomach got into a dither again. "Yeah?" I tried to sound nonchalant.

"Get over here, Al," he said. "Then I'll tell them you're coming here. I don't want you to go into Homicide."

"And neither do I," I said fervently. "I don't think they like me up there."

"I got that impression, too," Parker said. "Why is that?"

"I don't have the faintest idea," I said. "I'll come right in, Cap."

I hung up and felt suddenly old.

The ballistics boys were good. They could match the slugs to my gun—prove the gun had been fired recently. I didn't have a gun, I thought, I'd lost it.

Where?

I lit a cigarette while my stomach tied itself into knots. Where had I lost the gun? I lost it yesterday, I thought. I had it on my hip, instead of in a holster. Maybe I lost it when I was looking around James Kirkland's room.

I took the gun and holster off. I put the holster in a drawer, then went out into the kitchen. I found a file and carefully filed off the serial number of the gun. I unloaded the slugs left, cleaned the gun carefully, then put it into my pocket. The slugs went with it.

I went out to the prowl car, got in and headed toward the river. I parked and walked over to the bank. I'd chosen a deserted spot—a crumbling wharf that was overdue to be pulled down and wasn't being used. I tossed the slugs in one by one and then finally the gun. But before I tossed it in, I wiped the gun clean with a handkerchief.

Then I got back into the prowl car and drove down to the Precinct. I went straight into Parker's office.

Parker was there, Lavers was there, and another guy I had met before.

"Sit down, Wheeler," Parker said. "You know Commissioner Lavers, of course."

"Good morning, sir," I said.

"Morning," Lavers grunted. His eyes watched me shrewdly.

"This is Lieutenant O'Malley from Homicide," Parker went on. O'-Malley glared at me.

"Good morning," I said. He still just glared at me.

"Let's get to the bottom of this," Lavers said. "I'm much more concerned with the Offenheim case. The fact that some hoodlum who was already facing a first-degree murder rap got himself shot is something I'm not particularly concerned with."

O'Malley glared at him. "It's still murder, sir. Of course, we haven't been consulted on the Offenheim case. Perhaps that's why we're more interested in finding out who killed Rubens."

Lavers grunted and lit himself a cigarette.

O'Malley looked at me. "Lieutenant," he said in a hard voice. "You're accused of murdering Rafe Rubens."

"Who by?" I asked him.

"Rowlands says ..." He repeated the story of the phone call. I lit myself a cigarette when he'd finished.

"The Commissioner," I said mildly, "just remarked that Rubens was a hoodlum facing a murder rap, anyway. Now you're taking the word of his boss—a super-hoodlum—that I killed him. You'll forgive me, Captain, if

I don't understand your bias. Your preference for hoodlums, rather than cops."

O'Malley's face went a dull red. I saw Lavers' lips twitch.

"Listen," O'Malley roared. "We have to check any statement made in connection with a killing—even you dumb hicks in the Precincts should know that."

"I'll remember it, Lieutenant," I said earnestly. "I'll write it down in my little notebook."

Parker bent his head suddenly and his shoulders began to heave.

"The Lieutenant is a very bright lieutenant," O'Malley said. "He is so bright he should know that there's one quick way to clear this thing up."

"You tell me, Lieutenant," I said. "We hicks in the Precincts are always eager to learn."

O'Malley moved his shoulders impatiently. "Rubens was shot with couple of .32 slugs," he said. "You've got an issue .32. Let's have it—Ballistics can check it. If it wasn't your gun, you're in the clear."

They all looked at me.

"Come on, Wheeler," Parker said impatiently. "Give them the gun and let them take it away. Then maybe we can get some work done around here."

"I'd like to oblige," I said, "but I don't have it."

"What!" Lavers almost shouted.

I grinned feebly. "This sort of proves Homicide's point about hicks in the Precincts, doesn't it?" I said. "I lost it yesterday." I looked at Parker. "I have an idea it was somewhere around the time I had a look at Kirkland's room."

There was a heavy silence.

"Rubens was shot somewhere close to midnight," O'Malley said. "Just where were you, Lieutenant, around that time?"

"Do I have to answer that?"

"Yes," Lavers said suddenly.

"I hate doing this to a lady," I said. "I was at my girlfriend's place."

"What time did you get there?" O'Malley asked.

"A little after eleven," I told him.

"And what time did you leave?"

I averted my eyes modestly. "Around seven this morning."

O'Malley's eyes glittered. "We can check this, of course?"

"I guess so," I said. "Handle it gently, will you? She's a nice girl."

"She's got a name?"

"Mona Gray." I gave him the address.

"That's her home address," O'Malley said, writing it down in his notebook. "You know where she works?"

"Sure," I said. "Offenheim and Berkeley, attorneys-at-law."

"What." O'Malley looked up again, his eyes bulging.

I shrugged my shoulders. "She's a stenographer. You've heard of them, Lieutenant?"

He ignored me. He got to his feet, looking at Lavers.

"We'll check the alibi, of course, sir," he said. "Wheeler is under your jurisdiction, so what happens to him meanwhile is up to you, sir."

"I'll take care of it," Lavers said. "You'll let me know about the alibi?"

"Yes, sir," O'Malley nodded.

"Good." Lavers nodded in dismissal. O'Malley went out of Parker's office.

Parker looked at me grimly. "You lost your gun," he grated.

Lavers clenched his fists and pounded them on his knees. "I was crazy to listen to you, Parker," he said. "Wheeler got away with it once, on the Ralston case. But this time he won't get away with it. And it leaves me out on a limb—right out on a limb."

"Yes, sir," Parker said.

Lavers glared at me. "You're suspended from duty, Lieutenant, as of now. I almost hope they do pin this murder on you. And if they don't, I can promise you one thing—you won't be a lieutenant very much longer. I'll have you back in a uniform and pounding a sidewalk."

"That O'Malley," I said. "Has anyone had a look at his bank account lately?"

"What the hell has that got to do with it?" Lavers snapped.

"I just wondered," I said.

Lavers got to his feet. "I'm going back uptown, Captain. Seems to me there should be quite a lot of reorganization around the Twelfth Precinct. I shall look into it."

"Yes, sir," Parker said stolidly.

The Commissioner stamped out of the room, slamming the door behind him.

I lit another cigarette and stared at the ceiling.

"The unorthodox cop," Parker said. "I should have my head read for giving you the Offenheim case."

"Has Kirkland turned up yet?"

"Not a sign," he said sourly. "And don't change the subject. The Commissioner isn't kidding about reorganization, and I'm too old to start pounding a beat again. He'll probably think that, too. So he'll retire me eight years before I'm due. What does a retired captain of police do, Al?"

I took a draw on the cigarette. "O'Malley is running Homicide at the moment?" I asked him.

"Yeah," Parker nodded.

"Rowlands was operating in Chicago before he came here," I said. "O'-Malley might have some information on that—but we wouldn't get it if we asked for it."

"How do you know he was operating in Chi?"

"Rubens told me so."

Parker stared at me, "Then you did ..."

"I don't know what you're talking about, Captain," I said.

He shook his head bewilderedly. "Sometimes I can't figure you out, Al. There must be a reasonable explanation."

"No," I said. "But there will be."

I got to my feet. "I'm suspended—right?"

"You heard what Lavers said."

"I don't mind," I said generously. "There isn't very much that O'Malley will be able to do. My alibi will stand up."

"You were with the girl at that time?" Parker asked hopefully.

"I said the alibi will stand up—and I'll tell you something else, if you're interested, Cap. Given another forty-eight hours, I think I could bust the Offenheim case wide open."

"You've got plenty of time," he said. "You're suspended—your time's your own."

"There's just one other thing I need," I said.

"What's that?"

"A gun," I told him.

Parker looked at me for a moment, then shook his head. "I'm sorry, Al," he said.

"No dice?"

"No dice," he agreed.

"Well," I drifted toward the door, "I'll be seeing you, Cap."

"Sure," he said sourly. "You in your blue uniform, and me in mine."

CHAPTER 10
Redhead Alibi

I walked around for an hour, maybe two. I didn't know where I walked. When I became conscious of my surroundings again, I wasn't very far from the Twelfth Precinct. I stood still, staring into a shop window, and started to think again. I needed to think—and fast.

With the mood she was in, Mona might burst my alibi wide open at any time, and I couldn't blame her for doing it.

O'Malley. But it wasn't any use letting it get me. I had to do something constructive.

It was Twelfth Precinct territory—my own stamping ground. I knew where to stamp for most things around there. I started walking again, this time with an objective.

It had the three brass balls conventionally hung above the door. In the dark, musty window were a thousand cheap wristwatches and a couple of dozen baseball bats. The perfect commentary on civilization—the pawnshop.

I pushed open the door and walked inside. Inside it was dark and musty. A bell tinkled as I closed the door. Footsteps shuffled from out of the back room and Eli came to the counter.

How old he was, I never had figured out. He looked old enough to remember the flood. He wore a shapeless jacket over an old woolen muffler, wound close around his throat, and his rimless glasses were perched halfway down his nose. He never looked any different.

He hadn't looked any different the day we'd got Harry Morton in his shop. Harry had taken a bank and shot two tellers while he took it. He'd been holed up close to the pawnshop and had gone in to hock his watch. He had fifty grand in his room, but he dare not touch it because it was all high-denomination stuff and was hot. A patrolman had recognized him and rang the Precinct.

We had piled down to the pawnshop and Harry had pulled a gun. He was riddled before he got anywhere close to pulling the trigger and old Eli had watched imperturbably, and hadn't even complained about the blood on the floor afterward.

He nodded in my direction. "Hullo, Lieutenant."

"Hullo, Eli," I said. "How's business?"

He shrugged his shoulders. "Not good—but then it never is."

"It might be looking up," I said. "I want to buy something."

"So?"

"A gun," I said.

"Lieutenant, you know I don't sell guns."

"I know you buy them," I said. "Along with a lot of other things that come into the back of your shop late at night, instead of over the counter in the daytime."

"What does a policeman want buying a gun?" he asked. "You get one for free, don't you?"

I grinned at him. "Just say I'm stupid, Eli. I lost mine. I want to buy another one—not as a cop, just as a private citizen."

"You have a good name in this district, Lieutenant," Eli said gently. "Even those who do not like the law in any shape or form, they say, Lieutenant Wheeler, he is not a bad sort of a guy."

"You've got me crying again, Eli," I told him.

His eyes watched me carefully. "They say Lieutenant Wheeler is a man of his word."

"Yeah," I said.

"But I am not talking to Lieutenant Wheeler?" he asked. "I am talking to Mr. Wheeler?"

"Who wants to buy a gun," I said, "for private reasons."

Eli nodded, satisfied at last. "Come into the back room, Mr. Wheeler," he said. "I might be able to help you."

I followed him into the back room, which was even darker and more musty than the shop. Eli shuffled around, then came back with a drawer which he emptied out onto the table.

I stared. There were half a dozen guns there—a Navy Colt, too badly knocked around to be a collector's piece. A nasty-looking sawn-off shotgun. A couple of .22s, a Luger .38 and a Smith & Wesson .32.

I picked up the Smith & Wesson. The serial number had been filed off. "You got some ammunition for this?" I asked.

Eli nodded. "Sure, Mr. Wheeler."

"How much for the gun?"

"Twenty dollars."

"You've made yourself a deal," I said.

He gave me the slugs. I broke open the gun, loaded it, slipped the safety on, then put it into my hip pocket. Eli escorted me to the door of the shop.

"A pleasure to do business with you, Mr. Wheeler," he said.

I walked down the street, the .32 heavy in my hip pocket. I wasn't enthusiastic about this walking—I was missing the prowl car. I didn't have enough to hire a self-drive car. The twenty bucks for the gun had left me exactly fifteen in my billfold. I knew my bank balance—nineteen dollars and thirty-five cents. I had a monthly paycheck due in two days' time.

I picked up a cab and gave him the address of the rooming house where James Kirkland lived. The same miserable-faced old woman opened the door.

"There's a policeman up there now, Lieutenant," she said with a sniff. "But I can tell you this—that man Kirkland hasn't been back and if you ask me, I don't think he's ever coming back."

"I think you could be right at that," I agreed with her.

"And who's going to pay his back rent, I'd like to know?" she sniffed.

"Charge it to experience," I suggested, then went on up the stairs.

Patrolman Rorke opened the door with a gun in his hand. "Oh—it's you, Lieutenant." He relaxed.

"Yeah," I agreed. "It's me."

I walked past him into the room. It didn't look any different. I lit a cigarette. "How long you been on duty?" I asked him.

"Four hours," he told me. "It takes a hell of a long time to go around, Lieutenant. Just sitting in here is beginning to drive me crazy."

I nodded. "Captain Parker has had a call out for him," I said. "They've checked the highways, the railroad, airport—everything that usually gets checked. But the guy has disappeared. How do you figure that, Rorke?"

"I figure he got away before we started looking for him."

"Either that or he's dead," I said. "I'd like to find out."

Rain started coming down outside in sheets, driving through the open window onto the floor.

"Better shut the window," I said. "The landlady will raise hell if she sees her floor wet."

"Yes, Lieutenant," Rorke said reluctantly. "Though if it's all the same to you, I'll take my chance on the old turnip downstairs and leave the window open."

"It doesn't worry me," I said. "I never knew you were a fresh-air fan."

He wrinkled his nose. "I am in here, all right, Lieutenant. With that window closed." He made a face. "I don't know where it comes from—the place seems reasonably clean and ..."

"Shut the window," I said.

"Huh?" Rorke looked at me blankly.

"Shut the window," I repeated.

"OK, Lieutenant—whatever you say." He shut the window and looked at me out of the corner of his eye.

I dropped my cigarette and trod on it. Then I sniffed. I saw what he meant. I sniffed again, looking around the room.

"You sure you're OK, Lieutenant?" Rorke asked anxiously.

"I'm a sucker," I said, "and so are you. And so is every cop who's been in here." I lit a fresh cigarette. "OK—open up the window again."

He opened it up with a sigh of relief. "I don't know where it comes from," he said, "but, brother. It sure is high."

"How long since you've been in the morgue?" I asked gently.

He wrinkled his forehead. "Oh—maybe six months ago. Traffic smash—bad one it was and ... Hey. So that's it."

I took a draw on the cigarette. "I looked in the cupboards the first time I was here," I said. "But I wasn't looking for a cadaver."

I looked around the room again. "I don't think anybody dug up the floor-boards and then replaced them. So what does that leave us with, Rorke?"

"I don't know, Lieutenant." His face was greenish.

"It leaves us with a bed," I said. "That brass-railed monstrosity over there. Give me a hand to lift it out."

We lugged it sideways. And there he was.

He lay on the floor quite peacefully, his arms stretched out at his sides, his knees up. There wasn't a mark on him, but I had a strong feeling that when the doc took a closer look, he'd find a faint scratch somewhere.

Rorke's face had gone a deeper stain of green. "And I've been sitting here for four hours," he said, "and all the time—under the bed."

"Yeah," I said. "It breaks my heart, too. Go down and ring Captain Parker and tell him what we've found. Then come back here and wait until the meat-wagon arrives. I've got other things to do."

"Sure, Lieutenant," he said eagerly and hustled out of the room. I lifted Kirkland's wallet out of his inside pocket and took it over to the window with me. There was around fifty bucks in cash in it, a driving license, a couple of letters. I unfolded them and read them. They both started off with "My Own Darling Jimmy" and finished up with "From your ever-loving Lola."

Maybe they'd met up again by now.

There was nothing else in the wallet. I refolded the letters, put them back, returned the wallet to his inside pocket. Then I went out of the room, closing the door behind me.

The landlady was beside the front door. "What was the matter with that cop?" she sniffed. "He went past like the house was on fire or something."

"You ever clean under the beds?" I asked her.

She sniffed angrily. "Of course I do. Let me tell you that this house is one of the cleanest in the district."

"You should have cleaned under Mr. Kirkland's bed," I said. "You'd have got a surprise."

"Oh?" she said.

"Yeah," I said. "Mr. Kirkland."

"You mean he's been hiding under that bed all this time?" she gasped.

"I mean, he's been dead under that bed all this time," I said.

She moaned softly and her eyeballs turned up. She fainted in an ungainly heap on the front doormat. I stepped over her and out into the street. I thought she was going to have one hell of a time telling the neighbors as soon as she woke up.

I got another cab uptown again. It was five-thirty when I reached the offices of Offenheim and Berkeley. I wondered if he would have gone home, but he was still there.

I walked straight through the outer office and into his office without bothering to knock. He jumped as I came in.

"Hullo, Lieutenant," he said. "I didn't hear you knock."

I lit a cigarette. "Did you buy the curare from Kirkland, or was he in on the whole thing as well?" I asked him.

He jumped again. "What are you talking about, Lieutenant?"

"The curare," I said. "The stuff Kirkland filched from Morgan and

Scheer's plant. The stuff that killed your partner, his mistress and her lover."

"I haven't the faintest idea what you're talking about," he said.

"You know," I said, "this thing is going to bust wide open any time now. If I hadn't actually killed anybody, I'd do the smart thing—I'd start talking to the nearest cop."

"Are you ill, Lieutenant?" he asked.

"Not me," I said, "I'm fine. Don't you feel lousy about Kirkland? He took the bother to come in and see you. He told you you had to protect him—and what happened to him? He wound up dead under his own bed. That's one hell of a thing to have happen to you, Berkeley. Don't you think so?"

"Get out of my office," he said. "Get out." He was shaking all over.

"Sure," I said, "I'm on my way. But think it over. Tomorrow it might be the cops doing all the talking—and they won't give you a chance to make yourself heard."

I walked out of his office again and down the stairs. I got into the street and wondered. I looked up at his office windows. I wondered again and thought maybe I could try it, anyway. Lavers could only say no.

I walked the six blocks to the city hall. The building was nearly deserted— the nine-to-five boys and girls had long gone. I walked the corridor until I came to the door with the frosted panel marked "Commissioner of Police." There was a light in the office. I knocked and waited.

"Come in," Lavers bellowed.

I opened the door and went in. The Commissioner didn't look exactly enthusiastic to see me.

"You're just wasting your time, Wheeler," he told me curtly. "Nothing will make me change my decision."

"I thought you might still be interested in breaking the Offenheim case," I said.

He glared at me. "You know damn well I am."

"Found Kirkland's body this afternoon," I said. "Under the bed in his room. Nobody thought of looking there before."

"How was he killed?"

"There wasn't a mark on him," I said. "I left before the doc arrived— but I wouldn't be surprised if it was curare again."

"You came in to tell me just that?"

I shook my head. "I came to ask you to listen to a proposition."

"What sort of proposition?"

"To help break this Offenheim case."

He took a cigar out of his drawer and lit it carefully.

"I'll listen, Wheeler," he said, "but I don't guarantee anything else."

"Get hold of O'Malley," I said. "Tell him you've got some fresh evidence on the Offenheim business. Tell him it's pretty hot and you want the lawyer Berkeley brought in straight away for questioning. Tell him to bring Berkeley straight to your office."

Lavers stared at me. "What the hell's the idea of that?"

"It's a straightforward proposition," I said. "I think it will help break the Offenheim case."

"So what questions do I ask Berkeley when he gets here?"

"It's my belief he never will get here," I said soberly. "But if he does, then ask him why Kirkland came to him and told him he'd have to protect him, because the police would find out that he had easy access to curare in the plant where he worked."

"I never heard this before," Lavers barked.

"Because I never told you before," I said. "I'm telling you now, Commissioner. Is it a deal?"

He stared at me for a long moment, then picked up the phone.

"Lavers," he growled into it. "Lieutenant O'Malley there? Yes, put him on."

He chewed his cigar and looked at me again. "I'm wondering if I should have you tossed into a cell," he said.

Then he listened. "O'Malley? Lavers here. I want you to do something right away—it's important. Do it yourself—it's in connection with the Offenheim case. I want a lawyer brought in for questioning—man named Berkeley—Offenheim's partner. Yes, right away. When you've got him, bring him to my office. I want to be present while he's questioned. What? No, I don't give a damn whether you go by yourself to bring him in or take a dozen men with you. What I want is Berkeley here in my office as soon as possible. Good."

He put the phone back on the cradle. "What happens now?" he asked me.

"We wait, Commissioner," I told him.

CHAPTER 11
Dirty Work Afoot

It was a long half-hour.

I smoked four cigarettes and Lavers finished his cigar, then lit another. The phone jangled, making us both jump. He picked it up and barked "Lavers" into it. I heard the excited voice at the other end. It talked for quite a while and Lavers listened.

"All right," he said finally. "Find him." He dropped the phone back again and looked at me.

"Berkeley wasn't in his office," he said flatly.

"You surprise me," I said.

"Yes?" he said sharply. "How did you know?"

"I just guessed," I said.

I got to my feet. "Thanks, Commissioner," I said, and headed toward the door.

"Wait a minute," he roared. "This needs some explanation."

"Have you had a look at O'Malley's bank account yet?" I asked him, then closed the door quickly before he could think of an answer.

I got another cab. I bought eight dollars' worth of ride up to Cone Hill. That left me five bucks precisely in my billfold. A policeman's lot is a hard one, as somebody once said.

I got the cab to drop me four blocks from Rowlands' house. I walked a block and found a phone booth. I got inside, found a nickel and dialed the number.

A pleasant feminine voice answered. "Mr. John H. Rowlands' residence."

"Johnnie?" I said in a husky whisper.

"Yes," she said. "Who is that?"

"Just a pal," I said. "Give you some advice."

"Who is that?"

"Pack your bags, honey," I whispered. "He's getting all ready to move in with the Offenheim dame. You've had it."

"What," she gasped.

"You know what John H. is like," I whispered. "Once he stops liking people, they get in his hair—and you know what happens to people when they get in John H.'s hair." I managed a wheezing chuckle. "Curare." Then I hung up.

I walked out of the booth wondering if it was me who was nuts and thinking it probably was. I walked the three blocks to the house without hurrying. There were no cars on the drive. I walked up the drive and rang the bell.

The door opened a couple of moments later and the silver-blonde stood there, a worried expression on her face. She was wearing a black sweater and a pair of red shorts. She looked ready to play games. I thought it would be fun to play games with a silver-blonde, but business is business, as the pie-lady used to say to Sweeney Todd.

She raised her eyebrows. "Yes?"

"You might remember me," I said. "Lieutenant Wheeler."

"Yes," she said.

"Is Mr. Rowlands home?"

"No."

"Then I'll wait." I walked toward her and she instinctively stepped back. I closed the door behind me, then turned around.

"Where would you like me to wait?"

"In here," she said and walked toward the study. I followed her, trying to keep my mind on my work and my eyes off the rear view of the red shorts.

I walked into the study and looked instinctively at the floor. There were no signs of blood anywhere. I lit a cigarette. She stood and watched me, making up her mind whether she should stay or go.

"I don't expect Mr. Rowlands home for quite a while," she said. "You may have a long wait, Lieutenant."

"I'm in no hurry," I smiled at her, "particularly with a beautiful silver-blonde to keep me company."

Her lips curled and she didn't bother to answer.

"I've been over talking to Mrs. Offenheim," I said.

Johnnie still didn't bother to answer.

I sat down in the most comfortable-looking chair and blew a smoke ring toward the ceiling. "She's a beautiful woman," I said. "I can understand Rowlands' feelings about her."

"What?" she said.

I looked at her. "She's a remarkably frank woman, that Mrs. Offenheim."

"What were you saying," Johnnie asked tautly, "about Mr. Rowlands' feelings?"

"I was just quoting her," I said. "She made no secret of the fact that she never got on with her husband. She seemed so bright just now that I asked her if she'd backed a winner or something. Then she told me."

"Told you what?" Johnnie stamped her foot with impatience.

"Why," I said, "that they're going to be married, of course."

"It's a lie," she said loudly.

"Sure," I shrugged my shoulders. "It's only a rumor."

"It's a downright dirty lie," she said.

"OK, OK," I said. "You asked me what she said. Maybe she is nuts—I don't know, or care."

"He wouldn't dare marry her," she said. "He wouldn't dare."

"Lady," I said, "this is not my fight. I wouldn't care who he married—you, even."

Her cheeks were a blazing red. "If he thinks he can get away with this, I'll ..."

"Look, honey," I said. "I'm only a dumb, hard-working cop, but one thing sticks out a mile."

"Yes?"

"You're his housekeeper, right?"

"Yes," she said tightly.

"Then it doesn't make any difference what he does—there's nothing you can do to stop him marrying her, or anyone else he feels like marrying. You start arguing and he says, OK—quit. The party's over—pack your bags and beat it. And sister," I said heavily, "there's nothing you can do about it."

She gnawed her lower lip. "Do you know a man with a husky voice, by any chance?" she asked suddenly. "Talks almost in a whisper?"

I thought for moment, then shook my head. "Offhand, I can't say I do."

"I'd like to meet him," she said. "I'd like to know where he comes from."

"Honey," I said gently, "you're a nice-looking girl with a good future. Why don't you quit now—before he gives you the rush?"

"You won't get rid of me so easily as all that," she said.

"Be sensible, Johnnie," I said. "What can you do to stop him?"

"You'd be surprised," she said darkly. "With the things I know about him, he wouldn't dare try and boot me out." She laughed unsteadily. "He wouldn't dare."

"I'd be awful careful about how you put that to him," I said slowly.

She glared at me. "What do you mean?"

"If what you say is right," I said, "then there's always another alternative, isn't there?"

"I don't follow you."

"If he doesn't want you to stay and he doesn't want you to go in case you start talking about him, then there's another thing he can do," I explained patiently. "He can send you out of the door feet first and be sure you'll never talk to anyone."

She looked at me for a long moment with fear dawning in her eyes, and at that moment we heard footsteps coming down the hall.

Rowlands came into the study, followed by Elmer.

"Johnnie, honey," he said, "I ..." Then he stopped when he saw me. "What the hell do you want?" he asked curtly.

"I just dropped by," I said casually. "I happened to be in the neighborhood."

"Then you can drop out the front door," he said curtly.

Elmer made a grunting noise. "This is da guy who fixed Rafe," he said. "I ..."

"Shut up," Rowlands told him. "On your way, Wheeler," he said. "You're cluttering up the carpet."

"That's no way to talk to a lieutenant," I said mildly.

"A suspended lieutenant," he sneered. "A busted lieutenant soon to be a goon in a blue uniform directing traffic."

"You know an awful lot for a guy who doesn't belong on the force," I told him.

"Scram," he snapped. "Before I have Elmer toss you out."

I got out of the chair leisurely. "You bury Rubens today?"

"It so happens we did," he said. "I haven't forgotten you killed him, Wheeler."

"Not me," I said. "You must be getting confused, Rowlands. You're thinking of some other guy. But I almost wish I had killed Rubens."

I started to walk toward the door that led into the hall. "How you finding our great city?" I asked Rowlands. "Much different to Chi?"

"What was that?" he asked quietly.

I turned around and leaned against the door frame.

"I wish I'd killed Rubens," I said. "Tell you why. The way I figure it, Rubens had the drop on the guy who did it, and then somehow the guy got the drop on Rubens."

Rowlands' eyes narrowed but he didn't say anything.

"Yeah," I said. "Well—during the time Rubens had the drop, he'd have probably been in an expansive mood. So the other guy could have asked him lots of questions and probably got lots of good answers. Rubens wouldn't worry about telling the truth, because he'd be thinking the other guy would be dead in a couple of minutes, anyway—see?"

"I see," he said slowly.

I turned around and walked into the hall.

"I like that theory," I said over my shoulder. "The psychology of it appeals to me. You know the one—tommy guns and bombs are old-fashioned stuff. You need something subtle to kill 'em off with. You kill a couple and the rest get so frightened you don't need to kill any more."

I reached the front door, opened it, then looked back down the hall. Rowlands was standing in the doorway of the study, watching me intently.

"How did you ever think of curare?" I asked him, then stepped out to the porch and slammed the door shut behind me, before he could answer.

"I'm not a ladylike sort of dame," she said calmly. "Maybe that is one of the reasons my late husband and I didn't get on together very well. He wasn't exciting enough for me."

I took a draw on my cigarette. "That Rowlands," I said. "He's exciting, isn't he?"

"Just what do you mean by that?" she demanded.

"That he's exciting—is that a crime?"

She started to walk back to the house. "I don't like to be rude, Lieutenant," she said. "But if this is a social call, I'm afraid my evening is already taken up."

I walked along beside her. "It's not really a social call," I said. "I wanted to check a few things with you."

"Such as?" she said. "I really am in a hurry."

"Kirkland's dead," I said. "I thought you might care to know."

Her step faltered for a moment. "Oh," she said in a low voice.

"And your husband's partner," I said. "He is missing."

She stopped still. "Is this your idea of a joke?" she asked icily.

"I never think murder is funny," I said mildly. "Your husband was murdered and now his partner is missing—and by a coincidence, missing just when the police were going to pull him in for questioning."

We reached the house and went in. She made a beeline for the bar.

"I need a drink," she said. "A visit from you is as refreshing as meeting a ghoul."

"I'm glad you like my company," I told her. "You think I'm exciting?"

She looked at me for a moment, then laughed contemptuously. "You?" she said. "What can you do?"

It seemed a stupid sort of question to ask. I took hold of her arms, just below the shoulders, forcing back the robe so that it slid down, leaving her shoulders bare. I bent her backward almost to an angle of forty-five degrees and kissed her. The way a blonde who looked the way Gail looked should be kissed. Thoroughly.

When I finally let go of her she straightened up slowly, a dazed look on her face.

"I take it all back," she said.

CHAPTER 12
Black Widow

The butler opened the door. "Good evening, Lieutenant," he said politely.

"Good evening," I said. "Mrs. Offenheim home?"

"She's out at the pool, sir," he said.

"Fine," I said and gave him my hat. "I'll go see her there."

I walked through the house and out on the terrace, where a spotlight shone over the pool. I came up to the edge of the pool and watched Gail swimming, a spot of whiteness against the dark background.

She reached the edge of the pool and pulled herself out of the water with a lithe movement, almost at my feet.

I wondered if she was wearing the bikini again or something different. She stood up and at the same moment saw me.

"What are you doing snooping?" she demanded. I handed her the robe, reluctantly.

"I can't figure why your late husband ever went away."

She slipped on the robe and knotted the cord around her waist. "Light me a cigarette," she said.

I lit two and gave her one. She took a deep inhalation, letting the smoke trickle from her mouth.

"What are you doing here again?" she asked.

"You'd better take some of that robe back," I said gently. "Before you catch cold."

She shrugged the robe back onto her shoulders. "Now I really need that drink. How did you ever get to be a lieutenant?"

"What makes you ask?" I busied myself with a bottle and two glasses.

"It must have been a full-time job getting the experience that went into that kiss," she said. "I just wondered how you had the time to be a policeman as well."

"I combined both jobs," I said modestly.

"I see," she said. "Do it again."

I put the bottle back on the bar and did it again. We were interrupted by a discreet cough from the doorway. I let her go and looked up. The butler stood there.

"Will that be all tonight, madame?" he asked.

"Yes, Cedric," she said calmly. "You can go now."

"Thank you, madame," he said. "Good night. Good night, sir."

"So long, Cedric," I said.

He went out, closing the door gently behind him.

"His night off?" I asked her.

"One of his nights off," she said. "I'm really spoiling him."

"Does that leave just the two of us in the house?" I asked her. She picked up her drink and nodded.

"How cozy," I said.

"You shouldn't have done that to me," she said suddenly.

"What?"

"Kissed me like that," she said. "I was going out."

"Anything to stop you going out now?"

"Yes—you."

I drained the drink in one gulp. "Well," I said, "well." Then I refilled the glasses.

"Still," she said, "I suppose I can always go out."

"It might rain again," I said. "It's a good night to stay at home."

"I think so, too," she agreed. She ran her hand lightly down my arm. "You've unsettled me, Aloysius—that's what you've done."

"I've unsettled myself, Abby," I snarled. "We made a pact, remember?"

"Sorry, Al," she purred. "I forgot."

I drank some of my second drink. I wished I'd stopped somewhere to eat before I called—I was hungry. The liquor was hitting an empty void which should have been packed with food.

"You'll excuse me?" she asked.

"You haven't changed your mind again?"

"No. You wait here and have another drink. I won't be long."

"Promise?"

She squeezed my arm gently. "I promise."

She went out of the room. So I had another drink—two more drinks. Then I heard her voice calling. I went out into the hall.

"Al." Gail's voice floated down to me.

"Yeah?"

"Come on up here for a moment, will you?"

"Where's up here?"

"The room straight across from the top of the stairs."

"I'm on my way."

As I started up the stairs I heard a phone start to ring, then stop again. I kept on going, made the top of the stairs and walked into the room straight across from where I stood.

It was her room. She was lying on the bed, talking into an ivory phone.

"All right," she said, "you do that." She put the phone back on the cradle and smiled at me. "Where have you been? I've been waiting for you."

I looked at her with a tightening in the back of my throat. She lay back, wearing a negligee of black lace and nylon that emphasized she was a blonde—a blonde with curves.

"Don't be frightened," she said huskily. "Come a little closer. I won't bite."

I went a little closer. I went to the edge of the bed and looked down at her. She raised her hands toward me in a welcoming gesture. Light flashed from one of her fingers. She saw me looking at it.

"Like it?" she asked. "It's my good-luck piece." She turned her hand and I saw the ring with the huge egg—like stone in a claw setting.

"Be careful you don't scratch yourself," she whispered, and her hands came up to wind around my neck.

They never did. I clipped her under the jaw with a roundhouse right. She dropped back on the pillow, out to the world. I thought it wasn't the sort of bedroom etiquette that Emily Post would have approved of, but there it was. Necessary.

I slipped the ring from her finger carefully, wrapped it in my handkerchief and shoved it into my pocket alongside my billfold. She slept peacefully on. I hoped for her sake she didn't bruise. A bruise would have spoiled that magnificent profile.

I went down the stairs and out of the house. I walked half a dozen blocks, looking for a cab and not finding one. I kept on walking. The rain came down suddenly again, soaking me to the skin. I thought a copper's life was a hell of a life, but a suspended copper's was far worse. Finally I made a bus station, waited half an hour and then caught a bus back to town.

I reached the house, thinking of nothing else but a shower and a drink. I pushed the key into the lock, opened the door and stepped inside.

I switched on the light and saw I had a visitor sitting in the living room. He wasn't playing hi-fi, he wasn't drinking. When I got closer and had a good look at him, he wasn't even breathing.

I thought it was an untidy way for a lawyer to wind up his affairs. There were no visible marks on him, not that I expected any. One thing about this curare, it did a neat job—and it had done a neat job on Berkeley.

Somebody pushed a gun into my ribs.

"Relax, Lieutenant," Elmer's voice grated, "unless you want a hole right through you."

I relaxed. I'm very good at relaxing when there's a gun pointing at me, let alone pushing my ribs in.

I was giving a party and I didn't know it. They must have been in the bedroom. I'd had my back to the door while I took a close look at Berkeley's corpse. It was my mistake.

Elmer was the guy pressing the gun in my back. There was another hood who looked just as vicious. And there was someone else, too—the second guy brought her into the room. Mona, with a gag tied across her mouth and her hands tied behind her back. That I didn't like.

The other hood pushed her into a chair, then came across and stood in front of me. He patted my pockets, lifting the gun from my hip pocket. Then he hit me across the face with the barrel. It hurt. I felt a trickle of blood run down my cheek and into the corner of my mouth. It was a hell of a way to get a drink.

"Copper," he said softly, then hit me again.

"Don't waste time," Elmer said harshly. "The boss said we got to hurry back."

"OK," the hood said. "It's just that I don't like coppers." He hauled off ready to hit me again.

"I said can it," Elmer said. "Listen, Hymie—go get the car and bring it up outside the gate."

"OK," Hymie said reluctantly. He put the gun in his pocket and went out.

I stood in silence, feeling the pain in my face getting worse and seeing Mona's eyes looking at me helplessly. If I'd had a prowl car, I thought, and I hadn't had to wait for a bus, then ... What the hell was the use of thinking maybes? It had happened, hadn't it?

Hymie came back inside. "The car's ready," he said. "Do we go?"

"Take the dame and put her in the back," Elmer said. "You get in the front and drive."

Hymie walked over to the chair and hauled Mona on to her feet. "OK, sister," he said. "Start walking for the car." Then he pushed her in the back so that she stumbled toward the door.

"All right, copper," Elmer said softly. "You walk out there and get in beside the dame. Try anything and it'll be a pleasure to let you have it. I'm sitting right beside you when we get into the car—with a gun in your ribs."

So that's the way it was.

We rode in silence. The rain started again and the monotonous click of the wiper nearly drove me nuts.

"You mind if I smoke?" I asked Elmer.

"Help yourself," he said.

I fumbled around in my pockets before I got the pack out and managed to get my handkerchief with the ring inside it into my hand before I lit the cigarette.

We got back to Cone Hill. I thought for an exclusive district it was packing a lot of mayhem around the place. The car turned into the drive of Gail's place, ran up close to the front porch, then stopped.

Elmer got out, the gun still in his hand, and held the door open.

"Come with me, pal," he said. "I get lonely."

We walked up to the porch and he rang the buzzer. Nobody answered. He tried a couple more times, then grunted, "Nobody home—maybe she's already over at the boss's place."

So we went back to the car.

At Rowlands' house, there was a reception committee waiting for us when we were ushered into the lounge room. There was Rowlands and Gail. And standing behind them was Johnnie.

Hymie dumped Mona into a chair and took off her gag. Elmer stood with his back to the door, the gun still in his hand, watching me stolidly. As we'd got out of the car, I'd managed to drop the handkerchief onto the floor. I hoped nobody went back to look.

For a moment we made a tableau like so many waxworks, then Gail stepped forward and let go with a swinging right. The back of her open hand cracked against the side of my face, jerking it around quickly.

"That's for you," she said. "Wise guy."

Rowlands grinned. "You don't seem popular, Lieutenant. I wonder why?"

"Even my best friends wouldn't tell me," I said, "and now it's too late."

"Too late is right," he agreed cheerfully.

"Where is my ring?" Gail asked tautly.

"I dropped it someplace," I said. "When I left your house, I guess. I was running in the rain and it must have dropped out of my pocket."

"You're lying," she said.

I shrugged my shoulders. "I dropped it, lost it. That's all I know."

She went through my pockets until she was convinced I didn't have it with me. Then she hit me again. "You clumsy fool."

"Skip it, Gail," Rowlands said. "We've got other things to do, more important things."

She stepped back, a nasty look on her face. I was glad she stepped back out of range—my face was beginning to feel like a piece of raw steak.

I felt around and found another cigarette, then lit it.

"Do me a favor," I said. "Tell me something—how the hell do you expect to get away with all this? First Offenheim, then Lola Laverne, Kirkland; and after him, Berkeley."

"We'll get away with it, copper," Rowlands said softly. "It's like Dale Carnegie says—all a question of influencing people. Death is the biggest influence I know. Then there's always the character they used to refer to in Chi as the fall guy."

"Don't tell me you're fixing me as the fall guy," I said. "That I'd like to hear."

He shook his head. "You're going to quit. Suspended cop gets bitter is the story. Throws in his hand, beats it out of the city limits, swearing he'll never come back. And that's for sure," he added softly. "You'll never come back."

"You still need a fall guy," I said.

"Supposing Lola killed Offenheim," he said, "for the dough he was going to leave her. And supposing Kirkland found out and blew his top when he did. Supposing he killed her, then got remorse and killed himself?"

I shook my head. "It's got more holes than an exploded paper bag. How about Berkeley, then? Why did he die?"

"Because he'd told Lola the terms of Offenheim's will," he said. "Maybe even suggested to her that she could hasten nature along. That the quicker Offenheim kicked off, the quicker she'd get the dough. He wanted the business for himself, of course. So when the cops told him he was wanted for questioning, he panicked— and killed himself—thought they knew he was an accessory before the fact."

"You've got all the terms right," I said. Then I asked as casually as I could, "And how about Mona here?"

"She went with you when you quit the big city," he grinned. "That will add up OK. She's a great friend of yours, isn't she? You spend your time together."

"Yeah," I said slowly.

Rowlands nodded, with a satisfied look on his face. "We don't think we'll have any real trouble, copper. You've got an added reason for quitting town—you bumped off Rubens, remember?"

I thought maybe he could make it work.

Rowlands looked at his watch. "We've got plenty of time," he said. "I've got to go to town and pick up a guy first."

He turned to Hymie. "Take them down to the study—tie 'em up to chairs in there. They'll keep in there until I come back."

"Sure, boss," Hymie said.

"I'll give you a hand," Elmer said. He picked up Mona and escorted her from the room again. They'd taken the gag off, but still left her hands bound.

Gail stepped forward and hit me again. "You were lucky you hit me," she said. "You don't know how lucky."

"I've got a fair idea," I said. "Anyway—let's not have any hard feelings, Gail. I wish you the best of luck in your new marriage."

"New marriage?"

"Go on." I grinned at her. "You told me you and Rowlands are getting married just as soon as this business is cleared up."

"You're crazy," she said.

"OK," I sighed. "If that's the way you want it—I'm crazy."

I saw the look of hatred in Johnnie's eyes as she glared at Gail's back.

A gun poked me in the ribs. "Come on, pal," Hymie said. "We don't have all day."

CHAPTER 13
Snakebite

We sat in the study, facing one another. They'd left the light off, so I could only see a faint white blur which I knew was Mona's face. My hands were tied together behind the chair and my feet tied separately to the front legs of the chair.

"Al?" Mona said in a small voice.

"Yes, honey?"

"Will they do it?"

"Do what?"

"Take us outside the city, then let us go?"

"Sure," I said. "They just want us out of the way."

"I wish I could be so damned naive as that question," she said. "They're going to kill both of us, aren't they?"

"I guess so," I said.

She was silent for a while. "My head aches trying to work the thing out," she said. "Do you know what it's all about?"

"I've got a fair idea," I said. "How did they get you?"

"There was a knock on the door," she said. "I thought it was you come back. I hoped it was you, after all the terrible things I said to you."

"I asked for everything you said," I told her. "I got you into this thing in the first place."

"I don't mind," she said almost fiercely. "I'm glad."

There is no accounting for dames, as Solomon said, and he should have known—he had one for every mealtime of the year.

"You were going to tell me what it's all about," Mona said.

"Yeah," I agreed.

I was wondering how long O'Malley was going to be and I was hoping it was going to be a long time. The longer the time he was, the longer the time Johnnie had to burn. And I hoped she was really burning by now.

"Well?" Mona said.

"A lot of this is guesswork," I told her, "but I think it's more or less right. Take a successful lawyer—that's Offenheim—and take his beautiful wife, who is bored by life in general and him in particular. Take his partner, whose ambition it is to own the business—and take his mistress, who only wants his money. And there you have a setup that spells trouble."

"Go on," she said.

I cleared my throat. My face still ached like hell.

"That's the keg of dynamite," I said. "Then along comes the fuse. A bright new racketeer in town—John H. Rowlands, all the way from Chicago. One of his boys is in trouble, a murder rap, so he goes to the lawyer. The lawyer sees a lot of work and a lot of dough in a guy like Rowlands, so he cultivates him—takes him home, introduces him to his wife. Gail was so careful to tell me she never met Rowlands that I wondered why.

"So Rowlands sees that the wife is bored and beautiful and attracted to him. And Berkeley, watching carefully from the sidelines, sees too. So now the fuse is smoldering. He fans it into flame by letting Rowlands know the terms of Offenheim's will. That he leaves a hundred thousand bucks each to his wife and his mistress. Rowlands mentions it to Gail, and they get their heads together."

"You should get a job with a radio session, Al," she said. "You make it sound good."

"At least that's something," I said. "I haven't handled things very well. OK—then another guy appears in the picture. An earnest young man who loves but loves Lola Laverne, and his name is James Kirkland. He's a manufacturing chemist. He sees Gail, tells her he wants to set Lola free of Offenheim's clutches. And Gail suggests there might be a way.

"Rowlands is also busy establishing himself in the gambling rackets around the town and meeting some opposition. From his training in Chi, he figures that opposition is best eliminated but he also favors a psychological approach. Kill them in a nasty sort of way or a frightening sort of way and a lot of the living scare. It's economical, as Rafe Rubens so proudly told me."

The white blur across the room from me moved. "It sounds like it's getting complicated," she said.

"It is," I agreed. "But sooner or later Rowlands and Gail click on the point that Kirkland is a chemist. I guess he told Gail what sort of work he did—processing curare into anesthetics and so on. And to Rowlands it must have been a gift from the gods. So they persuaded Kirkland that the only way to true love was the removal of Offenheim from the scene—permanently. And some curare was just the stuff to help him on his way.

"So he got them the curare—they gave it to Offenheim. You only need a scratch and that's it. And Offenheim died. So far so good. I bought into the case at Parker's directive. I questioned Gail, then Berkeley. I got the name and address of Lola Laverne.

"Now there'd been a snag. Kirkland must have told Lola what had happened—or what was going to happen—and she was in a panic. That put Kirkland in a panic, so he told Rowlands. And Rowlands sent a couple of his boys around to tell her to keep quiet—or else. When she answered the door to me, she said something about you can tell Johnny to ... and then I told her who I was."

The blur nodded. "I'm still with you—I think. But who killed her?"

"Whoever it was," I told her, "was already there when I called. They hid in the bathroom, telling Lola to either get rid of me or distract me so I could be tapped on the skull. Lola was in a panic but she did it quite successfully, so that whoever it was in the bathroom could knock me out. But then they decided that Lola was too much of a risk, so she was disposed of, as well.

"They got away with that one. But then Kirkland panicked. When I questioned him and found out what he was, he knew it wouldn't take long for the police to find out exactly what it was he manufactured. He was scared solid by then—scared of me, the police, and Rowlands. He ran yelling, you remember, to Berkeley, saying that Berkeley had to protect him. And I don't doubt that Berkeley passed the good word to Rowlands—and Kirkland was taken care of."

Mona didn't say anything for a moment. "You still with me?" I asked her.

"It's horrible," she whispered. "Horrible."

"Murder is," I agreed. "You can throw in for good measure that Rowlands had a pipeline into Homicide—O'Malley. I got Lavers to order O'Malley to bring in Berkeley for questioning. If O'Malley was the leak in

Homicide, then he'd tip off Rowlands so that he could grab Berkeley before the cops. Which he did—and shut Berkeley's mouth permanently for him."

"You mean, you deliberately engineered it so that they would go out and kill him?"

"There was a chance that they wouldn't," I said. "I had to be quite sure about O'Malley, you see."

"But—but you sentenced Berkeley to death by doing that."

"He had it coming," I said. "He was as much to blame as the person who actually killed the others—anyway, so there we are. That's the story and a lot of good it'll do us."

"It's something to know, anyway," she said.

We were silent again.

"What time is it?" she asked finally.

"I wouldn't have the faintest idea," I said. "It must be late."

"I guess so. Al?"

"Yeah?"

"Do you love me?"

"I guess so."

"You don't sound enthusiastic."

"I have things on my mind," I said heavily.

"Well—do you?" she persisted.

"Yeah," I said.

"Enough to marry me?"

"I don't think Rowlands would send out for a preacher," I said carefully.

She made an impatient sound. "Don't be stupid. I just want to know—if this hadn't happened. Would you have married me."

"I don't know, honey," I said. "I don't think I can afford hi-fi and a wife."

"You," she said. "You're nothing but a—"

"Shut up," I said.

"What?"

"Shut up," I repeated. "Somebody's coming in."

She was quiet and I listened tensely. I thought I'd heard the door creak and as I listened I heard it creak again. Ghostly footsteps came toward me and I felt the hair on the nape of my neck beginning to rise. Had they changed their plans—decided to kill us now rather than later?

A soft hand touched mine and I nearly jumped out of the ropes that held me to the chair.

"Don't make a sound," she whispered.

"Johnnie?"

"Yes," she said. "You were right. I can see it now—when this is finished, they'll be together. I can see the kiss-off in his eyes every time he looks at me now. He thinks he can empty me out of his life like an ashcan." Her voice broke. "Well, I'm going to show him just how wrong he is."

"Sure, Johnnie," I said. "Sure."

She was around the back of me. "I'll loosen these ropes," she said. "I don't want to cut them because they'd see if they'd been cut as soon as they came in."

"Sure," I said.

She fumbled around for what seemed a hell of a long time. "Where is everybody?" I asked her.

"She's in the living room," she told me. "Elmer and Hymie are there, too. They're still waiting for Rowlands to come back—he's bringing his friend with him."

"O'Malley," I said. She was still playing around. The sweat was beginning to drop from my forehead. I thought anytime now one of the others will come in and that will be that.

At last I felt the ropes loosen.

"How's that?" she asked.

"Fine," I said. There was enough play for me to free my hands.

"What are you going to do?"

"I'm getting out," she said, "right now."

"Do something else for me," I said.

"What's that?"

"Ring Captain Parker—Twelfth Precinct. Tell him what has happened and where we are."

"I was going to ring the police, anyway," she said. "Captain Parker?"

"Twelfth Precinct. And thanks a million, Johnnie."

She moved almost noiselessly toward the door again. I heard it creak, then she was gone. I started to loosen the ropes around my wrists a little bit more so I could untie the ropes that held my legs to the chair, when the light suddenly went on.

I froze, blinking against the light, looking down to see if it was obvious that the ropes around my arms were loose. It wasn't. That was something, anyway. Not much—but something.

My eyes got used to the sudden light and I looked up as the door closed with a click. Gail stood there, leaning against the door for a moment, then she straightened up and walked into the room. She was wearing a wine-red gown that molded her figure from the bosom to the hips, then relaxed just enough to allow her to walk. She looked like a million.

She came into the center of the room between the two of us and smiled.

"You kidded me, Aloysius," she said reproachfully. "You said you'd lost my ring and all the time it was in the car." She held out her hand and I saw the rock glittering in the light.

"I'm glad you found it," I said. I had difficulty in talking—my tongue seemed stuck to the roof of my mouth.

"Naughty Al," she purred.

She turned around slowly, with all her reflexes not quite functioning a hundred percent. She was high. I didn't like that.

I wished she was sober. She was dangerous enough sober, but near drunk I thought she'd be ten times worse.

"How are you, honey?" she cooed at Mona, who glared back at her without saying anything. "Huh," Gail said. "You've sure got a dumb girlfriend, all right, Al. She can't even speak."

"I've got nothing to say to you, you murderess," Mona said,

"Oh, my," Gail said lightly. "The way you do talk." Then she turned around to look at me again. "How is she, Al?" she asked. "In the clinches, I mean. Good?"

"OK," I said.

"Do you have to talk to the woman?" Mona asked me frostily. I had to talk to her. For a reason Mona didn't know anything about—yet.

"Sure, Gail," I said. "She's not bad in the clinches—almost as good as you are."

"Huh." Gail swayed slightly on her feet. "Nobody could be that good—'cept me. You know that, Al. You sweep a girl off her feet until she's all ready to surrender, then what do you do? Knock her out."

"That was a mistake," I said.

"You've made a lot of mistakes, Al," she said. "A whole lot. And it's too late to do anything about them—but I'm going to do something for you, Al. Something for you and the child bride here. Make things easier for you."

She held her hand up under the light and watched the sparkle of the rock for a few moments.

"Pretty," she said.

"Is Rowlands back yet?" I asked her for something to say. My tongue still wanted to stick to the roof of my mouth.

"Not yet." She shook her head. "We're getting tired of waiting for him. You know something, Al?"

"Not a thing," I said.

"You know, that Rowlands is cruel. He's planning on tipping you both on the city dump—right at the bottom of it, he says, where the rats will get rid of the evidence."

Mona's scream was cut off as she bit down on it.

"I don't think it's right," Gail went on indignantly. "All that mental trouble. I'll be thinking about it all the time you're riding in the car up there." She smiled woozily at me. "But never you mind, Al pal." She nodded to herself. "Little ol' Gail's going to fix everything up so you won't feel a thing."

She walked toward Mona, her hand outstretched in front of her. "Look at that, honey," she purred. "Isn't that a pretty thing?"

"Gail," I said. "No. "'

"Why not, Al?"

"Me first," I said. "Please."

She stopped for a moment, undecided. Then slowly she turned around and walked toward me.

"OK, Al, if that's the way you want it—don't ever say Gail doesn't do things for anybody."

She came toward me, her hand outstretched. She got within a couple of feet of my chair and stopped, looking down at me for a moment.

"You knew, didn't you?" she said.

"Yeah," I said. "Hence the sock on the jaw."

"It would have been so much easier for you, Al," she said. "You could have died in my arms."

"You killed them," I said, "all of them?"

She looked at the ring again. "Such a pretty bauble," she said, "and so deadly. A touch of the curare on that claw setting—an accidental scratch—and it's all over."

"I figured it," I said. "I wanted to make sure."

"Never mind, Al," she said. "Your troubles are nearly over." There was a look in her eyes that I'd never seen in any woman's eyes before and I never wanted to see again. A gloating, evil look.

The look in the eyes of a snake the moment before it strikes.

She drew her hand back and then it flashed toward my face, the ring glittering, throwing shreds of light into my eyes.

At the same moment I pulled against the ropes and they parted. My hands caught her wrist and stopped her hand a few inches from my face. She was off balance and maybe the alcoholic reflexes didn't help, either. She stumbled forward and her face came down sharply, hitting her hand.

She straightened up again abruptly and I let go of her wrist. There was a jagged scratch across her right cheek. Her trembling fingers touched it.

"No," she whispered hoarsely. "I ... No. No. No." Her voice hit a rising crescendo, then stopped suddenly.

The color drained away from her face as the muscles suddenly relaxed. Her mouth sagged open and she looked for a moment like a child who has lost her favorite toy.

Then she dropped dead at my feet.

CHAPTER 14
One-Man Police Force

I frantically untied the ropes that held me to the chair. I tumbled onto my feet, feeling the pins and needles as the blood started to circulate again. I walked over to where Mona sat, her face a mask of horror.

"You stay right here," I told her. "I'll be back."

"Don't leave me, Al," she pleaded. "Don't leave me."

"Honey," I said, "it's better this way. If anyone comes in, you drop your head and play dead." Then I had a sudden inspiration. "Here." I scratched my thumbnail across her cheek and she gasped.

"Are you crazy, Al?"

"If anyone comes in," I said, "you play dead. They'll see Gail dead and they'll think that she killed you first, then I killed her. This is the best way, baby—it's safest."

I went out of the room quickly before she could argue anymore, closing the door after me. I stood in the hall for a moment. I could hear voices coming from the living room—slurred voices. I guessed the boys were hitting the bottle while they waited for Rowlands. That was fine.

I went out the back way, letting myself out the kitchen door, then cat-footing along the drive by the side of the house until I reached the front.

I went a little way down the drive. Now was the time when I wanted Rowlands to arrive. I waited for five minutes, ten minutes, chewing my fingernails. Then I saw headlights coming down the street outside.

I ducked down behind a large shrub in the center of the lawn. The headlights slowed then turned into the drive. The car rolled past me about five yards, then stopped. O'Malley and Rowlands got out.

As they took a step toward the house, I saw that O'Malley was in front and Rowlands had a gun in his back.

"Look," O'Malley said, his voice a fear-driven whine. "You won't get away with it—you can't."

"I didn't expect you to get soft, pal," Rowlands said softly. "I thought you were tough."

"I didn't mind taking your dough to tip you off when it was just a question of some graft," O'Malley whined. "But murder's different."

"You got your conscience just a bit too late, pal," Rowlands said. "You can take the same ride another lieutenant's going to take. It should be nice for you. You can swap stories with Wheeler about the days when you both pounded a beat."

They walked up onto the porch. Rowlands reached out with his free hand and rang the bell.

I stood up and cupped my hands to my mouth, and yelled so it practically uprooted my lungs.

"All right, men," I screamed. "Go get 'em. Shoot on sight. Murphy. Get that spotlight on the door. Joe. Get your men around the back."

They spun around, startled, craning their necks to see the carloads of cops they expected for the moment. But it wasn't their reactions I was interested in.

I ducked and ran to the car, opening the door and sliding into the driving seat. The key was in the ignition. I kicked over the motor, reversed down the drive, switched on the headlights and drove forward, going off the drive and heading toward the front.

The headlights bathed the porch in brilliant light. O'Malley and Rowlands shielded their eyes against the glare and I thought desperately if it doesn't happen now, it never will happen.

And then it did happen.

One of the front windows was flung open and a hail of lead poured across the porch. O'Malley went down, his arms and legs jerking grotesquely. Rowlands staggered forward, then straightened up and started to run toward the car. I let in the clutch and stamped on the gas pedal. The car surged forward.

For a fleeting moment I saw the horror and fear on his face and then I saw nothing. I only felt the bump.

The house surged forward to meet me. I kept my foot down on the gas pedal until the last moment, then flung myself down between the front seat and floor of the car.

There was a terrific impact and I felt as if I was being pushed forward into the engine. There was a rain of falling glass and the agonized screech of bending metal. Then silence.

The offside door was hanging open, bent out of shape. I wriggled forward and dropped to the ground. Lead poured from the front window into the car. I was glad I had the car between me and that window.

I wriggled forward on my stomach, onto the porch. My hands touched something wet and sticky. A pool. A moment later I found O'Malley. He was dead, almost cut to pieces by the lead.

I dove my right hand inside his jacket and pulled out the .32. I thumbed back the safety and got going. I made the front door which was shut. I fired a slug into the lock, then kicked and the door swung open.

I lurched forward into the hall.

The door of the living room was half open. Hymie appeared suddenly, a Luger in his hand. I pumped my finger automatically, seeing his face disintegrate. I still kept on going. I didn't have a cohesive thought in my head. Only that nothing could stop me.

I kicked the door wide open and plaster dribbled down from an inch above my head, where somebody's slug had bitten into the wall.

Suddenly it was quiet again, except for the roaring in my ears. I looked around slowly—the room was deserted.

So Elmer wasn't there.

I remembered I'd left Mona then, tied hand and foot in the other room. I went out of the living room in a stumbling run, heading toward the study. The door was shut tight. I tried the handle—it was locked. I pounded on it with my fist.

"Open up," I shouted. "You've got no chance, Elmer. The place is lousy with cops."

There was no sound from inside.

I thought he was waiting for me the other side of the door. A guy can only have so much luck. I had it when I made the front door. I had it again when I made the living room and got Hymie, instead of him getting me. I didn't want to crowd that sort of luck.

I pounded on the door and yelled some more for the effect, then catfooted out the back, through the kitchen. I went along on the grass until I faced the window of the study. The curtains were drawn and I couldn't see in.

"Here goes nothing," I told myself and started to run.

About four feet from the window I took a running jump, and tucked my head into my shoulder as I did so.

I felt my shoulder hit the glass, then there was a terrific noise as it splintered in all directions and the next moment I felt sharp little pricks all over my face. And the moment after that I hit the floor of the study.

I rolled a couple of times, then came up on my feet, remembering the way the judo expert had taught me in the marines. He would have been proud of me that night. I came up on my feet in one smooth movement, the gun ready in my hand.

And then I saw what was happening in the room.

Mona sat slumped in her chair and in the fleeting second that I looked at her I saw her cautiously open one eye to see what was going on, and my heart sang, as some lame-brained poet once said.

In the center of the floor sat Elmer, with Gail's head cradled in his lap. He looked at me dully while his hand held one of hers and stroked it, gently.

"She's dead," he said softly.

"And so will you be if you don't get on your feet," I told him. He looked at me and his fingers carefully slid the ring from Gail's finger. I watched him do it. I saw him hold it, look at it and shudder.

I was curious. So I still waited ...

He lifted the ring slowly and then his head dropped onto his hand in a dead faint. The scratch on his face showed livid for a moment.

"Congratulations, pal," I told him. "You have saved the State some considerable expense."

He didn't hear me.

I walked over to Mona's chair and started to untie the ropes that bound her.

"What happened?" she asked. "Did the marines arrive?"

"Just me, baby," I told her. "Everything's under control now."

I heard the dull thump as Elmer keeled over and wondered if he'd be missed by any of the boys in Chi. I went on undoing the ropes.

"I'm not a boasting man, honey," I said. "But you remember those two characters Rowlands and Hymie? Well, I took care of them."

"They're dead?" she asked.

"Definitely," I said.

The wail of sirens split the night.

"What's that?" Mona asked as she stood up painfully, massaging her wrists.

"The boy scouts," I told her. "They must have stopped to do a good deed on the way."

CHAPTER 15
Wedding Belles

I had made a mess of my face.

They'd got a doc to take out the bits of glass and then they'd stuck iodine over the little holes and plaster over the bigger ones. I looked like an unfinished jigsaw puzzle.

Parker had had the sense to get some coffee, buckets of it, and I was well into the third bucket. Mona sat opposite me, looking proud, and beside her sat Johnnie, looking sad for the guy she'd loved.

Lavers was there, and the D.A.

In between cups of coffee, I told them the story—more or less.

When I'd finished, Lavers smiled. It was quite an event—it was the first time I'd ever seen him smile.

"That's good work, Lieutenant," he said. "Good work."

The D.A. frowned. "What I'm not quite clear about," he said, "is how Rowlands died?"

"He committed suicide," I told him. "Threw himself under the wheels of a moving vehicle."

"Oh," the D.A. said doubtfully. "Who was driving the moving vehicle?"

"It just so happened I was," I said. "I shouted to him to get out of the way, but he wouldn't listen. Then it was too late."

"I bet you shouted real loud," Parker said, grinning into his coffee cup.

"Real loud," I said innocently.

Lavers lit a cigar. "It's quite obvious to me," he said flatly, "that one of them killed Rubens and tried to fix the blame on Wheeler here, knowing that he was hot on their trail."

"Quite," the D.A. said.

"So there is no reason for the Lieutenant to remain suspended," Lavers went on. "Or in fact to have ever been suspended."

"Quite," the D.A. agreed.

"So," Lavers continued, "there only remains the question of Wheeler having lost his gun. I consider a reprimand is sufficient to cover that."

"Quite," Parker said quickly and the D.A. gave him a hostile look for stealing his line.

Lavers looked at me severely. "Lieutenant," he said, "you were careless in losing your gun. Please don't do it again."

"No, sir," I said earnestly. "I won't."

Lavers looked at the D.A. "One further point remains," he said. "We're short of a detective in the Homicide squad. Furthermore, we need someone to boss it. I have a certain man in mind. I'd like your views on it."

"I heartily concur," the D.A. said. "I think Wheeler deserves it." His face glowed. "To have rid the community of an evil like that propagated by Rowlands is a great thing. It will further strengthen the faith of the community in their chosen officers, appointed to maintain law and order. Law and order, gentlemen, that must be tempered with justice and mercy. But in this case, there was no question of mercy for ..."

I wondered if he'd suddenly gone nuts, then I remembered the elections came up in a couple of months. No wonder the D.A. was happy and already practicing his speech.

"Yeah," Lavers said hastily, shutting him up. "So far as this girl is concerned," he nodded in Johnnie's direction, "she was instrumental in saving Wheeler. I think there is no case against her. None at all."

"Quite," the D.A. agreed.

Mona took hold of Johnnie gently by the arm and led her out of the office.

The D.A. got onto his feet. "Well, gentlemen," he said, "I'm proud to be associated with you." He looked down at his watch. "I think I'll go straight to my office and get a statement ready."

He stroked his moustache gently. "The press, of course, will want all the information they can get."

He went out of the office, whistling happily to himself.

Lavers watched him go. "You'll be lucky if you get a mention, Wheeler," he said drily. He hauled himself onto his feet. "I'm glad they got O'Malley," he said. "I don't like a cop standing trial—it doesn't look good."

"Sure," I said.

He looked at Parker. "I want him up at Homicide as soon as I can get him. They'll be restless up there."

"OK," Parker sighed. "If you want him, Commissioner, you got him, I guess. I'll have to make do with orthodox cops from here on." He smiled wryly. "I have a feeling that life is going to be dull around the Twelfth Precinct."

"Well," Lavers said, "I'll leave you boys to sort it out. When you're ready to take over, Lieutenant, come in and see me in my office."

"Yes, sir," I said, "and thank you."

"No," his lips twitched, "thank you."

He went out of the office. I looked at Parker.

"I guess you had it coming, Al," he said. "I'm sorry to lose you, but I guess life will be a lot quieter."

"I won't have to argue about prowl cars anymore," I told him. "Imagine. I'll just give myself permission to use one."

I walked out of Parker's office and past the guys on night shift grouped in the detectives' room.

"Well," Rigorski said in an awed voice. "Look at him. Flash Gordon of the Homicide squad."

"Next time you say that," I bared my teeth at him, "smile ..."

I went on out of the Precinct. There was another day outside, with the sun filtering down onto the streets. The streets looked clean and deserted—almost.

Mona stood on the curb, waiting for me. "Where's Johnnie?" I asked her.

"I gave her the key to my place," she said, "and sent her there in a cab."

"Oh," I said. "What are you going to do?"

"Listen to some hi-fi," she said cryptically.

There was a prowl car against the curb. "Wait a minute," I said. I went back inside the Precinct.

Sergeant Macnamara looked up at me from his desk. "Was there something else, Lieutenant?" he asked.

"Yeah," I said. "Will you tell Captain Parker that the chief of the Homicide squad just requisitioned one of his prowl cars?"

"Sure, Lieutenant," Macnamara said with a straight face.

"Only don't tell him for five minutes or so," I said. "Not until after I've gone."

"Sure, Lieutenant," he winked slowly.

I went outside again, bundled Mona into the prowl car and drove home.

It was still a nice morning when we got there.

I put some Dave Brubeck on the turntable, while Mona went into the kitchen. I had a shower—a shave was out of the question—then put on some clean clothes.

The smell of coffee drifted in from the kitchen. I sniffed it appreciatively. It was bolstered by the smell of frying bacon and I sniffed that even more appreciatively.

Boss of the Homicide squad. That would lift my seniority—give me a raise. If I didn't pull any boners, I'd be a captain within a year. That would be another substantial raise. With a permanent prowl car for my own use, I could almost afford to get married.

Be nice having somebody else cook the breakfast—make the bed, put the discs on the turntable. Maybe there was something in it at that.

I went into the kitchen. "How's it going, baby?" I asked her.

"Fine," she said. "Two minutes. You watch the bacon while I shower."

"OK," I said.

I watched the bacon, I served it. I had everything ready by the time she came back. I nearly dropped the percolator when I saw her.

She was wearing one of my shirts.

"What's the idea?" I asked her.

"I thought I would get into something comfortable," she said complacently.

"Yeah," I said. I suddenly realized I wasn't half so tired as I thought I was.

We finished breakfast and lit cigarettes to go with the second cup of coffee.

Mona crossed her legs. I noticed the tan was slightly fainter. "You're losing your tan," I told her.

"I need some more sun," she said.

"Miami's a good place for sun," I said. "They have lots of it down there."

"So I hear," she agreed.

I cleared my throat a couple of times. "Mona," I said.

"Yes?"

"I love you."

"That's nice," she said.

"Nice."

"Well—you wouldn't want me to think it was horrible, would you?"

I cleared my throat a couple of times more. "Mona," I said.

"Yes?"

"Will you marry me?"

She looked at me for a moment and I saw the tears in her eyes.

I thought that's great—she loves me so much she ... But then she couldn't hold back the suppressed laughter any longer.

She sat there and laughed until she nearly cried. I would have thrown the percolator at her, but there was still a cup left in it.

Finally she subsided.

"What's so funny about being married to me?" I asked indignantly.

"It would be fine," she told me. "Wonderful. Never a dull moment. After what I've been through the last couple of days and you want me to make a career of it. You think I'm crazy?"

"But ..." I said.

"Being questioned by police under bright lights—insulted by them. Kidnapped at gunpoint. Nearly murdered by a crazy woman. Gunshots everywhere. People hurtling through windows into rooms. You think I want to buy that for the rest of my life?"

"Well ..."

"Because if you do, you're a lot more crazy than even I thought you were," she said.

Then her face softened. "I have to admit that I'm very flattered at your wanting to marry me, Al," she said. "If you had any other sort of job, I'd jump at the chance. But I couldn't stand up to it. That Captain of yours at the Precinct says you're unorthodox and he's so right. You would die of boredom after six months of marriage."

In spite of myself, a feeling of relief stole over me. "Maybe you're right," I said. "Maybe you're right."

"But if you're talking about a vacation in Miami," she said, "count me in."

"Sure," I said. "Just as soon as I get that Homicide squad licked into shape and ..."

"You've fixed up three more murders," she sighed.

"I know."

She got up and walked into the living room. There's something about a girl in a shirt walking. The girl, I mean, not the shirt walking. The hell with it. There was something about Mona, anyway.

Brubeck was signing off as we came in and the speakers were silent.

"Well," Mona turned toward me, "what do we do now?"

I walked past her to the window and carefully pulled down the blind. I went into the hall and carefully locked the front door. Mona followed me around, her eyes wide.

"Al," she said, as I took her into my arms.

"You know me," I told her. "Unorthodox."

The End

Delilah Was Deadly

— — — —

Carter Brown

When they open the safe and find a guy inside strangled by a nylon girdle nobody remembers putting him there for safe-keeping.

Me, I'm not surprised.

It's an unorthodox murder and it looks like the Commissioner's giving it to me. This bright theory they got that it needs an unorthodox cop to solve it. That one, and the following three murders. Someone's throwing corpses around so fast I'd call a cop only I'd look sort of silly if I did.

Getting back to the first corpse. He worked for a fashion magazine and their set-up makes less sense than a Salvador Dali original.

The only things that made sense, like always, were the dames around the place. All over the place: my place ... their place ... it got confusing when I couldn't remember their names. But who wants to talk to a beautiful blonde, brunette, or redhead ...?

Then the Commissioner wants to fire me just because I don't report a murder I eye-witness, something about me being in charge of Homicide and setting an example. I'm setting an example all right—I figure I might even work out who'd done it. If I live that long.

CHAPTER 1
Exclusive

Cameron sat there with a sort of stupid look on his face.

"Let's take it easy, Lieutenant," I said patiently. "Take it from the beginning."

"Sure," he muttered. He cleared his throat a couple of times. "Well, there was the corpse."

"That's a good starting point," I said encouragingly.

"This little guy," he winced, "wearing pink silk pyjamas with a rosebud on the pocket."

I winced with him.

"Strangled," Cameron said wonderingly, "with a pink nylon girdle."

"I'm glad they didn't destroy the colour harmony," I said.

Cameron lit a cigarette. "He was in the office safe."

"It's understandable," I agreed, "anybody as precious as that."

We both winced again.

"One of the dames in the office opened the safe at ten this morning," Cameron continued, "and found him. She had hysterics and after they'd thrown some scented water over her, they sent the call into Homicide."

"And you got the job," I said. "What did you find out?"

"Skirts will be shorter this year," he said, avoiding my eyes.

I looked at him for about ten seconds.

"That's encouraging news. But what about the murder?"

"Skirts will be shorter this year," he repeated.

"If you say that once more," I smiled at him, "you'll have the downtown traffic all to yourself this afternoon."

"So help me, chief! That's all I could get out of them. They're crazy. The whole damned lot of 'em are crazy. They wouldn't talk any sense—no sense at all. All they could talk about was fashion and what Christian Dior is showing in Paris or something. I tell you, chief, right now that downtown traffic almost looks good to me."

I lit myself a cigarette and didn't say anything.

"Look, chief," Cameron pleaded. "You don't have to take my word for it—just give me the traffic. But take a look for yourself, just once."

I thought about it—it was a tempting thought. Three months back when Commissioner Lavers gave me the Homicide Bureau, I thought life could be beautiful, too. Now I wasn't quite so sure. Sitting around behind a desk all week got monotonous. The most excitement I'd had in three months was getting a tooth filled.

"You know something?" I said. "I might do just that."

"Thanks, chief." Cameron gave me a haggard smile.

"And you can get behind this desk," I told him, "and think up smart answers for the Commissioner every time he asks why we've got such a bunch of slobs masquerading as lieutenants in Homicide!"

My watch said it was noon.

I took Sergeant Podeski with me just for somebody to talk to.

If Cameron hadn't got any further with his fact-finding than skirts would be shorter this year, at least the others had. The fingerprint and photography experts and so on. All the science boys had finished with their science and gone back to the bureau.

We got there at twelve-thirty. At twelve thirty-two I stood in front of a receptionist's desk, looking at the receptionist. She was a brunette whose hair looked as if it had just had an argument with a hurricane and lost.

"Yes?" She tilted her nose high in the air as she looked at me.

"I'd like to see the manager," I said.

"Business, editorial or advertising?"

"You have three?"

She didn't bother to answer that.

"I'm Lieutenant Wheeler," I said.

"Navy, Army or Air Force?"

I gritted my teeth. "Police, honey. Homicide Bureau. I'm the guy that runs it."

"What is your business here, Lieutenant?"

"You had a murder this morning—maybe the guy thought that skirts should be longer this year and you had him knocked off. Who do I talk to about a murder?"

"I'll enquire," she said.

I was beginning to see what Cameron had been hinting at.

The brunette played around with an intercom, then looked up again.

"Miss Walker will see you," she said in a hushed voice.

"Who is Miss Walker?"

She looked at me blankly. "You don't know Elise Walker, the editor of *Exclusive*?"

"I know I haven't been around much," I said humbly. "Where do I find her?"

"I'll have someone take you to her, Lieutenant."

She pressed a bell on the desk and a moment later a redhead appeared. Her hair also looked as if it had just lost a violent argument with a hurricane.

The redhead took us to Miss Walker's office, announced us and left us.

"I can give you five minutes," Miss Walker said crisply. "I'm expecting Antoine."

"You even know the sex," I said wonderingly.

She coloured slightly. "If you consider that amusing, Sergeant, I'm afraid I don't."

"Lieutenant," I said patiently. "This is Sergeant Podeski."

"I suppose it's about the murder," she said.

I eased myself cautiously into a chair which appeared to be defying the law of gravity.

"Have a look around the place, Podeski," I told him.

"Huh?" he said.

"You heard me." I saw no reason to share Miss Walker with him.

Miss Walker was a honey-blonde with a white skin. She didn't look like the *Exclusive* models at all—she had a figure—from where I sat it looked the sort of figure any cop should investigate. It looked too good to be true. Better than that, it looked as if it was true although it looked too good to be.

"Haven't you ever seen a woman before, Lieutenant?" she asked with a touch of frost in her voice.

"Once," I admitted, "in Hoboken."

She breathed deeply and the lace of her blouse fluttered in alarm.

"I can't understand why it's necessary for more policemen to come here," she said. "We've already had a truckload earlier this morning."

"And now you've got me," I said, "the guy in charge of Homicide—you should feel flattered."

"Only alarmed," she said. "You've just destroyed my faith in the police."

I lit myself a cigarette while I tried to think of an answer to that one—and couldn't.

"This corpse that got filed in the safe," I said. "Who was he?"

The door shot open and a tall lean guy with a beard and a look on his face as if he always got lost Wednesdays shot into the room.

"Elise!" he almost sobbed. "It's too much. It's intolerable, it's, it's …"

"Wednesday?" I suggested helpfully.

"Wed—" He looked at me. "Please don't interrupt! Elise! You don't know what they've done to me!"

"Whatever it is, it's no improvement, pal," I told him.

His beard positively waggled as he glared at me. "Will you please, please, keep quiet!"

"Elise!" He was back to Miss Walker again. "They've given me Helene to model the Antoine chantilly. On her it looks like a sack! Am I supposed to illustrate a sack?"

"But, darling," Elise said, "Helene is definitely the best we have. Antoine insists that whoever models the chantilly must have verve and flair."

"Verve and flair!" He tore a handful of hair out of his beard and scattered it onto the carpet. "Helene! Shall I tell you what Helene has got?"

"There are ladies present," I said warningly.

"Crowsfeet under the eyes!" he went on, ignoring my interruption. "And her figure—it sags! Sags, I tell you!"

"Then you'll just have to use your imagination a little, Hubert," Miss Walker said briskly. "Now run along—we're coming up to a deadline quite fast, you know, and we must have the chantilly."

Hubert tore some more of his beard off, groaned loudly and tottered out of the room.

"Do you keep him to frighten away the mice?" I asked.

Miss Walker sniffed distinctly. "Hubert is an artist. That is something you probably wouldn't understand, Lieutenant."

"I met an artist once," I said. "In Hoboken."

I dropped the butt of my cigarette into the porcelain ashtray and lit a new one. I could see where Cameron got his information on skirts. I thought I could only try again.

"This guy," I said, "in his pink silk pyjamas."

The door shot open again and a brunette with haunted eyes and a build like a pouter pigeon shot into the room. She was an improvement on Hubert, anyway.

"Sweetie!" she said desperately to Miss Walker. "We just have to have another two pages of colour for Antoine! We cannot possibly do him justice in black and white!"

"Why not a pale mauve?" I asked. "With a chartreuse green around the edges?"

The brunette looked at me coldly, then back to Miss Walker. "What is that?" she asked interestedly.

"A policeman," Miss Walker said. "Pay no attention."

"Well."

The telephone tinkled and Miss Walker lifted the pale lemon receiver to her shell-pink ear. "Yes? No!" She replaced the receiver back on the cradle.

"I'll bet that's the fastest brush-off a guy ever had," I said admiringly.

The brunette came into the attack again. "Just two more pages of colour, darling!" she pleaded.

Miss Walker shook her head firmly. "The budget won't stand it, angel—sorry."

"But, Elise!"

"No can do!"

The brunette beat doleful retreat from the room. I followed her as far as the door and carefully locked it behind her. I came back to the desk as the phone started to ring. I picked up the receiver before Miss Walker had a chance to.

"Miss Walker says she'll fire whoever puts the first call through to her during the next half-hour," I said firmly.

I replaced the receiver and looked at a pair of blue icebergs.

"Just what ..." Miss Walker started to say.

I relaxed back into my chair.

"Now we have plenty of time without being interrupted," I smiled at her. "Tell me about the cadaver with the pink rosebud on his pocket."

CHAPTER 2
Suspects—I Got a Million

"He was Henry Parker," Miss Walker said. "He was our social editor."

"What did he do?"

"I just told you."

"I guess you did. Okay—what does a social editor do?"

"He keeps up with the social round—debs, parties, nightspots; you know the sort of stuff."

"Not really," I said, "but I can imagine. Why would anybody want to kill him?"

"I haven't the faintest idea." She lit herself a cigarette that smelled like Chanel Number 5.

"Did he have an apartment in the building—in your offices, I mean?"

"Of course not," she said. "What a ridiculous idea."

"How come he was in his pyjamas? If you tell me he used to come to work in them and a homburg hat, I'm not going to believe it."

She shook her head. "I really have no idea why he was wearing pyjamas—he was always immaculately dressed."

"Who found him?"

"Prudence. Prudence Foy, one of the girls in the accounts section. She had to go to the safe for something."

"And found Henry instead. What happened then?"

"She had hysterics—everyone rushed over to find out what was the matter. Finally, Joe Sutton rang for the police."

"Joe Sutton?"

"The accountant."

I lit a third cigarette of my own to try and combat the joss stick she was burning. "Was Parker in the office yesterday?"

"I saw him about two-thirty," she said. "He told me he was going to the party Janice Milbray was giving for Antoine."

"Who is Antoine?"

Miss Walker shook her head sadly. "You don't get around much, do you, Lieutenant? Antoine's one of the top five designers living. It's a great honour that he's visiting America. A very great honour."

"And I never knew,' I said wonderingly.

She looked down at her wristwatch. "That's all I can tell you, Lieutenant. That was the last time I saw Henry alive. Hubert was a friend of his—he might be able to help."

"The character with the face fungus?"

"Hubert Snell," she told me. "One of the most well-known illustrators in the country."

"Where does this Janice Milbray live?"

She gave me the address and I made a note of it. "Okay," I said. "Thanks. I'll probably be back."

"I was afraid of that," she said. "Good morning, Lieutenant."

I unlocked the door and let myself out.

I found Podeski gazing open-mouthed at the dame with the build like a pouter pigeon, while she tried to explain to him that layout wasn't what he'd thought it was. I took him gently by the arm and led him out of the office.

We got back into the prowl-car. I told the driver to take us to the morgue. It was a chore I preferred to get rid of before lunch.

Like Cameron had said, Parker was a little guy still wearing pink silk pyjamas. Hank, the morgue attendant who always looked right at home among his customers, peered over my shoulder and grunted.

"I seen a hell of a lot of cadavers, Lieutenant—but this is the first one who got knocked off with a girdle."

"What sort of girdle?" I asked him.

Hank grunted again. "I ain't an expert, Lieutenant—the thing didn't look much bigger than a pocket handkerchief to me. But it was made of elastic. I guess that helped whoever pulled it tight around his neck."

"I guess so," I said.

I had one more look at Henry Parker before Hank closed the drawer again. Parker had been a guy in his early forties, with carefully pomaded hair and a neat line of moustache across his upper lip. I took a closer look at his face.

"Yeah," Hank grunted. "That's rouge on his cheeks. You figure the girdle was his own?"

"I don't figure anything about this one, Hank," I said. "Not anything at all."

I left the morgue and had some lunch. I went back to the bureau and found Cameron in my office looking unhappy.

"What's the matter with you?" I asked him.

"The Commissioner rang twice while you were out," he said. "Wants a full report on this Parker case—the newspapers are on him, I guess. That sure is a screwball place."

"Yeah," I said again. "You can go out and do some work. Find out if Parker had any relatives—check his home, wherever that is; the magazine ought to be able to tell you, I forgot to ask. And see if you can get a line on that girdle."

"Girdle?" he asked hoarsely.

"The one Parker was strangled with—it had to come from somewhere, didn't it? Find out the make and so on—anything you can. If you think you're too young, you can send Podeski out."

"Okay, chief," he said.

"The editor last saw Parker at two-thirty yesterday afternoon," I went on. "Check and see if anybody saw him in the building after that time. There's probably a nightwatchman or something. Parker either walked back into the building or was carried. And check who knows the combination of that safe in the office. Find out if Parker knew it himself."

"You think it might be suicide, chief?" he asked hopefully.

"Oh, sure," I said. "I figure Parker strangled himself first, then opened the safe and climbed into it—not forgetting to shut the door behind him!"

"I only wondered," Cameron said in a hurt voice.

"Policemen should never wonder," I said. "Before you know where you are, you quit being a cop and get a job that pays money. I want a written report with the answers in it by tonight."

"Yes, sir," Cameron said miserably and went out of the office.

I picked up the phone and rang the city hall.

"Wheeler, sir," I said politely when the Commissioner answered the phone.

"How far have you got with this Parker case?" he asked.

"Not very far, sir," I said. "Still checking the facts."

"I'd like to see you close the case fast," he said. "The papers will make a field day out of it. A corpse in a safe, strangled with a girdle!"

"Yes, sir," I said.

"Keep in touch with me at least once a day, Wheeler," he said.

"Yes, sir."

"And Wheeler!"

"Yes, sir?"

"Where were you this morning?"

"Interviewing the editor of *Exclusive*."

"That's what Cameron said—you'd gone to look for yourself. I wouldn't normally approve of the Lieutenant in Charge of Homicide handling a case himself. But this one seems to be the exception. I agree with you—handle it yourself."

"Yes, sir."

"Control of the Homicide Bureau is really a captain's job, Wheeler. I would say that the successful conclusion of this case might see a promotion."

"Thank you, sir."

"On the other hand," he said gently, "an unsuccessful conclusion might see a new face in control of the bureau. Good afternoon, Lieutenant."

I didn't say anything.

"Good afternoon, Lieutenant!" he repeated sharply.

"I'm sorry, Commissioner," I said. "I find it hard to talk with my throat cut."

He laughed gently and hung up.

I should have left the case with Cameron.

Office routine caught up with me for the rest of the afternoon.

I got away around five-thirty and had a meal. I took a prowl-car with me and drove to the address Miss Walker had given me. It was a penthouse in Kyle Bay. Kyle Bay is so exclusive that even the lawns are given a French dressing.

A maid answered the door, a coloured girl who could have been Eartha Kitt's sister but undoubtedly wasn't. I told her who I was and that I'd like to see Miss Milbray. She asked me in, showed me into a room and left me there.

Then the door opened and she came in.

"Miss Milbray?" I said automatically.

"That's right," she said. "What can I do for you, Lieutenant?"

She was a brunette for midnight. She wore an evening gown of white jersey that was draped around her to subtly emphasise her figure was perfect. It was cut low in front and a diamond necklace gleamed against the whiteness of her throat.

"I'm investigating Henry Parker's murder," I told her. "I guess you've heard about it?"

"The evening papers are full of it," she said. "Poor Henry!"

"He was at a party last night," I said. "Here?"

She nodded. "Yes. I'm not sure when he left—it would have been some time after midnight, though."

"You knew him well?"

She shook her head. "Not really. He was always around at parties and things, of course. He used to call me darling, but then he called everybody that."

"Who else was at the party?"

"There were quite a lot of people. It was given in Antoine's honour—he was here, of course. And so was Hubert Snell—you know, the artist?"

"I know," I agreed.

"There would have been around fifty or sixty people here," she went on.

"Would you have a list of the guests?"

"I think so," she said. "There was a list for the invitations." She got up and went out of the room, then came back a couple of minutes later and gave me a typewritten list. I folded it and put it into my billfold. "Thanks," I told her.

"I wish I could help you more, Lieutenant," she said. "But I'm afraid I can't."

"You might have helped me quite a lot with that list." I got up onto my feet and walked towards the door. "Thanks again, Miss Milbray."

The maid let me out.

I stopped off for a couple of quick drinks at a bar on my way back and got into the bureau around eight-thirty. There was a stack of stuff on my desk. Doctor's report, the science boys' report and a memo from the Commissioner which said we were using too many typewriter ribbons.

No report from Cameron.

I pressed the buzzer and a cop came in. "Send Lieutenant Cameron in," I told him.

"He's not in, Lieutenant," he said.

"Where is he?"

"I don't know, sir. He went out maybe a couple of hours ago."

"Then send Sergeant Podeski in."

Podeski came in a few seconds later. I told him to sit down. "Where's Lieutenant Cameron?"

"He told me he was going to take a look at Parker's place."

"Where is Parker's place—on the forty-ninth parallel?"

"An apartment uptown, Lieutenant," Podeski said.

"What else has been happening?"

He cleared his throat a couple of times and looked as being near to embarrassed as a Pole who's built like the side of a house can.

"That girdle," he said.

"Yeah?"

"It's called Playgirl," he said huskily. "The Lieutenant had me check on it this afternoon. Made by a company called Playgirl Unlimited. I saw their sales manager. He figures they've sold over twenty-five thousand of them in this city alone. Says they figure they have sold over half a million throughout the country in the first four months it's been on the market. Almost every store in town sells them, including Buckman's."

"So there's no lead in the girdle?"

"Guess not, Lieutenant," he said.

I lit myself a cigarette. "What else have you been doing?"

He shuffled his feet. "Nothing very much, Lieutenant. I got back around five forty-five. Lieutenant Cameron tells me he's going to look over Parker's apartment and for me to stick around. I figured he'd be back before this." He blew out his cheeks. "I was off duty at five."

"You have the address of Parker's place?"

"Sure." He took out a piece of paper and shoved it across the desk towards me.

The address was Kyle Bay. Being a social editor must have paid off, too.

"Okay," I said. "You'd better get off duty."

"Thanks, Lieutenant," he said gratefully and beat it out of the office.

I picked up the doctor's report and read it. Parker had been strangled to death. The only thing in the doctor's report was his term for a girdle—he called it an elastic instrument.

The science boys had a hell of a lot to say about nothing, as usual—or maybe I'm just an old-fashioned cop. They'd found an army of fingerprints on the outside of the safe, which included Parker's. They'd analysed his pyjamas and his moustache among other things, but they didn't draw any conclusions from their analysis except that he was wearing pyjamas and a moustache.

I thought we'd made a hell of a good start on the case. So far we'd narrowed down the suspects to about a million—the population of the city—unless it was an out-of-town job, of course.

I tossed the reports into the wastepaper basket and lit another cigarette. I thought I might as well go out and see what Cameron was wasting his time at, as stick around twiddling my thumbs in the office.

Before I went, I dictated a memo into the dictaphone. "Memo to Commissioner Lavers from Lieutenant-in-Charge, Homicide. First report on Parker murder. Progress none."

Then I put on my hat and went out to the prowl-car again.

The apartment block wasn't quite up to the standard of the one that housed Janice Milbray's penthouse, but it was definitely Kyle Bay. The apartment was on the sixth floor. I rode the elevator up to the sixth floor, then walked along the cork-tiled corridor to the apartment.

The door was slightly open.

I pushed it open a little further until it opened wide, then went into the apartment. There were no lights on. I ran my hand down the wall and flicked on the switch. Soft light flooded the room.

The room was empty of people. On a wall opposite me was a Salvador Dali woman with snakes for hair and a body made out of butter-boxes. The rest of the furnishings looked like refugees from a psychiatrist's nightmare.

I lit a cigarette and walked across the room, opened the door which led into the bedroom.

There was somebody in the bedroom, on the bed. Underneath him was a blue satin drape which was stained red in places. There was a knife-hilt protruding from between his shoulder-blades.

His face was turned sideways and his eyes were wide open, staring at nothing. I felt automatically for a pulse but there wasn't any.

I'd found out what Cameron was wasting his time at, anyway. He'd been wasting his time being murdered.

CHAPTER 3
Kathi

The following morning bright and early I was in Commissioner Lavers' office. I was early, but I wasn't feeling bright. I'd had exactly three hours' sleep and even the bags under my eyes were tired.

"Take it from the beginning, Wheeler," Lavers growled at me. I took it from the beginning, up to when I'd found Cameron's body.

"He was stabbed, sir," I went on. "No fingerprints on the knife. Nothing the science boys could turn up, as usual."

"I know your feelings about the lab, Wheeler," Lavers said. "Just stick to the facts."

"Nobody in the apartment block saw Cameron come in—or anybody else they didn't know—and they didn't hear anything unusual. We don't have a single lead on why he was killed or who killed him."

The Commissioner grunted. "How about the Parker case?"

"The nightwatchman says that nobody came into the building that night. My guess is he must have been asleep and doesn't want to admit it for obvious reasons."

"So you don't have a single lead on why Parker was killed or who killed him, either?"

"That's right," I agreed.

Lavers banged his desk violently with his fist. "Is this what we have a Homicide Bureau for? Is this what you're given the job of Lieutenant-in-Charge for?"

"At a guess," I ventured, "I'd say not."

For a moment I thought he was going to choke. Gradually the colour of his face started to come back to normal.

"I'll give you exactly seven days starting from today," he said slowly. "I want both murders solved by then. If not, you are no longer the Lieutenant-in-Charge of Homicide. In fact, you will no longer be a Lieutenant! In fact—"

"I get the drift," I told him. I heaved myself onto my feet. "Okay, Commissioner—you've put it on the line. You want results in seven days or else!"

"Exactly!"

"How about playing it straight?" I suggested. "I have a free hand for those seven days?"

"Just what do you mean?"

"I can do what I like—towards solving the murders. I don't have to waste my time sending you reports—being on call at my desk and so on?"

"You can handle it anyway you want to," he said. "For seven days."

"Thanks very much," I told him.

It was only nine o'clock when I got into the bureau. I went into my office and sent for Lieutenant Hanlon. He came in a couple of moments later and sat down, eyeing me cautiously. He's one of the guys who figured he rated higher than me for the job I got, and hasn't forgotten it.

"As from now and for the next seven days," I told him, "you will sit at this desk and be the acting Lieutenant-in-Charge of the bureau."

He looked at me, not quite sure what to make of it. "It's not a promotion," I said. "I hope."

"What will you be doing?" he asked.

"I'll be working on the Parker case—and the Cameron case."

"Keeping the glory to yourself, Lieutenant?" he asked softly.

"Or get my throat cut," I agreed.

I got up from the desk and headed for the door. "It's all yours, pal," I told him and went out before he could argue. I took a prowl-car and drove home.

So far it had been a routine investigation and all it had got us was a cop murdered. A good cop, too.

It wasn't so long ago I'd had a sort of reputation for being an unorthodox cop. I figured it was time I started being unorthodox, again. But I needed some sleep first. So when I got home I went straight to bed.

I got up at nightfall, had a shower and a shave, made some coffee, and put some Kitty Wyatt on the hi-fi to listen to while I was drinking the coffee.

By the time I'd finished the coffee, I was feeling a little better.

I rang the office of *Exclusive* and asked to speak to Miss Walker.

Her voice fingered my spine lightly when she came through.

"How is the world of fashion today?" I asked her.

"The same as it was yesterday," she said. "What can I do for you, Lieutenant?"

"You could have dinner with me," I said. "I want to talk to you."

"I'm afraid that's impossible. I'm having dinner with Antoine at the Cafe Rouge. I could make an appointment for you in the morning, Lieutenant."

"For dinner?"

"For a talk!"

"I can never talk on an empty stomach," I said. "Is that tame artist of yours around—Hubert?"

"He left about an hour ago, Lieutenant."

"Can you give me his address?"

"Of course—hold the line a moment."

She came back a few seconds later and gave me the address. I made a note of it. "Thanks," I told her.

"Goodnight, Lieutenant," she said and hung up.

Half an hour later I was outside the apartment block where Hubert Snell brightened the world with his illustrations of chantilly or tantilly or whatever it was.

The block itself wasn't imposing, halfway towards a tenement. I found the apartment on the first floor and rang the buzzer. The door opened soon afterwards and a blonde stood there.

A blonde wearing a black cotton shirt and pirate pants painted black and white. I would have walked a gangplank for her any time.

"Why, Hubert," I said. "You've changed—and for the better, too!"

She gave me a level gaze. "If you're a friend of Hubert's," she said in a low voice, "he's out. He should be back in an hour or so. You can wait if you want to."

"I'd love to," I told her.

I followed her into the apartment. It had the same sort of furnishings that Parker's place had.

"I didn't know Hubert had a girlfriend," I said. "He's been playing you close to his vest."

"I'm his sister," she said. "I'm Kathi Snell."

"Al Wheeler," I said.

We shook hands formally. I offered her a cigarette and lit it for her and one for myself.

"Would you like a drink?" she asked.

"Rye, thanks."

She moved over to the bar and poured a couple of drinks. I sat down on a backless sofa and wondered how nature could make Hubert and this dame brother and sister. It didn't seem natural, somehow.

She gave me my drink, then sat down beside me.

"Poor Hubert's dreadfully upset about Henry Parker," she said.

"They were friends?"

"The best of friends," she said.

"I sort of figured that," I said.

She looked at me curiously. "Do you know Hubert well?"

"Not very well," I admitted.

"Oh," she said.

I lifted my glass. "Here's to us, anyway."

She raised an eyebrow. "Why us?"

"We have a natural affinity," I told her. "I feel it!"

"Maybe I'm sitting too close," she said thoughtfully and moved six inches further away.

"I don't think Hubert will be home," I told her. "He's a very unreliable character regarding time."

"I've never known him to be," she said.

"But you're his sister," I said. "You wouldn't know him very well."

"Why not?"

I couldn't think of an answer to that one, so I ignored it.

"The obvious thing is for me to take you out to dinner," I said. "That way we both eat and give that affinity a chance to improve itself."

"What do you do for a living?" she asked.

"Does it matter?"

"I just wondered if you sold vacuum cleaners," she said. "The technique seems familiar."

"Have I once been familiar?" I asked indignantly.

"No," she said, "but I've been watching you!"

I finished my drink. "Aren't you hungry?" I asked hopefully.

"I could be," she said. "Where were you thinking of taking me to dinner?"

"The Cafe Rouge," I said.

"Now that sounds a reasonable proposition," she said. "I can never afford to eat there myself." She got up from the sofa. "Give me fifteen minutes to change."

"I'll count the minutes."

She disappeared into what I presumed was her bedroom. I got up and poured myself another drink. A couple of minutes went by and then I heard a key grate in the outside lock.

I made faster time than a superjet and was there when the door opened.

Hubert looked at me vaguely. "What are you doing here?"

"You remember me?" I whispered.

"In the office yesterday," he unconsciously whispered back. "Yes, you're a policeman or something, aren't you?"

"I am," I agreed. "We think that Parker's killer is after you."

"What!" Hubert's eyes bulged.

"That's why I'm here," I went on. "You daren't stay here tonight—hideout some place and come to the Homicide Bureau at ten tomorrow morning—exactly ten—and ask for me, Lieutenant Wheeler."

"But where will I hide out?" he asked.

"Just curl up in your beard under a park bench," I suggested. "Go someplace where nobody will recognise you—a barber's shop or something. But whatever you do, don't come near this apartment tonight!"

He gulped noisily. "But shouldn't I have police protection?"

"We aren't sure we could stop him," I said. "Your only chance is to disappear—quick!"

"All right." His beard twitched like it had squirrels inside. "And be at the Homicide Bureau at ten in the morning?"

"Not a minute later—or earlier!" I told him.

His beard twitched again and then he was gone.

I closed the door gently and tiptoed back to the bar.

"Did somebody call?" Kathi called from her room.

"Some character looking for Hubert," I said.

"What did he look like?"

"Hubert."

"I didn't think Hubert knew anybody who looked like Hubert."

"Maybe he's twins and you never knew?" I suggested.

"If I wasn't so hungry!" she said.

Kathi appeared ten minutes later. She was wearing a strapless short evening gown in pale blue with a cherry-red stole over the top. I was glad I'd put on the suit back from the cleaners.

"You look terrific," I told her.

"I know it," she said complacently. "Now let's go eat—otherwise I shan't be in a fit condition to support this gown much longer!"

The Cafe Rouge is so expensive that you have to make a choice of eating there or paying your taxes. I'd made my choice—if I solved the case within seven days, maybe the commissioner would agree to the bill going on the expense account. If I didn't solve the case within seven days, the unpaid taxes would be the least of my worries.

The head waiter showed us to a table which had a reasonable view of the dance-floor. A waiter supplied us with menus and I tried not to look at the prices.

"I'm so hungry." Kathi looked at the menu enthusiastically. "I'm going to eat my way right through this."

It upset me so much, I actually drank half a glass of water before I tasted it for what it was. We finally ordered the food and two dry martinis to keep us company until the food arrived.

The drinks were duly served and I killed the taste of the water gratefully.

"You in the same line of business as Hubert?" I asked Kathi.

She shook her head. "I'm in the advertising business. I'm a copy-writer."

"Soap?"

"Fashion," she said. "Sometimes I wish it was soap!"

"Must be interesting," I said.

"Only ulcer-making! What do you do?"

"Me? I'm a cop."

"I'm serious!" she said.

"So am I," I told her.

"All right," she shrugged her shoulders. "If you don't want to tell me what you do, that's your business."

A vision in a black gown with a mink stole draped carelessly over her shoulders sat down half a dozen tables away from us. Her escort was a tall, good-looking guy with dark wavy hair.

"Well, look who's here," Kathi said. "The man himself—and with Elise Walker, no less."

"You know them?"

She nodded. "That's why I'm down here—the agency sent me down; I'm writing Antoine's copy—that's what's driving me nuts. Elise Walker is the editor of *Exclusive*. You've heard of *Exclusive*, haven't you?"

"Sure," I said. "Hubert illustrates for them, doesn't he?"

"That's right," she agreed.

She looked at me curiously. "How did you get to be a friend of Hubert's? You don't seem to be the artistic type."

"But I am," I said indignantly. "I paint towns."

"Towns?"

"Red!"

She winced. "You sure you're not in vaudeville?"

"Not for the next seven days, anyway," I said. "After that, anything can happen."

At least half a dozen waiters were converging on Antoine's table. Maybe this dress-designing had something. I thought—I should try it sometime—it would be a change from having designs on a dress, or whoever was wearing it.

The food arrived and there was a logical development—we ate. An hour later we were with the coffee and cigarettes.

"I feel better," Kathi sighed. "Much better."

"The gown can be supported without any further worry?"

"Right until breakfast-time," she said.

I looked across at the table where Antoine and Elise Walker sat in close conversation.

"Now I remember," I said. "Didn't they have a corpse in their magazine or something?"

"In their office safe," Kathi nodded.

"I wonder why he got knocked off?" I mused.

"Henry Parker? Did you know him?"

"No," I said.

She took a puff on her cigarette. "If you'd known him, you wouldn't have asked that question. Parker was one of the most repulsive characters I ever had the misfortune to meet. What my brother ever saw in him, I don't know!"

"You said earlier they were good friends?"

"I think Hubert was impressed with him," she said. "Hubert is very impressionable."

"What did Parker impress him with?"

"His airs and graces, I suppose. Being the social editor of *Exclusive*, he got around in society circles somewhat. He knew everyone by their Christian names. Hubert's only a kid from the sticks, really."

"He would be at home sleeping under a park bench?" I asked hopefully.

She stared at me for a moment. "Why do you say that?"

"I just wondered. Hubert strikes me as the sort of guy who'd sleep under a park bench, just for the hell of it."

"I think you're crazy," she said.

I ordered another couple of drinks.

"Do you think we should go back and see if Hubert's home?" I asked her.

"You want to see him?"

"No."

"Then why should we go home?"

"I thought the drinks would be cheaper at the apartment."

"One thing about staying with your brother," she smiled, "it makes a girl feel safer!"

"Sure," I said smugly.

People stopped by our table. I looked up and saw Elise Walker and Antoine standing there.

"Having a good time, Kathi?" Antoine asked, with only the faintest suspicion of an accent.

"Wonderful, thanks, Antoine," she said. "I'd like you to meet Al Wheeler. Al, this is Antoine."

I got onto my feet and we shook hands.

"And this is Elise Walker," Kathi went on.

Miss Walker smiled at me. "So you made a dinner date after all, Lieutenant?"

"Yeah," I said.

"What did you say?" Kathi asked Miss Walker sharply.

"She said I made my dinner date," I said quickly. "We were talking about food and I said the Cafe Rouge was good."

"I mean after that!" Kathi said.

"Did you say Lieutenant?" Miss Walker laughed softly. "Don't tell me he's been keeping it a secret, Kathi! Didn't he tell you he was a policeman?"

"No," Kathi said slowly. "He didn't tell me he was a cop."

There was a nasty, metallic note to her voice.

Miss Walker and Antoine made their farewells and departed.

"Care to dance?" I asked brightly.

"No, thank you, Lieutenant," Kathi said, with emphasis on the word Lieutenant.

Her fingers beat out a call to arms on the table.

"But, baby, you wouldn't believe me!" I said quickly.

"I wouldn't believe anything you told me!" she said doggedly. "I suppose Hubert is your chief suspect, Lieutenant?"

"Now wait a minute!" I said.

"I think I've waited long enough. I'm going home. Thank you for the dinner, Lieutenant, or should I thank the State?"

"I'll drive you," I said.

"No," she said firmly. "I'd much rather take a cab."

She picked up her purse from the table and started to get to her feet. I had as much chance of arguing with her as could with Rocky Marciano.

"Okay," I sighed. "If you see Hubert on your way home, tell him it's okay for him to come in out of the rain."

"What?"

"Tell him he's safe, he can sleep comfortable."

"I don't understand," she frowned.

"Hubert will," I sighed. "That's what happens to good organisation when some dilly dame busts into the picture. I just hate Miss Walker!"

"You're talking nonsense," Kathi said. "Sheer, unadulterated nonsense!"

"You tell Hubert," I said. "He'll be grateful."

She put the stole around her shoulders and walked off towards the door. I watched her go regretfully.

"Your check, sir," a hovering waiter said politely. I looked at it and shuddered.

"You have an hourly rate for washing dishes in this joint?" I asked hopefully.

CHAPTER 4
Hubert

I thought the hell with it as I pressed the buzzer. If I couldn't have an evening out with Kathi Snell, I knew one other beautiful woman I could visit—even if I did have to plead business.

The door opened and the coloured maid didn't open it. The guy who stood there was around six feet, two inches in height, nicely dressed in a tuxedo with the trimmings. He had iron-grey hair and a face some Red Indian must have carved with a hatchet. He was in his early forties, maybe.

"Yeah?" he said.

That's what I always like—the courteous touch.

"I'm calling on Miss Milbray," I said. "Are you she?"

His lips curled. "A wise guy, eh?"

"Just a cop," I told him and showed him my shield. "If you are not she, I would like to see she."

He turned around and walked back into the apartment without answering.

A couple of minutes later Janice Milbray appeared at the door. She was wearing a white negligee trimmed with what looked like mink. Maybe I was busting into something or busting something up. What the hell?

"Lieutenant," she said. "You are working late."

"I thought of some more questions I'd like to ask you," I said.

"Oh," she didn't sound enthusiastic. "Won't you come in?"

"Thanks," I told her.

I took off my hat and followed her into the living-room.

"Eddie," she said, "this is Lieutenant Wheeler. Lieutenant, this is Eddie Buckman."

He nodded sourly. "We met at the door."

If you'd put a bit of the silence that followed onto a pair of scales, it would have weighed heavy.

"Don't let me keep you," I said to Buckman, "if you were just leaving."

His lips twitched. "As a matter of fact, I was."

Janice Milbray looked at him, startled. "Do you have to go, Eddie?"

"Yeah," he said. "Too much noise and too many people around here."

He started towards the door and she went with him. I lit a cigarette and waited patiently. They whispered together for a couple of minutes and then she came back. I heard the sound of the outer door closing.

"I must apologise for Eddie," she said a little breathlessly. "I'm afraid he can be very rude at times."

"Forget it," I told her.

She stood there twisting her hands. "Would you care for a drink, Lieutenant?"

"That would be wonderful," I said.

I sat down on the couch and relaxed. She went over to the bar and poured two drinks, bringing them back with her. She gave me mine, and took hers to an easy chair that faced the couch.

When she sat down, the folds of the negligee loosened and I saw her knees had dimples where knees should have dimples but often don't.

"You had some questions, Lieutenant?"

I tried to think of some. "Hubert Snell and Parker were good friends, weren't they?"

"They always seemed so."

"Did Parker ever have a girlfriend?"

"Henry!"

"Did he?"

"I never saw him with one or heard of one," she said.

"Do you know if he had any enemies?"

"I'd say he had a million," she said simply. "He had an acid pen and used it that way most of the time. Apart from Hubert, I don't think there was anyone that liked him."

I sipped the drink. "Eddie," I said. "A friend of yours?"

"Yes," she brought the folds of the negligee together. "Is it a crime to have friends, Lieutenant?"

"If it is, it's a new one," I said. "What does he do for a crust?"

"You mean, you've never heard of Eddie Buckman?"

"You'd be surprised at the people I've never heard of," I assured her. "Tell me about him."

"Well, Eddie's in the fashion business—in a very big way."

"Buckman's—the store?"

"That's right," she nodded. "The big store here in the city and six branches throughout the State."

"Are you in the fashion business, Miss Milbray?"

"Only from a personal angle," she smiled. "I just like to wear nice clothes, Lieutenant. It's an expensive hobby."

"I can imagine," I said.

I seemed to be running out of questions.

"Was there anything else?" she asked.

"I guess not," I said. I finished my drink. "Thanks, anyway, Miss Milbray."

"It was a pleasure," she said. "I didn't know policemen worked so late."

"Never stop," I said. "That is, once we get started."

She walked with me to the door. "Goodnight, Lieutenant."

There was a door just off to my right. It was half-open and there was a light on inside the room. I opened the door a little wider.

"It's okay to come out now," I said, "I'm going."

I caught one glimpse of Eddie Buckman's infuriated face before I gently shut the door again.

I smiled at Miss Milbray's obvious embarrassment.

"That's a trick they teach all the rookie cops on their second day at school," I told her.

She recovered. "And what do they teach them on their first day, Lieutenant?"

I looked at her speculatively. "Never hope for a mink-trimmed brunette, because you'll never make enough money to be able to afford her. Goodnight, Miss Milbray."

I stepped out into the corridor and heard the door close gently behind me. In the moment before it closed, I heard her laughing.

I drove the prowl-car home—it was only eleven-thirty when I got there. And Hubert's sleeping under a park bench for no good reason, I thought disgustedly. I put some Sinatra on the hi-fi and thought that "Mood Indigo" was so right.

I poured some rye over some ice and took it back with me into the living-room, kicked off my shoes and plunked down on the sofa. It was times like these a guy thought of getting married. That shows how depressed I was.

The phone rang.

I allowed myself a couple of seconds of glorious anticipation before I answered it. It could be Kathi telling me all was forgiven and forgotten and to come around straight away. It could be Miss Milbray even, telling me Eddie Buckman had gone home and was I interested in mink.

I picked up the receiver and said. "Well, hello."

"Lieutenant Wheeler?"

"Yeah."

"Hanlon here."

"Yeah?"

"Trouble!"

"Okay," I snarled. "Stop gloating and tell."

"You remember that artist guy who works for the magazine?"

My hands felt cold and clammy. "Hubert Snell?"

"That's right. He's been knocked off. Guess where they found him?"

I closed my eyes. "Not under a park bench?"

"Are you kidding? What the hell would he be doing under a park bench?"

"I don't know," I snarled. "What would you be doing under a park bench?"

Hanlon made a sort of snorting sound. "They found him in the office safe—same place as they found Parker."

"Not another girdle!"

"Stabbed. The same way Cameron was stabbed."

"It's one way of narrowing down the suspects," I said. "How long ago?"

"Got the call about five minutes back. I've sent out Lieutenant Murphy and the boys."

"Who found him?"

"The editor—Walker, that her name? She and that designer guy. They went back to the office to look for something and they opened the safe."

"And there he was. Okay, I'll drive myself over."

"You want me to tell the Commissioner?" In spite of himself, Hanlon couldn't keep the satisfaction out of his voice.

"I guess so," I said. There wasn't anything else to say. I dropped the receiver back on the cradle and picked up my hat.

"Ol' rockin' chair's got me!" Frankie sang.

"Think yourself lucky it's not the Commissioner, pal!" I told him, then switched off the hi-fi before I went out to the car.

It was after midnight when I got there. Murphy looked glad to see me. He showed me the gory detail. The rest of the boys were about through. I told Murphy to go and see Kathi Snell and break the bad news and I'd take over in the office. He even seemed glad at that prospect. I guessed the word had got around Homicide that this was a hot one and nobody wanted any part of it—I could have it all.

Miss Walker was in her office with Antoine. They both looked worried and I didn't blame them—I felt exactly the same way. I went in, lit a cigarette and sat down in a chair and looked at them.

"Okay," I said. "Tell the story again."

"We were at the Cafe Rouge," Miss Walker said, "as you know, Lieutenant. We were talking business, of course, and Antoine was a little worried about some sketches—he didn't think they were quite right. So I told him they were in the safe and if he liked, we could come back and look at them. So we did. And found," her lower lip trembled, "poor Hubert!"

"And then?"

"And then, Lieutenant," Antoine said, "we rang the police."

"Who let you into the building?"

"The nightwatchman."

"You have keys?"

"Yes," Miss Walker nodded. "But after ten every night, the watchman slides the bolts on the inside of the door."

"I think I'll go talk to him," I said.

"Can we go?" Antoine asked.

"Not yet," I said. "Stick around. Maybe you could make some coffee, Miss Walker?"

I went outside again. The boys had gone, leaving a sergeant and a couple of uniformed cops behind.

"Meat-wagon's on its way, Lieutenant," Sergeant Holden said.

"Anything you want done?"

"Where's the nightwatchman?"

"Downstairs, Lieutenant."

"Put one of these guys on the door and bring the watchman up here," I told him.

I found an empty office and put on the lights, then sat down behind somebody's desk. A couple of minutes later Holden came in with the nightwatchman. He was a guy touching sixty, a thin, wizened-up character with a bad attack of the shakes.

"Sit down," I told him.

I looked at Sergeant Holden. "There's a guy called Sutton who is the accountant of this place. Find out from Miss Walker his address and get him."

"Get him?" Holden asked.

"Get him here, I want to talk to him. I left a prowl-car downstairs—take that. But I want Sutton here as soon as you can get him here!"

"Yes, sir," Holden went out of the office and closed the door behind him.

I lit another cigarette and stared at the watchman. He shuffled his feet and his hands shook more so.

"What's your name?" I asked him.

"Dewlap," he muttered.

"Sure it's not Rip Van Winkle?"

"Look, Lieutenant," he wheezed, "I ..."

"Night before last somebody came in here and put a corpse the safe," I said. "They've done the same thing tonight. You're the watchman—the guy with the keys, the guy who shuts the bolts across the door every night after ten. You tell me how they got in?"

"I don't know, Lieutenant," he said almost tearfully. "So help me, I don't know!"

"You know something?" I said gently. "I figure you go to sleep nights."

"I don't!" he almost shrieked. "I swear it!"

"Look," I said. "Getting fired off this job would be the least of your troubles. Lying to the cops in a double murder case could be really serious. I've known guys fetch a three-to-five for that sort of thing. You look kind of old to start doing a stretch in the pen. Your health doesn't look so hot, either. Come clean, Dewlap."

He plucked a handkerchief out of his pocket with a palsied hand and mopped his brow. "Honest, Lieutenant," he said. "I wasn't asleep the night before last and I wasn't asleep tonight. Sure, some nights I get a couple of hours, maybe. This building's kind of lonely in the early hours and it's all locked up. But during the times you figure they got these corpses into the joint, I was awake. I swear it."

He looked like he was sincere. But so many guys look like they are sincere—insurance salesmen, politicians ...

"If you were awake," I said thoughtfully, "then there's only one other theory that's workable."

"What's that?"

"That you've been an accessory to both murders! That you opened the door and let them in both times!"

"No!" he shrieked.

I leaned slightly forward, towards him. "I'll tell you something," I said. "Everybody's mad about this trio of murders. A cop was the second one and that makes all the cops mad. And the Police Commissioner's the maddest of the lot. If I take you down to the bureau now, the Commissioner will be only too happy to let me hand you over to a couple of tough cops and see if they can get the truth out of you."

The handkerchief was rapidly getting limp in his hand.

"You got to believe me, Lieutenant," he said. "You got to! I've told you the truth!"

Like I said, he sounded sincere. I let him sweat a bit longer. "Somebody got into the building," I said. "Maybe one or two or three—we don't know how many. They got into the building and they brought a corpse with them—twice. Those are facts, right?"

"I guess so, Lieutenant," he said. "But I don't know how the hell they did it."

"You'd better figure out how they did it, pal," I said. "There are other doors, other windows into the building. Go take a look and see if you can figure it out. I'll give you an hour. But if you haven't got it figured out by then, I'll just have to think you're lying and take you down to the bureau with me."

"But ..."

"You've got exactly fifty-nine minutes."

Dewlap got off the chair and shuffled out of the office. For a moment I almost felt sorry for him but I was feeling too sorry for myself to have any left over.

CHAPTER 5
I Get Fashion—Conscious

Sutton was a nice, intelligent-looking guy in his early thirties. Sergeant Holden brought him into the office and went out again.

"Sorry to drag you out of bed," I said.

"That's all right, Lieutenant," he said easily. "I wasn't in bed, anyway."

"Fine," I said.

I lit yet another cigarette—my mouth was beginning to taste like old stable week.

"I don't know what it is about your safe that attracts corpses," I said, "but it sure does!"

"It certainly looks like it," he agreed. "Poor Snell."

"I wanted to ask you an obvious question I should have asked you yesterday morning," I said. "How many people know the combination of the safe?"

He thought for a moment. "I do, of course. A couple of my staff, Prudence Foy and Larry Marshall. Miss Walker does, too."

"Anybody else?"

"Not that I know of," he said. "The directors, of course, but at the moment the three of them are in the New York office, so I guess they don't matter."

"Did Henry Parker know the combination?"

"That's right—he did."

"How about Hubert Snell?"

"I don't think so. It wasn't a very complicated combination to learn. I guess if anybody in the office had really wanted to find out, they could have by watching one of us open the safe."

"But nobody outside would have known?"

"Not unless someone in the office told them."

"Did you like Parker—as a man, I mean?"

He looked at me quizzically. "No."

"They tell me that nobody did much," I said.

"I guess that would be right, too," he agreed. "Parker wasn't a likeable character. He had the biggest ego of anybody I've ever met. And in this business, that's saying something!"

"I guess so," I said. "It makes it all the more difficult to get a lead on who would kill him—or why."

"I suppose so," he said. "Did he have any friends?"

"Only Hubert Snell."

"Was their friendship—er ...?"

"No," he shook his head decisively. "I'm sure of it, Lieutenant. Parker wasn't the type—or Snell either, for that matter. Matter of fact, Parker used to talk about a girlfriend, but I never heard who she was."

"Do you know anybody who hated Parker enough to murder him?"

"No," he said flatly, "I don't."

"Okay," I said. "Thanks for coming down, Mr Sutton. Tell Sergeant Holden to have one of the men drive you home."

"Thanks, Lieutenant."

I got up and went out into the general office. The safe stood with its door wide open. The meat-wagon had obviously called; the corpse had gone.

I looked inside the safe for a few moments. Then I went back to Miss Walker's office. She and Antoine were still sitting there, looking impatient.

"No coffee?" I said.

"No coffee!" Miss Walker said venomously.

"Can we go now, Lieutenant?" Antoine asked.

"Got some questions," I said. I sat down and pushed my fedora to the back of my head. "Why were those sketches in the safe?"

"Because they're valuable," Miss Walker told me in the sort of voice you explain obvious things to very young children.

"Why valuable?"

"They're sketches of Antoine's new collection."

"Why do they have to be kept in a safe?"

She gave me an exasperated look. "I've just told you!"

"Perhaps I can explain to the Lieutenant?" Antoine suggested. "I am presenting my new collection here in America, instead of Paris this year. I want to keep the designs secret, the materials secret—everything connected with them must remain a secret until the showing of them. My show will coincide with the release of the issue of *Exclusive* that contains the sketches and photographs and so on. It is good publicity for me."

"Tell me more," I said.

He cleared his throat. "These days a designer can't make a fortune out of originals, Lieutenant. I make a collection of, say, thirty gowns? I will, if I am successful, be able to sell them at prices from perhaps as low as two hundred and fifty dollars to as high as three or four thousand. But even if I sell every one—and they represent a year's work by myself and by my staff—should not be able to pay my overhead expenses. So as well, I make an agreement with a manufacturer to give him certain designs that will be mass produced. And he pays me a percentage on his sales. That is where the real money is. But one is necessary to the other. I have to produce the exclusive collection to keep my name in the magazines and make people wish to wear my gowns. I have to have some of those gowns mass produced so that the return will be great enough."

I thought about it for a moment. "So if somebody stole your ideas, it would cost you a lot of money?"

"Precisely," he said. "That is why we must be so careful. Miss Walker I can trust; the advertising agency I employ here I can trust. But one never knows who will try and bribe staff. That is why the sketches are kept in a safe until it is absolutely necessary for them to be used in the production of the magazine."

"How much is a lot of money?" I asked him.

"Pardon?"

I lit another cigarette—who cared about the stable, anyway?

"If somebody got hold of your collection or the sketches—got enough information about it to know what it contained—what would they do?"

"Pirate them!" he said. "Rush into production before my own manufacturer was producing."

"And that would cost you a lot of money—how much?"

He shrugged his shoulders. "It's difficult to estimate—if my collection is a success, the mass market could easily be worth a million dollars or more."

Miss Walker moved her shoulders impatiently. "What has this to do with the murders, Lieutenant?"

"Quite a lot," I said. "For the first time, somebody's come up with a motive."

"My collection ..." Antoine's face went grey at the thought.

"But that's ridiculous!" Miss Walker said.

"Would you like me to edit your magazine for you?" I asked.

"What's that got to do with ..." She stopped suddenly. "I see."

"Sure," I said. "I'll do the detecting—such as it is. We've got the thought. Why don't you two go home and sleep on it? If you have any ideas about it, you know where to find me. And I do hope you have some ideas!"

"The only idea I have is about some sleep," Miss Walker said.

I watched them go. Five minutes later, I heard shuffling feet shuffling along in a hurry. The watchman came into the office, almost out of breath.

"I got it, Lieutenant!" he gasped. "I got it!"

"Don't worry," I told him. "People have been known to get over it!"

"How they got in, I mean!" he said breathlessly. "I got it all figured out!"

"This had better be good," I told him.

"You come with me, Lieutenant."

I went with him out into the corridor to the elevator. We rode down to the basement and then got out. Half the basement was a garage with room enough for about ten cars. A Cadillac was there gathering dust.

Dewlap almost pulled me over to the outside wall. "See that?"

"Sure," I said. "It's a shutter."

"That's right, Lieutenant. A power-operated shutter—you push that switch on the wall over there and it shuts, and when the shutter makes contact with the steel track set in the floor, it locks automatically."

"Okay, genius," I said. "So what?"

He was trembling with excitement. "I got it figured, Lieutenant. Came to me in a flash! Supposing somebody puts something on the track—don't have to be anything big. Just a little thing but it stops the shutter making contact with the steel track, see? Maybe stops it a couple of inches above the track. That shutter's counter-weighted. A couple of inches is enough room for somebody to get their fingers underneath the shutter and lift it.

"I figure that's the way it was done, Lieutenant. Once they got inside they could dump the corpse, come back here and get out. They could take away whatever they used to put on the track so the shutter would shut properly behind them."

I tried it, using a spanner on the track. I stood outside and the watchman closed the shutter. The spanner held the shutter two inches or so off the track, enough to get my fingers underneath. With the counter-balanced weights, it was child's play to lift the shutter again from the outside.

"Okay," I said after I'd finished trying it. "Looks like you won the bet. You don't go down to Homicide. I'm even prepared to believe you stay awake on the job."

Dewlap gurgled his thanks.

Half an hour later I was back at the bureau.

I went into my office expecting to find Hanlon and found the Commissioner, instead. It looked like being my lucky night. He had an overcoat on over his pyjamas and he was smoking a cigar. "Okay," he grunted. "You tell it, Wheeler, and it had better be good!"

So I told him what I'd found out. When I'd finished he grunted and puffed cigar smoke towards me.

"So you've maybe established a motive," he said. "What else do you figure?"

"I was wondering why the two corpses were put in the safe," I said. "Seemed a pointless thing to do."

"No accounting for a maniac's mind," he said.

"If our motive is right," I replied diplomatically, "then maybe there is some accounting. Maybe the guy wanted to see what was in the safe—the sketches and so on. But he didn't want anybody else to realise that. So he put the corpse in the safe, instead of leaving it wherever he had committed the murder. He hoped that when the corpse was found in the safe, everyone would think he had opened it just to put the corpse inside—not to see what was in the safe itself!"

"Could be," Lavers grunted. "Got a reason for Cameron being murdered?"

"Only the obvious one," I said. 'That when he walked into Parker's apartment, he also walked in on the murderer. But don't ask me what the murderer was doing there."

The Commissioner got onto his feet. "You seem to be making some progress, anyway. Keep going, Wheeler—you've got six more days."

And he walked out of the office, leaving me with that cheering thought. I went home to bed.

Next morning I got up around ten and was ready to go out around eleven. I was almost out of the door when the phone rang.

I went back and answered it.

"Lieutenant Wheeler?"

"Sure," I said.

"This is Kathi Snell."

"Hello, Kathi," I said softly.

"I'd like to see you," she said.

"Sure—when?"

"As soon as possible," her voice was flat and emotionless.

"I'll come around now if you want?"

"That would be fine," she said. There was a sharp click as she hung up.

I got there about a quarter to twelve. She opened the door and I followed her into the living-room. She was wearing a dark suit with a dark sweater underneath. Her face was pale.

"I'm sorry about Hubert," I said.

"So am I," she said flatly. "I won't say we were terribly fond of each other, but it's been a shock—quite a shock."

"I imagine," I said.

"Would you like some coffee?"

"Sounds wonderful," I told her.

She went out into the kitchen. I lit a cigarette and waited for her. She was back ten minutes later with the coffee, and it was good.

"What did you want to see me about?" I asked her.

"About the murder," she said. "Hubert's murder. When I got back here last night, he wasn't in. He didn't come back, either. The first thing I knew about it was when a Lieutenant Murphy called sometime after midnight and told me what had happened."

"Tough," I said.

She drank her coffee and lit a cigarette.

"I was rude to you last night," she said. "I apologise."

"It doesn't matter," I told her. "Maybe I had it coming."

"I'd like to help," she said.

"Help?"

"Help you find who killed Hubert."

"What do you think you could do?"

"I don't know," she said wearily. "But I would do anything—anything at all to help."

I finished my coffee. "Do you know any reason why Hubert should get himself murdered?"

"None at all," she said. "I've only been here two or three days. The agency sent me down—they've an agreement with *Exclusive* to use Hubert's sketches for advertising after the Antoine issue is published. As I told you, I'm writing the copy for the ads. The idea was I could familiarise myself with the gowns and talk to Antoine about them, too."

"Yeah," I said.

She got up and began to pace up and down the room.

"Hubert was terribly upset about Henry Parker's death," she said. "They were very close friends."

"So I heard."

"But he didn't say anything much about it—to me, anyway."

"Did he say anything—anything at all?"

She thought for a moment. "He did say a couple of things that didn't make sense, but then Hubert was always saying things that didn't make sense."

"Such as?"

"He said something about Henry being too ambitious and he'd made too many enemies. I thought he was talking about Henry's job—he never did have a very kind pen. Most of the time he was very sarcastic about people."

"Did Hubert say anything else?"

She stubbed her cigarette in an ashtray. "It's hard to remember. Hubert talked nonsense most of the time and I don't know if the things I remember now have any significance or not."

"Don't worry about that," I told her patiently. "Just try and remember." She thought again. "He said something else the other morning, something about Henry's trouble had been that he'd got too smart and Hubert hoped he wouldn't make the same mistake."

"Anything else?"

"Nothing that I can remember," she said.

It looked like a wasted visit except for the coffee.

I got up. "If there's anything you can do to help, Kathi, I'll let you know."

"Please!" she said. "I think I'll go crazy just sitting around the apartment and thinking about it all the time."

"You don't have to do that," I told her. "Why don't you have dinner with me tonight?"

"Thanks," she smiled faintly. "I promise you this time I won't run away."

"This time I'll run after you," I told her. "There's never been a blonde get away from Wheeler yet."

CHAPTER 6
Leave 'em Guessing

Buckman's was quite a store. I rode one of the elevators up to the top floor and finally found the office of the great man himself. He had a secretary who would have made a Hollywood talent scout drool. I drooled a little myself and I'm no talent scout—well, not from Hollywood, anyway.

"I'm sorry," she said. "Mr Buckman is very busy."

"I'll let you into a secret," I told her. "So am I." I showed her my shield and told her who I was.

She rang through to his office and spoke to him for a moment. Then she put the receiver back and smiled. "He'll see you right away, Lieutenant."

"That's a pity," I said.

She looked puzzled. "I beg your pardon?"

"I was hoping for five minutes to spend looking at you," I said.

"I'll bet you say that to all the girls."

"But only one at a time," I said and walked on into Buckman's office. He sat behind a massive desk in a massive office. I wasn't impressed.

"Yes, Lieutenant?" he said stiffly.

"I wanted to ask you some questions," I said.

"I'm very busy this afternoon," he said. "Will it take long?"

"It depends how long you take with the answers," I told him. "Or perhaps you would prefer to come down to the bureau and answer them there?"

Buckman's grey hair bristled. "You can't talk to me that way, Wheeler! I happen to have some influence in this town! I'm not some drunken tramp you've pulled in out of the gutter!"

"It's all a matter of opinion," I told him. "You going to answer my questions or do I take you in?"

"All right," he growled. "Ask your questions."

I hooked my foot under the rung of the visitor's chair and pulled it towards me. When it got close enough, I dropped into it and lit a cigarette.

"Miss Milbray's a friend of yours?"

"Yes."

"You were at her party the other night—for Antoine, the dress designer?"

"That's correct."

"Henry Parker was there—you knew him?"

"Vaguely."

"What did you think of him?"

He shrugged his shoulders. "I never thought very much about him—he was a poisonous little brute."

"You mean, the way he wrote?"

"The way he talked, the way he looked, acted—everything about him was poisonous."

Buckman looked as if he meant it.

"You have any theories why someone might have killed him?"

"I figure he walked around asking for it," he said. "You ask me, I wonder he lived as long as he did."

"There's been an epidemic," I said. "First there was Parker and then a cop who was looking over Parker's apartment—and then Hubert Snell, the artist. Did you know Snell?"

"I think I might have met him at Janice's place," he said. "Had a beard, didn't he?"

"That's right."

I managed to blow a smoke-ring—most times I miss. I watched it float towards the ceiling until it dissolved.

"This is quite a store you've got here," I said. "You've got other branches throughout the state as well?"

"That's right," he said. "Business is good."

"Do much in the way of fashion goods?"

"Sure—backbone of the business." He looked at me sharply. "Why do you ask that?"

"I thought you might be able to help," I said, with my best poker face showing.

"I'd be glad to help the police in any way I can," he said, with all the enthusiasm of a platinum blonde being offered a synthetic stone.

"This guy Antoine," I said. "*Exclusive* is running his collection in their next issue. I understand he'll release it at the same time. And soon after that his manufacturer will release copies on the cheap market."

"It's the usual practice," Buckman agreed.

"If somebody got hold of those designs and released them on the cheap market before Antoine's own manufacturer could, he'd make a lot of money, wouldn't he?"

"Sure," Buckman said. "A hell of a lot of money. Antoine is really big news in fashion over here right now. The fact that he's releasing his collection here instead of in Paris, gives it a terrific edge."

"I'm looking for a motive for the killings," I told him. "I'm wondering if that's it?"

Buckman stared at me for a long moment.

"Cops are guys without much imagination," I explained. "We like to see a nice solid motive behind a murder—particularly when there are three murders. And a million dollars makes three murders an occupational risk. It seems to fit a lot more neatly than the fact that a lot of people disliked Parker and therefore might have knocked him off because of their dislike. Don't you think, Buckman?"

He peeled the cellophane off a cigar and lit it carefully. "I guess so, Lieutenant. I guess so."

"I'm glad to have your opinion," I said. "It's a great help." I stubbed out my cigarette and got onto my feet.

"You're going, Lieutenant?"

"Thanks for your time," I told him.

"No more questions?"

"Not one. I've asked you the questions I wanted answers for. Thanks again."

"What will you do now?" he asked curiously.

"We'll keep following up what leads we have at the moment," I said. "But I'll tell you one thing, Buckman. If anybody brings pirated Antoine designs on the market, they're going to have to answer a lot of questions—an awful lot of awkward questions. Good afternoon, Mr Buckman."

"Good afternoon, Lieutenant."

I looked back just before I closed the door behind me. He was still staring at me, the cigar burning down unnoticed between his fingers.

I wondered if I'd given the guy something to worry about. I hoped so. I thought a guy with all the dough that Buckman had deserved some worries—it would sort of even the score for him.

It was three in the afternoon when I got back to the sidewalk.

I got back into the prowl-car and drove across town to the offices of *Exclusive.*

The windswept blonde knew me by now. It took me only a minute to get from reception into Miss Walker's office. She was seated behind her desk, wearing a navy worsted suit which looked efficient and exclusive.

"Back again, Lieutenant," she said. "Not more trouble, I hope?"

I was getting used to visitors' chairs. I sat down in hers and lit the inevitable cigarette.

"Do you have coffee in the afternoons?" I asked her hopefully.

"I can arrange it," she smiled and picked up the phone.

Miss Walker had the sort of job I'd always wanted—where you can pick up the phone and order anything you want—coffee, a drink, a blonde—anything at all.

The coffee arrived a few minutes later—in a silver pot with white and gold cups for the serving. They do it differently at the bureau—there it comes in cardboard containers. She poured the coffee and handed me a cup. I sipped it gratefully; it was good.

"How long to go before your Antoine issue is on the streets, Miss Walker?"

"Why, Lieutenant!" she smiled. "I didn't know you were that interested in high fashion."

"I'm interested in the people who wear it," I said, giving her my old-fashioned look. "Particularly blondes."

She didn't say anything to that. I sipped some more coffee. "The Antoine issue will be out in ten days," she said finally.

"So if somebody has pirated his designs, they haven't got much time to produce them?"

"They'd have to be quick," she agreed. "They'd want to get them on the market not longer than a week after our issue hits. Antoine himself has arranged for the mass production through his own manufacturer, to be on the market three weeks after the issue is out."

I finished the coffee and put my cup back on the tray.

"Would you like some more coffee, Lieutenant?"

"I'd love some more coffee," I told her, "and I'd like to meet Prudence."

"Prudence?"

"Prudence Foy."

"Oh, of course," she nodded. "The girl in accounts."

"The girl who opened the safe and found Parker, instead of whatever she was looking for," I added.

"Do you want to talk to her in here, Lieutenant? It would give you some privacy. I can fill in time elsewhere."

"Thanks," I told her. "It would be a help."

She went out of the office and came back a couple of minutes later with a girl walking behind her. Miss Walker introduced us, then left.

Prudence Foy was a brunette with hair that hung down below her shoulders. Her eyes were too wide and too bright and her lips too red. Her figure looked around ninety-eight per cent. I deduct two per cent for the possible aid of figure-control garments. I am nothing if not a cautious assessor.

I asked her to sit down and she did. I asked her if she'd like some coffee and she said she wouldn't. I offered her a cigarette and she didn't. I was tempted to ask her what she *did* do and thought maybe it was a little early in our relationship.

"You found Henry Parker's body in the safe, Miss Foy?"

"Yes, Lieutenant," her eyes widened still more. "I'll never forget it."

"What did you go to the safe for?"

"A ledger."

"You knew the combination?"

"Yes," she nodded. "I'm Mr Sutton's assistant, you see."

I didn't, but I let it pass. "Who else knows the combination?"

"I'm not really sure, Lieutenant. Mr Sutton does of course, and Miss Walker. I guess the directors would know it, too."

"Yeah." I lit another cigarette—hell, they say that smog can have the same effect, don't they?

"Did you know Henry Parker very well?"

She shook her head. "Not very well, Lieutenant. You see, he was editorial and I'm accounts."

"Don't they mix?"

She smiled. "Not really. We consider we're sane—if you get what I mean?"

"I think I'm with you," I said. "Did you know Hubert Snell at all?"

"Hardly," she said.

"He was editorial, too?"

"That's right," she agreed.

"Okay," I said. "That's about all the questions I can think of, Miss Foy—thanks."

"A pleasure, Lieutenant," she smiled.

She got up from the chair and started towards the door.

"Do you drink, Miss Foy?" I asked.

She spun around, still wide-eyed. "Alcohol? Certainly not."

"Girl scout?"

"I'm a Ranger!" she said with dignity.

"I thought so," I nodded. "What a waste."

Miss Walker came back into the office a few moments later.

"What have you been saying to Prudence?" she almost grinned at me. "She seems quite upset."

"I was just working out why she works in accounts," I said. "That safe of yours must have personality or something—it has attracted two corpses already."

She winced. "I wish you wouldn't put it like that, Lieutenant. We've had enough publicity already."

"Don't you like publicity?"

"Not that sort. It doesn't do a magazine like ours any good at all."

"You have the combination, Sutton has it, Prudence Foy has it, your directors in New York have it. Anybody else?"

"I gave it to Hubert Snell," she said, "while he was working on the Antoine drawings—it was essential they were locked up."

"Nobody else?"

"Not that I know of, Lieutenant."

"It sort of narrows down the field of people who could have opened the safe and put Parker's body inside, doesn't it?" I asked casually.

Miss Walker stared at me for a moment and then her mouth dropped open. "I'd never thought of it that way before."

"We can doubt that Snell stabbed himself in the back and then bundled himself in," I went on. "That leaves us a choice of three, doesn't it? We can discount your directors in New York."

"You mean," she gulped, "Joe Sutton, Prudence—or myself?"

"You're right on the ball."

"But—but that's ridiculous!"

"Prove it," I said.

"Well, in the first place ..." her voice trailed away into silence. I watched as her hand crept up to her throat. "I can't believe it," she said. "Surely somebody else must have known it? Hubert could have told somebody else, couldn't he?"

"So could you," I said gently. "Did you?"

She shook her head. "No—I've never told anybody else the combination."

"It's just a thought," I said. "I'd like you to think about it and if you have any ideas, let me know."

CHAPTER 7
Watchman! What of the Night?

She had her hair in tight curls on top of her head. She was wearing a simple little number in blue sharkskin—if it had fitted the original shark as tightly as it fitted her, the shark would have got cramp.

She stood there and looked around the living-room.

"Cosy," she said. "I didn't realise this was where you meant when you said somewhere nice and quiet for dinner."

"What could be quieter than my place?" I said. "Like some music?"

"Where from?"

"Out of the wall there," I told her. "It's my hi-fi set-up that keeps me poor!"

"That and women," she smiled slightly.

"That and women," I agreed.

I stacked discs onto the turntable—Andre with his strings and sweet, sugary Sammy Kaye. It would last us through dinner, anyway.

"What are we eating?" she asked.

"Kathi," I told her, "you have a mundane mind!"

"Also an empty stomach," she said. "I haven't eaten since this morning—the food had better be good."

"Oysters, lobster, strawberries," I said. "How does that sound?"

"Good," she said. "Don't tell me you can cook?"

"No," I admitted, "I can't. But that guy who runs the delicatessen down on the corner—can he cook!"

I opened a bottle of rye and poured two drinks, handed her one and raised my own glass. "Here's to dinner."

"To dinner," she agreed. "Surely it doesn't end so abruptly, Al?"

"It's brief and to the point," I said.

"What does it stand for?"

"The last dame who asked me that ended up dead," I said. "A two-time murderess, no less. You have been warned."

"Forget I ever asked," she said.

Kostelanetz gave out with "Summertime."

"I'll just check the lobster's dead," I said, "and be back.'

I went out into the kitchen. I had everything highly organised, all ready to serve. I put the champagne into a bucket and packed ice around it. I served the oysters and took the plates into the living-room, where I had the table already set.

"Food," I announced.

She walked across towards the table. The blue sharkskin rustled as she walked.

"Did anyone ever tell you that you're beautiful?" I asked her as she sat down.

"Hundreds," she said. "Is that the pepper over there?"

Okay, Wheeler, I told myself. So try and get romantic when the dame's hungry. "Yeah," I passed her the pepper.

I brought the champagne with the lobster. Kathi took one look at the bottle and raised her eyebrows.

"I see I shall have to watch my step," she said. "This looks like a campaign."

"Champagne!" I said, and winced with her.

Some three-quarters of an hour later the meal was finished. I tossed the dishes into the kitchen, served the coffee and we sat on the sofa—to drink the coffee, drink the benedictine and listen to Sammy Kaye. Or maybe that's why Kathi sat there—my motives were different.

I lit a cigarette for her and one for myself. "How do you feel, Kathi?"

"Wonderful," she said. "I hand it to the guy in the delicatessen. His food is good."

"I carried it all the way home," I said defensively.

"Well, half a cheer for you."

I thought a rye would help. I got up and poured myself one and absentmindedly switched off the overhead light at the same time.

"Hey," she said sharply.

"I can't stand bright light," I explained as I sat down on the sofa again—six inches closer to her than I'd been before. "Don't you think we've got enough light with the table-lamp?"

"No," she said.

"What do you want light for? What are you planning to do—read?"

"Have you got any good books?" she asked.

I was losing my grip. There was no doubt about it. We sat there—smoking.

"I was thinking about Hubert today," she said finally.

"Yeah?"

"I told you we were never very close, but he was my brother, after all."

"Sure."

"He was a funny guy—what's an 'animist'?"

"Huh?"

"I asked him if he believed in anything once, and he said he was an animist."

"I never heard of it."

"Neither did I."

We sat in silence again.

"He had a talent, you know," she said after a while. "A real talent—he was a very good artist."

"Sure."

"You don't sound very interested."

"Would you like another drink?" I suggested hopefully.

"No, thanks. I think I've had enough."

There was a gentle click as the last disc shut itself off.

"More music?" I suggested.

"No, thanks."

"What, then?"

"I'd like to go home, I think."

I got up and switched on the overhead light. I poured myself a double rye and drank it down in one shuddering gulp.

"Okay," I said.

She stood there, watching me with a slight smile on her face.

"Poor Al," she said. "It's not your night, is it?"

"It never was," I growled.

Half an hour later I dropped her outside her apartment block. She didn't ask me up. I wasn't even surprised.

"Thanks for the dinner, Al," she said. "It was wonderful."

"A pleasure," I said.

"Ask me again some time," she said. "Maybe I'll be in a better mood."

"Sure," I said, and kangaroo-hopped the prowl-car away from the kerb.

I thought I didn't have to waste all the evening. If I couldn't play it cosy with hi-fi and rye, I could play it tough with a certain guy I'd had on my mind since the night before.

I figured I had given him long enough to think he'd got away with it, so the psychological shock might be greater when I hit him with it tonight. I could try, anyway. I was in the mood to be mean.

There was a nightbell outside the front door of the office block. I pushed it and left my thumb hard against it for about twenty seconds, then let go— the silence inside the building must have been a relief.

I lit a cigarette and maybe half a minute later a peephole in the door opened and Dewlap's watery eyes looked out at me.

"Open up," I told him. "Lieutenant Wheeler here—remember me?"

"Sure, Lieutenant," he said.

The door swung back and I stepped inside. He closed the door and bolted it again. I looked at my watch automatically—it was just after eleven.

"You want to take a look at the magazine office?" he asked.

"No," I said. "I just wanted to have a talk to you."

"What about, Lieutenant?"

"Let's go down to the basement," I said.

We went down the steps into the basement. He switched on the overhead lights. The place looked empty and cold. Our voices echoed as we talked.

"You know something, Dewlap?" I said. "I think you're one smart guy."

"How's that, Lieutenant?"

"Working out how they got into the place—through that shutter."

He laughed nervously. "Guess you had me worried, Lieutenant. I didn't hanker after getting third-degreed down at headquarters. No, sir!"

"You were smart all right, Dewlap," I said. "Just a little too smart."

He stopped laughing suddenly. "How was that, Lieutenant?"

"You were too smart," I said. "Nobody could have worked all that out in half an hour."

"What're you driving at, Lieutenant?"

I looked at him carefully. "How much?" I asked.

"Huh?"

"How much did they pay you—or did they threaten they'd kill you as well?"

He was starting to shake again. "I don't know what you're talking about, Lieutenant."

"You do!" I said. "I'll give you a break, Dewlap. Tell me the truth now and maybe I can swing it for you. Maybe there won't even be a charge in it. But I want the whole truth."

"I still don't know what you're talking about," he quavered.

I was beginning to feel tired.

"Don't give me that," I said. "It's the same as last night—only worse! We can play this thing two ways, pal. You can tell me and like I said, I'll try and give you a break. Or you can come down to the bureau now and I'll let the boys work you over until they sweat it out of you. Then I'll throw the book at you. False witness, concealing evidence, accessory after the fact and maybe before the fact as well. You want to die in the pen?"

His palsy was acting up worse. For a moment I thought he was going to pass out. I looked at my watch carefully.

"Ten seconds, Dewlap," I said. "If you haven't started talking by then, I'll take you down to the bureau. I don't aim to spend my night in a basement."

He wiped his forehead with the sleeve of his shirt. "You—you were on the level about giving me a break?"

"As much as I can—so long as you come clean."

"They didn't give me very much," he muttered. "Five hundred bucks was all they gave me."

"Go on."

"You got a cigarette?"

I gave him a cigarette and had to light it for him; his hands were shaking too much to hold the match.

"They came in here the way I showed you last night," he said. "That's the truth, Lieutenant. They was out of luck—or I guess I was. I happened to be down here when they came in. I saw the two of them get out of the car and I nearly died with fright. I saw 'em carrying this other guy in his pyjamas. They carried him up the steps and I was over there," he pointed with one hand, "behind the boiler. I guess I should have rang the cops then, but I wondered what the hell they was doing. I thought maybe it was a gag or something."

"Why did you think that?"

"The things they had over their faces."

He stopped talking suddenly and I saw the naked fear in his eyes as he looked over my shoulder. Two shots hammered out and his face seemed to suddenly blur and dissolve into a red mask. The next moment the lights went out.

I flung myself sideways and down flat on the cold concrete. I rolled a couple of times and finished up on my chest. I clawed the Smith and Wesson out of my shoulder-holster and waited.

Nothing happened. There was no sound in the basement at all. I remembered that I'd been standing with my back to the steps. Whoever had fired the shots must have come down the steps and Dewlap had seen him—or her—and must have seen the gun in their hand.

The silence persisted. I noiselessly got to my feet again and began to edge my way towards where I thought the steps must be. I wondered where in hell the light switches were—probably beside the steps.

I had the gun in one hand and the other hand stretched out in front of me. I felt the wall and then moved along beside it until it turned a right-angle. I had to be at the foot of the steps then.

I ran my hand over the wall gently until I found the switches and clicked the two of them on. Light flooded the basement again and I stopped breathing for a moment, then relaxed. The basement was empty except for me and the body of the nightwatchman.

A moment later I heard faintly the sound of the bolts on the front door on the ground floor being drawn, then the sound of the door slamming shut again. The killer had got out—there was no point in chasing after him. By the time I got into the street, he could be four blocks away.

I walked over to Dewlap and knelt beside him. He was dead all right. Both slugs had smashed into his face and were probably lodged in his brain.

There was nothing much left for me to do now except shout, "Copper!" I thought about it and decided against it. It only meant hanging around and probably having the Commissioner give me another of his talks. It wouldn't help find the killer. I thought right now what I needed was a drink.

I went back up to the ground floor and let myself out. There was nobody in the street. I got back into the prowl-car and drove away slowly.

I thought I was the bright boy and just how much Lavers would appreciate me if he only knew. I'd kidded Snell to stay out in the rain because I'd hoped of better things from his sister—and while he'd stayed out in the rain, he'd been murdered.

I'd figured the night before that Dewlap was just a little too smart, but I'd been so smart I didn't try to break him down then.

I had to wait until tonight. And he got killed right under my nose before he'd given me any real information at all.

Life was just a bowl of cherries.

I found myself driving aimlessly around the block. I decided I still needed a drink, but I didn't want to go home. I didn't want to go to a bar, either. I was just being difficult. I thought the hell with it, I'd buy myself an expensive drink—at the Cafe Rouge.

And I did.

The head-waiter gave me a table for two right beside the dance floor. That was a break—the floorshow started ten minutes later.

I ordered a double Scotch and got it just before the floorshow started.

The show wasn't bad, not bad at all. In particular, the last act was a strip by a tawny blonde who looked as if she'd be right at home in an African jungle, with Hemingway stalking her with a rifle. It was a high-class strip all done with mirrors and drapes and you probably didn't get to see as much of the tawny blonde as you would on a beach, but the customers seemed to like it.

When the show was finished I looked around to order another drink and saw a guy standing there, smiling down at me.

"I'm Marty Shore," he told me. "I own this place. I thought I might be able to buy you a drink, Lieutenant?"

"I never refuse an offer like that," I told him. "Won't you join me?"

He slipped into the chair opposite me and gestured to the drink waiter. "What are you drinking, Lieutenant?"

"Scotch, thanks," I said.

"A double Scotch for the Lieutenant and a martini for me."

"I didn't know my fame had spread so wide," I said. "Or is it my ugly face?"

He grinned. "One of the waiters heard Miss Walker telling the girl you were with the other night that you were Lieutenant Wheeler. I'm always interested when the police visit me. It makes me wonder if I'm doing anything I shouldn't?"

"Not that I know of," I told him. "Although with that lioness in your floorshow, I wouldn't be surprised."

The waiter returned with the drinks.

"Here's cheers," Shore said. "You waiting for your girl tonight, Lieutenant?"

I shook my head. "I thought I'd like to buy myself an expensive drink before I went home to bed," I said. "That's all."

"If you'd like Sherry to join you," he said, "I'm sure she'd be delighted."

"Sherry?"

"The lioness you were talking about," he explained.

"What is this?" I asked. "Bribery and corruption?"

He laughed easily. "I like to be on good terms with the cops, Lieutenant." He snapped his fingers and the waiter surged forward. "Tell Miss Blair I'd like her to join us for a drink."

He offered me a cigarette and lit it for me.

"You're working on the Parker murder case, Lieutenant?" he said. "I read about it in the papers. I'm interested—Miss Walker comes here regularly and Parker was here quite often—not that he ever gave us a plug in the magazine."

"Sure," I said, "I'm working on the case."

"How's it progressing, Lieutenant? Not that I'm expecting any secrets, of course."

"Okay," I said, "I think."

"You're expecting to make an arrest soon?"

"That's what it says in the papers, doesn't it?"

He laughed again. "I guess I shouldn't have asked."

"Did Hubert Snell ever come here?"

"The artist? The other guy who was murdered? Once, I think, Lieutenant. He was with Parker. I remember him; he had a beard, didn't he?"

"And a worried look," I added.

Someone stopped beside the table. I looked up, then stood up. The tawny blonde was wearing a black sheath that seemed to leave more uncovered than the strip had done. The waiter tucked a chair underneath her and she sat down.

"Sherry," Marty Shore said, "I'd like you to meet Lieutenant Wheeler."

"Hello, Lieutenant," she smiled slowly at me, revealing white, even teeth with slightly accented canines. "I just love policemen."

CHAPTER 8
Lavers Loves Me

I pulled back the drapes and staggered back to get out of the blinding glare of sunlight. There was a dwarf inside my head with his thumbs pressed against the back of my eyeballs. He'd just finished coating the inside of my mouth with tar and when he wasn't pressing my eyeballs, he was twitching all my nerve ends so I twanged like a guitar.

I looked at the two empty bottles and the two half-empty glasses on the table and shuddered. I lit a cigarette, inhaled and shuddered again.

I could hear the shower running. I tottered back into the bedroom, put on a robe and went into the kitchen. I heaped coffee into the percolator, ran water over it, then switched it on.

Then I went back into the living-room, turned a chair so that it faced away from the daylight and sat there, listening to the terrifying irregularity of my heartbeats.

Five minutes later somebody padded into the room. The drapes were flung wide open and I winced as the increased light hit my eyes.

"Gosh!" she said enthusiastically. "What a beautiful day!"

I turned my head slowly, ignoring the knives that stabbed into it, and looked at her.

"You feel healthy?" I croaked.

She took a deep breath. "I feel wonderful!"

I pointed a shaking finger at the two empty bottles. "Did we drink all that?"

"About a bottle each, I guess," she said. "Then you wanted to take your prowl-car and go rob a liquor store." She purred deep in her throat. "But I had other ideas, honey. And finally you saw things my way."

"Sherry," I said wonderingly, "where do you get your vitality from?"

"My folks were circus-folk," she told me. "The old man was a lion-tamer and Ma was the strong woman. You should have seen it when they had a fight. Folks used to come from miles around just to watch."

"I imagine," I shuddered.

She looked groomed, immaculate and fresh ... I felt like a discarded champagne cork beside her. She was wearing the black sheath.

"I guess I ought to be going, Al."

"I'll drive you home," I said.

"Don't worry," she said. "I can get a cab—you look like you need aspirin and rest."

She came over, leaned down and kissed me gently on the forehead. "So long, Al. It was fun. See you around, huh? Maybe you'll ring me—or come see the floorshow again?"

"Sure," I said. "So long, Sherry."

She went out, whistling.

I leaned my head back against the chair and closed my eyes. My heart-beats sounded terrible. I wasn't sure which was worse—the sound it made when it beat or the sound it didn't make when it missed a beat.

The phone rang and I climbed two feet in the air. I managed to stagger over to it and lift the receiver.

"If that's the morgue," I said, "I hope you've got room for one more."

"Good morning, Lieutenant Wheeler," a smooth voice said. "It is now precisely eleven twenty-nine and thirty seconds. I do hope I haven't disturbed your sleep?"

I gurgled something indistinct into the mouthpiece.

"I wouldn't have worried you, Lieutenant," Lavers continued smoothly. "But another corpse has turned up—such a nuisance!

"Another?"

"The nightwatchman at the *Exclusive* building. Shot dead in the basement! I use the word in a geographical sense rather than anatomical, of course."

"Yes, sir," I mumbled.

There was a moment's pause.

"If it should interest you in any way," he went on, "Hanlon has the facts. May I remind you, Lieutenant, that I foolishly agreed to give you seven days in which to solve these murders by your own methods. Three of those days have already gone. Just how far have you got?"

"Nothing definite yet," I muttered.

"You mean, you haven't got anywhere?"

"I wouldn't say that."

"I would," he said gently. "Tell me—what do you consider is the major problem out of the now four murders?"

"Parker," I grunted.

"Parker, eh? Why Parker?"

"The way he was murdered," I said.

"We know that—he was strangled!"

"Yeah—how?"

"With a girdle." Lavers was getting impatient again.

"That's the problem," I said.

"Why? Why with a girdle?"

The silence lasted about ten seconds. Then there was a bull-horn roar in my ear. I hastily held the receiver away—I could still hear his voice quite clearly.

"Why!" he thundered. "Are you crazy, man? What possible significance has that got? Four men murdered—one of them one of your own Homicide lieutenants—and you're playing around with inconsequential riddles! Why, you ..."

I didn't think he was going to say anything instructive, so I hung up on him gently, hoping the click wouldn't interfere with his argument.

I stood under the hot shower for ten minutes, then the cold shower for five minutes. I had a shave. I cleaned my teeth. I even got dressed.

I went into the kitchen and drank three cups of black coffee.

I lit a cigarette and wondered if I felt any better. If I did, I didn't notice it. I went out to the prowl-car and drove down to the bureau at a screaming twenty-five miles an hour.

Hanlon's smug look was more so.

"Well, good after ..." he looked at his watch carefully. "Sorry, Lieutenant. I mean good morning."

"You have a short memory, pal," I told him. "I am still the Lieutenant-in-Charge of the bureau."

"Yes, chief," he said. "Did Commissioner Lavers contact you?"

"He did."

"He seemed a little upset when he rang here earlier for you," Hanlon murmured. "I told him we hadn't seen you in a couple of days, but I was sure if he rang your house he'd find you. He did find you home, didn't he, chief?"

I saw a pair of bloodshot eyes staring at me from a chalk-white face and realised I was looking into the mirror. I turned away quickly and lit a cigarette.

"Hanlon," I said gently, "I can see that sitting behind my desk has been too much for you. Sitting behind a desk is bad for any cops—they grow corns where no corns should grow. You don't want corns there, do you, Hanlon?"

He didn't say anything. His dirty look penetrated my shoulder-blades just like a knife.

"So you can get up from that desk," I continued, "and go out into the big wide world and do some work. I want to know things about a dame called Janice Milbray, another called Elise Walker and another called Kathi Snell. I also want to know about a guy called Antoine, a guy called Eddie Buckman, a guy called Joe Sutton and another guy called Marty Shore. I want to know how much dough they have, how they live and where their dough comes from. I want to know if they are married or if they have any other arrangements. And I want to know by tonight—early!"

Hanlon came out of the chair in one jerk. "Now wait a minute, chief! Do a check like that on seven people! That'll take a couple of days ..."

"I can give you their addresses," I said. "I can tell you what they do or don't do for a living. You can use anybody else you like, as well—take Murphy and Podeski if you want. But I want that information by this evening—say six! And if you haven't got it, I'll make a report to that effect to the Commissioner."

Hanlon started to walk towards the door.

"It's okay for you," he muttered. "You don't even come inside the damned office in two days and then you—"

"You write your report to the Commissioner," I said gently, "and I'll write mine."

He got as far as the door, then looked back. "Don't you even want to hear about that nightwatchman?"

I raised my eyes and stared at the ceiling. "His name was Dewlap," I said. "He was around sixty years of age. He was shot dead in the basement of the *Exclusive* building last night, somewhere around eleven o'clock. Two bullets in the face, probably lodged in the brain, death being instantaneous …"

Hanlon stared at me with bulging eyes. "How the hell did you know all that?"

I shrugged my shoulders casually. "Work that out, pal," I said, "and you'll know why I don't need to come near the office in a couple of days."

He went out with the look of sheer bewilderment still etched on his face.

I sat down in the chair he'd just vacated and lit another cigarette from the stub of the first. I could handle Hanlon okay, but I wasn't doing so well with the Commissioner.

I tried to think of something constructive to do and came up with the answer almost right away. I leaned my head back and went to sleep.

I woke up around three, went out and had some lunch and one Scotch, then felt a little better. I sat around the office waiting for Hanlon and he showed up on time. He looked harassed as if he'd really been working hard and that made me feel even better.

"I got it," he said. "I had Murphy and Podeski help me, as you suggested. But some of it took some getting in an afternoon."

"I'm sure it did, Lieutenant," I said generously. "Why don't you sit down and ease some weight off your brains?"

He glared at me, then slumped into a chair. He pulled out his notebook and flipped over the pages.

"Who do you want first?" he asked.

"Take 'em as they come," I told him.

"Okay. Buckman, he was easy. Owns Buckman's Stores—they're an incorporated company, of course, but he has a fifty-two per cent shareholding. His income, as close as we can get, is somewhere around a hundred thousand a year—after taxes," he added in a hushed voice. "Unmarried. Quite a guy with the dames but nobody could pin any one dame down for us. He lives high, but he can afford to."

"Okay," I nodded. "Who's next?"

"Janice Milbray." He flicked the page of his notebook. "Hard to find out where her dough comes from. Money is paid into her account regularly—in cash. She lives high—her own penthouse, throws big parties, and so on. Bit of a mystery—she isn't married, either.

"Elise Walker, she's the editor of *Exclusive*, as you know. Unmarried—income of thirty thousand a year, plus bonuses. Has a nice apartment and so on—living within her income, has a nice holding of bonds lodged with the bank. She doesn't have any particular male interest as far as we could find out.

"Kathi Snell, copy-writer with the Advance Advertising Agency in New York. Salary of twelve thousand a year. Has her own apartment. Sent here to work on Antoine's account—staying with her brother, or in his apartment now. Not married and doesn't have any attachment here. I wouldn't know about New York.

"Joe Sutton, accountant with *Exclusive*. Salary of twenty thousand. Not married. Nobody knows anything about how he lives or what his interests are—keeps himself to himself. Has his own house—nice place on the edge of Kyle Bay, must cost him a lot of dough."

Hanlon cleared his throat a couple of times and looked up at me.

"Go on," I told him.

"Antoine," he went on. "I guess we don't know anything more about him than the newspapers do. He's a French fashion designer and he's got a place in Paris. Over here to launch his new fashions. He's staying at the Hotel Montford."

He flicked the last page. "Marty Shore, owns the Cafe Rouge, been there about twelve months. Plenty of dough in the bank and the place is doing all right—making plenty. Came here from New York—no police record but nobody knows what he did in New York. There's a stripper works in his floorshow, name of Sherry Blair—she lives on the premises and there's talk that she's Shore's girlfriend."

He closed his notebook and looked at me. "That what you wanted, chief?"

"I guess so," I said. "Thanks."

He shuffled his feet around. "Tell you anything, chief?"

"Nothing that helps," I said wearily. "Out of that bunch you've been through, would you say any of them needed dough?"

He thought for a moment, then shook his head. "No, chief, I wouldn't."

"Would you say any of them needed dough so badly that they would murder for it—not once but four times?"

"I guess I wouldn't," he said.

"Neither would I," I sighed. "And that's a pity."

"How come?"

"Because I had a million bucks odd set as the motive for the murders," I told him. "And none of the suspects need that sort of dough."

He was trying to make up his mind whether I was kidding him or not and he wasn't sure.

"Marty Shore," he said. "Where does he fit in as a suspect?"

"He doesn't," I grinned. "I just threw him in to make it harder for you."

Hanlon's face went a dull shade of red and he got up out of his chair and stomped out of the office. I let him go.

I waited five minutes, then walked outside. Lieutenant Murphy was talking to Sergeant Podeski. He looked up and grinned when he saw me.

"Hi, chief—you're a stranger around the place these days."

"I guess so," I said. "Had a busy afternoon?"

"Busy!" Podeski bellowed. "I'll say. That Hanlon, the slob. He ought to be ..." he stopped suddenly and swallowed. "Sorry, sir," he added stiffly.

"Forget it," I told him. "It's my fault, anyway. I told Hanlon I wanted the answers by six tonight, or else."

"I sort of figured it might be something like that," Murphy grinned. The grin faded. "Maybe I should keep my big mouth shut, chief. He went out of here five minutes ago—on his way to the city hall."

"Maybe he's got a friend there," I said. "He's ahead of me, if he has."

I nodded to them and walked towards the outer door. Murphy caught up with me as I walked down the corridor.

"Maybe it's none of my business, chief," he muttered. "Maybe like I said just now—I should keep my big mouth shut. But that Hanlon, you know whose job he's after."

"I can make a shrewd guess," I said. "But thanks all the same."

"The rest of the boys are happy the way things are," he went on. "But that Hanlon's ambitious. Anything the rest of us can do, chief."

"Thanks," I told him. "I appreciate it."

CHAPTER 9
Prudent Prudence

I was home with Brubeck's version of "Fare Thee Well, Annabelle" playing on the hi-fi. I almost wasn't hearing it—I was thinking. That's something I'm not used to doing and it hurt.

When you're getting no place fast, you have to skip the routine alleys that are closed anyway and try something else. That's being unorthodox—or something.

Dewlap had been too smart to be true. I wondered about the other characters—if any of them were too something to be true? I had a thought; it wasn't much of a one, but I was desperate.

There was somebody who was too good to be true, maybe.

I looked up the phone directory, but she wasn't listed. So I looked up Elise Walker's private number and rang her. She was home.

"Lieutenant Wheeler," I told her.

"Good evening, Lieutenant," she said.

"A piece of routine I forgot," I said casually. "Can you give me Prudence Foy's address?"

"I think so," she said. "I keep a list of the staff's home addresses here somewhere." She was back half a minute later and gave me the address.

"Thanks," I said. "It'll keep our records straight."

I hung up, grabbed my hat and went out to the prowl-car. Prudence Foy lived in an apartment block about six miles out of town. I parked across from the apartment block, turned off the motor and lit myself a cigarette.

The apartment block was across the road. I got out and walked across, up the front steps into the entrance. Her apartment was on the second floor.

I walked up the two flights of stairs and knocked on her door.

There was the sound a radio playing inside. I knocked again and the door opened.

She was wearing a towelling robe and she had a comb in her hand. Her eyes were just as wide as they had been when I saw her in the office.

"Why, it's Lieutenant Wheeler, isn't it?"

"That's right," I agreed. "I wanted to ask some more questions, Prudence. Cops are one hell of a nuisance like that."

She hesitated for a moment. "Won't you come in?" she asked doubtfully.

"Thanks," I said and walked into the apartment. She closed the door behind me and followed me in.

"I was just out of the shower," she said. "Will you excuse me for a few moments, Lieutenant?"

"Sure," I said. "If you feel safer with clothes on, that's okay by me."

She disappeared into the bedroom. I lit a cigarette and had a look around the apartment. The furnishings were sombre—but expensive. If she'd furnished it on her salary from the magazine, I wondered if Joe Sutton could use another assistant.

A radiogram stood against one wall. I walked over to it and had a look—I'm always interested in any form of reproduction.

There was a disc on the turntable. I had a look at the title—"Night On Bare Mountain." Not the sort of music for a girl scout.

She came back into the room a couple of minutes. later. She was wearing a form-fitting dress of pale blue silk. Her hair, just combed out, seemed even longer.

She smiled nervously at me. "I'm ready for the questions now, Lieutenant."

"Sit down and relax," I told her. "You seem all tensed up."

She sat down. "I guess I'm not used to policemen around the apartment, Lieutenant."

I looked over at the radiogram. "You like music?"

"Why, yes," she nodded. "Serious music, that is."

"Like 'Night On Bare Mountain'?"

"Yes," she nodded.

"You know what it's about? All the evil spirits and things that go 'eck! in the graveyards!"

"Of course!" Prudence sounded almost offended.

"I'll bet you don't get taught that sort of musical appreciation in the Rangers."

She smiled warily. "Now you're making fun of me."

"I'm not really making fun of anybody," I said. "I've got four murders to solve and none of them is really very funny."

"I'm sorry—you must be terribly worried."

"Yeah," I said, "I guess I am. I'm worried about that safe in the office. I'm worried that both Parker and Snell were found inside it. And only four people ever knew the combination. We can skip the directors in New York. The four people are Elise Walker, Joe Sutton, Hubert Snell who's dead, and you!"

I stubbed out my cigarette and watched her carefully.

The too-bright eyes were wide open. "You mean that the three of us are major suspects, then?"

"I can't figure it any other way," I said. "Can you?"

"It seems sort of ridiculous," she said in a small voice. "I mean, Miss Walker and Mr. Sutton; you couldn't meet two nicer people anywhere."

"Let's include you in that," I said, "and we'll say we couldn't meet three nicer people anywhere. But one of the three of you must have opened that safe, or given the combination to someone else."

Prudence just sat there, staring at me.

"You're sure you didn't give the combination to anyone else?"

"Of course I'm sure," she said coldly. "I'm not the sort of person who abuses a trust, Lieutenant."

"Ranger's honour?"

She flushed. "Now you're making fun of me again."

I climbed onto my feet. "Well, I just wanted to make sure. Thanks for your time, Miss Foy."

She walked with me to the door. "Goodnight, Lieutenant."

"Sweet dreams," I told her. "And I wouldn't play that disc just before you go to bed, if I were you."

I went back to the prowl-car. I felt I wanted female company. The sort of female company that smoked cigarettes and drank hard liquor and whose idea of fun wasn't "Night On Bare Mountain." In fact, I realised as I accelerated hard, I wanted the sort of company a professional stripper could give.

I got the same table and the big-wheel treatment from the head waiter. I ordered a bottle of Scotch to save the waiter getting tired hefting glasses to and from the table. I had myself a couple of drinks and then the floorshow started. Sherry was just as good as she'd been the night before.

I sent a smoke signal via the waiter after the show was over, saying that maybe if she wanted a drink I had one. I settled back to wait and poured myself a third drink.

Somebody arrived at the table, but right away I could tell it wasn't Sherry: she didn't have five-o'clock shadow—even at eleven.

"Back again, Lieutenant?" Marty Shore grinned as he slid into the chair opposite me.

"Don't think I'm making too much of a good thing," I said. "I'll pay my own bill tonight."

Shore waved it aside.

"I insist," I told him.

"If you insist, Lieutenant," he shrugged his shoulders. "Are you waiting for someone?"

"Are you kidding?" I asked him.

He grinned. "Sherry, a charming girl!"

"I called her a lioness last night," I said. "I've had no reason to change my mind."

And at that moment the lioness appeared. Wearing a simple little number that advertised all the physical advantages of Sherry Blair with the subtlety of a full colour page ad in *Post*.

"Hi, there, cop!" she said as she sat down.

"Hi," I said. I nodded towards Shore. "You know your boss, don't you?"

"We've met," she admitted. "He's a nice guy when he's not saying no to me making more money."

"The liquor I have to sell to employ you," he sighed heavily. "You have no idea."

"You've got that wrong somewhere," she said sweetly. "It's me that sells the liquor for you. All the men get so burned up, they drink themselves stupid trying to put out the fire!"

Shore sighed heavily again and looked at me. "That's the ego I have to contend with." He stood up, still shaking his head. "I'm running for cover. She's all yours, Lieutenant. Have yourself a time!"

The waiter poured Sherry a drink, then discreetly disappeared. She raised her glass. "Here's to your stamina. From the way you looked this morning, I'd have taken an even bet you'd have stayed in bed for the next three days."

"We Wheelers are tough," I said hollowly, "I hope. How is life with you?"

"Just about the same," she said. "It was nice of you to drop by."

"Just to see you," I told her.

"Al," she smiled warmly, "that's real nice of you."

"Underneath this brittle facade," I said slowly, "is the desperate yearning of the timid timberwolf."

She frowned at me. "What does that mean?"

"I don't know," I admitted. "I read it some place."

"I get the wolf part all right, all right," she said darkly.

We had another drink.

"This is quite a joint, isn't it?" I said, taking a look around.

"The plushest in town," she agreed. "Not that that's saying a hell of a lot."

"Don't insult the dump I was born in," I told her. "We have our local pride."

"You have?"

"You mean, you haven't met the district attorney yet?" I raised my eyebrows. "That is an experience you shouldn't miss. You'll understand then just how twisted local pride can get!"

Sherry got out a cigarette and I lit it for her.

"Did you have any plans for tonight, Al?" she asked. "You know— Scotch, hi-fi and catch-as-catch-can?"

"Not tonight, honey," I said. "I just wanted a quiet drink with a beautiful companion."

"You keep saying the nicest things," she murmured.

We didn't seem to be getting anywhere. I carefully topped up her glass.

"Is this place legitimate?" I asked casually.

She raised her eyebrows. "Al! Don't tell me you've gone all nasty and copper on me."

"Cross my heart," I assured her. "I'm interested—but I'm not going to raid the place. I just like to know what goes on."

Sherry shrugged her bare shoulders. "It's legitimate as far as I know, Al. It's a nightclub and they charge four times the value for the liquor and the food—but what club doesn't?"

"Check," I agreed.

"There's a couple of private rooms upstairs that get hired out for private parties," she said. "I wouldn't know how the parties go—I've never been invited."

"Probably for visiting firemen by local firemen. Nothing more interesting than that? No dope on the side? No phone numbers and a call-girl racket or anything?"

"If there is," she yawned, "I haven't heard."

"Pity," I said. "I wanted something to dream about."

"And what," she asked coldly, "is wrong with me?"

She had a point there. I gave us one more drink that emptied the bottle.

"Well," I said, "here's to our further meeting, honey."

"Sure," she said. "When?"

"I don't know," I said. "But I'll call you in a couple of days or maybe drop by for a drink, huh?"

"Fine," she said. "I'll pine until I hear from you." She got up from the table. "Goodnight, Al."

"Goodnight, honey," I told her.

CHAPTER 10
Back Where I Started

I got into the bureau bright and smiling at nine the next morning and the desk sergeant's mouth dropped open so wide he nearly lost his bridgework.

I breezed into my office and found Hanlon seated at my desk. "Well!" he said. "Good morning, chief. Any orders?"

"Yeah." I bared my teeth at him. "Get lost!"

He went out, his face going that shade of red it always seemed to be going lately. For a cop he was sensitive.

I doodled on the desk calendar and discovered it was Thursday, the twenty-eighth day of April. It's amazing the things you find out by just looking.

I pressed the buzzer and a uniformed cop came in with a stunned look on his face.

"Who did you think it was?" I asked him. "Termites!"

He was smart enough not to answer that. "Send in Lieutenant Murphy," I told him.

"He's not in yet, sir."

I glanced at my watch. "Why not? It's five after nine, isn't it?"

His mouth opened and he made gobbling noises.

"Well, send him in here as soon as he appears!" I told him.

The cop staggered out of the office and I hummed a merry tune to myself. This was the way to run a Homicide Bureau, I thought. Efficiency was the keynote. A place for everything and everything in its place. I wondered if I should clear a room and put up a sign. "Corpses Please Park Here." That way we could have things tidy from the beginning.

At nine-thirty Murphy came into the office. He looked stunned the way the others had looked stunned.

"You wanted me, chief?" he asked.

"And furthermore," I said pleasantly, "I wanted you at nine o'clock, the time you were due to start work. Where were you?"

"I was down at Joe's place on the corner," he said. "Having breakfast."

"Why didn't I think of having breakfast?" I said bitterly. "The guys that work for me can afford to have breakfast."

"Sorry, chief," he gulped.

"That's okay," I told him. "In future, Lieutenant, I expect you to be on time on the days that I'm here on time."

"How will I know when you're going to be here on time?" he asked dully.

I thought about it for a moment. "I'll give you a ring the night before?" I suggested.

Murphy sat down and I offered him a cigarette and let him light it and mine as well.

"I want you to go out into the big wide world and find out things for me," I said.

"Such as?"

"You know the Rangers?"

"The Forest Rangers?"

"No!"

"The Texas Rangers?"

"Do I look like Davy Crockett?" I thought about that for a moment. "You'd better not answer. The Girl Guide Rangers, I'm talking about."

He looked at me wonderingly for about ten seconds. "The Girl Guide Rangers?" he repeated huskily.

"Yeah," I snarled. "When they get too big to be Girl Guides any more, what happens to them?"

"They get names like Marilyn Monroe and Jane Russell?" he said hopefully.

"They join the Rangers," I almost shouted. "There's a girl called Prudence Foy," I gave him her address. "I want to know if she's a Ranger. Find out for me."

"Okay, chief," he wrote it down carefully in his notebook.

"And find out what an animist is," I added.

"A what?"

I spelled it out for him.

"Where the hell would I find out a thing like that?" he asked.

"A dictionary might help," I said doubtfully, "but I don't think it would be enough—go ask at the University or somewhere."

He wrote that down, too. "Anything else, chief?"

"Yeah," I said. "Take another look at Parker's apartment. Only be careful—remember what happened to Cameron."

"I'll remember," he said soberly. "What am I looking for?"

"Something we never found before," I said. "A hiding-place—a wall safe, a secret drawer, a hollow floorboard."

"Okay, chief," he said doubtfully and wrote it all down.

"That's about all, pal," I told him.

He went out into the big wide world and I leaned back in my chair and thought it was nice to be a boss and order other guys to do the work. That lasted me thirty seconds, then the phone rang and my boss was on the other end of the line.

"Wheeler," Lavers purred. "I must congratulate you, I really must. In your office at this time in the morning. In fact, in your office at all!"

"Thank you, sir," I said. "I can only say I am doing my duty as I see it. As a law-enforcement officer holding the sacred trust of the people of this State, I ..."

"That will do," he said coldly.

"Yes, sir."

I listened to him breathing heavily for a while. "Progress?" he said finally.

"On what, sir?"

"On what!" he bellowed. "Four murders unsolved and you say on what!"

"Oh—that."

"No—them!"

"Yes, sir."

For a moment he sounded as if he was gibbering to himself. "Three days to go, Wheeler. You're fortunate I'm a man of my word, otherwise you'd be an ex-cop so fast you—"

"Yes, sir."

"The D.A. is grinding his heel into my face," Lavers went on. "The Governor is pressing me for results. I can't even send him a progress report. You know why? Because you haven't made any blasted progress."

"Yes, sir."

"If you 'yessir' me once more," he said heavily, "so help me, I'll—"

"Commissioner," I said quickly. "Have you figured out why Parker was strangled with that girdle?"

"No," he said. "Have you?"

"No!"

There was an awful ringing note in my ear as he slammed the receiver back on the rest. I put the phone down gently and lit a cigarette.

So I was unpopular. Well, I'd been unpopular before. But not this unpopular, an uneasy voice muttered inside of me. Brother! If you don't turn something up in the next three days, our heels won't touch as you fly out the door.

And hurray for Hanlon.

I thought I should get back to efficient thinking. But it wasn't easy. I decided that the whole atmosphere of the bureau was depressing me and I needed wide open spaces in which to think clearly—some place like a bar.

I went out of the office. There were half a dozen guys sitting around in the detectives' room, including Hanlon.

"I'm going out," I told him. "It's okay with me if you'd like to go back into my office and practise."

Hanlon got up stiffly, trying to ignore the guffaws around him and disappeared in the direction of my office.

I wondered why I had to keep needling the guy and decided it was because I figured I didn't have much time left to do it.

I had the prowl-car topped up with gas and drove downtown. I stopped off at a bar I know—not that there are many I don't. I had a double Scotch to take the taste of Commissioner out of my mouth. When I'd finished the drink, I thought it was a beautiful day and I should do something constructive. Like taking coffee with a blonde.

Kathi was home, which was helpful. She was wearing a skin-tight sweater and blue jeans. I looked her up and down.

"How did you get them so tight?" I asked her wonderingly. "Shrink them?"

"How did you know?" Kathi asked. "It's still a hot tip in the women's magazines. You wear them under the shower, then let them dry on you."

"How do you take them off?"

"That's none of your business," she told me. "And talking of business—what do you want?"

"Coffee," I said. "And that's a hell of a way to greet an old friend!"

"Who said you were an old friend?" Kathi asked. "Old—yes. Friend—doubtful!"

"Do I get some coffee?"

"I guess so," she said. "That's the trouble with me—I'm kind-hearted."

"I don't remember it," I said.

"If you're referring to the evening I went to your house for dinner," she said, "I am not *that* kind-hearted."

She went into the kitchen to make the coffee and I sat down on the sofa to do nothing. That's the way it should be, I figure. And maybe that's why nobody will marry me. I even asked a dame to marry me once. I still wake up nights shuddering, thinking how it would have been if she'd said yes.

Ten minutes came by and Kathi came back with the coffee. She put the tray down on the low table and sat down beside me. The coffee was good.

"How are things?" I asked her.

"Not too bad," she said. "I'm almost through with the Antoine copy—be finished at the weekend. I'll be going back to New York on Monday."

"That's a shame," I said.

I lit a cigarette for her and one for myself.

"How are you doing, Al?"

"Not good."

"I thought you'd come to tell me something exciting!"

"I only came for the coffee," I told her, "and you in those blue jeans."

She relaxed against the back of the sofa.

"I never met a screwball like you before, Al," she said wonderingly. "How did you ever get to be in charge of the Homicide Bureau?"

"Genius," I said modestly. "Some guys have got it—about one in every thirty million. I was just that much better than 29,999,999 other guys!"

"I give you coffee and you give me that," she said disgustedly.

"That brother of yours," I said. "Was he short of dough?"

"Not that I know of," she said. "Why?"

"I just wondered," I said. "There was a way for him to make dough—a lot of dough, if he'd wanted."

Kathi sat upright. "*Exclusive* paid him well, very well. How could he have made all this money, anyway?"

I told her the theory. About Antoine's exclusive collection and then the mass-production of some. How if somebody had pirated the designs, somebody else could get in first on the mass market.

"So I thought just maybe Hubert was short of dough," I went on, "and if he was, then somebody might persuade him to let them look at some of the designs he was sketching for Antoine's collection and ..." I stopped talking and looked at her.

Kathi was leaning back against the sofa and gurgling with laughter.

"Did I say something funny?" I asked her.

"Al!" she gurgled. "You may be one hell of a good cop, but you don't know much about fashion or the mass-production of fashion goods, do you?"

"Put it that way," I admitted, "I don't."

"How long before the issue containing his collection gets onto the bookstalls, Al?"

"Two, maybe three weeks, according to Miss Walker."

"Do you know how long after that the cheap editions will be in shops all over the country?"

"Antoine said something about a week, or maybe a couple of weeks—I don't remember."

"Let's say five weeks from now," she said. "Let's say six, even seven weeks before Hubert started the drawings—before Antoine arrived in the country—okay?"

"Okay," I nodded.

"I'll guarantee Antoine's manufacturer had the designs three months ago, at least," she said. "Do you realise how long it would take the manufacturer to produce them in mass quantities? Why, distribution throughout the country alone would take at least six to eight weeks. If anybody was going to pirate those designs they would have to have done it a couple of months ago at the absolute latest. Three months ago as a minimum to make sure they got them out ahead of Antoine's own manufacturer."

I sat there looking at the wall opposite me.

"That's on the level, Kathi?" I said. "You wouldn't kid me?"

"That's on the level, Al," she assured me. "Is it important?"

"I hadn't got very far with these murders," I said slowly. "But I did at least have a theory why all these guys had been murdered—and you've just destroyed it!"

"I'm sorry," she said.

"You should be glad," I told her. "It stops me climbing a hill that isn't there, I guess."

I got up onto my feet. "Mind if I use your phone, Kathi?"

"Of course not," she said.

I rang the Hotel Montford. Antoine was in his room and I got through to him.

"Lieutenant Wheeler," I said. "Remember me?"

"Of course, Lieutenant."

"Your theory of somebody trying to pirate your designs."

"My collection!" he interrupted.

'Whatever you like to call it. It doesn't add up." I went on and repeated Kathi's theory to him.

There was a short silence after I'd finished.

"What do you think?" I asked him.

"I don't know how to thank you enough, Lieutenant," he said in a pleased voice. "Of course! You are absolutely right. Now I have no more worries. I was a fool to be worrying! Thank you again, Lieutenant. I can't tell you how happy you've made me!"

"And nuts to you!" I snarled and slammed down the receiver.

Kathi was smiling innocently when I came back to the sofa. "Guys like that," I muttered, "should be strangled before they can talk. That way they wouldn't get into the hair of goods cops who—"

"Would you like some more coffee?" Kathi interrupted.

"I'd like a drink," I told her. "Long and straight."

"I have a bottle of rye?" she suggested.

"Just remove the cork, honey," I told her, "and wheel it in!"

I had two-thirds of the bottle of rye and some lunch with her.

Around three in the afternoon I thought I should go out and do something, so I left.

Kathi walked with me to the door.

"You haven't forgotten what I said?" she asked. "Anything l can do to help—let me know. I mean that, Al."

"Sure," I said. "You helped enough this morning."

"Well, don't forget."

"I won't, honey." I looked at her reflectively. "Just wearing those jeans helps quite a lot!"

I was still looking when she gently closed the door in my face.

I got back to the bureau around four and went into the office. Hanlon wasn't there. That was something. I sat behind my desk, pressed the buzzer and the uniformed cop came in.

"Lieutenant Murphy been back yet?"

"No, sir."

"Send him right in when he gets back."

"Yes, sir."

"Where's Lieutenant Hanlon?"

The cop almost smirked. "Commissioner Lavers sent for him about an hour ago, sir. He left straight away for the city hall."

"Okay," I said.

"Will that be all, sir?"

"It's enough for me to get along with for the time being."

Murphy came in around five. I told him to sit down and he sank gratefully into a chair.

"How did you get on?" I asked him.

"About a seventy-five per cent score, chief," he said cautiously. "The easy ones first. Prudence Foy isn't a Ranger, never has been and furthermore, was never a Girl Guide even."

"That sounds pretty positive," I said. "Okay—what next?"

"The apartment," Murphy said, looking pleased with himself. "I found it!"

"A hiding-place?"

"That's right, chief. Hollow panel behind the bedhead, operates on a weighted swivel—you press one side and it swings around."

"That's great," I said. "What was in it?"

"Nothing."

"I sort of figured that."

"I took one of the fingerprint boys up there afterwards, chief."

"Whose prints?"

"Parker's, of course. A couple of other sets we can't match, and Cameron's."

"I figured you'd find Cameron's," I said.

Murphy looked a little crestfallen—also disbelieving. "How'd you figure that, chief?"

"Whoever knocked off Cameron must have had good reason," I said. "More reason than just being found in the apartment when Cameron arrived. So I figured the guy had found something—or gone to remove something that was evidence as to why Parker was killed—and Cameron caught him. Or Cameron found it and the guy caught Cameron with it—that looks like being the way it was."

"Yeah," Murphy grunted.

I lit another cigarette. "I take it we've got the seventy-five per cent?"

"That's right, chief," he nodded. "I went up to the University, like you said. I told them what I wanted and they put me onto a runt of a character with a head two times too big for him. Name of Professor Borosin. I figured it would be easy."

Murphy shook his head slowly. "I see him and tell him who I am and what I want to know. He looks me up and down like I was used flypaper and says why do I want to know? So I tell him my chief, Lieutenant Wheeler who's the boss of the bureau, he wants to know."

"So this little runt says calmly. 'Then tell him to come down here and talk to me and I'll tell him.' Then he ups and walks out, leaving me standing there like a sleepwalking drunk waking up in the middle of a temperance meeting."

"Never mind," I grinned at him. "You've done a damned good job finding that secret hiding-place. And I'm glad to know that Prudence Foy isn't a Ranger, after all."

"Why, chief?"

"She didn't strike me as being the type," I replied. "Okay—go home and rest your feet."

I waited until he'd gone out of the office and then I rang the University and asked to be put through to Professor Borosin. I waited half a minute and then a cultured voice said, "Borosin."

"Lieutenant Wheeler, Homicide," I said. "I have a question to ask, professor. I understand you insist on me asking it personally."

"I never deal with subordinates, Lieutenant," he said crisply. "It only creates confusion."

"Well," I said evenly, "I'll tell you how we can overcome it, professor. I'll send a squad-car out now and have you picked up and brought back here to the bureau. That way I can ask you personally."

"I don't think I can spare the time," he said coldly.

"You misunderstand me, professor. This is police business. I'm pulling you in—you don't have any choice in the matter."

"Now, look," he protested.

"Of course," I went on, "we just might be able to compromise, professor. Do you drink?"

"Alcohol?"

"What else?"

"Yes, I drink."

"If you cared to name a bar somewhere about halfway between here and the University, maybe we could meet there?"

Borosin chuckled dryly. "A policeman with a sense of humour, Lieutenant. All right—you know the Blue Parrot?"

"Sure," I said.

"I'll meet you there in, say, an hour?"

"Fine; professor," I said and hung up.

CHAPTER 11
Borosin

I recognised him from Murphy's description. You couldn't have missed him, anyway. A little guy with a head much too big, but a sort of air about him.

I walked over to the booth where he was sitting and introduced myself.

"Sit down, Lieutenant," he said after we'd shaken hands. "What are you drinking?"

"Scotch, thanks."

He ordered and we waited until the drinks arrived. Then he looked at me interestedly.

"You want to know what is an animist, Lieutenant," he said.

"Why?"

"Because a guy who was murdered claimed he was one," I said.

"That sounds very interesting," he said. "Well, briefly, animism is a primitive belief that the spirit may inhabit other bodies—at least temporarily. And in particular, the bodies of animals."

I couldn't have looked very bright.

"An animist believes he can become an animal," Borosin went on. "Or at least, inhabit an animal's body. In primitive religion, for example, many tribes of savages would wear masks representing various animals that they identified themselves with. The lion, the leopard, the wolf, and so on. It was really the first, crude conception of the soul. It became perverted in some cases, of course. The leopard-men of Africa who wore claws and leopard skins and murdered in an orgiastic frenzy. The legend of the werewolf in the Carpathians still existed until the beginning of this century. It may still do so, quite possibly."

I sipped the Scotch. "Thanks, professor," I said. "Could you explain why this particular man, a commercial artist, would claim he was an animist?"

"You're referring to Hubert Snell?" Borosin said shrewdly. "I have followed the sensational newspaper reports of these murders, of course."

"Check," I agreed.

His face sobered. "I don't know, Lieutenant. I'm afraid I would not like to hear any man claim to be an animist."

"Why not?"

"Well," he spread his hands wide. "No civilised man is going to claim he belongs to a state of savagery that has only just begun to recognise the existence of the soul, would they? That's merely claiming to be many thousands of years behind the rest of mankind. So he must be claiming something altogether different."

"A perversion of the belief?" I suggested.

"I see you're staying with me, Lieutenant," he smiled. "Yes—he would be claiming membership of some cult organisation which would be, to say the least, unhealthy! Either that or he's in a very advanced stage of neurasthenia."

"Yeah," I said and waved to the barman to refill our glasses.

Borosin looked at me over the top of his glass. "Does that help you at all, Lieutenant?"

"Maybe yes and maybe no," I said. "At the risk of seeming even more stupid than I look, I'd like to ask you another question."

"Go ahead," he said. "I'm finding this very interesting, believe me, Lieutenant."

"If you met a girl," I said, "who was beautiful and nervous—beautiful in a wild-eyed sort of way and extremely nervous—and if you had a job like mine and had to ask her a lot of questions and during that questioning you found out she didn't drink and didn't smoke and she told you she was a Ranger as well ..."

I grinned almost sheepishly. "I'm taking one hell of a long time to get around to asking the question, aren't I? And then if you found out she wasn't a Ranger and never had been. And later if you called at her home and found it furnished on a scale obviously far beyond her salary and looked at the radiogram and saw 'Night On Bare Mountain' sitting on the turntable. What would you think?"

Borosin chuckled. "I'd think she was a very smart girl who got awfully worried that the Lieutenant might find out about her boyfriends. So she overdid the story of sweet and pure innocence. It isn't a crime to play 'Night On Bare Mountain,' is it?"

"Not according to the book," I admitted. "It just seemed so out of character that I wondered."

"It's a fascinating piece of music," he said. "You know the significance, of course?"

"All the goblins and what-have-you rising out of the graveyard or something," I said. "I remember seeing Disney's *Fantasia* years back."

The professor pressed the fingertips of both hands together and looked all set to enjoy himself by giving me another lecture.

"The Bare Mountain is the Brocken, in Germany," he said. "A most impressive sight, Lieutenant. A colossal granite dome rising above the trees that surround it. Heidenheim is the nearest town. In the year 780, Saint Waldburg, the Abbess of Heidenheim, died there.

"Her death was accidentally associated with the popular superstition that the Devil called his meeting on one of her feast days, that is the first of May. Really the night of the thirtieth of April and the first of May, of course. It's known as Walpurgis Night—the night the Devil summons the witches on broomsticks and the he-goats to the ancient places of sacrifice, of which Brocken is reputed to be the oldest."

I took a gulp of Scotch. "That's very interesting," I murmured politely.

"Walpurgis Night is the big night of the year for Satan Worshippers," Borosin continued. "The celebration of Black Mass and so on."

"Kind of makes you feel glad you live in the twentieth century, doesn't it?" I said.

"Why?" the professor asked benignly.

"Well," I laughed, "all that sort of stuff died out years ago!'

"What makes you think that, Lieutenant?" he asked gently.

I stopped laughing. "Didn't it?"

"There are undoubtedly still sects which practise Satanism," he said. "In civilised countries they would be very small, no doubt. But they do exist. If one could have access to all the psychiatrists' notebooks, I think you would find all the proof you want."

"Why would anybody belong to such a sect?" I asked.

He shrugged his shoulders. "Very hard to generalise on that point, Lieutenant. I think firstly that where such groups exist, their main reason for existence is to practise excess. By having or pretending to have such beliefs, it gives them the excuse to practise the excess. And undoubtedly some of them do firmly believe that they can receive power from the Black Host. They believe in such things as the curse of Saint Secaire, for example."

"What's that?" I felt my eyes beginning to bulge.

He grinned. "I think we should have another drink."

"I'll second that," I told him.

He ordered again and then continued when the barman had set up the drinks.

"The curse, which has a prolonged and very unpleasant ritual involving sacrifice," he said soberly, "is believed to bring about the death of an enemy. It's a common belief among primitive peoples that death can be wished upon another person. The Australian Aborigines believe it—'pointing the bone' is the phrase they have, as I remember.

"One of the necessary things to any such group who wish to enjoy actual power," he said casually, "is to have among them an elemental."

"What's that?"

"An elemental is a human being who is attuned to the black arts—the power can be drawn through them, so to speak. They become the lightning conductor, if you like. Often they can be quite innocent and not even realise their own peculiar properties. They can be used by others and not even know it."

Borosin grinned again. "Those are the theories and the ancient beliefs. Modern psychology would have different and probably far truer explanations. They would say the elemental lacks willpower, personality. Is a taut, highly-strung person who is remarkably susceptible to hypnosis and auto-suggestion. You can make your own choice, Lieutenant."

"Well, well, well," I said wonderingly. "And I never knew!"

"Very few people know or are interested," he said. "I happen to lecture on primitive culture for a living, Lieutenant. Therefore I know something about these things."

"I'll look under my bed tonight," I told him.

He laughed. "Everything has its opposite, of course. There are the powers of white magic, you know. There are safeguards—the sign of the cross, holy water—many things which will overcome the powers of darkness. Mistletoe is another one."

"I'll feel safer come Christmas!"

Professor Borosin looked at me for a long moment.

"You asked me a silly question a little while ago," he said. "Or you claimed it was silly, anyway. So if I may, I'd like to be silly as well."

"Go ahead, professor."

"If I were you, Lieutenant," he said soberly, "and I was taking the self-professed animism of Hubert Snell seriously and if I were still wondering about the wide-eyed girl who claimed such perfect innocence and who plays 'Night On Bare Mountain' on her radiogram ..."

"Yeah?" I said.

"I would say that Snell had been a Satanist," he said calmly, "or belonged to some group that played around with similar ideas. If I wanted to connect the girl with that group, I could do that quite easily, too."

"How?"

"Elementary, my dear Watson," he grinned. "I'd say she was an elemental!"

I sat there, staring at him.

"Do you know the date, Lieutenant?" he asked gently.

"Sure," I said. "I took a look at the desk calendar this morning. It's the twenty-eighth of April."

"Just two more nights," he said softly, "and then it's Walpurgis Night."

CHAPTER 12
Janice Wants Security

I sat at home with Louis blowing his trumpet sweet and hot on the hi-fi and me hardly hearing it. I had a drink in front of me and it was the same one I'd put there an hour ago. That was how worried I was.

I'd left the little professor with the head that was too big in the bar and driven home. I might as well have tossed myself into the lake for all the good the thinking had done me up to date.

Borosin was nuts. Okay.

Hubert Snell had talked animism to his sister for a gag. Okay.

Prudence Foy got frightened at the idea of a cop finding out about her sugar-daddy and she thought that record was a Stan Freburg version of "Jingle Bells." Okay.

So that left me with four unsolved murders and three days, cutting down to two, to solve them in. And no theories.

The phone jangled and I shot out of the chair like Marilyn Monroe had just walked into the room. I went over and answered it.

The voice was nice and husky. "Lieutenant Wheeler?"

"Sure," I said.

"This is Janice Milbray. I hope you remember me?"

"Of course."

"I wanted to apologise to you, Lieutenant. The last time you were here, there was rather an embarrassing situation."

"I wouldn't call Eddie Buckman an embarrassing situation," I said politely. "I'd call him a slob!"

She laughed softly. "I like your approach, Lieutenant. Are you doing anything right now?"

"Other than drinking—not a thing!"

"I wondered," she paused. "Why don't you come over to my place and do nothing with a martini here? I'm bored to death sitting here alone and I'm sure you can tell me thrilling stories of your investigations—or something?"

"It sounds a wonderful idea," I said. "Just put a sign on your door—'No Buckmans Allowed'—and I'll be right over."

"I'll keep the martinis cool," she promised.

It sounded a much better proposition than sitting with myself, quietly going nuts.

Some forty minutes later I was there. She opened the door and let me in.

Janice was wearing a green negligee that fitted tightly from shoulder to ankle and was slit up one side so she could walk in it.

We went into the living-room. There was one shaded wall-lamp alight. The rest of the room was a nice, friendly gloom.

I sat on the sofa and she brought over a shakerful of martini and two glasses. I watched, fascinated, while she set them up on a small table in front of us. Then she sat down beside me.

"That saves us all the bother of having to get up for another drink, doesn't it?" she said.

"You ought to copyright the idea," I told her. "It's strictly inspirational!"

Janice smiled. "Please, can I call you by your Christian name? Lieutenant sounds so formal."

"Al is the name."

"Short for what?"

"Al!"

"All right," she smiled. "It's your secret." She filled up the glasses. We drank.

When she'd sat down, the split in the side of the negligee had opened. I could see enough of her legs to find it hard to look at anything else. She was aware of it, the way she was aware of the exact effect she had on me, right down to the last zing.

I sipped the martini—it was really dry, around six to one. I hope it wouldn't start an argument with the Scotch when they met.

"What have you been doing, Al?" Janice asked. "Anything exciting?"

"Not a thing," I replied. "Except trying to find out why four people got murdered and who murdered them."

"Have you found out?"

I shook my head. "Just between you and me, I'm not very far ahead at all."

"Poor Al," she said. "You sound as if you're having a tough time right now."

"You can say that again."

She laughed suddenly. "Eddie thinks you have him in mind and he's worried sick."

"What makes him think that?"

"Didn't you tell him that the murders were committed because somebody wanted to pirate Antoine's designs and mass-produce them?"

"I might have done," I said cautiously.

"He's sure you think it was him. He's lost about ten pounds in weight already!"

"That's some consolation," I said. "Or do you like Eddie?"

"Like him?" she said softly. "Do you think it would be possible for anyone to like Eddie?"

"Now you mention it—no!"

Janice finished her drink and poured herself another.

"If you don't like him, either," I said, "how come he's around here so often? Or is that a personal question?"

"It's a personal question, Al," she said, "but I'll answer it. He's around so often because it's his apartment. That is, he pays for it." Her tone grew bitter. "He buys my clothes, my liquor, my car."

"Okay," I said, "I have the picture."

"I suppose you're shocked, Al?"

"Me?" I looked at her, surprised. "Me—a cop! I couldn't be shocked at anything."

She smiled. "Well, if you're not shocked you must disapprove."

"I gave up disapproving of people a long time ago," I told her.

"Do you really think Eddie killed all those people?" she asked suddenly.

I grinned at her. "That's a state secret."

She swayed towards me and our lips met. A moment later my glass was taken gently out of my hand and put on the table, and then she was in my arms.

If kisses can burn, Janice was a forest fire.

It was some time later when I groped feebly for the glass and finished what was left of the martini.

"For a policeman," she said softly, "you must have had a lot of experience."

"Training policewomen," I told her, "and before that—bloodhounds!"

She refilled the glasses again and sat close enough to me to be in my lap. Her left hand tousled my hair gently.

"Please, Al," she said. "Tell me about Eddie."

"What do you want to know?"

"That's better," she said. "I can be awfully nice to people who do what I ask."

"How nice?"

"Nice enough," she said. "Tell me."

I drank some more martini. "I don't think Eddie killed any of them. I don't think anyone's going to pirate Antoine's designs. I think neither they nor Eddie had anything to do with the four murders."

"Thanks, Al," she said, and wound her arms around my neck.

"Now I'll keep my promise."

I stood up abruptly, so that she slid off my lap onto the floor and landed with a distinct bump which must have penetrated the negligee hard enough for her to take her meals off the mantelpiece for the next couple of days.

When she landed on the floor with her arms flailing, she knocked over the small table and the drinks with it. The carpet began to look a mess.

She looked up at me, her eyes black with hate. "How dare you do that to me!" she almost spat. "You!"

"Save it for Eddie!" I told her.

"I didn't want to know for Eddie!" she snapped.

"Sure," I agreed. "You wanted to know for little Janice's sake. You wanted to be sure Eddie would be around to keep paying for the apartment, the clothes and the car. You wanted to be sure that nobody was going to make a grab and whisk your stake-money away. And the easiest way to do that was to finesse a dumb cop who'd get so dazzled by a martini and a negligee, he'd tell you anything at all."

Janice struggled onto her feet and stood there glaring at me, breathing heavily.

"Get out!" she snarled.

"Sure," I said, "I was on my way. Thanks for the drink. You can take it that the information I gave you about Eddie is free. I won't say it's strictly accurate, but it's free."

She picked up the shaker and hurled it at me. I ducked and it sailed over my head. The next moment there was a splintering crash from behind me as a vase disintegrated.

"Careful," I said. "Eddie won't appreciate his property being smashed up like that."

"Get out!" she screamed. I got.

I went back to the prowl-car and drove a block, then pulled into the curb and stopped. I switched off the motor and lit a cigarette. I forgot about Janice Milbray and her security worries.

My watch said eleven-thirty. In another thirty minutes I'd have exactly forty-eight hours left to crack the case. And that didn't leave me much time.

I had an idea. I didn't like it any more than I liked Professor Borosin's theories, but the idea could help me prove the professor was either right or nuts.

I started the motor again and drove on. I arrived at the door of Kathi's apartment just after midnight. I pressed the buzzer three times before she answered. She stood there in silk pyjamas and no robe, yawning gently behind her hand.

"What is this?" she demanded. "A frontal assault!"

"Believe me, honey," I told her, "this is business—fool that I am."

"In that case," she said, "you'd better come in."

I followed her into the living-room.

"There's the bottom half of that bottle of rye left," she said.

The martinis knifed me in alarm at the thought.

"I'd rather settle for coffee," I said.

"It must be business."

She put on a robe, then went out into the kitchen. I smoked a cigarette down until she came back with the coffee. Then we sat on the sofa. Lately I seemed to be spending most of my time sitting on a sofa with a dame. That's the advantage of being a cop. You can always claim that your questions are official.

We drank the coffee.

"Okay," Kathi said. "Don't let's while away the small hours with silence. Make with the business."

"I met a guy tonight," I said. "A professor, by the name of Borosin."

"I knew a guy named Smith in New York once," she said. "But he wasn't a professor, he was a garbageman and ..."

"There's some point to my story!" I said coldly.

"Well, I'll give you another thirty seconds to prove it," Kathi said. "Otherwise you're going to get Smith's story and like it!"

"Borosin gave me the definition of an animist," I said, "and the sort of animist he thought Hubert might have been."

I went on and told her the whole lot.

She shivered when I'd finished and moved closer to me, tucking her arm through mine.

"Just don't take advantage of this, Wheeler," she told me. "If I wasn't so scared, I wouldn't chance it."

"You've got time to get more scared," I told her.

"Of course," she said, "it's all a gag—isn't it?"

"I don't know," I said honestly. "I'd like to find out."

"How are you going to do that?"

"That's where you come into the picture, honey."

"Me?"

"You wanted to help—remember? You'd do anything to help anything at all—unquote!"

"I guess I did say that," she said slowly. "Okay—what?"

I cleared my throat, lit two cigarettes and gave her one.

"If you don't like the idea," I said, "say so and we'll forget it."

"Tell me the idea first," she said. "That way it will be easier for me to make up my mind."

I sucked smoke into my lungs. "Let's suppose for a moment that Borosin's hit on the right idea. That there is the group and Hubert did belong to it. Okay?"

"Okay," she shivered and held my arm tighter. "Go on."

"Well," I said, "the only one we know of for sure is Prudence Foy—the elemental. Right?"

"Right," she agreed.

"But being an elemental, she may not even realise exactly what goes on; she may be in a sort of trance when they have their meetings and so on."

"So?"

I sucked some more smoke into my lungs.

"I want you to call on her tomorrow evening," I said. "I want you to tell her that you knew all along Hubert belonged to the group—that he was an animist. Since he's dead, you've decided you want to join the same group. Say that Hubert had nearly converted you before he died, and now you feel you want to belong even more."

"And then what?"

"Maybe a number of things," I said slowly. "Maybe she says okay, we'll let you know—just fill in an application for membership and post it. But if Borosin is the red-hot boy he may be, then I figure she'll look at you as if you're nuts and tell you she doesn't know what you're talking about. If that happens, don't argue about it. Tell her that whatever she thinks, she must tell them."

"Who is them?" Kathi asked.

"That," I said impatiently, "is what I hope you're going to find out."

"That's fine," she said. "Just fine. I'm the fall-guy, huh?"

"In a manner of speaking," I said cautiously. "But don't worry, I won't be very far away. Nothing will happen to you!"

She held my arm tighter still. Then she shivered again. "I've a nasty sort of feeling I'm not going to like this at all, Al. But I'll do it. If it's true and this sort of thing has been going on, Hubert would have been weak enough to be led into it. I want to see whoever killed him get the electric chair."

"Sure," I patted her arm gently. "From tomorrow evening we have to play this carefully. When you leave her apartment, come straight back here and ring me. Whatever you do, don't try and see me. I'll keep in touch with you by phone and tell you what to do, okay?"

"Okay, Al," she said.

"That's my girl," I told her.

"I think I need a drink after all," she said.

She got up and collected the bottle and two glasses, then came back again. She poured herself four fingers and drank it neat.

When the colour came back to her face and she could speak again, she gurgled gently. "I feel better."

"I would imagine," I said in an awestruck voice.

"You know something, Al?" she asked.

"What?"

"You did make a frontal assault after all!"

"I don't get it."

She shivered and moved still closer to me. "Every time I close my eyes, I see witches on broomsticks. You don't leave this apartment until daylight, Al Wheeler, even if I have to knock you senseless to keep you here!"

"That won't be necessary," I told her. "I'm a cop, remember. I have a sense of duty."

"In that case," she said, "you can sleep on the sofa."

"I had a sense of duty," I said quickly.

"You still sleep on the sofa!" Kathi said firmly.

And I did.

CHAPTER 13
Fired

I got into the bureau around eleven and sent for Murphy—it wasn't necessary to send for Hanlon, he was sitting behind my desk. I lit a cigarette while I waited for Murphy to come in.

"The Commissioner sent for me yesterday afternoon," Hanlon said smugly.

"So I heard," I grunted.

"He was pretty guarded in what he said," Hanlon went on. "But he seemed to think there were going to be some changes around here soon—very soon!"

"He's putting you back into traffic?" I suggested.

I think," he said happily, "if anyone goes back into traffic, it won't be me."

Murphy came in then and grinned. "Good morning, chief!"

"Hi," I said.

"You want me?" Hanlon got onto his feet.

"Yeah," I said. "I've got a job for both of you—it starts this evening."
They both looked at me. Murphy expectantly, Hanlon with raised eyebrows.

"Kathi Snell," I said, "Snell's sister. This evening she's going to call on Prudence Foy, the girl who works in the accounts section of the magazine."
I gave them both addresses. "I don't think she'll be there very long—I don't know. I want her tailed from the time she leaves her apartment. I want her tailed from then on, twenty-four hours of the day. I want one of you to be close behind her all the time. I want you to report back to me whenever she goes out of her apartment."

Hanlon's eyebrows went up still further. "But this is a job for Podeski or another sergeant."

"This is a job for a lieutenant," I said. "For two lieutenants. The changes haven't taken place around here, Hanlon, and until they do, you take orders from me."

"This is important, chief, huh?" Murphy asked.

"It's damned important," I replied. "From the time Kathi Snell leaves Prudence Foy's apartment, she may be in danger. She'll go straight back to her own apartment. I want whoever is tailing her to be on the same floor—and stay there. If anything looks like funny business, don't be polite about it. Okay?"

"You think there may be trouble?" Hanlon asked.

"I think somebody might try and get at her," I said. "I think somebody might even try to murder her. I could be all wrong about this, but I can't take any chances."

"Right," Murphy said. He looked at Hanlon. "Who takes first tail?"

"You can," Hanlon said promptly. He looked at me. "When do we start?"

"Six tonight," I told him.

"You take it to midnight," Hanlon said to Murphy. "I'll pick you up in the apartment block then and take it till nine. Okay."

"Okay?" Murphy said disbelievingly. "Why, it's downright generous!"

"I have a date at seven," Hanlon almost smirked.

"Hell!" I said. "You could be human yet!"

I mooched around the bureau for rest of the day and even did a little routine work before I went home. I sat down beside the phone and let Kitty Wyatt try and ease my nerves on the hi-fi.

At seven the phone rang. I lifted the receiver almost before it had rung once. "Yeah?"

"Murphy, chief."

"Yeah?"

"She went into the Foy dame's apartment ten minutes back. I'm across the road in a phone booth."

"Good," I said. "If she comes out within half an hour, don't worry about phoning in again—just keep with her. If she doesn't come out within half an hour, ring back."

"Got you, chief," he hung up.

I lit another cigarette, poured myself a drink and began to pace up and down the room. I was wondering who was crazy in the whole set-up and kept coming up with the nasty thought that I was the close favourite.

The phone didn't ring again for an hour. When it did ring, I almost jumped down it.

"Al?"

"Yeah."

"How are you?"

"Just fine," I growled. "You're okay?"

"I'm fine," she said. "Except a man followed me home."

"That's okay," I said. "That was a cop; he's somewhere outside in the corridor now."

"You might have told me!" she said.

"Didn't want to worry you," I said. "What happened, Kathi?"

"She's seen me around in the office a couple of times," she said, "and she knew who I was, so that made it a bit easier. I told it to her the way you said—you know, about Hubert telling me and so on."

"Sure, sure!"

"She acted the way you said she probably would. She looked straight through me and said she didn't know what I was talking about. So I said to her very slowly and carefully that she was to tell them what I had said to her. I said it a couple of times and she still just shook her head and said I must be crazy. So then I gave up and left."

"That's okay," I said, "that's fine. Now if anybody rings about it, you play along and fall in with any suggestion they may make. Then ring me as soon as they've hung up. Do the same with anyone that calls—and remember, if things look sticky at all, just scream. That cop in the corridor will be into your apartment in under five seconds."

"That's an interesting thought, Al," she said. "If I feel lonely during the night, all I've got to do is scream—huh?"

"Ring me at midnight," I said. "Whether anything's happened or not. And ring me at eight in the morning the same."

"Okay," she said. "I'll go now, you're making me feel nervous."

"Relax, honey," I said. "Nothing's going to happen to you." I hung up and wished I was sure of that.

I poured myself another drink.

It was a long four hours to midnight and then she rang again. "Hi," she said.

"Hi," I croaked.

"You sound as if you've been drinking."

"I have," I admitted.

"Huh! Not worrying about little Kathi at all!"

"Not a care about Kathi!" I lied.

"Well, nothing's happened, so I'm going to bed. Goodnight, Al."

"Goodnight," I said. "Sleep tight."

I hung up again—I thought I might as well go to bed, too. I wouldn't sleep, of course, but I might as well lie down, anyway. I woke with sunlight streaming through the window. I looked at my watch and saw it was five to nine. I made a dive through into the living-room and dialled Kathi's number.

The phone rang and rang and no one answered.

I slammed the receiver back on the cradle and grabbed some clothes. Five minutes later I was in the prowl-car heading towards the city, with the siren going full blast.

I parked outside the apartment block and ran into the foyer. I took the elevator up to her floor and ran down the corridor. The door was closed. I pressed the buzzer a couple of times, then took out my gun and blew off the lock.

I had time to make sure the apartment was empty before a herd of people arrived, including the janitor who wanted to know if I had any authority to go around blowing locks off doors.

I told him in a few terse words exactly what authority I had, and told him to clear the other people out of the apartment and off the floor.

"There was a Lieutenant on duty in the corridor last night," I said, "watching this apartment. Did you see anything of him?"

He scratched his head. "I wasn't up on this floor last night at all, Lieutenant."

"When I find him, I'll break him into little pieces!" I snarled.

There was a faint drumming noise from somewhere. "What the hell's that?" I asked.

"Hot-water pipes again," the janitor said dismally. "Need to get the plumber back."

The noise seemed to get louder. "You sure?" I said.

"I'll go look," he said.

We stepped into the corridor. The noise was definitely louder out there.

"Hell, no!" the janitor said suddenly. "That's coming from the broom closet down the hall."

He shuffled down to the closet, with me following him. He jerked the door open and a bundle fell out at his feet.

"Well, I'll be ..." the janitor muttered.

"I don't know about you, pal," I said, "but he will, for sure."

Hanlon made gurgling noises from behind the gag and shuffled his taped feet and hands apologetically.

Half an hour later we were at the bureau.

I put out a general alarm for Kathi and a full description, but I didn't feel optimistic.

Murphy came in and took one look at my face and didn't say anything. Hanlon stood there, his face pale, watching me.

"Okay," I said to him. "How did it happen—and when?"

"Must have been just after five this morning," he said. "I was down at the end of the corridor when I heard the elevator coming up. I walked down to the doors and waited. The elevator stopped and the doors didn't open." He touched the back of his head gently. "Next thing I was gagged and taped up inside that broom closet."

"One guy takes the elevator to attract your attention," Murphy said patiently, "while the other guy comes quietly up the stairs."

"We can all get smart after it's happened," I said. "Where the hell were you, anyway? You were supposed to relieve Hanlon at nine ... it was after nine when I got there."

"That was my fault, chief," Hanlon said. "I was two hours late, I didn't get there till two. I told Murphy not to relieve me till eleven."

I lit a cigarette.

"Chief," Hanlon said, "I'm sorry. It was my fault. I should've known better than fall for the sucker-trap with the elevator!"

"Forget it," I said. "I guess it's my fault if we're going to argue about it. I should've put you inside the apartment. I didn't think they'd try strong-arm tactics and kidnap her. I was expecting somebody to either phone her or call. I wanted to know who it was."

Murphy looked at me curiously. "Chief, what's this all about?"

"Yes," a voice boomed from the door, "I'd like to know that, too, Wheeler."

The Commissioner pushed his bulk into the room and slammed the door behind him. "What's this general alarm out for Kathi Snell?"

Hanlon told him the story of what had happened during the night. He took all the blame himself. I was beginning to wonder if I'd finish up liking Hanlon, after all.

Lavers grunted when he had finished. "All right, Wheeler," he said.

"Why?"

"You aren't going to like it when I tell you," I told him. "You aren't even going to believe it."

"I'll be the judge of that," he snorted.

I didn't have any choice. I told him how it had been.

There was a moment of awful silence.

"I never heard so much nonsense in all my life!" Lavers roared. "You're supposed to be in charge of this bureau and you're running around looking for witches on broomsticks!"

"Now wait a minute," I said. "There's another angle, too. The caretaker of the *Exclusive* building—you know, Dewlap?"

"Yeah," Lavers growled.

"I broke him down that night," I said. "In the basement. He was telling me he saw them come in carrying Parker's body. He said he followed them but he couldn't tell who they were because far as he ever got because somebody shot him right then.

"Don't you see?" I went on. "Dewlap was going to say they were wearing masks! It ties in with Borosin's theory—they identify themselves with some animal and they wear a mask depicting that animal so that ..."

"Wait a minute, Wheeler," Lavers said softly. "Did I understand you to say that Dewlap told you this much just before he was shot?"

"Yeah," I agreed. "Whoever shot him switched off the lights straight afterwards. When I got back to the steps and found the switches, the guy had gone—I heard the front door on the ground level slam shut."

"And what did you do then, Wheeler?" Lavers asked gently.

"I left the building and went ..."

And all too late I realised what I'd said.

"You left the building and went home," Lavers repeated. "You left the building and went home! You—the Lieutenant-in-Charge of the Homicide Bureau, witnessed a murder so you went home! You didn't report it—of course not! It was none of your business, I suppose?"

There wasn't much point in answering that one.

"This is one time you've been just a little too unorthodox," he said. "I've put up with a lot from you, Wheeler. For the last six days I've been crucified by everyone in city hall and the press. I've tried to ignore the newspapers and I've told city hall that my brilliant Lieutenant-in-Charge of Homicide would have the whole case sewn up inside a week, but secrecy was essential. And I find that you've been crystal-gazing with some maniac of a professor, instead."

Lavers took a deep breath. "You admitted in front of witnesses that you were an eye-witness to a murder. You didn't report it. All right, Wheeler, that's enough for me to act on. As from now, you're dismissed! Right now, you're plain Mr Wheeler! I can do that to you and I've done it!"

"Wait a minute, Commissioner," Murphy said. "You can't ..."

"If I hear one more word from you," Lavers said coldly, "I'll put you out into the eighth precinct as a uniformed sergeant!"

Murphy closed his mouth.

"Hanlon!"

"Yes, sir?"

"As from now," Lavers said, "you are acting-in-charge of the bureau. I want you to press the investigation of these murders as hard as you can. I want every available man on the job—got it?"

"Yes, sir," Hanlon said.

I looked at his face. There wasn't any pleasure showing on it. I thought maybe I'd been all wrong about the guy—he could've been ribbing me before, just for the hell of it.

Lavers fixed his eyes on me. "Mr Wheeler," he said. "You have no right here—this is the Homicide Bureau. Only police officers are allowed in here. I must ask you to leave."

"Sure," I said, "I was just leaving."

"I'd like a statement left with a stenographer," he went on. "A statement concerning the murder of Alfred Dewlap—your eye-witness report. We may charge you with withholding vital evidence later, Mr Wheeler. The D.A. will have to look at it."

"Tell him to leave no stone unturned," I said. "He might find the Police Commissioner under one of them."

Lavers' face began to turn purple. "Get out!" he roared.

"I'm going," I told him. "But just for the record—you are the biggest slob I have ever met! And I must say I have met some slobs in my time!"

"Get out!"

I got.

Twice before I'd been suspended, but this was the first time I'd been fired. I also had the nasty thought it could probably be the last because it would be permanent.

Then I started to worry about Kathi again and I forgot about Commissioner Lavers.

CHAPTER 14
Sherry, I Love You

I spent that day and that night worrying.

I rang Murphy and he promised me he'd let me know as soon as they had any news of Kathi Snell. I hung around until eight that evening, then I had an idea. I took a cab out to the University and found Professor Borosin was home.

He had a nice, book-lined study which suited his head.

"Ah, Lieutenant," Borosin said as I came in. I didn't bother to disillusion him. "You're just in time for a drink."

He pulled a book off the shelf, then reached into the recess and came out with a bottle of Scotch. He got two glasses and poured the drinks.

"Thanks," I said. I slumped into a chair and lit a cigarette.

"You look dispirited. Trouble?"

I told him of the idea I'd had of sending Kathi around to see Prudence Foy. Then I told him how Kathi had been kidnapped and so far the police hadn't found any trace of her.

Borosin filled his pipe carefully while he listened.

"So all I've done," I finished, "is probably organised the fifth murder."

"They would know she was lying about wanting to join them, of course," he said.

"The cop in the corridor," I nodded. "Sure."

"If it's any consolation to you, Lieutenant," he said, "I think she is safe for the moment. Safe until tomorrow night."

"Why?"

"You've forgotten what tomorrow night is?"

I sat up with a jerk. "Walpurgis!"

"Exactly," he nodded. "If they intend to harm her, they won't harm her until then."

"You mean, they'll kill her as part of a ritual?"

He avoided my eyes. "Walpurgis demands a sacrifice. The most valuable sacrifice of all is, of course, a human being."

I got to my feet. "I don't know how the hell you can just sit there and say things like that!"

"Calm down, man!" Borosin said coldly. "Losing your head won't get you anywhere. This is the time you've really got to think if you hope to save the girl."

"I guess you're right," I slumped back into the chair. "But she could be anywhere—anywhere at all."

"You say the only one you're sure of is the elemental, Prudence Foy?"

"That's right," I agreed.

"She wouldn't tell you anything," Borosin said. "I'm inclined to believe she couldn't—but if she could, she obviously wouldn't."

"So where does that get me?"

"I don't know," he said, tamping down the tobacco with one finger. "You should know better than I, Lieutenant. Personally, I find it very hard to believe that there isn't something else that might help. Some other lead, however small, which might open up a path of investigation."

"There isn't one," I told him.

He shook his head. "If you'll forgive my saying so, Lieutenant, I don't think you're reasoning clearly. There may be a lead that isn't obvious to you now because you're obsessed with trying to work out who else besides Prudence Foy, is mixed up with the Satanists. Try and forget them for a little while."

"Sure," I said. "Thanks." I finished my drink and stood up.

"If there is anything I can do," he said.

"I'll let you know, professor," I told him, then let myself out.

I went back home and rang Murphy in case he might have rung me, but he hadn't. The situation was unchanged. I stayed up until two, then went to bed. In spite of myself, I slept.

It was nine in the morning when I got up. I showered, shaved, then rang Homicide. Murphy had gone home but I got through to Hanlon. There was genuine regret in his voice when he told me nothing had happened.

It was around eleven that I remembered.

I remembered the first time I ever went to the Cafe Rouge, I went with Kathi. I remembered that Miss Walker and Antoine had been there. The second time I went I was on my own—and Marty Shore had introduced himself to me. He had known my name—the waiter had overheard it the first time, he said.

Marty had gone out of his way to be friendly, insisting that I drink on the house. And he'd practically thrown Sherry Blair at me. So maybe, if Marty was one of them, Kathi would have been suspect from the very beginning—from the time she approached Prudence Foy.

I had to find out if Sherry was one of them, too. If she wasn't, she might be a help—a big help.

I had to hand it to the professor. I was thinking the way he'd said I should think. The apparently unconnected event might be the key.

I crossed my fingers and rang the Cafe Rouge. I asked to speak to Miss Sherry Blair. I waited a few moments and then she came on the line.

"Hi," I said as lightly as I could.

"Who's that?"

"A fine thing," I said indignantly. "You don't even recognise the voice of the law."

"Well," she said, "if it isn't my friend the cop. It's Saturday morning, isn't it? You don't work on Saturday mornings—what are you doing awake at this time?"

"It's a beautiful day," I said. "It just naturally made me think of a beautiful woman to share the beautiful day with. So I rang you."

"You keep on flattering me with the truth, Al," she said. "Don't forget I'm a working girl tonight—Saturday's our big night."

"I was thinking of lunch," I told her. "How about that?"

"Sounds good," she said. "Give me an hour to get up and be ready."

"Sure," I said.

"Pick me up at the club?"

"In an hour."

I was there on the dot. She was waiting for me on the parking lot. She was wearing a dark suit with a sweater underneath. I'd hired a sedan and she raised her eyebrows as she got in.

"What? No prowl-car?"

"This is a special for you," I told her. "Where will we eat?"

"I'm not awfully hungry," she said. "Why don't we pick up a couple of bottles of Scotch and go back to your place? We can music then, too."

"Sounds wonderful," I agreed.

Half an hour later we were back at the house, with the first bottle of Scotch opened and Kostelanetz giving out on the hi-fi.

"This is what I go for," Sherry said. "The simple life!"

"Sure," I said. "No food!"

"They been keeping you busy, Al?"

"So-so," I grunted.

We had a couple more drinks. She took her jacket off, then took her shoes off and curled up on the sofa, leaning her head comfortably against my shoulder.

"I wish I didn't have to work tonight," she said. "This business of earning a living sure is tough."

"It sure is," I agreed. "But then tonight's a very special night, isn't it?"

"How did you know?" she asked.

"I just did," I said, feeling my throat muscles tighten.

"I've rehearsed and rehearsed, Al," she said. "I just hope it goes okay."

"Huh?" I said blankly.

"Who told you I was going to do a vocal with the strip?" she asked. "I thought it was a secret."

"I guess somebody must have told me," I said weakly.

I waited the space of another drink and tried again.

"The one night in the year," I said, "and the most significant."

"What's that?" Sherry turned her head slightly so that she was looking at me.

"Walpurgis, of course," I said. "You couldn't have forgotten!"

Her face was pleasantly blank. "Say it again?"

"Walpurgis! You know—Bare Mountain and everything?"

"Al," she said softly. "What are you babbling about?"

I had been watching her face as if my life depended on it—or more to the point, maybe Kathi's life depended on it. Nobody could be that good an actress. I thought Sherry was genuinely puzzled.

"Honey," I said, "I'm a cop."

"I heard," she nodded.

"And right now I'm being a cop. Believe me when I tell you that a girl's life depends on you telling me the truth."

She sat upright. "What is this?"

"You remember the first night we met?"

"Sure—in the club."

"Marty sent for you, didn't he?"

"Marty does that sometimes," she said. "It's a command—be nice to an important customer—you know?"

"Sure," I said.

"But I'm not half as nice to the rest of them as I am to you," she smiled. "You lucky guy."

"I appreciate it," I said. "Did Marty say anything about me to you?"

"Yes," she nodded.

"What?"

"He said you were an important cop and I was to try and find out how your murder investigation was going," she said soberly.

"Did you tell him anything?"

"No," she shook her head. "He told me he thought maybe a friend of his might get mixed up in it and he'd like any news he could pass along. But I told you you were tighter than a clam and I couldn't move you at all. He seemed sort of disappointed but he told me to keep trying."

"Thanks, honey," I told her. "Thanks a lot."

Sherry squeezed my hand. "Anything for a cop. You weren't kidding about a girl's life, Al?"

"I wasn't," I told her.

"I don't see I've been much help," she said.

"You've told me enough to get after Marty," I said. "I'll be in the club early tonight, looking for him. You'd better not tell him I've been with you—and keep out of my way tonight."

"Whatever you say, Lieutenant." She relaxed again and leaned her head back against my shoulder. "But you'll have to be early to see Marty tonight."

"Why?"

"There's a big private party and he's going to be there."

"Yeah?" I said. "Where?"

"In the private rooms. They have taken over both of them. Marty was giving his instructions this morning because he won't be downstairs at all tonight."

I licked my lips carefully. "What time does it start?"

"Somewhere around ten, I think," she said. "They're doing all their own catering—it must be very exclusive; the staff have been given strict instructions to stay out of the way."

"Sherry," I said. "I love you!"

"That's nice, Al," she said. "Some dame is giving the party. She must have plenty of dough."

"I guess so," I said.

"Janice Milbray is her name," she added casually. "A brunette with come hither and go thither eyes."

"Sherry!" I said. "I love you, I love you, I love you!"

"You keep on saying that," she pouted, "but you don't prove it."

I couldn't think of a better way to spend an afternoon.

CHAPTER 15
Walpurgis

I got a cab to take Sherry back to the club around seven.

I cooked myself a steak after she'd gone, to settle the liquor I'd drunk during the afternoon and to waste time. I'd thought of ringing Homicide not once but fifty times. Each time I had realised the futility of it. Lavers would still say I was crazy. So it looked like there was going to be a new act at the Cafe Rouge on Saturday night. Al Wheeler giving his celebrated impersonation of a one-man band. I checked my Smith and Wesson issue thirty-two and felt grateful that Lavers had forgotten to haul it off me when he fired me.

I ate the steak slowly, made some coffee and drank three cups. I lit a cigarette and looked at my watch, seeing that the time had crawled around to eight-thirty. Half an hour's drive to get to the club. If the party was due to start at ten, it wouldn't warm up until later.

I had a very simple plan of campaign. I aimed to bust in on the party with a gun in my hand and take it from there. But if I busted in too early, I'd look fully stupid if a lot of people were just sitting around drinking and there was no sign of Kathi.

The worry was that I'd be either too early or too late.

I gnawed my fingernails for another half hour, then I couldn't stand it any longer. I went out to the sedan and drove slowly in the direction of the Cafe Rouge.

It was a quarter to ten when I arrived. I put the sedan on the parking lot and lit a cigarette. I had to wait half an hour before I could really move with any safety. It was a long thirty minutes.

When my watch said a quarter after ten, I got out of the car and walked towards the club. There was a back entrance Sherry had told me about. I walked around the side of the club and then around to the back. I got within a few paces of the door when somebody stepped out of the shadows.

"Where you going, pal?" he asked.

"In there," I said.

"Try the front way, pal," he growled. "Private party upstairs tonight."

"Sorry," I said and turned away.

I swung back quickly and my balled fist caught him in the throat. He staggered back, his eyes bulging as he struggled to take a breath. I hit him again just above the heart. He sagged onto the ground and I caught him under the shoulders and dragged him around the side of the club, away from the door.

I hadn't expected him and Sherry hadn't expected him either, because she hadn't mentioned him. I wondered what the hell to do with him.

Finally I had a bright idea. My watch said it was only twenty after ten—I had plenty of time. I dragged him back to where I'd left the sedan and bundled him into the back. I drove three blocks and then parked it on the edge of an intersection, a couple of feet away from the traffic lights.

I dragged the guy over into the front and draped him around the wheel. He started to lift his head, so I tapped him with the butt of the Smith and Wesson and he went to sleep again. Then I got of the car and walked quickly away.

Behind the sedan, the traffic was beginning to bank up and the noise of the horns was bedlam. I hoped a cop came along soon and picked up the guy in the sedan. I figured it was certain that a cop would be along soon—the noise of those horns would be heard away over in the Homicide Bureau.

I walked the three blocks back to the Cafe Rouge and went around the side to the back door. This time nobody stopped me going inside. I walked down a corridor, then up a flight of stairs to the corridor above. I remembered what Sherry had told me about the layout. I kept walking swiftly, turning left at the top of the stairs and walking down towards the end door, which was the door to the men's changing-room.

I opened the door and stepped inside, then closed it behind me quickly. There was a character already in the changing-room.

"Who the—" he started to say.

He didn't get any further than that. I hit him with a haymaking right— his eyes got that glassy look and his knees buckled under him. I let him drop to the floor.

He was a guy in his middle thirties, running fast to fat, with loose lips and a receding chin. There was a bag on the bench beside him.

I ripped open the bag and it was the Fourth of July. I pulled out a magnificent mask which would have made Pluto drool with envy. It was the head of a wolf—a complete head. I wondered what else he wore with it.

I was getting a bright idea. When I'd first come into the room, I'd figured on hiding out there for a while, then trying to get into the private rooms. But this wolf-mask made a difference. I figured with that over my head, nobody could tell me from Gregory Peck—not if I stood on tiptoe, anyway. The only problem was what I was supposed to wear with it. But there was another problem which needed attention first.

I dragged the guy over to the row of lockers against the far wall. I went through his pockets and found a couple of handkerchiefs. I tied one around his mouth as a gag and hoped he could breathe through his nose. I tied his hands behind his back with the other. I took his shoes off so if he kicked he wouldn't make so much noise.

Then I bundled him into the locker.

I got back to his bag just as someone turned the handle of the door. I whipped the wolf-mask over my head the moment before somebody stepped into the room.

The new character closed the door behind him and looked at me. He was a small, bald-headed runt with dirty mud pools where he should have had eyes.

"Greetings!" he said.

"Greetings," I said, the voice distorting inside the mask.

He dumped his bag on the bench and started to get changed. I also started to get changed, but more slowly. The bald-headed guy didn't waste any time. A couple of minutes later he was the working example of what the well-dressed Satanist was wearing this year.

One mask was a leopard, complete with whiskers—a pair of scarlet tights and a black cloak draped over his shoulders. He looked like he should crawl back into the woodwork.

I dived my hands into the bag belonging to the guy who now lived in the locker and came up with an exact replica of the tights and cloak.

I quickly changed into them. I turned my back on my leopard pal and managed to lift the thirty-two out of my trousers' pocket and tuck it into the waistband of the scarlet tights. I twirled the cloak around my shoulders and I was ready.

I followed the other character to the door, feeling like Gina Lollobrigida's stand-in.

We walked a few yards down the corridor and then my pal opened another door. A gorilla-mask stood just inside the door.

"Secaire," he said.

"Walpurgis," my pal answered.

I followed and repeated the password or whatever it was. The room was big—maybe sixty by thirty—and there were a dozen or more people inside, men and women in approximately equal numbers, all wearing exactly the same sort of fancy suit—the only difference being in the masks. The women seemed to favour bird-masks.

The walls of the room were covered in crimson drapes and no windows showed. At the far end was a raised dais and upon it an incense-burner gave off a steady cloud of pungent smelling incense.

It all looked like a third-rate carnival show and you sort of waited to hear a husky barker start telling you to roll up and it only cost you twenty-five cents admission.

Yet it wasn't quite like that.

The men and women stood around in groups, some of them talking and some of them just standing. The huge masks cast grotesque shadows against the drapes. The light inside the room was dim and red-coloured. I couldn't work out where it came it from.

Everyone seemed to be waiting for something.

Then from somewhere the music came, softly. My old friend, "Night On Bare Mountain."

Instinctively the people inside the room stopped speaking and began to move towards the dais. I mingled with a group of three. A goat's-head, a pig's-head and an eagle which sat on top of a beautifully proportioned female torso. I thought any time she cared to quit the Satanists she could make real dough in burlesque, but right now didn't seem to be the time to suggest it to her.

The music came louder. At the back of the dais, heavy drapes moved and someone came forward onto the dais, carrying a large piece of rock. The guy carrying it wore the mask of a satyr. He put the rock down carefully and then a porcelain bowl beside it. And beside the bowl, a small black box. Then he disappeared behind the drapes again.

I thought if that was his act, it was lousy.

The music grew louder and louder, reaching a crescendo which assaulted the ears with almost physical violence. Then it stopped abruptly.

The room was hushed.

Then the drapes were thrown aside. A woman came forward, her mask the mask of Medea, with the writhing snakes for hair. Sanity told me that the snakes were no more real than the rest of the mask, but in the flickering light they seemed to writhe and move with a horrible semblance of life.

She held her arms high, the black cloak falling back across her shoulders.

"We are together to celebrate the Night of Walpurgis," she said. "To worship our Master, to take the Black Host!"

No one moved.

"It is near the Witching Hour," she continued. "On this night of all nights, we are the most powerful. On this night of all nights so is our Master. And we must make sacrifice worthy of him. And tonight, that shall be done!"

She stepped back dramatically, one arm flung back pointing to the drapes. They parted suddenly and two men came forward—one the satyr and the other Beelzebub, complete with horns.

But I didn't even see them for a moment—only what they were carrying.

They were carrying a girl who was limp in their arms. She wore a single, white diaphanous garment that covered her from neck to ankles and wasn't really a covering at all. They lay her across the rock, one holding her arms above her head and the other her ankles, so that she was helpless.

I saw the stark fear in her eyes, the way her mouth writhed hopelessly. I remembered I was the guy who'd persuaded Kathi Snell to let herself in for this and I didn't feel bright.

The music started again on a low throbbing note. The curtains parted and another girl came on to the dais. She wore the same type of garment as Kathi. Her dark hair hung below her shoulders like the wings of an angel of death. Her wide eyes stared on brokenly ahead of her. In her right hand she carried a knife. A wicked-looking knife.

She came to the rock and stood still, perfectly composed, still staring straight ahead of her. It looked like the professor had been dead right about Prudence Foy.

Then the music became merely a muted rhythm and Prudence began to speak. It was gibberish—a language I had never heard before and never wanted to hear again. Her voice held an unending cadence like the rise and fall of the tide, seemingly going on forever.

Then suddenly she stopped.

Beelzebub stepped forward and picked up the bowl. He knelt down beside Kathi, holding it ready.

Slowly Prudence's arm rose into the air and the edge of the knife gleamed in the reddish light.

I fumbled with the waistband of my tights and got a grip on the butt of the thirty-two. I thumbed back the safety and held it ready.

The muffled beat of the music stopped.

Prudence's eyes seemed to grow even wider. Her arm reached the limit of its arc and was held there motionless, ready for the plunge downwards.

I thought the only way I could stop it would be to shoot her.

But then I had another idea. The room was silent, without sound of any description.

"Prudence!" I shouted suddenly at the top of my voice. "Mr Sutton wants those accounts immediately! Prudence!"

There was a confused babble of voices around me. I watched her tensely. Her eyes widened still further. For a moment she remained motionless, then the arm that held the knife slumped suddenly down to her side.

She looked around wonderingly. "Is this a nightmare?" she said in a small voice. "What ..."

She saw Kathi then, stretched across the rock. She turned and saw the masks of the others on the dais with her for the first time, then she screamed and kept on screaming.

Beelzebub leapt forward from the dais. "Who shouted?" he demanded hoarsely. "Who defiled the Host?"

"He did!" the eagle-mask woman screamed beside me, her hand clutching my shoulder and pushing me forward.

I dug her in the solar plexus with my elbow and she lost interest suddenly.

Beelzebub ploughed through the people in front of me and I let him come. Brother, this was going to be strictly self-defence!

I let him get within a couple of yards of me and then I pulled the trigger twice.

He seemed to keep on coming and panic hit me for a moment. I thought maybe he had some supernatural, evil power that made him immune to bullets. But then his knees went from under him and I realised it was only his own momentum that had carried him a few steps further.

I started towards the dais and the satyr, seeing me coming, let go Kathi's wrists and grabbed the knife from Prudence's hand.

He jumped towards me, swinging the knife into the air, and I fired a couple of shots that seemed to stop him momentarily in mid-air.

He crashed down onto the floor in an untidy heap, the knife dropping from his hand.

There was bedlam inside the room. Everyone seemed to be shouting or screaming. There was a general stampede towards the door. Half a dozen of them reached it, then seemed to stop. The door burst open and I could see other people rushing into the room.

I turned back towards the dais and saw Medea halfway through the drapes. I jumped up on the dais and lunged for her, catching her cloak, ripping it from her shoulders.

I lunged again and this time caught hold of her arm. I jerked around with enough force to knock her off her feet. As she fell, the mask slipped suddenly and rolled on the floor.

"My, my!" I said. "Fancy seeing you here, Janice!"

She said something I won't repeat.

Then the whole room seemed to be lousy with cops.

I went over to Kathi and helped her onto her feet, then held her in my arms. She was trembling violently.

"You okay, honey?" I asked.

"I think so," she said, then passed out.

I seemed to be seeing familiar faces—Hanlon, Murphy and—I didn't believe it—Commissioner Lavers, and behind him a head that was too big to belong to anybody but Professor Borosin.

"You were dead right, professor," I told him.

"I can't believe it," he said in a quavering voice. Then he sighed gently and slid to the floor.

"What have you been trying to do, Wheeler?" Lavers grunted. "Save the state the expense?"

"What are you talking about?" I asked him.

"Buckman and Shore," he said. "They're both dead!"

"It was strictly self-defence!" I said quickly.

"For once," he grinned, "I won't argue with you."

I watched uniformed cops herding them out of the room. The professor recovered and stood there dabbing his forehead with a large handkerchief.

Prudence Foy walked past me, being led gently by a burly cop. Her face was a complete blank and she was singing softly to herself. "Mary Had a Little Lamb."

Borosin looked at her, then looked at me. "What happened?"

I told him how I'd yelled to try and pull her out of the trance before she murdered Kathi and what had happened after that. He nodded without saying anything.

"Is she all right?" I asked.

He shrugged his shoulders. "She's in a catatonic state at the moment—the shock of realisation was too much obviously—she's retreated to childhood where she can feel secure. Whether she'll stay there or not—who knows?"

"Maybe I would have been better off shooting her," I said.

He shook his head. "It is not for you to judge, Lieutenant. You acted as mercifully as you could. In three months she may not even remember any of it. She may be perfectly sane with a blank spot in her memory which she thinks of as her breakdown."

"You're a comfort to have around, professor," I told him.

I glared at Lavers. "Which is more than I can say for some of the other ghouls around here!"

CHAPTER 16
She Loves—Me Not

We sat around in Commissioner Lavers' office the following morning. Lavers and the D.A. were there; so were Hanlon and Murphy. So was Kathi Snell. The other two people in the room were a wardress and Janice Milbray.

"I don't know what I'm doing here," I said as soon as I got into the office. "I'm just a citizen."

"Stop that twaddle, Wheeler," Lavers growled. "You're the Lieutenant-in-Charge of the Homicide Bureau and you know it."

"Did you or did you not," I said as evenly as I could, "fire me the other day?"

Lavers grinned suddenly. "Well," he conceded, "maybe you thought so— and so did Hanlon and Murphy. But I was desperate, Wheeler. We had to crack the case. The last two times you had a tough case, you cracked both of 'em after you'd been suspended from duty. This one seemed the toughest yet, so I thought the only way I could really spur you on was to fire you. I couldn't let Hanlon and Murphy know until afterwards that it was a gag, because I wanted it to look good."

"What a character!" I said.

The D.A. took off his glasses, polished them carefully, then put them on again.

"All very interesting," he said coldly, "but the press is screaming for a statement."

"Got any ideas, Wheeler?" Lavers grunted.

"Sure," I said. "Now I have. We know the prime organisers were Poison Ivy here," I jerked my thumb in Janice's direction, "Shore and Buckman. I'll take a bet that all the members paid plenty to belong to the group. That's where Janice's dough was coming from—not as she so carefully tried to tell me, from Eddie Buckman."

I looked at her and her mouth framed a nasty word.

"You know something?" I said to her. "You don't look any different to me with that mask off."

I turned back to Lavers. "Parker belonged to the group—Snell, too. Parker got ambitious and decided he could make some dough out of it— blackmail.

"But Parker got a little too ambitious when he started trying to blackmail the three who ran the show—so they killed him. Then they had the problem that all murderers have—what to do with the body. Somebody got a bright idea. Let's plant it where it has no connection with us—and let's make it look as zany as we can so the cops can tear their hair out trying to connect things that can't be connected."

"So they put it into the office safe in the *Exclusive* building and they put a girdle around its neck because they thought it appropriate to a fashion magazine, maybe."

Lavers snorted. "That's what you were getting at when you kept on asking me why he was strangled with a girdle?"

"Yeah," I grinned, "but I didn't know it. It worried me because it was so zany I thought it must hold the key to the murder ... which was exactly what they wanted us to think.

"Cameron was searching Parker's apartment. I'd say he found the secret recess and inside it he found Parker's mask. And one of the unholy three walked in on him, realised what had happened and killed him to keep his mouth shut and get hold of the mask."

I looked at Lavers again. "I have a confession to make." I told him how I had kidded Snell that night so he wouldn't be in the apartment when I came home with Kathi—or I thought then I'd be coming home with Kathi.

"Snell must have suspected what had happened to Parker—he told his sister Parker had got too ambitious. I figure that I put the fear into him, telling him somebody was after him. He couldn't believe it, didn't want to believe, so he went around to see Janice, to ask her if it was true."

I smiled at her. "With his beard fluttering in the wind, he was playing Samson to your Delilah, wasn't he?"

She didn't answer.

"By going around to see her, Snell committed suicide," I said. "When Janice heard the story, she'd be worried about why I had told Snell that—and she'd see that Snell was so frightened that if the police pulled him in, he'd blurt out the whole story of the group. So Snell had to go."

"Who killed him?" Hanlon asked.

I shrugged my shoulders. "One of the three of them. Two of them are dead, so I say it's the third who killed him."

"It's a lie!" Janice said.

"Honey," I smiled at her, "it doesn't matter—you'll fry on that one just the same."

"You ..."

The wardress clamped a firm hand across Janice's mouth, cutting off the words. "Naughty!" she said reprovingly.

"Then there was Dewlap, the nightwatchman. We know why he had to die—because he saw them carrying Parker's body into the building. They bribed him first and probably put the fear of death into him to keep his mouth shut. The thing he knew was that they had worn the masks. But when I questioned him in the basement, I frightened him even more so he was going to talk. I think one of them trailed me into the building that night, then overheard the conversation and put a couple of slugs into Dewlap before he could say any more."

"How'd they get the combination of the safe?" Murphy asked.

"Easy," I said. "Prudence Foy was their elemental. A girl who could be hypnotised at the toss of a hat. All they had to do was put her under and ask."

The D.A. polished his glasses some more. "That all seems quite satisfactory," he said. "We are holding Miss Milbray on a first-degree murder indictment, I take it?"

"We are," I agreed. "And we have a valuable character witness in the shape of Miss Snell. Once she's recounted her experiences of last night, I think Poison Ivy will be lucky if the jury don't decide to take the law into their own hands and lynch her right there and then."

The D.A. rubbed his hands. "Fine. I like a nice watertight case. I'll go and talk to the gentlemen of the press, if you'll excuse me."

He bustled out of the room, slamming the door behind him. I lit another cigarette. "Anything else?" I asked Lavers.

"Couple of things," he grunted. "You'd better take a week off. Hanlon can take over." He grinned. "I'm grooming him for the captaincy of sixth precinct. That was another needle we hoped to jab you with—pretending he was being groomed for your job."

"I couldn't work with a nicer bunch of guys," I said bitterly.

I turned around and saw Janice Milbray's eyes were two dark holes of hate as they stared at me.

"Do we need that anymore?" I asked Lavers, pointing at her. "Looking at her puts me off my food."

"Take her away," Lavers grunted to the wardress. They went out and the door closed behind them.

"Yeah," Lavers said. "Take a week off and come back fresh, Captain."

"Sure," I said. "What did you say?"

"I said take a week ..."

"I heard that part," I said. "It was just that last word—for a moment there I thought you said *Captain*."

"I did," he grinned. "When you come back."

"Hell!" I replied. "That means I'll have to start calling you sir again!"

We got out of the office ten minutes later and I drove Kathi back to her apartment.

"Coffee?" I said hopefully.

"Okay," she said and went out into the kitchen.

I followed her out. "It must have been dreadful for you," I said soberly.

"It was," she shuddered. "It wasn't what they did to me—they didn't touch me. It was what they were going to do. The Milbray woman would keep on going over and over it in detail!"

"Nobody will miss her when she's gone," I said. "That won't be long now, either."

Kathi made the coffee, carried the tray into the living-room and put it down on the table. I noticed the bedroom door was open and I also noticed a couple of bags on the bed.

"Hey," I said. "You're not leaving?"

"You bet your sweet life I am," she said. "I've had enough of this town to last me a lifetime. If I have to come back for the trial, I'll come back. But I'm catching a New York plane this afternoon."

I sipped my coffee thoughtfully. "What a wonderful coincidence it is."

"What?"

"That you should be going to New York," I said slowly. "Here I am with a week's leave and wondering where to go. New York is the answer, of course." I looked at her anxiously. "I hope your apartment's big enough for two?"

She smiled sweetly at me. "Why, of course it is, Al."

"Well, that's fine then," I said. "All I have to do is make plane reservations."

"If my apartment wasn't big enough for two," Kathi mused, "where would my husband live?"

"Huh?"

She smiled sweetly again. "I've been married for the last fifteen months, Al. Secretly, of course—the agency doesn't approve of married women working for them, and the money is so useful."

She squeezed my hand. "You will keep my secret for me, won't you, Al?"

"To the grave," I said hollowly, and spilled coffee down the front of my suit.

She looked at her watch. "I'd better hurry my packing or I'll miss the plane. I don't want to rush you, Al, but you know how it is?"

"Sure," I said bitterly, "I know exactly how it is."

We shook hands at the door and I went down to the prowl-car. I drove home and put the first disc I came across onto the hi-fi.

It was a mistake. I got Sinatra singing, "Memories are made of this!"

A long grey week stretched ahead of me into infinity.

I poured myself a drink, up to the brim of the glass, and drank it down with three gulps and two shudders. I slumped into the chair while Sinatra obligingly gave forth with "Mood Indigo."

"Ain't it the truth, brother!" I muttered.

Then I suddenly came out of the chair in one movement which carried me to the phone. I had rocks in the head! What was I doing?

I rang Miss Walker at *Exclusive*.

"Hello, Lieutenant," she said.

"You hear the news?" I asked her.

"Wonderful, isn't it?" she said enthusiastically. "I'm surprised you heard so soon."

"Huh?"

"I mean, you must have a spy on the magazine!"

"Huh?" I said again. "What news are you talking about?"

"Why," she said rapturously. "It's definitely right—they will be two inches shorter this year!"

"What will?"

"Skirts, of course. Isn't it colossal?"

I made a face at the mouthpiece of the phone. "Sure," I said. "But I was talking about the murders."

"Oh, that," she said disinterestedly. "Yes, I heard about that. About time, I must say. I thought you were going to drag on forever without catching them."

I let it lie. "I was wondering if you'd care to have dinner with me tonight?"

"I'm sorry, Lieutenant," she said. "I'm flat out on a new issue. Two inches shorter—that's really news! Bye now." She hung up.

I filled the glass up to the brim again, slumped back into the chair again and then came out of it again just as suddenly as the first time.

I dialled the Cafe Rouge.

"Al here, honey," I said a moment later.

"Well, hello," she said. "I believe you were slightly terrific last night?"

A dreamy smile started out of its own volition across my face. "Well," I said modestly. "It was your help, honey."

"I helped myself out of a job," she said. "But things aren't so bad. I've got a new job—in a joint in Chicago. I'm leaving in a couple of hours."

"Well, that's fine," I said with my hollow voice working again. "Say, that's a wonderful coincidence."

"What is?"

"I've just got a week's leave. I can spend it driving you to Chicago. How about that?"

"It sounds wonderful, Al, but Chicago's only a hundred and eighty miles away from here."

"Well?"

"It's only half a day's drive."

"Not the way I drive, honey," I said. "Why, it takes me three days to get started."

"Oh," she said.

I crossed my fingers and waited.

"Stack them on the turntable, honey," she said, "and call me a cab!"

The End

Allan Geoffrey Yates Bibliography
(1923-1985)

As Carter Brown/
Peter Carter Brown

Series:

Al Wheeler (no U.S. edition
unless otherwise stated through
to Chorine Makes a Killing)

The Wench is Wicked (1955)
Blonde Verdict (1956; revised for
the U.S. as The Brazen, 1960)
Delilah Was Deadly (1956)
No Harp for My Angel (1956)
Booty for a Babe (1956)
Eve, It's Extortion (1957; revised
as Walk Softly, Witch!, 1959,
and further revised for the U.S.
as The Victim, 1959)
No Law Against Angels (1957;
revised for the U.S. as The Body,
1958; 1st U.S. Wheeler)
Doll for the Big House (1957;
revised for the U.S. as The
Bombshell, 1960)
Chorine Makes a Killing (1957)
The Unorthodox Corpse (1957;
revised for the U.S., 1961)
Death on a Downbeat (1958;
revised for the U.S. as The
Corpse, 1958)
The Blonde (1958; reprinted in
the U.S., 1958)
The Lover (1958)
The Mistress (1959)
The Passionate (1959)
The Wanton (1959)
The Dame (1959)
The Desired (1959)

The Temptress (1960)
Lament for a Lousy Lover (1960)
[includes Mavis Seidlitz]
The Stripper (1961)
The Tigress (1961; reprinted in
the UK as Wildcat, 1962)
The Exotic (1961)
Angel! (1962)
The Hellcat (1962)
The Lady Is Transparent (1962)
The Dumdum Murder (1962)
Girl in a Shroud (1963)
The Sinners (1963; reprinted in
U.S. as The Girl Who Was
Possessed, 1963)
The Lady Is Not Available (1963;
reprinted in U.S. as The Lady Is
Available, 1963)
The Dance of Death (1964)
The Vixen (1964; reprinted in the
U.S. as The Velvet Vixen, 1964)
A Corpse for Christmas (1965)
The Hammer of Thor (1965)
Target for Their Dark Desire
(1966)
The Plush-Lined Coffin (1967)
Until Temptation Do Us Part
(1967)
The Deep Cold Green (1968)
The Up-Tight Blonde (1969)
Burden of Guilt (1970)
The Creative Murders (1971)
W.H.O.R.E. (1971)
The Clown (1972)
The Aseptic Murders (1972)
The Born Loser (1973)
Night Wheeler (1974)
Wheeler Fortune (1974)
Wheeler, Dealer! (1975)

The Dream Merchant (1976)
Busted Wheeler (1979)
The Spanking Girls (1979)
Model for Murder (1980)
The Wicked Widow (1981)
Stab in the Dark (1984; Australia only)

Larry Baker

Charlie Sent Me (1965; revised from Swan Song for a Siren, 1955)
No Blonde Is an Island (1965)
So What Killed the Vampire? (1966)
Had I But Groaned (1968; reprinted in the UK as The Witches, 1969)
True Son of the Beast (1970)
The Iron Maiden (1975)

Barney Blain (no U.S. editions)

Madam, You're Mayhem (1957)
Ice Cold in Ermine (1958)

Danny Boyd

Tempt a Tigress (1958; no U.S.)
So Deadly, Sinner! (1959; reprinted in the U.S. as Walk Softly, Witch, 1959, 1st U.S. Boyd; rewritten as Terror Comes Creeping, 1960; different version of the Wheeler title)
Suddenly by Violence (1959)
Terror Comes Creeping (1959)
The Wayward Wahine (1960; published in Australia as The Wayward, 1962)
The Dream Is Deadly (1960)

Graves, I Dig (1960; revised from Cutie Wins a Corpse (1957)
The Myopic Mermaid (1961, revised from A Siren Sounds Off, 1958)
The Ever-Loving Blues (1961; revised from Death of a Doll, 1956)
The Seductress (1961; published in the U.S. as The Sad-Eyed Seductress, 1961)
The Savage Salome (1961; revised from Murder is My Mistress, 1954)
The Ice-Cold Nude (1962)
Lover Don't Come Back (1962)
Nymph to the Slaughter (1963)
Passionate Pagan (1963)
Silken Nightmare (1963)
Catch Me a Phoenix! (1965)
The Sometime Wife (1965)
The Black Lace Hangover (1966)
House of Sorcery (1967)
The Mini-Murders (1968)
Murder Is the Message (1969)
Only the Very Rich (1969)
The Coffin Bird (1970)
The Sex Clinic (1971)
Angry Amazons (1972) [includes Randy Roberts]
Manhattan Cowboy (1973)
So Move the Body (1973)
The Early Boyd (1975)
The Savage Sisters (1976)
The Pipes Are Calling (1976)
The Rip Off (1979)
The Strawberry-Blonde Jungle (1979)
Death to a Downbeat (1980)
Kiss Michelle Goodbye (1981)
The Real Boyd (1984; Australia only)

Paul Donavan

Donavan (1974)
Donovan's Day (1975)
Chinese Donavan (1976)
Donavan's Delight (1979)

Max Dumas (no U.S. editions)

Goddess Gone Bad (1958)
Luck Was No Lady (1958)
Deadly Miss (1958)

Mike Farrel

The Million Dollar Babe (1961;
  revised from Cutie Cashed His
  Chips, 1955)
The Scarlet Flush (1963; revised
  from Ten Grand Tallulah and
  Temptation, 1957)

Rick Holman

Zelda (1961; 1st U.S. Holman)
Murder in the Harem Club,
  1962; reprinted in the U.S. as
  Murder in the Key Club, 1962)
The Murderer Among Us (1962)
Blonde on the Rocks (1963)
The Jade-Eyed Jinx (1963;
  reprinted in the U.S. as The
  Jade-Eyed Jungle, 1964)
The Ballad of Loving Jenny
  (1963; reprinted in the U.S. as
  The White Bikini, 1963)
The Wind-Up Doll (1963)
The Never-Was Girl (1964)
Murder Is a Package Deal (1964)
Who Killed Doctor Sex? (1964)
Nude—with a View (1965)
The Girl from Outer Space (1965)

Blonde on a Broomstick (1966)
Play Now... Kill Later (1966)
No Tears from the Widow (1966)
The Deadly Kitten (1967)
Long Time No Leola (1967)
Die Anytime, After Tuesday!
  (1969)
The Flagellator (1969)
The Streaked-Blond Slave (1969)
A Good Year for Dwarfs? (1970)
The Hang-up Kid (1970)
Where Did Charity Go? (1970)
The Coven (1971)
The Invisible Flamini (1971)
The Pornbroker (1972)
The Master (1973)
Phreak-Out! (1973)
Negative in Blue (1974)
The Star-Crossed Lover (1974)
Ride the Roller Coaster (1975)
Remember Maybelle? (1976)
See It Again, Sam (1979)
The Phantom Lady (1980)
The Swingers (1980)

Andy Kane

The Hong Kong Caper (1962;
  revised from Blonde, Bad and
  Beautiful, 1957)
The Guilt-edged Cage (1963;
  revised from That's Piracy, My
  Pet, 1957; published in Australia
  as Bird in a Guilt-Edged Cage)

Ivor MacCallum (no U.S.
  editions)

Sweetheart You Slay Me (1952)
Blackmail Beauty (1953)

Randy Roberts

Murder in the Family Way (1971)
The Seven Sirens (1972)
Murder on High (1973)
Sex Trap (1975)

Mavis Seidlitz

Honey, Here's Your Hearse
(1955; no U.S.)
The Killer is Kissable (1955; no
U.S.)
A Bullet For My Baby (1955; no
U.S.)
Good Morning, Mavis! (1957; no
U.S.)
Murder Wears a Mantilla (1957;
revised for U.S. as same title,
1962)
The Loving and the Dead (1959;
1st U.S. Seidlitz)
None But the Lethal Heart (1959;
reprinted as The Fabulous,
1961)
Tomorrow Is Murder (1960)
Lament for a Lousy Lover (1960)
[includes Al Wheeler]
The Bump and Grind Murders
(1964)
Seidlitz and the Super Spy (1967;
published in the UK as The
Super-Spy, 1968)
Murder Is So Nostalgic (1972)
And the Undead Sing (1974)

Unrelated Novels/Novelettes (all
non-U.S. unless otherwise noted)

Death Date for Dolores (1951)
Designed to Deceive (1951)

Duchess Double X (1951)
Forever Forbidden (1951)
The Lady Is Murder (1951;
reprinted as Lady is a Killer with
Murder by Miss Take, 1958)
Three Men, One Love (1951)
Uncertain Heart (1951)
Your Alibi Is Showing (1951)
Alias a Lady (1952)
Blackmail for a Brunette (1952)
Blondes Prefer Bullets (1952)
Hands Off the Lady (1952)
Kiss Life Goodbye (1952)
Larceny Was Lovely (1952)
Meet Miss Mayhem (1952)
Murder Sweet Murder (1952)
She Wore No Shroud (1952)
Sssh! She's a Killer (1952)
Chill on Chili/Butterfly Nett
(1953)
Cyanide Sweetheart (1953)
Dead Dolls Don't Cry (1953)
Dimples Died De-Luxe (1953)
Judgement of a Jane (1953)
Kidnapper Wears Curves (1953)
The Lady Wore Nylon (1953)
The Lady's Alive (1953)
Lethal in Love (1953; reprinted as
The Minx is Murder, 1956)
Madame You're Morgue-Bound
(1953)
Meet a Body (1953)
The Mermaid Murmurs Murder
(1953)
Model for Murder (1953;
different from 1980 Al Wheeler
title)
Moonshine Momma (1953)
Murder is a Broad (1953)
Penthouse Pass-Out (1953;
reprinted as Hot Seat for a
Honey, 1956)

Rope for a Redhead (1953; revised as Model of No Virtue, 1956)

Slightly Dead (1953)

Stripper You're Stuck (1953)

Widow is Willing (1953)

The Black Widow Weeps (1954)

Felon Angel (1954)

Floozies Out of Focus (1954)

The Frame is Beautiful (1954)

Fraulein is Feline (1954; reprinted with Moonshine Momma & Slaughter in Satin, 1955)

Good-Knife Sweetheart (1954)

Honky Tonk Homicide (1954; reprinted with Chill on Chili & Butterfly Nett, 1955)

Homicide Harem (1954; reprinted with Good-Knife Sweetheart & Poison Ivy, 1955; with Felon Angel, 1965)

The Lady is Chased (1954; reprinted as Trouble is a Dame, 1957)

A Morgue Amour (1954)

Murder—Paris Fashion (1954)

Murder! She Says (1954)

Nemesis Wore Nylons (1954)

Pagan Perilous (1954)

Perfumed Poison (1954)

Poison Ivy (1954)

Shady Lady (1954)

Sinsation Sadie (1954)

Slaughter in Satin (1954)

Strip Without Tease (1954; reprinted as Stripper, You've Sinned, 1959)

Trouble is a Dame (1954)

Wreath for Rebecca (1954)

Venus Unarmed (1954)

Yogi Shrouds Yolande (1954; reprinted with Poison Ivy, 1965)

Curtains for a Chorine (1955)

Curves for a Coroner (1955)

Cutie Cashed His Chips (1955; revised for U.S. as The Million Dollar Babe, 1961, as Farrel series)

Homicide Hoyden (1955)

Kiss and Kill (1955; reprinted with Cyanide Sweetie, 1958)

Kiss Me Deadly (1955; reprinted as Lipstick Larceny, 1958)

Lead Astray (1955)

Lipstick Larceny (1955)

Maid for Murder (1955)

Miss Called Murder (1955)

Shamus, Your Slip Is Showing (1955; reprinted with A Morgue Amour, 1957)

Shroud for My Sugar (1955)

Sob-Sister Cries Murder (1955)

The Two Timing Blonde (1955)

Baby, You're Guilt-Edged (1956; reprinted with Pagan Perilous, 1959)

Bid the Babe Bye-Bye (1956)

Blonde, Beautiful, and – Blam! (1956)

The Bribe Was Beautiful (1956)

Caress Before Killing (1956)

Darling You're Doomed (1956)

Donna Died Laughing (1956)

The Eve of His Dying (1956)

Hi-Jack for Jill (1956)

The Hoodlum Was a Honey (1956)

The Lady Has No Convictions (1956; reprinted with Slightly Dead, 1959)

Meet Murder, My Angel (1956)

Murder By Miss-Demeanour (1956)

My Darling Is Dead Pan (1956)

No Halo For Hedy (1956)
Strictly for Felony (1956)
Sweetheart, This is Homicide
(1956)
Bella Donna Was Poison (1957)
Cutie Wins a Corpse (1957;
revised for U.S. as Graves, I
Dig!, 1960, as Boyd series)
Last Note for a Lovely (1957)
Lethal in Love (1957; different
than 1953 title)
Sinner, You Slay Me (1957)
Ten Grand Tallulah and
Temptation (1957; revised as
The Scarlet Flush, 1963, Farrel
series)
That's Piracy, My Pet (1957;
revised as Bird in a Guilt-Edged
Cage, 1963, as Kane series)
Wreath for a Redhead (1957)
The Charmer Chased (1958)
Cutie Takes the Count (1958)
Deadly Miss (1958)
Hi-Fi Fadeout (1958)
High Fashion in Homicide (1958)
No Body She Knows (1958; with
Slaughter in Satin, 1960)
No Future Fair Lady (1958)
Sinfully Yours (1958)
A Siren Signs Off (1958; with
Moonshine Momma; revised for
U.S. as The Myopic Mermaid,
1961, as Boyd series)
So Lovely She Lies (1958)
Widow Bewitched (1958)
The Blonde Avalanche (1984)

As Tod Conway (western stories)

As Caroline Farr

The Intruder (1962)
House of Tombs (1966)
Mansion of Evil (1966)
Villa of Shadows (1966)
Web of Horror (1966; reprinted
in the U.S. as A Castle in Spain,
1978)
Granite Folly (1967)
The Secret of the Chateau (1967)
Witch's Hammer (1967)
So Near and Yet... (1968)
House of Destiny (1969)
The Castle on the Lake (1970)
The Secret of Castle Ferrara
(1970)
Terror on Duncan Island (1971)
The Towers of Fear (1972)
A Castle in Canada (1972)
House of Dark Illusions (1973)
House of Secrets (1973)
Dark Mansion (1974)
Mansion Malevolent (1974)
The House on the Cliffs (1974)
Dark Citadel (1975)
Mansion of Peril (1975)
Castle of Terror (1975)
The Scream in the Storm (1975)
Chateau of Wolves (1976)
Mansion of Menace (1976)
Brecon Castle (1976)
The House of Landsdown (1977)
House of Treachery (1977)
Ravensnest (1977)
The House at Lansdowne (1977)
Sinister House (1978)
House of Valhalla (1978)
Heiress Of Fear (1978)
Room Of Secrets (1979)
Island of Evil (1979)
A Castle on the Rhine (1979)

The Castle on the Loch (1979)
The Secret at Ravenswood (1980)

As Raymond Glenning (stories)

Ghosts Don't Kill (1951)
Seven for Murder (1951)

As Sinclair Mackellar

Prompt for Murder (1981)

As Dennis Sinclair

Temple Dogs Guard My Fate
 (1968)
Third Force (1976)
The Friends of Lucifer (1977)
Blood Brothers (1977)

As Paul Valdez (stories &
 novelettes)

Hypnotic Death (1949)
The Fatal Focus (1950)
Outcasts of Planet J (1950)
Jetbees from Planet J (1951)
Escape to Paradise (1951)
Fugitives from the Flame World
 (1951)
Kidnapped in Chaos (1951)
Killer by Night (1951)
Suicide Satellite (1951)
The Time Thief (1951)
Flight Into Horror (1951)
Murder Gives Notice (1951)
The Corpse Sat Up (1951)
The Maniac Murders (1951)
Satan's Sabbath (1951)
You Can't Keep Murder Out
 (1951)
Kill Him Gently (1951)

Feline Frame-Up (1951)
Celluloid Suicide? (1951)
The Murder I Don't Remember
 (1952)
Kidnapped in Space (1952)
There's No Future in Murder
 (1952)
The Crook Who Wasn't There
 (1952)
Maniac Murders (1952)
The Mad Meteor (1952)
Operation Satellite (1952)

As A. G. Yates

The Cold Dark Hours (1958)

As Alan Yates

Novel:

Coriolanus, the Chariot (1978)

Stories & Novelettes:

Client for Murder (Leisure
 Detective #7, 195?)
The Corpse on the Carpet
 (Leisure Detective #8, 195?)
Farewell, My Lady of Shalott!
 (Action Detective Magazine #6,
 1952)
Hush-a-Buy Homicide (Leisure
 Detective #9, 195?)
Margie (Action Detective
 Magazine #5, 1952)
Merger with Death (Leisure
 Detective #12, 195?)
Murder in the Family (Leisure
 Detective #11, 195?)
Murder Needs Education (Action
 Detective Magazine #2, 1952)

Murder! She Says (Detective
Monthly #2, 195?)
My Love Lies Murdered (Action
Detective Magazine #7, 1952)
Nemesis for a Nude! (Leisure
Detective #10, 195?)

Genie from Jupiter (Thrills
Incorporated #14, 1951)
Goddess of Space (Thrills
Incorporated #20, 1952)
No Pixies on Pluto (Thrills
Incorporated #22, 1952)

Planet of the Lost (Thrills
Incorporated #17, 1951)
A Space Ship Is Missing (Thrills
Incorporated #16, 1951)
Spacemen Spoofed (Thrills
Incorporated #23, 1952)

Autobiography

Ready when you are, C.B.!: The
autobiography of Alan Yates
alias Carter Brown (1983)